CONSPIRACY!

※   ※   ※

Still expecting a trap, Deralze made his way quickly to Brandon's suite, and the door obligingly slid open. No one was within. He crossed the outer chamber and entered the bedroom, where a single figure was outlined beneath the covers on the bed.

"Krysarch Brandon?"

Lenic Deralze leaned down, hesitated; then deliberately ignoring years of training, touched the bare shoulder of the young man lying asleep on the bed.

The reaction was instantaneous and violent.

Brandon flung aside the bedcover and lifted his arm as though sighting along a firejac. Taking aim directly at Deralze's face, he mumbled, "Under fire. Where's the com?"

Habit forced Deralze back a step before his eyes registered that there was no weapon in the Krysarch's hand.

Brandon collapsed back in the bed. The hand that pointed at Deralze now pressed against his eyesocket. "Hell. That you, Deralze?"

"Yes, Highness." The honorific came automatically to his lips, despite the ten year hiatus.

"Damn, what a headache," Brandon muttered. "And what a nightmare. Markham and I, under attack—" He squinted around the room as though shards of his dream-images still lingered in the silent, vaulted corners. Then he grinned, a twisted rueful grin that reminded Deralze suddenly of the adolescent Krysarch he had served. . . . He could kill the nyr-Arkad now, right here in the middle of the Palace Minor, stronghold of the Arkad family for nearly a thousand years, and no one would witness it.

EXORDIUM: BOOK 1

THE PHOENIX IN FLIGHT

SHERWOOD SMITH
&
DAVE TROWBRIDGE

A TOM DOHERTY ASSOCIATES BOOK
NEW YORK

THE PHOENIX IN FLIGHT

Lines from "The Second Coming" are reprinted with permission of Macmillan Publishing Company from *The Poems of W.B. Yeats: A New Edition*, edited by Richard J. Finneran, copyright 1924 by Macmillan Publishing Company, renewed 1952 by Bertha Georgie Yeats.

Quotation from Pierre Tielhard de Chardin's *The Phenomenon of Man*, Harper Torchbook, © 1965, used by permission of HarperCollins Publishers.

Cover art by Jim Burns.

A Tor Book
Published by Tom Doherty Associates, Inc.
175 Fifth Avenue
New York, N.Y. 10010

Tor ® is a registered trademark of Tom Doherty Associates, Inc.

ISBN: 0-812-52024-6

First edition: February 1993

Printed in the United States of America

0 9 8 7 6 5 4 3 2 1

With thanks to Marjorie Miller and Florence Feiler, who first got us launched, and to GEnie's SFRT, which kept us flying.

PROLOGUE

✳

We are the children of conflict. We have been shaped by struggle: against the Collective and its descendant, the Hegemony; against the Adamantines, their machines turned masters; against the Shiidra, ancient and alien beyond understanding; and against the diluting force of interstellar distance. To the student of humanity, it often seems that what we are depends as much on what opposes us as on what sustains us.

We are the children of the Exile. No matter how far diverged by their singular histories, every human culture in the Thousand Suns resonates to its tragic echoes. How else could it be? All of us—Downsider, Highdweller, even Rifter—are descended from the many and varied groups who rejected the sterile conformity of the Solar Collective and chose instead to flee in primitive starships through the Vortex.

We are the children of a mystery. We do not know what the Vortex was. Perhaps it was an artifact of the *race we call the Ur, or of the unknown enemy that destroyed them so long ago. The Vortex opened only twice: once, to bring humankind here from the other side of the Galaxy; once more, to disgorge a cybernetic horror engendered by the Hegemony. We do not know if it will ever open again. Without it, there is no return to Earth, if Earth even still exists.*

Thus we are a deeply praeterite people, fascinated by the bits of Earthly life our various ancestors carried with them through the Vortex. In the face of all the forces arrayed against us, these fragments keep us human, for they are sacraments of the deep realities that made our forebears choose Exile and remain rooted in the fertile ground of their natural cultures. Our languages, religions, social and political structures are grounded in these fragments; to the extent that an innovation departs from these roots, it is recognized as false, and fails.

We are the Phoenix, ever regenerate from the flames of conflict, which burn away the dross to reveal the gold of true humanity. Sundered from the mother of humankind by an immensity of spacetime, we yet remain the children of Earth.

> Magister Davidiah Jones
> Gnostor of Archetype and Ritual
> *The Roots of Human Process*
> Torigan Prime, A.A. 787

What would we do without our enemies?

> The Sanctus Teilhard
> (Pierre Teilhard de Chardin)
> *The Phenomenon of Man*
> Lost Earth, ca. 200 B.E.

N!Kirr was out of catalepsy into second sleep before he felt his own mind again. He fled the awareness of his other lives and rose slowly toward consciousness.

Pushing his way through first sleep, the aged Guardian folded himself upright, his movements almost involuntary through habit, and locked his secondary knees against his thorax with the deliberate grace of twenty millennia.

The air tasted foul, like a moldy *klopt* egg, and N!Kirr flexed his mandibles irritably. The harsh clatter echoed through a thousand images of the vault, as he registered the dust-laden sunbeams lancing into the cool darkness through the Sunset Arch.

Sunset? he thought. Disbelief wrenched his eyes into focus, and their iridescent facets glinted as the Guardian peered about, hissing with vexation. Had he lost a night and a day, then? Where were his underbearers, and his acolytes? Such a thing had never happened before!

"They shall have their shells broken for this! Sunset!" N!Kirr, confused and dizzy, spoke at last, his anger leaking away.

"Sunset," returned the vault, its echoes blurring the chattering syllables, and N!Kirr swayed, overcome by a sudden sense of wrongness. The sunset light was the color of an offworlder's blood; the setting Egg was entering Red Victory, one phase of the patient pulse of life that would one day hatch another demon.

A sudden swarm of acolytes scurried toward him, the edges of their chelae pale with confusion and fear, but N!Kirr ignored them. *A successor will see the hatching,* thought the Guardian dispassionately, *in that timeless instant before the star-born demon shall swallow him and all our race into its consuming fury.*

"All the stars shall mark our passing, and the fulfillment of our vigil and our trust." The Guardian spoke softly, to himself, but the acolytes milling about his dais subsided into a respectful silence, and N!Kirr saw several of them start scribbling on the writing plates hanging from their necks.

Droogflies! he thought angrily, vexed by their dependence on him. He had seen too many of their generations fleeting past him, their brief lives blurring into anonymity, and he was tired.

Still confused by the apparent loss of a day, N!Kirr looked down at the focus of the Shrine and of his people. At the base of his thorax lay the Heart of the Demon, partially sunk in the spiral-incised stone of the Guardian's dais. Its perfectly reflecting surface mirrored in curved distortion his anxious face as he bent over it, and the faces of his frightened attendants, waiting silently for his guidance. His age-reddened chelae stroked his throat patches in a rasping sigh, and he cautiously sank his mind into the small sphere, seeking the Pattern. The feeling of wrongness intensified and the stone-prisoned sphere assumed a numinous clarity to his eyes as he found only emptiness.

Without further thought, N!Kirr brought his forearms down and stabbed at the Heart of the Demon with his killing-thumbs. There was a muffled pop and the mirror-sphere vanished, leaving only its shape in the stone and a few silvery tatters. The acolytes shrieked in unison and fled in all directions, their limbs clattering in noisy terror against the inlaid stone.

The Guardian remained perfectly still for a moment as the shock overthrew the haze of ancient ritual endlessly repeated and left him completely alert. The Heart of the Demon had been stolen, and a simulacrum placed in its stead while he slept. The offworlders!

N!Kirr closed his eyes as flames of thought began to flicker through his mind. Twenty thousand years he'd watched, and generations of Guardians before him, and the Heart was gone. The Devourer would wake again.

The vault seemed to echo to many voices, all of them familiar though never heard before, multiplied by the carven wall of the Shrine to a tapestry of compulsion and demand. N!Kirr surrendered to them gratefully, yielding up the crushing knowledge of his race's failure, so near the end of their long vigil, and the voices swelled into a cold, blinding light that took him into oblivion.

❊   ❊   ❊

The next day, at the urging of its fellows, an acolyte crept timidly back into the Shrine. It found the Guardian still standing there, its carapace cold and lightless. Shortly after that, for the first time in ten million years, the Shrine was empty of life and movement, a hollow shell abandoned in the bloody light of a dying sun.

PART ONE

✳

ONE

✻

PARADISUM

Verin Dalmer stalked through the terminal, dodging easily through the throng of travelers. Far above the hurrying Rifter, crystal panels glinted as they shifted to follow the bloody light of Ouroborous in red eclipse.

" . . . ever eating its own tail. But in fifty thousand years or so the resulting expansion will vaporize Paradisum and the Shrine Planet." The pompous voice broke his train of thought, and Dalmer glared at the Tiklipti tour group milling about in his path as he pushed his way through them. Their obese guide's green-dyed face was a garish black in the red light flooding the Paradisum spaceport.

Like a vacuum-eaten corpse, the Rifter thought in disgust, and he stomped on the fat Downsider's foot and shouldered him aside. The reddish glare on Dalmer's scarred features must have compounded his normally savage expression, for the guide jumped back and gabbled an apology which Dalmer ignored.

Fifty thousand years. So what! He'd be long dead when the dying star swallowed Paradisum. Dalmer snorted and glanced up as he neared the DataNet parcelcom. The red giant and the ring of fire ripped from its surface by its now-eclipsed companion dominated the yellow sky. *Still,* he thought, *I'll be glad when we skip out tonight.* Paradisum was the only Doomed World Dalmer had ever visited, and if he had his way, it would be the last. What kind of race had the Ur been, to make an art form of destruction, on a scale that required a multimillion-year perspective to appreciate? And if they'd been powerful enough to remake solar systems, what could have wiped them out so completely?

The Rifter grimaced, impatient with himself. That damned Shrine Planet and those crazy Bugs had given him the shillies. Verin hated insects, and the memory of the Guardian towering above him, frozen by the gas bomb, made him unconsciously speed his pace a bit.

There was no line at the parcelcom, and the screen lit as it sensed his approach. *"Virtwandhi?"* The word scrolled slowly upward on the screen as the com spoke.

"Speak Uni!" snarled Dalmer. "D'ya think I'm a stinking Paradeezer?"

"Your pardon, *genz,*" replied the singsong voice, not sounding sorry or anything else. "Your parcel's destination?"

"Brangornie orbit, Class II, insured."

"Value?"

"Contract, cash."

"302.2 AU, please." The port below the screen dilated and accepted the box and the sunbursts Dalmer threw after it. In a moment the wait hum ceased and the voice resumed. "Martin Cheruld, Aegios Prime. 306-275 DataNet, Orbit Sync+5, Brangornie."

Dalmer glanced at the screen as the com spoke. "Correct. Timing?"

"Estimated 13.2 days, four nodes, SPC variance 0.15."

The Rifter scooped his change out of the hopper and turned away as the machine singsonged its meaningless thank-you. The yellow, cloudless glare of Paradisum's sky oppressed him as he headed for the field tubes. If it hadn't been for that slug Barrodagh, he'd have posted it at the DataNet in sync.

"From the city, it must be posted from the city," the Bori had insisted. "And Class II—no one must handle it, only machinery."

Well, thought Dalmer as he scowled at passersby, he could understand *that*. That mirror-sphere he'd stolen from the bugs was the weirdest-feeling thing he'd ever handled: even a Downsider would notice the dissonance between the sphere's heft and its apparent lack of inertia. Like most Rifters, Dalmer had a fine-tuned sense of mass and acceleration, and handling the sphere had made him a little queasy. He was glad to be rid of it.

What was hard to understand was sending it by DataNet in the first place. *Eusabian sends us clear across the Thousand Suns to steal it, complete with passcode for the Quarantine Monitor, no less, and then he has me entrust it to his enemies for shipment!*

He'd asked his navigator about it. Nalva was always reading chiptexts on something weird, and always had an answer, or knew where to find out.

She'd nodded. *Dol'jharian revenge customs—IeWilliam had a good account of it. The paliach, they call it. Have to give the other blit a chance to wriggle out of it or it's no good.* Nalva grinned wickedly at him. *Like blasting off your load too soon . . .*

Dalmer shrugged away the memory. *Well, his money's good, and that's all that counts. All Dol'jharians are crazy, anyway—and curiosity doesn't pay when you're dealing with the Lord of Vengeance.*

No doubt there was someone watching him—easier in the spaceport than at the Node in sync. The Rifter elbowed his way to the entrance of the field tube, feeling a distinct relief as the doors slid open. In a few hours he'd jump out of this stinking hole and take the *Bloodknife* back out to deep space and his reward.

Rifthaven, here I come, he thought happily, and the doors closed behind him.

✳   ✳   ✳

BRANGORNIE ORBIT: THE NODE

Martin Cheruld, by the grace of His Majesty Gelasaar III Aegios Prime of Infonetics at Brangornie Node through Re-Hamand, Archon Brangornie, and traitor to his liege, tapped the hold button and blinked groggily at the vidplate, his eyes burning from too many hours staring at the screen, his stomach churning from tension and from drinking too much strong Alygrian tea.

Bitter regret welled up in him as he looked around at the dim-lit elegance of his workroom, littered with papers. Near the door stood a small valise. There was nothing left for him here. He'd labored long for the Lord of Vengeance, now revealed as the Panarch's implacable enemy; now his betrayal in turn of Dol'jhar, while it might save the Panarchy, would not return to him the oath he'd broken.

He was forsworn, but he would have his revenge on those who'd gulled him. He'd spent three shifts undoing the work of five years, stretched his talents to the utmost in an attempt to negate the web Dol'jhar had spun around him, and he might still win. The decode algorithms—no matter that they didn't fit anything he could discover, and weren't even formatted for the DataNet—were on their way to Ares and Arthelion, along with a full recording of the coded messages he'd transmitted for Dol'jhar since he'd sold his loyalty, with a description of what little he knew; and the package from Paradisum had been diverted to the one man Cheruld thought might understand its contents. Most of his time had been spent deleting all traces of what he'd done; when he was finished, his actions would be irreversible, even if discovered. There would be no way of tracing any of it.

All that was left was to finish the message to Sara, to try to save the life of the man they both had more than ample reason to hate.

Cheruld looked at his hands and flexed them slightly. The same talent that had gained him his title, the almost unconscious, intuitive grasp of structure that enabled him to meld with the computers at the Node, and traverse the structures of the DataNet like a bird in its element—that same talent had brought him to the attention of Dol'jhar, and would now, he hoped, save him from the consequences of his treason and unravel the plans of the Lord of Vengeance.

"The Lord Eusabian wishes to deal with a more reasonable government than the one likely under Semion," the Bori had said, during their long negotiations. "His Majesty Gelasaar is willing to listen to reason, but he is old. He will pass soon, and his heir is harsh and inflexible. Dol'jhar wishes peace, and a resumption of trade, a goal incommensurate with Semion's military ambitions." It had seemed so reasonable, seen through the lens of his hatred for Semion and his love for Sara.

Galen, the Panarch's second son, the poet, the dreamer with his quicksilver sensitivity, had a core of very real strength. He had quickly won both their hearts, Downsider and Highdweller alike, that summer years ago on Narbon. Of course Galen would make a better Panarch—on that Cheruld and Dol'jhar could agree.

Cheruld glanced again at the screen. The wait hum of the computer's inanimate, inexhaustible patience formed a quiet backdrop to his thoughts. Now Galen too, and billions of others, were in danger. How could he ever have thought they could deal with Dol'jhar and escape unscathed? He should have known Eusabian would play a double game.

But somebody else in Dol'jhar's service was playing double game too, and the appearance in his mailbank of a decode algorithm, with no other information attached, had given him the key to some of the messages he'd inserted into the DataNet. He'd stolen hours of computer time from the Brangornie Node, protecting vast areas of memory from the scavenging circuits to give his search program room to work without attracting attention, and had been rewarded with twenty-two decoded messages, out of thousands. Included among the twenty-two were the commands detailing the plans for Galen's death, at the hands of a fellow Douloi in a rigged duel.

His hands flew over the console again, and a brightly colored spacetime graph windowed up on the screen. Red lines signified Dol'jhar's plots; green the progress of the information he would shortly dispatch to Sara on Narbon and the journey he himself would make to Talgarth; pale blue spheres, fuzzy with the indeterminacy imposed by relativistic communications, the various planets. The red lines fell short of both Narbon and Talgarth; the blue spheres of both Semion's and Galen's words were transfixed by green shafts of light and life.

Cheruld closed the window with a sudden stab at the console. Like most Highdwellers, he knew too well the fallibility of the graph. At this moment—a concept, he reflected grimly, that itself had no meaning—someone else halfway across the Thousand Suns could demand a graph of the same situation, and get a different answer. Where you stood—nothing more—determined the priority of events: The DataNet and all its complex calculations of Standard Time were just a gloss of the unyielding vastness of spacetime. But humanity persisted in imposing order on disorder, insisted on comprehension of the incomprehensible . . . and he could hope.

It was all he had now.

He turned his attention back to the screen, slapped the hold button off, and continued. "The only way I can save Galen now is to go to Talgarth myself. I should be there about the time you receive this." He paused, reluctant to continue, to plead for the life of the man he hated above all others. "You must tell Semion, regardless of what it costs me or you. Too much depends on us now—only he can mobilize the naval detachment at Narbon with any chance of stopping whatever is intended to follow his assassination—the deaths of the three heirs are only a small part of Dol'jhar's plan. It's the only way we can smash Eusabian's plot before it starts. I did manage to arrange a few unpleasant surprises for the Lord of Dol'jhar—we may win, after all."

He stopped and looked down at the holo of Sara on his desk—clear, sea-green eyes under a crown of red-gold hair, exquisitely formed features, and the hint of a smile playing around the corners of her mouth. He knew he would never see her again.

"If I get to Talgarth on time and can get Galen away, I'll contact you then." He swallowed convulsively and slapped the send plate. After a moment he keyed in the final sequence of his program. "Execute." The screen blanked.

He stood up abruptly, knocking the chair over, and strode out of the room, scooping up the valise near the door. At the door to his suite he took a last look around, at the elegance and quiet wealth he would probably never enjoy again, and then keyed the door open.

"Taking a little vacation, Aegios?"

Cheruld turned abruptly away from the viewport and the receding planet below, feeling cold and a little sick. He hadn't registered under his real name or title, and he didn't know these two men.

He glanced up and down the corridor, but there was no one else around. They had chosen their time well. One of them raised his hand and pointed a dull black tube at his face.

There was a soft click, and Martin Cheruld had just enough time to realize that he hadn't been killed before the jet of gas turned his mind off.

※   ※   ※

NARBON

Sara Darmara Tarathen looked back across the park at the ancient, dark-stoned manor that she'd been forced to live in for eight years. The golden roof tiles gleamed with thousandfold reflections of the westering sun, but she did not perceive the beauty. At the sight of the house the fear and anger that had been Sara's constant companions for eight years constricted her chest. She scanned the arched windows: no one visible. No last-minute panics or warnings.

Not that she had expected any. The whole plan had been startlingly easy to make, once Martin Cheruld had supplied the needed contact, and she did not believe it could go awry now. *Believe?* No. It would be so like Semion to play along until the end, then, with his coldest smile, expose them all . . .

She forced herself to stroll at a leisurely pace up the pathway toward the house, the fine, glistening-white gravel scrunching under her feet. The fear intensified into nausea, but she schooled her face and kept her walk slow.

Bear it. Soon you will be with Galen.

The name instantly released a measure of her tension, like the most powerful of mantras. Galen. Galen ban-Arkad, second son of the Panarch of the Thousand Suns, soon to be vlith-Arkad, heir to the Emerald Throne. Galen always knew without asking the moods of people around him, and wherever he was, music was not far distant. When he read poetry, one glimpsed—however briefly—stillness and harmony in the universe. Life around Galen meant peace, beauty, joy.

Eight years used as a hostage to force Galen's compliance.

Resolutely she stilled the anger as she approached the house. She walked slowly past the doorman, and for once she was able to ignore that detestable creature's hot gaze following her into the house.

At once a young serving-girl flitted out from the bedroom to meet her. One glance at her face told Sara that something was wrong, and alarm immediately kindled inside her again. The girl murmured, "Lady Sara, there's a publicode com for you."

Sara nodded and went into her wardrobe, her throat and

mouth too dry with fear for a word to be squeezed out. She made a start toward Semion's suite, thinking to exempt the call from the recording mechanisms that infested the house, using the Family security code she'd stolen some months earlier; then she stopped. *No use worrying about that anymore . . . if he knows, I'm wasting my time, and if he doesn't, he never will.*

She glided with outward calm into her own chambers, locked her wardrobe door, and palmed open the small paneled room which housed nothing more than a comscreen and chair.

Sara sat down and keyed in her code; her anxiety stretched out the fractional pause before the screen lit and she saw Martin Cheruld's face staring out.

Her alarm intensified into terror as her eyes ran over his always smooth blond hair now lying tousled and grimy on his brow, the sheen of sweat on his face and the exhaustion and fear in his slanted eyes. She had never seen him anything but immaculate, a gentleman coolly amused by the vagaries of the world. In control.

As he began to speak he half reached a hand out, as though to touch her. Though she knew the com had been sent days before, from an unimaginable distance away, the gesture gave her an unsettling sense of immediacy.

"Sara—I hope this will get to you in time. We're going to need Semion alive. I've been lied to . . . much more is involved than just Semion's assassination . . . we've unwittingly aided a massive plot aimed at the entire Panarchy. We've been used, used and betrayed by Jerrode Eusabian of Dol'jhar." His voice hardened as he spat out the faint gutturals of the name.

He clearly expected Sara to recognize it and hate it; and some faint recollection twitched at the back of her mind—but it would not surface, and Cheruld was going on. She did not know if she would have time for a replay. She must listen now.

" . . . I did not tell you that our aide, the contact for the assassin, and much besides, came from Dol'jhar, because I was afraid you would not trust this source." He paused, rubbing shaking hands across his eyes. "I wish I had. Dol'jhar intends to have Galen assassinated at the same time Semion was to die, and I believe he intends to kill the third son, Brandon, at the same time, at his Enkainion, on Arthelion. In the heart of the Mandala, the center of the Thousand Suns! All three of the Panarch's heirs . . . It's Eusabian's revenge against the Panarch for his defeat at Acheront . . ."

Sara's mind was caught like a faulty record chip. *They're going to kill Galen?* She forced her eyes back to Cheruld's face and tried to comprehend his words.

He gave her a swift description of the plot engineered for Galen's death, and his hopes to prevent it, then added, "You must tell Semion, regardless of what it costs me or you."

No! her mind cried. Blood sang in her ears, and the room grayed for a moment. She fought her attention back to the screen.

" . . . it's the only way was can smash Eusabian's plot before it starts." His teeth showed then, as he added savagely, "I did manage to arrange a few unpleasant surprises for the Lord of Dol'jhar—we may win, after all . . ."

Sarah did not hear his closing remarks. Her fingers automatically hit the code that would dump the com. Then, after taking a deep breath, she murmured, "Comp."

The green light glowed.

"Spacetime graph for . . ." Where was Cheruld? "Brangornie and Narbon, and Brangornie and Talgarth." She responded mechanically to the computer's queries: DataNet, commercial starflight, comparison timings delimiting the progress of the plot as outlined by Cheruld. The fact that he had said the assassinations were scheduled for the same time made it easier for her—too easy. A Downsider born and bred, she had been conditioned by the certainties of planetary seasons and the clockwork cycle of day and night: spacetime was merely an abstraction to her. On the screen a deceptively simple pattern of red and green lines grew from pale blue dots enhaloed by the uncertainty assigned by the program.

In obedience to its programming the computer calculated from what it was given, and Sara stared dully at the completed graph, the green light of Cheruld's flight falling short of Talgarth—a pale blue dot transfixed by the bloody red line of Dol'jhar's successful plot. Cheruld would not, had not, made it in time.

Galen is dead.

Her palm slammed down on the cancel pad and the light winked out. She rose, walked into the wardrobe. Semion was due back within an hour at most: she must make a decision now.

She moved through her bedroom, past the bain with its tub of clear, swiftly circulating water, out of the suite, and up to the back atrium. She laid her hands on the rail and looked down at the tile floor below, between the two pools. The chirps and whistles of the exotic birds confined in the conservatory echoed from the walls surrounding the atrium, but Sara did not hear them.

No one in sight. If Semion were back, one or two security men would be standing about. She glanced up through the ever-green leaves of the conservatory trees at the wall of glass, in time to see a bright pinpoint of blue light etch slowly down the purpling sky. Semion's yacht.

She retreated to her suite. It would take him a quarter hour to get in from the field. Fifteen minutes to calm herself . . . to decide.

She passed into the wardrobe and changed from her gown into a soft silk wrapper, then hesitated. Though she had seen nothing and no one out of the ordinary all day, she knew the assassin waited in her bedroom, concealed in the old dumbwaiter behind the ancient Charvannese tapestry. The air in that room seemed subtly different . . . charged.

Today she had swum naked in the atrium pools, well knowing that Semion's silent and seldom-seen valets spied on her when Semion was not present. Sara smiled grimly. The assassin had no doubt found his path quite clear: she had felt the pressure of unseen eyes, which meant there had been none to mark the arrival of the killer now waiting in her suite.

She wanted Semion to die, and she wanted to choose the moment when it happened. And it had to occur in her bedroom, where she had been subjected to eight years of little deaths.

And Cheruld wanted her to save him? *Is evil to win again?* she thought bitterly, stalking into her bedroom and sitting down at her ancient carved-wood desk.

What had Cheruld said? Eusabian of Dol'jhar. She remembered something now, about an attack on the Panarcy, when she was a little girl. Perhaps that was why Martin, who hated Semion almost as much as she did, wanted Semion to live. Semion held flag rank in the Navy, had ships at his command.

All the sons to die, and the Panarch too, no doubt.

She frowned sightlessly at the desk, remembering the existence of the third son, Brandon, whom she had never met. What could he do? She remembered the glow of pride in Galen's eyes when he talked of his younger brother's brilliance—despite there having been some sort of scandal that had resulted in Brandon's being removed from the Naval Academy ten years ago. Since then, it seemed, Brandon had done little but create new scandals with his excesses. *He can do nothing.*

She shook her head, fighting hard against the tears that burned her eyes. *Damn them all. If Galen is dead, then so is life, and joy, and meaning. Yet Martin wants Semion spared ... just to exchange one evil for another? Semion shall* not *live to triumph.*

Men's voices: in the hall, downstairs.

She lifted her head, recognizing in the echoing laughter a familiar hard edge. Semion always traveled with half a dozen formally uniformed officers around him, like minor planets orbiting a sun.

Sara picked up her quill and dipped it, and began writing random sentences. She had quickly embraced the aristocratic practice of penning one's own letters—how graceful and leisurely! And how extravagant, to send a piece of paper across star systems! But she wrote no letter now; he must only see the pose, and would not have time to read over her shoulder.

She heard the hard impact of his boots on the marble flooring of the hall, and smiled. *I'm sorry, Martin. Your news only hardens my resolve.*

Semion walked into the room. "Good afternoon, Sara. The panic was the usual Highdweller foolishness. We found no sign of Rifters anywhere in that sector. That bleater Wortley will have to be replaced, this time by a Downsider."

One of his hands was already unbuttoning his black tunic as he advanced into the room, and Sara, unnerved by the approaching climax of her plans, forced her face to assume the calm expression that had been her only shield for eight years.

But she wasn't entirely successful. Semion's hard eyes surveyed her face, and the thin lips tightened. "What's wrong, my dear?"

Without thinking, the words spilled from her mouth in a rush. "A com . . . Galen has been challenged to a duel!"

Semion gave his quiet, sardonic laugh. "Galen, it seems, will never learn: if he wants to get rid of irritants, he pays. Much less noisy."

"But it's Santyn—Archon Srakin's son—called him out in *public* . . ."

"It couldn't very well be a Rifter, now could it?" Semion shrugged, his eyes ranging slowly down her body.

She hugged her elbows to herself, no longer trying to stop her trembling.

"So he pays a little more." He smiled faintly as he reached out, dug his fingers into the flesh above her elbow, and pulled her toward him.

"But it may be a p-plot, Semion!"

"Why do you think I have guards around him, my dear? If he can't manage to settle it, they will. But how do you know this? Have you been doing a little of your own spying?"

The amused condescension in his voice cauterized her fear and replaced it with a flaming anger that flooded her entire body with new strength and resolution. She smiled straight into his eyes and laid her hands on his shoulders, pushing him so that his back was now squarely to the tapestry. His fingers ran up her sides and started to part her wrapper as he muttered, "Can you contrive to put Galen from your mind for a time? I require your attention . . ."

The words rolled over her tongue with a rare, rich taste: the vintage taste of the wine of vengeance, eight years in the aging. "For your pleasure," she said: the code words her assassin listened for.

She watched hungrily, drinking in his expression as the amusement became a mild puzzlement at the unfinished, unexpected sentence. She heard the faint *spit*; his face reflected surprise and momentary pain, then his eyes lost all expression and the dead fingers traced unfeeling down one of her breasts as he crumpled to the floor.

A moment later the assassin parted the tapestry and stood facing her, firejac still in hand. Between Sara and the assassin a thin curl of smoke rose from the tiny charred pit in Semion's back, like a sacrifice of incense to an unloving god. The assassin was a couple of years younger than she, with the queer cold eyes of a psychopath, and the pallid face of one who spent his time in darkness and secret byways unlit by any sun. His eyes slid down to the open "V" of her wrapper, which revealed her flesh in a clear line to her stomach. She made no effort to close it as she read in his eyes what was going to come next, and what she must do.

She lifted a hand to brush her hair off her forehead, smiling vacantly at him, watching lust quicken in his pale eyes as they followed the shifting movement of her clinging silk gown. She thrust one hip subtly forward and noted his hand clenching on his jac.

"I'm supposed to kill you too," he said, his voice already getting raw.

"Oh, please," she murmured, as though reading lines in a drama. "I'll do anything . . ."

His face reflected his thoughts as clearly as if he spoke aloud. The assassin kept the jac clutched in his hand while he used her, there on the bed next to the dead body of the Aerenarch. At the end she shut her eyes, thinking: *the last time.*

He stood up and straightened his clothing, and she lay there watching him, smiling with promise. He stood looking at her a moment, fingering his jac, then abruptly sheathed it and turned away to the corpse on the floor. She heard a brief shivery sound terminated by a soft crunch, then the rumple of cloth. Moments later the assassin straightened up, glanced at her with a sated smile, his eyes manic.

"I'll be back," he said hoarsely, and slipped out of the room, a sack dangling from one hand.

Sara lay there a moment longer, steeling herself, then sat up and looked at the corpse on the floor.

Much as she had hated Semion, the sight of his headless body filled her with horror.

Galen . . . Galen

The reality of violent death made her reach desperately across the gulf that separated her from Galen—who might also lie this very moment in the same slow-stiffening embrace of death.

Dry sobs tore through her. Ignoring them, she got up and stumbled over to the little safe in her desk. With shaking fingers she opened it and withdrew an old book from under her jewelry box. Under the cover was a tiny, hand-painted portrait of Galen. The serene face smiled out at her, the clear dark eyes looking beyond her into some dimension of unseen poetry, unheard music. Grief was crumbling the safety of her anger now, and it was impossible to control the strangling sobs or the contorting of her face as she carried the portrait into the bain.

Her fingers swept aside the tiny faceted bottles of perfumes and exotic cosmetics on a tile shelf and closed around a tiny scent bottle carved in the shape of a teardrop. She dropped her wrapper on the floor and stepped down into the cleansing embrace of the bath, kissing the portrait clutched in one hand until it glistened wetly with her tears. Then, with her teeth, she unstoppered the green bottle. A sharp scent pinched her nostrils and she tipped her head back, swallowing the contents without letting them touch her tongue.

She flung the bottle aside and her hands closed on both sides of the portrait as she gazed desperately on it, trying to fill her mind only with memories of Galen. Part of her fluttered in fear, noticing faintly how cold she felt despite the warm water bubbling around her, but pleased that the woman had told the truth. *There will be no pain,* she had said, and there wasn't.

Sara's eyes flickered away in a sudden spasm, then fixed hard on the portrait again, but her mind was slipping away from her, and she no longer noticed what was happening to her body. The painted face melted into Galen's features, alive and smiling, the first time he looked on her, the first time she sang for him, the first time they made love: an effortless swirl of remembered sound and feeling, then a sudden swoop of motion took her over the edge of an infinite fall with a barely registered sensation of relief.

Two

✳

DOL'JHAR

Barrodagh leaned back in his chair and inhaled the warm scents of jumari and arrissa that filled the room, trying in vain to ignore the shrill whine of the storm outside the triple-dyplast window. The incessant sound felt like a merciless grip on his neck, and a blinding point of pain was slowly growing behind his eyes. A sudden change in the wind caught savagely at Hroth D'ocha, and the Bori's stomach clenched again as the gravitors damped the swaying of the tower. He pressed his fingers into his neck and stretched, trying to savor the soft air of a summer night on distant Bori, but the chill of a Dol'jharian spring trickled through the window and along his spine as the stink of ozone slowly grew.

The conditioners are overloading again. Barrodagh swiveled himself away from his desk to face the opaqued window. He glared at the large deep-set pane, now counterfeiting the phosphorescent beach at Aluwor on Bori. Its frame vibrated under another blow from the wind, and he slapped the window switch. Why couldn't the Dol'jharians pour their buildings like everyone else, instead of fitting them loosely together out of wood and stone, like an Ur-be-damned puzzle, just because it had always been done that way?

The window cleared slowly, becoming a deep sill backed by a featureless gray that nevertheless gave an impression of rapid movement and intense cold. Barrodagh's reflection stared back at him, colorless and ghostlike. Dark hair, pale eyes, pale skin; the Bori saw these without noticing, hating the wind, the cold, and the planet that spawned them.

Without warning, the gray shroud outside thinned and whipped away, and the window flared savagely bright as the almost pinpoint sun broke through the storm. Barrodagh gasped and squeezed his tear-flooded eyes shut, groping for the window control. The pane dimmed too slowly—*the damned window must be all of five hundred years old,* thought the Bori angrily—but finally he could see again and looked out over the white, thaw-splotched expanse of the Demmoth Ghyri, the high plateau of the Kingdom of Vengeance. His back straightened unconsciously, almost a posture of defiance, as he surveyed the planet-sized prison that confined him. Bori was a gentler world, with mild seasons in its large temperate zone. None of its people adapted well to the harsh iron-bright winters and flame-ravaged summers of Dol'jhar.

Above the dark line on the horizon where the Ghyrian highlands dropped off to the narrow plains below, another wall of clouds was building, towering slowly toward the descending sun with the promise of yet another assault on Hroth D'ocha. Barrodagh watched as the wind flung tattered clouds across the green-gray sky at breakneck speed. He was the second most powerful man on Dol'jhar, more powerful than any of the so-called True Men save the Lord of Vengeance himself, whom he had served for nearly twenty years; but the least of those arrogant Dol'jharians could withstand temperatures that would kill him quickly.

A soft buzz sounded behind him and Barrodagh opaqued the window, feeling something he refused to acknowledge as relief. Power *was* his, for through him went out the commands of Jerrode Eusabian, Avatar of Dol, Lord of Vengeance and the Kingdoms of Dol'jhar. *The True Men may disdain me, but they obey, for who is to know which commands are Eusabian's and which are mine?*

Barrodagh smiled as he turned back to his desk and touched the ruby point that glowed in its dark, glassy surface. He tapped his knuckles on the desk as it slowly extruded the vidplate from a slot at the back. The screen flickered with a nauseating swirl of greenish-gray light as the electronics struggled to resolve an image. *Damned antique,* thought Barrodagh, thoroughly irritated by the almost continuous queasiness induced by the grav-damped swaying of the tower. *And damned Dol'jharians, too: if it had suited their thirdfathers, it suited them, unless, of course, it was good for killing people or inflicting pain—then only the best and newest would do.*

The Bori was drifting into a pleasant memory involving the use of some of the Dol'jharian technology of pain when the vidplate finally came to life.

"Serach Barrodagh." The voice was coldly formal, with no trace of the obsequiousness he was used to hearing, and Barrodagh started slightly as he recognized the angular, arrogant features of Evodh, Lord Eusabian's personal *pesz mas'hadni*. The claws and eyes of the *karra*-patterns lacquered on his skull gleamed dully as the Dol'jharian physician looked at him with a trace of disdain. He had used the "presumed equal" mode of address, an exquisitely shaded insult that was as close to civility as a Dol'jharian noble ever came in speaking to a Bori.

Barrodagh inclined his head and did not speak, as was fitting, but his mind was awash with pleasurable surmise. Evodh had been so certain that the last session in the pain machines would finish Thuriol off, especially the prolonged decompression/recompression cycles: had it merely been that the doctor could not believe a Bori capable of a paliach, the high Dol'jharian art of formal vengeance? Barrodagh felt excitement wash through him in anticipation of his enemy's next death as he waited for Evodh to continue.

"Your toy has just been decanted from the restoration process." The Dol'jharian's sneering emphasis on the word "toy" brought the Bori's head up in a quickly controlled motion of protest at the insult. "As I warned you, it is now an autonomic chunk of meat, nothing more."

Evodh smiled thinly and Barrodagh realized that he was failing to conceal his distress. He schooled his face into the noncommittal mask that had kept him alive for so long and said nothing. The physician continued after a brief pause. "Do you want to terminate it yourself, or shall I have a technician disconnect it?"

Barrodagh thought quickly, his mind ablaze with disappointment and rage: disappointment that Thuriol had only died three times, and rage at the physician's pleasure at his obvious loss of face. But Evodh was powerful, and Dol'jharian nobles were not to be trifled with, especially one whose title indicated his mastery of pain in all its intensities and forms. The paliach of such a man would be fearsome, and Barrodagh realized again that he was no match for a Dol'jharian in the execution of a formal vengeance— witness the fact that Thuriol had died only thrice.

A child's paliach, raged Barrodagh to himself. *A toy! That's how he sees my vengeance.* Well, he would lose no more face in this particular encounter. He inclined his head again briefly, and spoke in a quiet, controlled voice. "No, pesz ko'Evodh," he replied, indicating by his address the least possible difference in rank between them, which was the closest to insult that any Bori dared come when speaking to a noble of Dol'jhar. "You may disconnect it as you see fit."

Evodh nodded and blanked the connection. Barrodagh sat quivering for a moment, then slammed his fists down on the desk and shot to his feet. *Damn him! Damn them all!*

The vidplate chose that moment to jam in its slot, and the

ancient mechanism emitted a jeering squeal as it struggled to retract the screen. Barrodagh lunged savagely across the desk and grabbed the vidplate, wanting desperately to break something, but it jerked from his grasp and sucked his fingers into the slot with bruising force, leaving him sprawled across the desk in a welter of paper and record chips.

The Bori yanked his fingers out of the slot, levered himself back to his feet, and stepped around the desk. He stood stiffly for a moment, his face mottled with rage, looking around the room at the various objets d'art and plants that adorned it, and then selected a small jumari tree and began methodically shredding it. The plant writhed slowly in vegetable agony, its woody stoma gaping silently open as Barrodagh stripped off its leaves and snapped its scaly stems, hissing between his teeth in vengeful concentration. Finally, after he had stomped the remains deep into the plush carpet, leaving sticky yellow stains on the warm browns and greens of the intricate pattern, he took a final look around and hurried out, his rage still unsatisfied.

The gray-clad guard outside came to attention as Barrodagh stormed out of his office, and then stiffened even more as he saw the expression on the Bori's face, trying unsuccessfully to hide his fear. Barrodagh noted this with some satisfaction, but his frustration remained unabated. He'd proved his power over Dol'jharian commoners too many times to take any pleasure in terrorizing this one; not with Evodh's insulting tones still fresh in his mind.

The faces carved in riotous profusion in the stone of the corridor walls seemed to leer at him as he passed, their eyes mocking his impotence. The worst of it, Barrodagh decided, was that he could do nothing—he had no leverage in this case. If Eusabian ever found out what Thuriol had tried to do, in his year-long duel with Barrodagh for supremacy in the Bori bureaucracy that ran the Dol'jharian state; and that he, Barrodagh, had given him the opportunity to do so to maneuver his enemy into an untenable position . . .

The Bori shuddered, and not from the cold of the drafty hall. Eusabian's paliach against the Panarchy, twenty long

years in the making, might have crumbled to ruin. Barrodagh
turned the corner into the corridor leading to his quarters, almost running. Every breath would be a burden of insupportable, unending pain, if Eusabian found out.

He reached the door to his suite and pushed through
without pausing. As the door swung closed behind him he
stopped, letting the warm ambience of the room soak into
him. Here, deep within Hroth D'ocha, there was nothing of
Dol'jhar, except the occasional swaying of the tower, and
that was lessened. *No,* he thought, *Evodh is untouchable.
This matter must never reach the ears of the Lord of Vengeance, save perhaps as an amusing tale of a Bori's failed
paliach.*

Barrodagh gritted his teeth as he sat down in a lush chair,
relaxing as it adjusted to his form. Yes, let it be that:
Eusabian cared only that his commands were carried out instantly and efficiently. He need not know that a carefully
cultivated traitor to the Panarchy, key to Eusabian's plans,
had nearly discovered the true extent of Dol'jhar's plans—
knowledge that surely would have turned him back to the
Panarch's service.

The gentle sound of falling water from the fountain in
the next room worked its familiar magic on Barrodagh's
nerves, and the remainder of his rage leached out of him
as he leaned back and stretched. There was really no need
to worry, he decided. Thuriol had been stopped in time,
and the last movement of his lord's paliach had begun.
When the Heart of Kronos reached Cheruld, still unaware
of the true extent of his treason—*No thanks to Thuriol,* he
thought—he would hand it over to Eusabian's agents, and
Dol'jhar would strike.

*It will take them weeks just to understand what had hap-
pened.* Trammeled by the unyielding stubbornness of spacetime, limited to shipborne communications, their Panarchist
foes would crumble before the onslaught of Dol'jhar and its
Rifter allies, armed with the instantaneous communicators
and power relays left by the Ur when they vanished ten million years before. *Our ships are already more powerful than*

anything the Panarchy has, and Lysanter says the genera-
tor's only on standby. With the Heart installed, there will be
no limits to our power.

Barrodagh reclined further, happily anticipating the day—
not too far off now—when he, speaking for the Lord of
Vengeance, would rule the Thousand Suns. And someday,
inevitably, Eusabian would fall victim to his last remaining
son, Anaris; but he, like all the Bori, would continue, the
faceless power behind the throne. Perhaps, he thought, it
was time to leak a little more information to the heir, to
keep his gratitude alive until he grew powerful enough to
cultivate more openly.

A soft tone sounded, and the Bori grimaced as he reached
over and tapped the complate.

"Tillimar byn-Amal reports a change of command on the
Skullwind and requests the command ciphers for Fleet 10."
The voice shaded into amusement. "There's an interesting
visual, if you like."

Barrodagh energized the vidplate on the wall opposite
him. A moment later its surface swirled into a tableau that
surprised a snort of laughter from the Bori. The scene was
the bridge of the *Skullwind*, the Rifter destroyer posted as
the flagship of Fleet 10, on route to Nyangathanka for the
coming attack. The bulky figure of Tillimar byn-Amal filled
the screen, frozen by the circuitry as he held aloft the clum-
sily hacked-off head of his father, Amal byn-Serafiny, its
face frozen in a rictus of pain and surprise.

Barrodagh laughed again as he noticed that the corpse's
nose had been bitten off. The lurid emotionalism of their
Rifter allies was a source of endless amusement to the Bori,
accustomed as he was to the cool, almost passionless savagery of Dol'jhar. He lingered on the picture for a moment,
trying to decide which was uglier: the corpse's disfigured
face or the scaly, red-cracked visage of the parricide, distorted with both triumph and a loathsome skin condition.
Then he cleared the vidplate with a casual slap at the
comtab.

"Give him the ciphers," he said.

The voice acknowledged the command as Barrodagh settled back in his chair. *I definitely backed the right* ch'qath *in that fight.* He grinned again: byn-Amal's disease made him the very image of the scaly ch'qaths, the savage scavengers whose battles in the pits of the work-dorms were a favorite amusement of Dol'jharian laborers. Now he would activate the sleeper on the *Skullwind* to make sure he received regular and accurate reports on the true state of affairs on board, just as he had from byn-Amal while his father was in command.

The Bori stretched again, relaxing further into the soft embrace of the chair, secure in the knowledge that no Rifter was a match for one who had survived twenty years of infighting in the bureaucracy of Dol'jhar. He was hovering in the delicious half-minded state between wakefulness and sleep when the comtone sounded again.

"What now?" He allowed a measure of irritation into his voice.

"Senzlo'Barrodagh." The unaccustomed use of the honorific snapped him fully awake. "Cheruld has betrayed us." Barrodagh's heart slammed painfully in his chest, and his vision started to gray around the edges as the voice continued inexorably. "The Heart of Kronos is lost, and the Panarchists have been alerted."

When the Bori bureaucrat came back to full awareness of his surroundings, he found himself in the bathroom of his suite, kneeling over the disposer with a sour taste in his mouth and the wrenched-throat feeling that follows a violent spasm of vomiting. He moved to stand up, but his legs wouldn't obey, and he collapsed back onto the cool rim of the disposer, shaking uncontrollably, his mind filled with gruesome images of Dol'jharian vengeance.

Slowly and carefully he reviewed the commands he'd issued even as the anxiety attack had possessed him. The training imposed by twenty years of experience had been all that stood between him and a death too agonizing to contemplate. Slowly, too slowly, he began to regain his composure.

He tried to alert the Panarchists, but our communications are faster, and it may be—he allowed himself a small glimmer of hope—*it may be that the spacetime lag will work in our favor. Certainly the paliach against the sons is safe, and the attack is so close . . .*

He grimaced as he remembered the stuttering head computer tech laboriously explaining how impossible it was to give him the answers he needed in the time he demanded. The tech's stutter had choked him into silence when Barrodagh threatened him with the mindripper, and worse, and he had nodded jerkily and broken the connection. He would have the answers before dawn, as required.

But more important even than that was securing his own safety. He levered himself to his feet and haltingly made his way over to a small cabinet, from which he extracted a small box. He snapped it open and contemplated the brittle black capsule within. Then, after washing his face and cleansing his mouth, he sent a glance through the door of the bathroom at the sealed entrance to his suite before he pulled the capsule out and carefully placed it under his tongue, where it would remain until his underlings answered the questions he'd posed them just before the fugue had totally overwhelmed him.

A slight movement of the tongue and a gritting of the teeth, and Eusabian can do as he wills with my carcass. He didn't know or care if the poison was painless—anything was preferable to falling into the hands of Evodh, directed by the dark passions of the Lord of Vengeance.

Then the Bori made his way slowly back to his chair and sat, steeling himself to quietly await his destiny.

❊   ❊   ❊

Eusabian stood unmoving at the window, a black silken cord writhing with sinuous motions around his fingers as they wove it in an intricate pattern. Above him the light of the karra-fires flickered across the carven ceiling, stirring the ancient figures of gods and demons to fitful life; the rumbling crackle of the distant volcanos came muffled to his ears through the invisible monocrystal wall before him.

He stood at the edge of a dizzying drop: from his towertop the fortress walls fell sheer to the city below. There were no other towers; the low angular buildings gleamed dully in the gray-green dawn of a Dol'jharian spring, while beyond, the land rose in craggy, snow-streaked terraces to the fiery heart of his demesne.

Eusabian's gaze swept up, past the looming lightning-stitched clouds of ash on the horizon, and fixed on the bright point of light rising swiftly in the slowly lightening sky. It looked like a dagger pointed at Jhar D'ocha, threatening the heart of the Kingdom of Vengeance. The tower shuddered momentarily; as the gravitors compensated for the rolling quake he felt the slight pull in his inner ear—like the deadly tug of a ruptor pulse—like the battle of Acheront . . .

. . . the bridge jolted violently and his ears popped as he fell to his knees.

On the viewscreen the Panarchist battlecruiser grew swiftly; the picture shimmered at intervals as the computer tracked the ship that would shortly vaporize them.

"Hypermissile aborted, ruptor turrets one and two not reporting, drive one destabilized . . ." The damage-control monitor's voice was abruptly modulated by a shattering subsonic rumble as the edge of a ruptor pulse brushed past them, its main thrust spent deep within his flagship.

The lights went out, leaving the monitors at their posts briefly silhouetted against a galaxy of flickering status lights, most of them red or amber, and then came on again, dimmer. The sudden wailing of the radiation alarm shrilled in his ears.

"Drive two destabilized, battle reserve thirty percent and falling, shields oscillating . . ."

Eusabian waited for death . . .

The Panarchist Quarantine Monitor faded swiftly as its circumpolar orbit took it higher into the northern sky. Soon he would obliterate that symbol of defeat hanging insolently above his planet, and annihilate those who had placed it there.

Even now, his paliach against the Panarch Gelasaar was unfolding with crushing force, twenty years in the making: first his wife—that long since accomplished—then his sons, then his kingdom, and finally his life. Soon, perhaps today, he would receive new of the heirs' fates; much later, so would the Panarch, and he would wonder at the apparent simultaneity of their deaths.

Eusabian smiled faintly. Between his fingers the cord twisted, like a living creature trying to escape inevitable death, the knot growing ever more complex, shifting and changing as Eusabian contemplated his coming triumph. The timing of those deaths was a clue to the nature of what faced his enemy, if the Panarch had wit to see it. Little good would it do him. And how would he react to the knowledge that for fourteen days the key to his destruction had lain within his grasp, indeed, had been free for the taking for over seven hundred years?

The Lord of Vengeance scowled and turned away from the window as a subtle tone interrupted his thoughts. He frowned at the door, irritated by this intrusion into his early morning solitude, and his eyes narrowed as he considered what might have brought Barrodagh so early . . . perhaps the paliach, one step closer to conclusion; but that was no reason for the Bori to interrupt this Hour.

"Enter." As he spoke he turned back to the window, his fingers ceaselessly weaving the silken cord into an ever-more-intricate web.

Barrodagh tried one more time to rub the sleep out of his eyes and then abruptly dropped his hand to his side as he heard the edge of menace in Eusabian's voice. On Dol'jhar, among the nobility, the hour before dawn was the *orr narhach'pelkun turish*—the Hour of the Unsheathing of the Will, to be interrupted only for the most momentous reasons.

Barrodagh had never dared this before and wished he
didn't have to now. How had Thuriol done it? He'd been
sure he'd stopped him in time. At least there was no way
to link this disaster back to him—Barrodagh was sure of
that—but where had he slipped?

The door slid open silently, and a wash of light from the
corridor briefly illuminated the Lord of Dol'jhar's brooding,
strong-nosed profile as Barrodagh hurriedly stepped
through. The Bori felt his stomach gripe as he caught sight
of the *dirazh'u* in his lord's hands. *Has he been curse-
weaving all night?*

Barrodagh tried to calm himself as he bowed to
Eusabian's back. After a moment that seemed endless,
Eusabian spoke, a trace of irritation in his voice. "The heirs
are dead." It was only partly a question, and partly, to
Barrodagh's ears, a warning that no lesser news would ex-
cuse his interruption of Eusabian's mediation.

"No, Lord . . ." As always, Eusabian's lieutenant let nothing of his inner agitation into his voice, but he knew the
words betrayed it nonetheless. Barrodagh clenched his teeth
momentarily, feeling that they would chatter audibly if he
relaxed the aching pressure of his jaws. "That is not—"

"Then why have you disturbed me?" The irritation in
Eusabian's voice shaded into anger as he interrupted
Barrodagh's words, and the new dawn light flooding in
deepened the lines that absolute power and its exercise had
graven in Eusabian's face.

"Lord . . ." began Barrodagh; and for a panicky moment
he could not continue, for to his finely tuned senses, honed
by twenty years of service to the Lord of Vengeance, the
tower room was slowly filling with the force of his lord's
anger, and the promise of future pain. Then the words came
in a rush.

"Lord, Cheruld has betrayed us." At the words, Eusabian's
hands stopped moving and his fingers clenched whitely on the
dirazh'u, but he did not turn around. "Our agents on
Brangornie intercepted him trying to flee to Talgarth—he had

somehow discovered our intentions toward Galen and was trying to warn him."

Barrodagh swallowed painfully; Eusabian stood absolutely still, staring out the window at the tortured expanse of Jhar D'ocha, the kingdom his ancestors had held for two thousand years, the center of his power as the Avatar of Dol. "Since we do not have a hyperwave on Brangornie, this news has just arrived—it is four days old." This was as close as the Bori dared come to reminding Eusabian that he had recommended the placement of one of the Urian instantaneous radios at Brangornie, despite their scarcity. He'd been overruled by Juvaszt, captain of the *Fist of Dol'jhar*, who insisted that all the hyperwaves be shipborne for strategic reasons.

"They mindripped him and found that he had dispatched messages to Ares, Arthelion, and Narbon. However, the Panarch has stopped over on Lao Tse for a meeting with his Privy Council—none of the messages can have reached him yet."

Barrodagh hurried on, anticipating his lord's concerns. "There is no threat to your paliach upon the Panarch's sons. The message to Narbon may have been received, but our people are already standing by with a secondary plan should the woman attempt to warn the Aerenarch. We expect no difficulty on Talgarth or Arthelion: it is impossible for any warning to reach them in time."

Eusabian turned slowly and looked at him, expressionless, and Barrodagh felt his voice begin to fail him, as in a nightmare, when the scream so much desired, the scream that would wake one from the horror if but uttered, will not come.

"There is more?"

"Lord . . . he diverted the Heart of Kronos to Charvann— and we have no hyperwave there, either." The Bori's voice was hoarse. "We estimate it will arrive within a day. It was sent to a professor of Urian studies."

There was a long silence. "Who is closest to Charvann?" The Bori thought swiftly, poised on the cusp of decision.

Charterly's fleet was somewhat closer, but Hreem—Hreem's was the only flagship on which Barrodagh had no spy. *That damned pet tempath of his.* And Hreem's assignment was the shipyards in Malachronte orbit, where an almost completed battlecruiser lay in the ways. Even without a spy on board, Barrodagh was certain Hreem had more in mind than merely fulfilling the mandate of the Avatar of Dol.

"Hreem's fleet, Lord. His assignment is the orbital shipyards at Malachronte. He is presently five days from Charvann."

"Reassign Hreem to Charvann. Have him get the Heart of Kronos; do not tell him what it is. Are our other forces in position?"

Barrodagh began to relax. He had anticipated correctly the thrust of his lord's concerns: how would this development affect his planned attack on the Panarchy? It had taken the computer techs under Ferrasin all night to map out the complex interplay between the Panarchy's shipborne communications and the infinitely faster communications that Dol'jhar and its Rifter allies enjoyed.

Those coms are ten million years old, and they still work as well as the day they were made, Barrodagh thought, and continued, secure now in the knowledge of his reprieve, for he had the answer Eusabian would want to hear. No warning from a planet or base under attack could reach any other important Panarchist stronghold in time to warn it before it, too, was attacked.

"Not all, Lord, but our calculations indicate that their relative delays in arriving at their targets are less than the spacetime lag of Panarchist communications."

Eusabian looked down at the cord in his hands. After a long moment he pulled on the ends of the dirazh'u, and the knot vanished as the cord stretched taut between his hands. "Let the attack begin."

As Eusabian turned back to the window, already weaving a new knot, the Bori bowed deeply again and withdrew.

THREE

✳

ARTHELION

Crossing the Palace complex on the Mandala takes hours, even for a former bodyguard who knows most of the secret passageways, lifts, and doors added over the centuries.

Alone in a subterranean tunnel, Lenic Deralze sat silently as the gray walls whizzed by. Now he was passing beneath the Palace Major; that trip, he remembered well, took forty-two minutes.

Lenic Deralze was angry.

For ten years he had borne the white flame of rage, the righteous anger of the honest man betrayed, and when a smooth-voiced agent had encountered him on Rifthaven four years ago, offering him a place in a plot against Aerenarch Semion, he had joined willingly. It was Semion who had engineered the disgrace and expulsion of Krysarch Brandon and his best friend, Markham vlith-L'Ranja, from the Naval Academy ten years ago.

Markham . . . a vision of a laughing blond figure flickered through Deralze's mind. The Krysarch and Markham had been inseparable all through school, and together they had gone on to the Academy. It was Markham who was the leader, Brandon the willing conniver in all their outrageous practical jokery. From a distance, the Panarch had been amused, and from Semion there were only instructions on seeing that Brandon concentrated on his course of study, which was to be in the administrative branch of the Service. Brandon had never discussed his oldest brother in Deralze's hearing, he'd simply obeyed the increasingly frequent directives.

Deralze had always liked his charge; by degrees he had extended his loyalty to Markham, who embodied the very best of what the Panarchy had to offer. And Markham had unconsciously strengthened the bond by returning that loyalty: whether it was his nature or merely because he was from an obscure background, he was always quick to note people of low degree as well as high, to see the human being behind the face of the guard or valet that the Arkads had been trained to see as merely ubiquitous.

And then, with no warning, Brandon and Markham were arrested and formally charged, merely for sneaking some unscheduled training time in one of the atmospheric craft. On the books it was against the rules, but eager pilots had been known to boost their training by taking a craft out. Deralze had managed to find out that Semion was behind the arrest; Markham was finished in the Navy, but Brandon—protected from retribution by his status—was to be merely removed. And he did not react at all.

So when after a time it appeared that the assassination plot had been extended to include the death of Brandon, Deralze had concurred: his last sight of his former charge had been the Krysarch standing silently by while Markham was formally cashiered. And when, afterward, Deralze had broken twenty years of training and accused Brandon of complicity with Semion's plans—of cowardice—the nyr-Arkad had still made no answer.

Deralze's anger was not sparked by his own summary expulsion from the Marines, and near death (avoided only by evading Semion's "honor guard" coming to escort him to a fast ship to nowhere). He had expected that. What had destroyed his faith in his vows, and turned him against those he had sworn to protect, was that Markham—the brightest and most popular young officer in the Academy—had been ruined out of mere caprice, yet Brandon did not try to stop it. And from the Panarch, that living symbol of truth and justice, there had been no word at all.

Deralze breathed deeply, his hands clammy on his knees as the familiar walls raced silently by, shadow-chased like ghosts from the past.

He did not know who had engendered the assassination plot, or why. He did know that the universe would be better off without Semion. As for the murder of Brandon, who from all reports had embarked on a spectacular career of dissipation, was he not just a tool of his oldest brother?

But then two years ago, Deralze encountered Markham himself, at a high-powered gambling establishment on Rifthaven. Dressed like a swashbuckling escapee from a wiredream, Markham had laughingly included Deralze in his party, had introduced him to people he forgot a moment later, and had plied him with expensive liquors. At the end, after they had laughed over old times, Markham had managed to get him alone, away from friendly and unfriendly eyes, long enough to say: *Check on Brandy, will you? I've heard nothing, and I'm afraid Semion still has his teeth in Brandon's neck.*

Deralze had agreed, with no intention of complying. But old habits had a strange way of influencing perceptions: when the plots evolved to the point of selecting operatives Deralze found himself volunteering not for the unit going to Semion's fortress on Narbon, but for his old station, the Palace Major on Arthelion, where Brandon nyr-Arkad was to make his Enkainion.

Deralze looked up as the cart stopped. He had to know if the nyr-Arkad had conspired with Semion—or not. He stepped out of the cart and keyed the lift.

It had, after all, been so easy to arrange.

He knew exactly how to get a message to Brandon past Semion's spies; what he did not know was if Brandon would heed it. Deralze said nothing in the message beyond a request for a meeting, and a time, three months ago.

On the day named, he'd waited in a seedy bar on the edge of the civilian spaceport, armed and expecting either a squad of Semion's coverts or else nothing at all—but right on time, the familiar slim figure had entered alone, looking around with mild interest as if he were a tourist on holiday from one of the Highdwellings.

Remembering the things he had shouted into the aristocratic face he had guarded so closely for two decades, when Markham was expelled, Deralze had expected from Brandon anger, contempt, even curiosity about where the former bodyguard had been since he shook off Semion's guards and disappeared.

But before Deralze could even speak the lies he'd carefully prepared, Brandon had surprised him by saying, *You're the only one I can be sure Semion has never suborned. Will you execute a commission for me?*

Brandon, it seemed, wanted a private vessel for some private purpose—which gave Deralze reason to continue to stay in contact. And eventually, to be here this very night.

Deralze felt the lift stop.

He took a deep breath and keyed the door, which slid open silently. Deralze was unprepared for the blow to his emotions when he smelled the familiar air, saw the same elegant hallways he'd walked for two decades.

No one was about; the subsequent message from Brandon had promised that. Still expecting a trap, Deralze made his way quickly to Brandon's suite, and the door obligingly slid open.

No one was within. Deralze paused and looked around. The place looked unfamiliar without the usual swarm of valets and guards, though that did not explain the tightness in his chest.

Deralze crossed the outer chamber and made his way to

the bedroom, where a single figure was outlined beneath the covers on the bed.

"Krysarch Brandon?"

Lenic Deralze leaned down, hesitated; then deliberately ignoring years of training, touched the bare shoulder of the young man lying asleep on the bed.

The reaction was instantaneous and violent.

Brandon flung aside the bedcover and lifted his arm as though sighting along a firejac. Taking aim directly at Deralze's face, he mumbled, "Under fire. Where's the com?"

Habit forced Deralze back a step before his eyes registered that there was no weapon in the Krysarch's hand.

". . . Dream." Brandon collapsed back in the bed. The hand that had pointed at Deralze now pressed against his eye socket. "Hell. That you, Deralze?"

"Yes, Highness." The honorific came automatically to his lips, despite the ten-year hiatus. The habit of twenty standard years was not easily denied. "Just arrived."

"Damn, what a headache," Brandon muttered. "And what a nightmare. Markham and I, under attack—" He squinted around the room as though shards of his dream images still lingered in the silent, vaulted corners. Then he grinned, a twisted rueful grin that reminded Deralze suddenly of the adolescent Krysarch he had served.

Markham. Deralze stared down in some bemusement at Brandon, who sat naked in his bed, digging the heels of his hands into his eye sockets. *"Under attack?"* Deralze had spent his twenty years making sure that the nyr-Arkad had never seen any kind of action, had never experienced anything even remotely dangerous. Nor, if rumor was correct, had he since. Brandon's nightmare could not have been memory, could only have been a residue of some expensive wiredream.

Markham vlith-L'Ranja was the best of them all.

An idea gripped Deralze: instead of handing Brandon over to the rough justice awaiting him in the Ivory Hall of the Palace Major, he could in fact kill the nyr-Arkad, right now, right here in the middle of the Palace Minor, stronghold of the Arkad family for nearly a thousand years, and no one would witness it.

He looked down, caught a brief, speculative glance from the blurred, bloodshot blue eyes.

Does he see it, then? Anger gave way to curiosity. *He hasn't asked where I went after I disappeared from his service.*

"What did Eleris put in those cups?" Brandon asked the ceiling, and yawned.

"Shall I call from some detox, Highness?" Deralze spoke, trying to force the memories away. *Of course he just assumes my loyalty. Is he really so blind?*

"Detox." Brandon nodded, sitting up. "And coffee. Real, not caf. Bath." He thrust his dark hair out of his eyes, then winced as if even that much movement was painful. "Damn."

Deralze moved to the bedside console, tabbed the inlaid keys. A moment later he heard the sound of water running in the adjoining bain. The door stood open, and Brandon breathed deeply of the drifting steam.

Abruptly the wait hum ended and the dumbwaiter door opened above the console. Two glasses stood there, accompanied by the aromatic smell of real coffee, but Brandon picked up the cold glass of milky liquid first, winced at it, and then gulped it quickly. He shuddered, then reached for the coffee, his face relaxing slightly as the detox diminished what must have seemed a lethal hangover.

When Brandon looked up, his blue eyes were noticeably clearer. "Anyone see you come in?" he asked.

"No one, Highness," Deralze said.

Brandon grinned, once again looking young despite the puffy eyes and the bristle of day-old beard on cheeks and chin. "So you still know how to get in and out of here."

"None better."

"They thought I was crazy to insist on being alone before my Enkainion. You've done what I asked?"

"The ship sits at the booster field right now."

Brandon's next words took him by surprise. "Yet you don't ask why?"

Deralze hesitated, the question, coming so quickly, putting him on the defensive. Why did Brandon ask? Was this the closing of a Semion-contrived trap—or was Deralze merely about to lose the fantastic sum that Brandon had offered him when they'd made their unexpected bargain? "It is not my place. Highness." He took refuge in the emptiness of formality.

Brandon's eyes narrowed with sudden amusement, and he said, "Don't worry. You'll be paid."

Which seemed to close the subject. Brandon got up, carrying his coffee, and moved with leisurely steps across the room. "Want any coffee, Deralze?" he said over his shoulder. "Or anything else?" He waved at the console. "Help yourself." He turned and walked into the bain.

You do not realize that you are on trial here, not I. Yet the former guard felt a twinge of regret, as if he'd missed an important cue.

Deralze followed the Krysarch into the bain. He saw little of the effects of what gossip reported to have been a spectacular ten-year drinking orgy in the slim figure stepping down into the bath. Not quite as tall as his older brothers, Brandon, like Galen, did not carry Semion's mass. Deralze did not see any flab on Brandon's frame; somehow he'd managed to retain some kind of muscle tone, though of course the smooth light brown skin was innocent of any scars.

Brandon led the life of dreams. One long party, carried from one planet to another in glitterships that cost more than the lifetime pay of a thousand soldiers. Beautiful and willing sex partners everywhere he went, unlimited food, drink, and smoke . . . And in a few hours he was scheduled to go before the highest ranked of his peers—the Douloi of the Thousand Suns—to be formally accepted into the Ranks of Service. "Service" for Brandon, according to report, was to be a life of just the kind of thing he'd just spent ten years doing.

The Enkainion would be a pageant, and a party, so spectacular that the DataNet would carry it to every corner of the Panarchy, clear out to the fringes of the Rift.

Was to have been, Deralze thought grimly.

The sound of a quiet belltone interrupted Deralze's reflections.

"Yes?" Brandon said.

The house computer's even, singsong voice was just audible above the rushing of the water. "Holocom from the Aerenarch Semion vlith-Arkad, urgent, released 12-15-65 Standard from the planet Narbon."

Three days ago, Deralze thought. *And today, the agent promised, he was to die.*

"It can wait." Brandon ducked under the water. He came up again, water streaming down his face, when the bell toned again. Brandon's lips twitched. "Wager on this being Eleris?" This time the smile was ironic.

Deralze realized he could no longer read his old charge. Surprised that Brandon seemed willing to have a witness to his private communications, and not knowing how to respond, he said nothing.

"Ident?" Brandon asked the ceiling.

"Lady Eleris vlith-Chandreseki, urgent," the indifferent voice of the comp reported dreamily. The blue light on the little console indicated a two-way visual request, Deralze noted.

"Accept," Brandon said. "But voice only."

At once, a musical soprano filled the steamy room. "Brandon darling . . ." Deralze listened with interest. He remembered the heir to the once-prominent Chandreseki shipyards. *Looks of a holovid star and the morals of a chatz-house professional.* He sidled a glance at Brandon. Why didn't he take this com privately?

"Good morning, Eleris." Brandon grinned up at the afternoon light streaming in the high window on the other side of the bain.

Her laugh ripped for just a moment too long, Deralze thought. "Good *evening,* my love! You *could* have stayed.

Your special day is not yet over. I have many more delights planned for us."

"But I have to get ready. You knew that, I reminded you twice."

"Oh, Brandon . . . I didn't think you *truly* meant to leave so suddenly—were you a teeny bit angry that I fell asleep?" The beautiful voice sounded wistful until the last word, which sounded petulant to Deralze's ears. "You did say we were to spend your special day together."

"We did. This is night."

"Oh, Brandon! You could have sent for your things. I've disappointed you?"

"It was a wonderful day, Eleris, as was last night and the day before. I told you, I have to appear at this thing alone tonight—but that doesn't mean we can't continue afterward . . ."

Her musical laugh rippled again, as calculated and lovely as a waterfall onstage. "Only I know how much you value your independence, Brandon dear, for you know I am exactly the same way. But since the Enkainion is for *your* enjoyment, can we not forego allowing dreary protocol to dictate our lives, just this once?"

Brandon splashed water over his head, then sent an expressive look at Deralze. "Forgive my being stupid, Eleris," he said. "But I have to understand you. Are you suggesting we run away together—and kiss our hands to our relatives, and our lives of dreary Protocol—and the Panarchy?"

"Oh, Brandon!" The pretty sigh betrayed just a hint of exasperation.

Deralze suddenly remembered *semmata*-fishing one summer in the Gulf of Luan: the delicate play of man and massive fish, linked only by a gossamer thread that either could easily snap, but for the skill of the fisherman. Eleris would have made an excellent fisher, he decided.

"So you won't run away with me, then," Brandon said in a disappointed voice.

"Brandon, there's very little time left, and I must discuss

tonight with you. We were promised together for the whole of the day. And I am ready to accompany you."

Brandon hit the mute tab. "So it was the title, after all," he said softly. "Are you surprised, Lenic? Am I?"

The irony in his smile was unmistakable, but Deralze sensed disappointment in his old charge.

Then both expressions were gone as Brandon released the mute.

The voice became urgent, and as fluid as the bathwater. "Brandon my love, what we have is strong enough to survive the cold glare of the public eye. If we *were* to find ourselves bound to still tongues by entering a State Marriage, the strength of our love—certainly mine for you—would transcend the stifling trappings of state!"

"Eleris."

The aria stopped. "Yes, my darling?" Expectation made the voice as breathy as silk.

"I'm sorry, but an urgent holocom from my brother is incoming."

"Then I shall use the time to get ready for your Enkainion. But, my dear, please make haste, we've yet to arrange transportation for me . . ."

"Good-bye, Eleris." Brandon sat back, splashing idly, his gaze wandering across the richly patterned walls. "Well," he said aloud, "that's nearly the last of 'em. Archonei Matir, Flori, Archonei Tanian, Ahz-Ru, Eleris." Once again Deralze sensed, rather than heard, regret. "And leaves . . ."

The tone sounded again, and the computer softly identified the caller: "Dowager Archonei Inesset, urgent."

" . . . Phaelia." Brandon squirted water between his hands, watched it shoot into the air and splash down again. He sent a glance of triumph at Deralze, who felt an unwilling grin stretch at his mouth. *In some ways he hasn't changed.* "Fire away!"

"Your Highness," an imperious, slightly nasal female voice announced in a richly aristocratic accent. "I am calling you at the request of the Aerenarch your brother. He indicated that he was sending you a congratulatory holocom . . ."

There was just a hint of a question in the voice. Brandon smiled wryly at Deralze and once more hit the mute on his bathside console. "Semion must have dispatched a message to Inesset at the same time he sent the one now waiting in my mailbank," he said, as if discussing someone else's affairs—someone far away, not very well known, or liked. "No doubt the smart money in the Court is on Phaelia, with Semion and the Dowager backing her." Without waiting for Deralze to reply, he released the mute.

"I've not seen it yet," he said pleasantly, letting his head fall back on the soft tile surrounding the bath so he could gaze at the sunburst mosaic on the ceiling.

" . . . and he wished me to emphasize that should you wish to please your father, you would accede to the Aerenarch's express request and escort your cousin Phaelia to your Enkainion. As a member of the Family I believe I may speak frankly, and I think it ramshackle to be arranging these things at the very last moment. You might have answered anytime during these last three days; I find it difficult to believe that you had business that necessitated remaining incommunicado. But I do not intend to rebuke you on your day of honor—as a gesture of Family Unity, my daughter has expressed her willingness to have you escort her this evening. It will please your excellent brother, and it will also enable you to avoid the affront to the Family that would be occasioned by acceding to the demands of one of the various persons you are know to associate with in your private life."

"No danger of that."

Archonei Inesset's fastidious phrase *private life* had been delivered in the tone of voice usually reserved for the discovery of a sixteen-legged *sleggishin* in one's after-dinner mousse. Deralze shut his eyes, imagining her beady eyes screwing up tight in her puffy face, and at least one of her multiple chins disappearing under her famous scowl. He'd only met the woman once, but that once had sufficed for a lifetime.

"I must say, I am relieved to hear it," the Archonei went on. "You will send a phaeton?"

"One moment. How will Phaelia feel about this onetime gesture if the gossips see us enter together, her and the wastrel third son whose private life you all deprecate?"

There was the faintest of pauses. Then: "She has indicated she is willing to accede to the Aerenarch's request, but you know she has gained in her superlative training a clear view of the realities of our public lives and has never failed in her duty. Should you wish to discuss this privately with her . . . perhaps tomorrow, here, for tea, at five? But for now, time is growing short. May I . . ."

Brandon interrupted gently. "Since she's going to the ceremony anyway, a few minutes more won't matter, will they?" He paused a moment, then continued before she replied. "Excuse me, my com is flashing, perhaps it's from my brother."

"Very well. I shall tell her to expect confirmation from you momentarily."

Brandon terminated the communication, then once again the comp's inhuman voice spoke, with the typical redundancy of machine communications: "Holocom queue: from the Panarch Gelassar hai-Arkad, urgent, released 12-16-65 Standard en route to planet Lao Tse; from Krysarch Galen ban-Arkad, urgent, released 12-13-65 Standard from planet Talgarth."

"Execute," Brandon said.

Deralze said quickly, "Highness. Do you want to view these in private?"

Brandon looked up from his bath, his eyes blue and cold. His voice, though, was mild as he said, "Why? These messages weren't made in privacy."

Surprise, anger, all dissolved when the holo of the Panarch appeared before them. Deralze had not seen the man in person or in image for twice six years, and the effect of the short, slim, and dapper figure in his faultless white uniform, his silver beard neat, was profound.

A surreal sensation imbued Deralze with old memory and newer words reviewed: always in the past the Panarch had seemed very like a sun, remote yet benevolent, but also, like a sun, removed by unimaginable distance from the affairs of individuals.

The Panarch gazed out at them through blue eyes very much like Brandon's. Deralze felt prickling along the back of his neck and was glad he was still standing. Though this was only a holocom, and days old at that, the effect of the Panarch's presence was strong.

"Welcome, my son, to the ranks of those who serve." The Panarch's lined face was transformed by a sudden smile, one of humor and regret, that made the man look very much younger. For a moment it seemed as if he really did look across time and space to smile at his son, and again Deralze felt that preternatural tingle in the nerves down his neck.

With a swift surge of water Brandon rose from the bath and swathed himself in a towel, his eyes on the holo now projected directly before him.

"I will forbear a long preachment: I expect you will get your surfeit and more of well-meaning speeches today," the Panarch went on. "I wish I could be there: I wish tradition did not dictate that you must face your peers alone. But so it is, and there is a reason for this tradition.

"You will receive many gifts today, most of them costly and some of them even useful. I will leave you with two intangibles.

"The first, the words my mother spoke to me by holocom, on the eve of my own Enkainion: When you stand before your peers to speak the vows of Service, remember the Phoenix, ever consumed by the demands of Service, ever regenerate from the flames. Remember also the Polarities of our ancestor Jaspar Arkad.

"The second thing, from me, from my heart: remember

my love, and your mother's love, which is unending. I hope
and trust we will see one another before long."

The holo winked out. Deralze watched as Brandon stood
unmoving for a moment, then turned and tabbed the wall
console with unecessary violence, using his fist. "Comp!"
he said. "Call through to Steward Halkin."

A moment later the comp gave the confirmation tone.

"Hal," Brandon said.

"Sir?"

"My message to my father. Has it reached him?"

"We've not yet received confirmation, sir. He is still in
transit. Your message has been distributed on the Net along
with his itinerary, with projected convergence a day and a
half ago. I'll patch his reply through when it comes, but it's
likely to take at least two more days, unless he's changed
his plans."

"Thank you." Brandon leaned over and tapped the cancel
pad. Deralze saw his fingers hesitate, tendons rigid, then he
hit another tab and Krysarch Galen appeared in holo, tall,
thin, and dark-eyed. There was tension in Galen's high
brow, though his smile was gentle.

"Brandy," Galen said, "I hope you enjoy your Enkainion.
My own was filled with music and poetry, though nothing
was as splendid as the sunbird you and I used to try to catch
out in the sequoia gardens. Remember that?" He shifted position a little, to a more formal pose, and Deralze had a sudden thought, imbued with an unexpected sadness: *A code,
that about the sunbird. Both Galen and Brandon expect
Semion to view this holo himself.* "My best wishes to you
today, and I hope we will see one another soon." The holo
winked out.

For the first time, Deralze explored the perimeter of the
plot he was a part of. *Semion's death promised, a coin more
precious than mere gold, and Brandon to die for the greater
good. Did the unknown voices tell me the truth—would they
let Galen live?*

"Let's end this," Brandon said, and Deralze looked up
sharply.

But Brandon did not see; he walked into the spacious wardrobe, leaving Deralze to follow behind. "Comp," Brandon said. "Holocom to Krysarch Galen on Talgarth ... Wait ... N-no ... cancel. I'll call him when I'm free. I've an idea he'll enjoy that."

Brandon flung up one hand. "It's time to hear what my beloved brother has to say. You remember Semion?" This time the edge was distinct in his voice, a bitterness that Deralze had never heard there before.

And then, suddenly, there it was: an answer, given freely: "You and Markham disappeared, Deralze, and Semion won yet again. But it's taken me ten years to figure out that I can't fight him within the system, so I have to do it from without ... Except—" He tightened the towel around himself as he stared at the holopad where his father's image had stood. "Is the system worth saving, Deralze?"

An answer, not *the* answer. He was not Semion's tool now. Was he then? Why had he done nothing?

"Is the system worth saving?" That decision is out of your hands, Krysarch, Deralze thought, and for the first time, the inexorable weight of the justice he'd actively worked for pressed on him. *Not justice. Vengeance—* Vengeance? Where had he heard that, as a title—

"But first something suitable to wear," Brandon said, breaking the splintering trains of thought, as he looked slowly around the wardrobe.

Hanging next to the long wall-mirror in the wardrobe was a splendid tunic and trousers, maroon in color, with gold stitching on collar, cuffs, and down the seams of the trousers. Jeweled decorations lay on the low table below, along with Brandon's elegantly plain boswell, reflected darkly in the flawless obsidian surface. On another table sat a pair of beautiful single-seamed boots.

Brandon paused, looking at the tunic, the decorations. Then he stepped to the side of the mirror and touched a control. The mirror slid silently into the wall, revealing rows of neatly hung clothing ranging from formal to everyday. He reached in, pulled out a plain shirt, a well-made tunic bare of decoration, and some dark trousers, and tossed these on the table which held the medals.

Then Brandon smiled over at Deralze. "Comp," he said. "Run the holocom from Semion. Freeze."

He turned toward the slender inlay-patterned table by the door. A miniature projection of the heir to the Panarchy appeared. Deralze studied the hard face, thin lips with sarcasm ingrained at the mouth corners, the heavy-lidded blue eyes. Semion looked older than his forty-three years as he stood stiffly, his image frozen by the comp, the decorations glittering on his formal black tunic.

"Proceed." Brandon turned away as the image began speaking and went on with his dressing, slowly, thoughtfully, one item at a time, as he listened.

"Brandon, today you will make your formal entrance into the Douloi, the Ranks of Service, embarking on what will be a lifetime of commitment. I wish, of course, to congratulate you on your new status, and to express the wish that you enjoy the festivities arranged in your honor. It is not appropriate for any of us to be there, for you must face your peers alone. That is tradition. However, I desired Vannis to be there as my representative. Perhaps you have heard from her by now . . ."

Brandon looked up in surprise. "Correction: there's one I haven't heard from. You see, Deralze, I do have some luck."

"You will no doubt be receiving a congratulatory message from the Panarch our father. He has indicated to me in private communication his pleasure that you have at last chosen to assume your responsibilities. I understand you desire private audience: perhaps, after you have accustomed yourself to the demands of your duties, a meeting will be arranged."

Brandon's eyes narrowed and he paused, then went on with his dressing.

"One way to gain his favor would be for you to comply with our wishes and accompany Krysarchei Phaelia to your Enkainion. Should you decide to ally permanently with her, the family connection will be beneficial to everyone on Arthelion, and throughout the Panarchy."

Brandon laughed softly. He turned, rummaged in a drawer, lifted out some socks, then sat down and slowly pulled one on as his eyes stayed fixed to the holocom of his brother's face.

"I should like to add a word about your personal and private life . . ."

"By all means!" Brandon waved the other sock in a regal gesture.

"You must learn to keep your private and public lives separate. An alliance with Krysarchei Phaelia would be ideal—you need never see her except on public occasions, and your personal friends would be effectively silenced. Court expects to see Vannis Scefi-Cartano with me when I attend public functions, and no comment is raised when this occurs. My wife also serves as my deputation at those public affairs that I cannot attend.

"Sara Tarathen, in turn, knows that she will preside only at private affairs, for my personal friends. Therefore, though the Court may or may not know about her, she has her place, unseen by the public, and again there is no comment. I am passing along advice accrued from twenty years' experience of public life. I shall be on Arthelion in two weeks, if all goes well here, and we shall discuss this further. Have an enjoyable evening."

Brandon smiled faintly as the hologram disappeared. He pulled on the expensive boots, then turned to face Deralze. The humorless smile tightening the corners of his mouth increased the resemblance between him and Semion. Brandon must have seen something in Deralze's face change, for the expression deepened for a second, then disappeared as he laughed ruefully.

Brandon's eyes fell to his boswell lying on the low table. He picked it up, weighing it in his hand. "Do Rifters use these?" he asked.

"Yes," Deralze said, fighting a growing sense of unreality.

Certainly no Downsider or Highdweller would leave his dwelling without that indispensable combination of communicator, computer tap, and personal databank. Deralze's brain, though, caught on the word *Rifter*. It was hired Rifters who had made the Ivory Hall into a deathtrap. *But not Markham's group. His message seemed random, but was it? Now I see a circle—*

Brandon shrugged and dropped the boswell back on the table. "There's nothing in there that would do me any good out there, anyway," he said.

He keyed open the concealed drawer in the table and removed a huge sum in medium-denomination AU, and another in large, this last which he handed to Deralze, who stared down at the bills. They were the fashionable new Archaic Style notes from the Carretta Mutual Assurance Sodality; the visage of Brandon's ancestor, Jaspar I, founder of the dynasty, stared back at him. Some trick of the engraver's art imbued the formal portrait with the hint of a knowing grin.

"You know the Polarities of Jaspar I, don't you, Deralze? Begins 'Ruler of all, ruler of naught, power unlimited, a prison unsought.' My well-meaning father has never seen that those are polarized between his offspring: Semion has claimed the first and third, leaving Galen and me gripped by the other two." He shook his head. "Anyway, I find it singularly appropriate that it's one of old Jaspar's Unalterables that will help us leave no trace." Brandon smiled at the irony.

Thinking back ten years, Deralze said automatically, "The right of sentients to untraceable monetary exchanges shall not be infringed." Otherwise the boswell would long ago have made cash obsolete, rendering one's every move visible to the authorities. *And would have made it easy for Semion's coverts to catch up with me.* Deralze drew in a slow breath. "So you want to leave? Now?"

"There isn't a better time, is there?" Brandon countered. "Every one of my watchdogs is at the Palace Major, and none of them know what I'm doing—"

None of your watchdogs, or mine. But the search will begin soon. Still, he said nothing.

Brandon paused and looked back at his boswell.

Deralze watched him pick it up and weight it in his hand, then he said, "What have you recorded in it?"

"I'm not sure," Brandon said.

Deralze nodded, unsurprised. Brandon had the very best type of boswell made, and its data capacity was enormous. But it was possible that someone might be able to draw some conclusions about his intended destination from it.

Brandon crossed the room to the disposal and thrust the boswell in. The disposal emitted a warning trill, indicating the presence of something other than a document.

"Fanfare for a private Enkainion," he said, and tabbed the confirm. The muffled whoomp from the shredder fields was only a little louder than usual. Then he said softly, "Let's go."

The strained sense of unreality gripped Deralze, made clear thought difficult. He had come here seeking an answer, and he'd obtained it, but at the cost of larger questions he'd never faced and which now haunted him like the shades that would soon depart the Palace Major's Ivory Hall.

Stay with the immediate problem, then.

He said nothing, feeling as if he watched himself and Brandon on a vidscreen as they took the VIP elevator down to the maglev transport terminal deep underground.

When the door slid open, he saw and recognized two high-ranking naval officers crossing the quad from the military side of the complex. He and Brandon remained silent and still in the dim-lit doorway until they passed. Across the low-lit quad, through a line of attractive potted flowering shrubs arranged to screen off the less elegant portions of the terminal from the eyes of the guests arriving for the ceremony, Deralze caught sight of some of the personnel overseeing the arrival of the first wave of bejeweled and beglittered civilian attendees. Brandon paused, watching for a moment, then walked silently to the VIP sub-tube access. Deralze followed.

Brandon keyed it open with the Family override code, and inside the pod he stepped into the operator's booth and activated it with a quick and experienced hand. Outside, the heavy door slid shut with a subdued clank as the vacuum lock engaged, and the pod lifted off the rail, humming faintly.

After a moment, Brandon punched the drive button and sat back, as the pod shot toward the 285-kilometer-distant booster field.

Deralze glanced over at the Krysarch, who was staring pensively out the window at the featureless wall of the tunnel whizzing by.

The ghosts fled down the dim tunnel with Deralze, forcing him to review his own actions for the past ten years. He'd moved through life as if asleep, and now, though he felt as if he moved in dream time, his mind was truly awake.

Deralze saw that he had been imprisoned not so much by the agent's lying words, playing on his disappointment and twisting old loyalties, but by his own lack of vision. *I trusted Semion all those years, thinking he supervised his brother's training, but now I see it for the imprisonment it really was. And the Panarch was absent not from disinterest, but from disinformation.*

He thought again of the Polarities of Jaspar I—and the limits placed on one human being by the burden of a government more vast than anything history spoke of.

How far does this plot reach? I thought it merely encompassed the end of two Arkads—

His attention was caught by the buzzer announcing their arrival at the boost field.

The door hissed open and they walked out, both looking up at the empty control window. The booster field beyond, a smaller version of the vast complex on the other side of the capital, was equally empty and silent, except for a single ship resting in a launch pod.

"Oversaw the last modifications myself," Deralze said, trying to shake the now nearly paralyzing sense of unreality which gripped him. "One- or two-person operation, inter and intra-system . . . everything. Of course, the field comps show it still needs a week's work or so." He glanced up at Brandon. "The booster module's set for automatic lift, under ship control—it'll just be an anonymous blip on the screens at the Node." He paused. "Ready to boost." It was almost a question.

"Are you regretting your duplicity?" Brandon's smile was wide, his eyes intent. "Now's the time to make your choice."

Deralze stared back at Brandon, wondering if, after all, he had known about the plans. But that had been Semion's trick, to play along until the end, then close his fist on the plotters. And Semion would never knowingly place himself in any danger.

Deralze looked at the waiting blue eyes. Brandon exhibited no sense of danger. *He trusted me once, he trusts me still,* he thought.

Deralze looked out at the cloud-streaked sky, at the nightbirds wheeling over the wide field. How random, after all, were these events? *A circle*

"Choice?" he said. Swallowed. "Duplicity?"

Brandon's smile was twisted. "You made vows once to protect the system, and now you're helping me to escape from it: my oldest brother, at least, would classify that as duplicity. As for choices: well, either you take the money and run—or come with me. I've found out where Markham is, you see. He's done the Riftskip, and he has a base on a moon called Dis in the Charvann system."

"You want me to join you?"

"I'd like to have you," Brandon said lightly. "And so would Markham, I think."

Deralze thought suddenly of the Enkainion now gathering. If it was to begin now, how long would they have before he was missed?

Decision closed round him, shattering the paralysis.

Deralze knew he'd made a lethal mistake in assuming that Brandon had anything to do with the Aerenarch's machinations. He also knew that though both sides would now seek his blood, he would walk out of here with the Krysarch alive.

"I'll stick by you, Highness," Deralze said.

"Then call me Brandon. I've heard they don't use titles where we're headed."

For the first time in ten years, Deralze laughed, and he followed Brandon up the ramp.

Inside the silent vessel, Deralze watched, pleased, as Brandon looked around slowly at the yacht's neat proportions, then breathed in deeply, as if tasting the new-smell that lay with its own peculiar promise in the as-yet-uncirculated air.

Brandon accessed the navcomp to load his destination. Midway through the sequence he stopped, his hand hovering over the keys.

"There is one person who didn't come today who I wanted to say good-bye to," he said slowly. "By one of those curious coincidences, Markham's Dis is in the same system as Omilov's Charvann. Though I don't know if either of them is aware of the other. Mind if we make one stopover?"

Deralze gestured. "I'm ready," he said.

Brandon finished his sequence, then entered it. Moments later the boost light on the console came on, and a faint green light washed the field briefly before the viewscreen blanked automatically.

Both men strapped themselves into their seats. Brandon's hand hovered momentarily over the go-pad, then came down decisively.

FOUR

✳

Leseuer wasn't sure when it happened, but partway into the
Enkainion the last of her egalitarian cynicism vanished, and
she knew that whatever her planet's decision, she was now
and forever a Panarchist.

All around her the fulgent panoply of a wealthy, ancient,
and complex civilization blended in a synergy of color and
sound and scent. Exalted, she walked among the men and
women mingling and conversing in the exquisite pavane of
courtesy and grace that was second nature to the Douloi.

Behind her, the tall stained-glass windows of the Hall of
Ivory admitted the last light of a long summer day. Slow
cloud shadows lent animation to their colors and brought
the tapestries on the walls to polychromatic life. High above
her head the chandeliers, elegant structures of glass and
metal hovering without visible support, flamed and sparkled
in the sunset light. As she watched, a beam of light lanced
through a window and splashed against the massive doors
guarding the entrance to the Throne Room, picking out in

bold relief the riotously complicated abstract mural inlaid in them: the Prophetae Gennady's *Ars Irruptus*.

But the richness of the room paled in comparison with the sumptuous clothing and glittering decorations of the Douloi assembling to pay honor to the Krysarch Brandon nyr-Arkad. The traditions of a myriad of cultures and centuries of history were represented here, for the collective memory of the Panarchy reached back to a planet forever beyond reach.

Suddenly a hush descended on the Hall as the huge inlaid doors opened slightly, barely wide enough to admit one person, but no one emerged. It was time for the first of the Three Summons.

Leseuer triggered the *ajna* on her forehead to a narrow focus on the doors, feeling its delicate pull on her skin as the semi-living lens adjusted. Her boswell briefly flashed framing lines across her vision; she was pleased to see that her target was already centered.

(You've really gotten quite good at this.) Leseuer flushed slightly as the boswelled voice of Ranor, her tutor from Archetype and Ritual, interrupted her thoughts. There'd been a time when she'd thought she would never master the art of ajna-imaging. It was so subtle and hard to control compared to the primitive vidcams used back home.

(Hush!) she boswelled back to him. *(It's hard enough without you chattering in my ear.)*

(Not your ear, love.) He chuckled and fell silent. She glanced at the boswell on her wrist. Neural induction still felt like magic to her, despite the year of practice she'd had.

She returned her full attention to the scene before her. The floor in front of the doors cleared as the Laergon of the College of Archetype and Ritual strode forward with a measured pace. His arms were extended rigidly overhead, firmly gripping the glittering Mace of Karelais: the ancient scepter of the first kingdom to indite the Covenant of Anarchy that ushered in the Jaspran Peace. His gold-trimmed purple robe of state swirled around his stout figure as he stopped before the door. Behind him, the representative of the Polloi, stark in her uniform of black and white, her features hidden by a shimmermask, held aloft the golden manacles of Service on an ebon tau-shaped staff with a silver snake twined around it. The music that had formed an unacknowledged background to the gathering now changed, becoming slower, measured, laden with tonalities evocative of time and the long chain of lives that linked them all to Lost Earth.

The Laergon shook the Mace in a long arc over his head, bending so deeply to either side that its ends tapped the marble floor. The resulting spray of harmonics from its crystalline core, ranging from a deep booming that recalled the restless sea to teeth-aching supersonics, effectively stilled the last remnants of conversation in the Hall of Ivory. Then there was complete silence.

The Laergon straightened up and grounded the Mace in front of him. "His Royal Highness, the Krysarch Brandon Takari Burgess Njoye Willam su Gelasaar y Ilara nyr Arkad d'Mandala!" His voice echoed into a stillness broken only by the musical clangor of the Manacles as the Polloi brandished them at the partly opened doors to the Throne Room.

After a moment, the Laergon turned away from the doors and strode back across the room, followed by the Polloi, and the doors swung shut again. Around the perimeter people stirred once again, the machinery of state resuming, and Leseuer marveled again at the effortless combination of unstudied elegance and careful ceremony that was the hallmark of government in the Thousand Suns.

Who knows what will be decided here tonight? she thought. *The result of some carefully arranged encounter that I probably wouldn't recognize as significant even if it happened right in front of me.* Then she suppressed a little shiver of awe as she realized that one of the decisions reached tonight might be the status of her planet in the Panarchy.

(That's definitely on the agenda, but I think more people are wondering about the absence of the Aerenarch-Consort.) Ranor chuckled. *(You're subvocalizing again.)*

She flushed. Then, amazed that she had not previously noted her absence: *(Lady Vannis Scefi-Cartano? She's not here?)* Leseuer looked around the vast room again, as if she could have missed the familiar small, elegant figure. Seen from a distance, the Aerenarch's wife had always reminded her of a knife worn hidden in a sleeve. Nothing important happened at Court without her presence. *(What does her absence mean?)*

(That's what everyone is trying to figure out. It could be a message from the Aerenarch Semion, or it could be a message to him. Or it could be a message from the Cartano family to the other principal Mandala families.)

Leseuer repressed the chill of memory. She'd been presented to the Aeranarch on Narbon, on her way to Arthelion. She'd known almost nothing of Panarchic politics at the time, but had sensed a darkness around the heir and his Court, an impression only strengthened by her year at the court of Gelasaar III.

> *(The man that hath no music in himself,*
> *Nor is not mov'd with concord of sweet sounds,*
> *Is fit for treasons, stratagems, and spoils;*
> *The motions of his spirit are dull as night,*
> *And his affections dark as Erebus:*
> *Let no such man be trusted.)*

Ranor quoted softly, as if sensing her unease. Perhaps he had: the boswell's ability to indicate subtle muscle movements sometimes gave its use the quality of telepathy. *(But don't worry,)* he continued. *(It's unlikely to have any effect on the Ansonia question. Tonight's maneuvering is merely detail work.)*

(And?)

(Oh, I don't know what's been decided. I just know how these things work. This is far too high a ceremony to host a major negotiation.)

Leseuer shook her head. She didn't expect she'd ever fully understand Panarchic politics: the perplexing interplay of spontaneity and choreography amidst the splendors of Douloi ceremony, the wheels within wheels wherein a shrug or a lifted eyebrow could set off a swift interchange of events that would decide the fate of millions. But the politics merely reflected the nature of these people: shrewd, cosmopolitan, self-controlled, and wise with a weight of years and tradition that had no counterpart on her world.

Ansonia was fiercely proud of its hard-won democratic principles and devotion to rational government, and deeply suspicious of the bizarre Panarchist combination of anarchy, ritual, and absolute monarchy.

Her throat tightened as she realized how important it had become to her that her planet understand what was offered them, despite its strangeness.

Across the Hall she saw the gee-bubble of a nuller float through the entrance doors; he or she—so wizened by the great age conferred by life in free-fall that Leseuer could not distinguish—was upside down with respect to the Hall. She still didn't understand how these rare, almost immortal humans fit into the careful structures of Douloi life, with their disregard for the conventions of placement and preference.

The nuller's bubble hovered over a far group as a whisper, no more than a susurrus of summer leaves, rustled through the company. Leseuer felt it more than she heard it: some heads turned toward the great doors, so her head turned as well—

(The Krysarch,) Ranor said. *(He has not yet been seen.)*
(Isn't he supposed to appear after the third call?)
(But he should be here waiting for the last summons, and he is nowhere to be found. Perhaps he's en route through the complex via unorthodox ways—the Arkads are rumored to know most of the secret passageways this place is honeycombed with. If so, he'd better hurry and appear. The Household is in a panic.)

Just then a flash of livid green caught the edge of her vision and she saw a Kelly trinity entering the hall. She stared in fascination at the first nonhuman race she'd ever seen in the flesh, one of the few yet discovered in the Thousand Suns. The three aliens were short, rotund tripeds covered in a dense lacework of fluttering, tape-like ribbons. Armless, each had a single, long headstalk springing from its torso, crowned with a mouth like a fleshy lily with three bright blue eyes under the lip. They wore no clothing. As she watched, she suddenly became aware that they were heading directly for her.

The two larger, yellow-green Kelly pivoted in a waltz-like movement around the smaller, bright green one in the center of the trinity. Their headstalks—each adorned with a gaudy, bejeweled boswell—twisted in a constant helical motion, gently intertwining and touching each other with the soft pseudopods arrayed around their mouths. The constant caresses somehow reminded her of an infant playing with its fingers and toes. As they came closer she could hear their claws clicking on the floor in an elaborate trinary rhythm.

(*Threy want to meet you,*) said Ranor. (*Since I wasn't told in advance, we must assume this is a test, of you and of Ansonia.*)

(*But you haven't finished briefing me on the Kelly yet,*) she replied, a knot of panic forming in her stomach. All she'd seen was an ancient pre-Exilic flatvid—monochrome, yet—that was too silly for words, interrupted by a summons from her Ambassador for yet another meeting. Ranor had introduced the vid by remarking that it was the starting point for the ceremonials that Archetype and Ritual had developed to bind the Kelly into the Ranks of Service. He hadn't had a chance to explain further, and now the aliens were only a few meters away.

(*That is the Archon of Kelly. Threir adopted names are Lheri, Mho, and Curlizho. The one in the center, the intermittor, is Mho. She will speak for threm.*)

(*What! But that's the vid . . .*)

(*Yes. Threy use those human names because we can't pronounce threirs, and for other reasons that will become apparent. I haven't time to explain now. Just do exactly what I tell*

*you, no matter how strange it seems. Exactly! And don't move
unless I tell you to.)* She could hear an edge of panic in his
voice, which only intensified hers, and then the aliens halted
in front of her. The blason d'solei—the sunburst of direct
aegicy that marked those who received authority directly from
the Panarch, rather than by delegation—glittered brightly
against their green pelts. She wondered distractedly how the
decorations were fastened on.

"Well met, Leseuer gen Altamon," said the alien. "We
welcome you." Its voice was a mellow, reedy blat; its
breath and body scent were an odd mixture reminiscent of
cut herbs and burning plastic. Without warning it reached
out and slapped her hard on top of her head, waved its
headstalk up and down in front of her face, and then
tweaked her nose. Its lips? fingers? were warm and soft.

*(Now slap her on top of the body, wave your hand side-
to-side in front of her headstalk, fingers pointed at her, and
then poke her in the eyes with two fingers!)* said Ranor.
(Quickly! Like the vid. You won't hurt her.)

Confused and frightened, Leseuer reached out and hesitantly slapped the Kelly next to where the headstalk joined
the torso; belying their appearance, the glossy ribbons were
exquisitely supple and velvety. As she waved her hand back
and forth the Kelly's headstalk followed it with a sinuous
motion. It didn't flinch when she gingerly stabbed at it, but
her fingers were deflected by a hard, horny membrane flickering across the two of its three eyes facing her.

All three aliens burst into a quiet paroxysm of honking
and hissing, their headstalks slapping each other's torsos
frantically and twining about each other in a confusing
snarl.

*(That ancient vid was the breakthrough that enabled us to
develop rituals and symbols that Kelly and humans could
share,)* commented Ranor, relief audible in his voice. *(Threy
are very physical beings in whom the sense of touch is
highly developed.)* His boswell transmitted the strange
sound that indicated a sigh of relief. *(You did very well;
threy are quite pleased.)*

The mixture of plural and singular forms had merely added to her disorientation, and Leseuer groped for something to say as she tried to recover from the Kelly's greeting.

"Well met indeed, Your Grace," she finally replied as the snaky writhing of the Kelly subsided. "I am honored."

She was saved from the effort of further conversation by the Second Summons, which followed the pattern of the first. The Kelly did not change the position of their torsos; only their headstalks twisted to watch. As the great doors closed the second time and the Laergon strode past her she noted a look of distraction, even worry, on his face.

(Has the Krysarch been found?)

(No.) The short answer carried with it a wave of anxiety.

Mho twisted her headstalk back toward Leseuer. "You humans always do important things in threes. That's what convinced us you are truly civilized." The other two Kelly moved closer, and throughout the ensuing conversation they softly touched her shoulders and arms in a gentle, patting motion. Despite their strangeness—or perhaps because they did not at all resemble humans, and thus had nothing of deformity about them—she found the contact strangely comforting.

"Speaking of threes," continued the Kelly, "we congratulate you on your completion."

Leseuer kept her face blank as she tried to unravel the meaning of that comment. *(Completion?)* she subvocalized as the alien proceeded.

"We have met Ranor, and look forward to greeting your third."

(Third?)

(Our unborn child.) Ranor's love and delight bathed her in warmth.

(But we only just found out. But how did they know?)

(The Kelly often use ultrasound to sense attitudes—muscle reading.)

Recollecting herself, she bowed. "We are honored." She emphasized the pronoun.

Mho abruptly changed the subject. "Will Ansonia accept a Protectorate?"

Leseuer hesitated, sensing heightened alertness in the watching aristocrats. There was no comment from Ranor. "That is something my Ambassador would have to answer."

The three Kelly blatted; a derisive noise. "He is ribbonless," said Mho, her tape-like pelt fluffing out. "Sterile, a drone."

(The intermittor's ribbons are the genetic material of a trinity—essential to its reproduction, and their racial memory,) said Ranor suddenly.

"No," continued the alien, "it is you, and the other artists like you whom the Panarch is guesting, that will answer that question. You are the lips—excuse me, eyes—of your people." Mho's headstalk briefly caressed her cheek. "You in particular, Leseuer gen Altamon. Had you been born in the Thousand Suns, we've no doubt you would have been one of the Prophetae." The Kelly fell silent, and all three headstalks bent toward her, bringing nine lambent blue eyes to bear on her with grave regard.

Leseuer was stunned by the extravagant compliment. The Prophetae were the top level of Archetype and Ritual, gifted artists who explored the noumenal world, emerging with new and reinterpreted archetypes to unify the many cultures of the Thousand Suns. She sensed she was now the focus of attention for many of the Douloi nearby, and realized that the Kelly had, with the indirection typical of Panarchic politics, announced its support for an Ansonian Protectorate, rather than continued Probation and Quarantine.

"I hope we will," she finally replied.

"So do we. You have much to offer, and more to gain."

An eddy in the crowd around them revealed the stately figure of the High Phanist of Desrien standing to one side, the Digrammation of Aleph-Null bright upon his chest. Leseuer hoped he wouldn't approach her; she was an agnostic, and the preposterous religious eclecticism of the Magisterium, the religious authority of the Thousand Suns, both repelled and fascinated her. She didn't know what she would say to him. But the Kelly rescued her.

"But I've taken enough of your time," said Mho. "You

must observe and interpret." The trinity made a complex
motion that took in the whole hall. "We depend on you."

"Not at all, Your Grace. I would gladly continue."

The Kelly pitched its voice for her ears only. "As would
we, but I see the High Phanist there, and I sense your unease. We will distract him while you make your escape."

Leseuer realized with amazement that the almost preternatural sensitivity of the Douloi to body language extended
even to alien members of the aristocracy; and she realized
that their ultrasound perception gave them an advantage
lacking to humans.

Then she was fighting to suppress the worst attack of the
giggles she'd ever had as the Kelly withdrew with a full
formal bow, performed with an impeccable snaky grace.
Despite their alien conformation, and the triple echo of their
motions, she could read perfectly the mode: superior to inferior modified by acknowledgment of primacy of function.
It was precisely the mode that would have been appropriate
to a Prophetae, and she heard a murmur of comment from
the people nearby as she returned the deference.

(*Do you still think that Ansonia represents that much of
a challenge?*) Ranor's tone held cool amusement mingled
with affection. (*Compared to the Kelly, integrating your
people into the Panarchy will be child's play.*)

(*I hope so,*) she replied, (*but you may have misjudged the
depth of our prejudice.*)

(*We've dealt with rationalist democracies countless times—
it's a developmental stage all cultures go through. The princi-
ple is always the same: those who deny the role of ritual and
symbolism in their lives are helpless against it.*)

A swirl of motion at the entrance indicated that another
group of people had entered, at their center a tall man she
didn't recognize. He wore a severe black tunic with the
blason d'solei its only decoration. She framed him with the
ajna and triggered an interrogative.

(*That's Myrradin, Demarch Cloud Achilenga,*) said
Ranor. (*Perhaps the most powerful Highdweller in the
Panarchy, with almost a thousand oneills under him.*)

As she watched the tall Douloi make his way into the room she was struck again by the contrast between Arthelion and Narbon. Here the blason d'solei was a common sight, there it was rare. Here there was a mix of Highdwellers and Downsiders mingling in harmony, there a predominance of Downsiders, close-mouthed and even more close-minded.

Now the Douloi were slowly forming a double line centered on the Throne Room doors as the time of the Third Summons approached. As she was carried along by the motion of the assembly, she noticed a hesitation to the movements of the people around her that was foreign to the usual nature of Douloi ceremony. The sound of the crowd had changed too: harsher, somehow, on a note that made her neck hairs lift.

(What's going on?) she subvocalized.

Ranor didn't answer for a moment. When he did, she could sense the tension in him. *(Enough of them, like you, have boswell contacts outside the room and the word is spreading: no one knows where the Krysarch nyr-Arkad is.)*

The Laergon entered the Hall of Ivory, followed as before by the representative of the Polloi. His face was composed, but his eyes darted about like trapped fireflies.

(Then why are they continuing? Why don't they delay the third Summoning?)

Ranor's voice was resonant with helplessness. *(There's no precedent for this. If his delay or absence is his own choice, it's unforgivable: the entire top level of government is here tonight, except for the Privy Council. If it's not . . .)* She could hear the noise that indicated him swallowing. *(If it's not, if it's related to the absence of the Aerenarch-Consort, it could be the first blow of a Family coup.)*

(Vannis—and Krysarch Brandon?) she queried in total disbelief, trying to pair the diamond-cold Aerenarch-Consort and the handsome, blue-eyed third son who always seemed half-asleep. In her year at Court, though she'd seen the two of them at several functions, she could not recall ever having seen them speak to one another.

The Laergon stopped before the vast doors now slightly

ajar, the Mace held overhead, his posture somehow radiating hopelessness. Once again he bent from side to side, silencing the increasing buzz of comment in the Hall with the strange music of the Mace.

The Laergon straightened up and grounded the Mace. "His Royal Highness, the Krysarch Brandon Takari Burgess Njoye Willam su Gelasaar y Ilara nyr Arkad d'Mandala!"

In the long pause that followed, the tension in the room increased so sharply that at first Leseuer thought the faint whine she heard was the blood singing in her ears. Then she noticed a blue glow slithering around the edges of the doors to the Throne Room as they swung shut. Overhead, the immense chandeliers, not yet lit in deference to the latesummer light, began to flicker with an eerie fluorescence.

Now the complex lineaments of the *Ars Irruptus* blazed with lurid glimmers of livid blue light, running along the inlaid metal strips of the mural with fervent energy. The double line of Douloi disintegrated as they began to back away from the strange display of energy; and as they moved a strange piping chatter spread among them. For a moment Leseuer puzzled at the sound, and then her boswell joined the chorus. She looked down with momentary incomprehension at the device now glowing an angry red, and realization hit her simultaneous with Ranor's anguished cry.

(Leseuer, my love! Get out of there!)

But it was too late. The boswell dispassionately announced her fate in the privacy of her inner ear: *PLEASE SEEK MEDICAL ATTENTION IMMEDIATELY. LETHAL RADIATION LEVELS PRESENT;* and still the light from the deadly doors intensified.

She read the same resignation on the faces of the people around her that she knew must be on her own. Now she could feel her skin prickling, like the first warning of a sunburn. A smashing sound twisted her around in time to see the nuller's bubble punch through a stained-glass window, fleeing the deathtrap of the Hall of Ivory.

Then a triple, anguished howl snapped her head back and she saw the Kelly trinity in the throes of an incomprehensible agony. The two larger Kelly were tearing great clumps of ribbon off of Mho, assisted by the smaller Kelly in a savage act of self-mutilation, throwing them into the air, where they fluttered frantically away in every direction. Gouts of yellow blood erupted from the intermittor as the motions of her head stalk gradually lost coordination and she slumped unmoving, supported only by her companions as they continued flaying her.

At the point of death, from sorrow and shock as much as from the energy now flooding the room, amidst panic and rage, Leseuer's talent, which the Kelly had rightly ranked with the Prophetae, asserted itself. Without awareness of her actions she faithfully recorded the death throes of the Douloi, both those who clawed their way toward unattainable escape regardless of those they trampled, and those attempting to shield their loved ones from the penetrating rays with futile heroism.

(*It's too late, Ranor beloved,*) she replied. (*Let this be my final gift to you, and to your wonderful, complicated, elegant, doomed world.*)

So it was that all her experience of the Thousand Suns and its people flooded her inner being, and she saw with the single eye for the last time. In the agony of her own dissolution, she pronounced the epitaph of the Panarchy as it had been. And since her art was visual, not verbal, she borrowed the words of a man long dead before the Vortex swallowed the Exiles of ancient Earth and delivered them to the loneliness of the Thousand Suns.

> (*The blood-dimmed tide is loosed, and everywhere*
> *The ceremony of innocence is drowned. . . .*)

She saw a flare of light that filled her vision, felt the briefest possible sensation of heat, and then there was nothing; nothing but a man's anguished weeping transmitted to a ruined boswell.

FIVE

❋

CHARVANN

Sebastian Omilov, Doctor of Xenoarchaeology, Gnostor of Xenology, Chival of the Phoenix Gate, and Praerogate Prime (Occult) to His Majesty Gelasaar III, lifted his brandy snifter and stared through it at the huge reddish-gold sun hanging at the horizon. The light reflected and refracted through the amber liquid within, washing his hand with flares of golden light.

He lowered the crystal to take a long and savoring sip, then turned to face his son.

"Why did you not to go Arthelion for the nyr-Arkad's Enkainion?" Osri asked again.

"It should be sufficiently obvious," Omilov said. "I was not invited."

The frown on Osri's face deepened. Omilov, looking dispassionately at his straight-backed son still in his Academy uniform, wondered if he ever wore civilian garb anymore.

Omilov saluted Osri with his crystal. "Watch it on the vids with me tomorrow. Will you drink, my boy?"

Osri shook his head once. "There must be a reason. Your position as friend to the Panarch, as tutor to the Krysarchs—it's an insult."

It's a warning, Omilov thought, but he said nothing. He'd tried to stand against Semion in the Lusor affair ten years ago, and had lost. The retreat to Charvann was to spare his family; Osri's best protection was his ignorance.

Not that he would have confided in his only son if he'd had the chance. Looking down at Osri's face, he thought a little sadly, *You've too much of the Ghettierus love for the sound of rules, and too little of the Omilov savor of their sense.*

Osri rubbed his hands down the arms of his chair, staring out over the grassy compound beyond the verandah. The evening breeze was rising; as Charvann's primary touched the distant horizon a flock of *jezeels* winged their way raucously over head: dipping, deceptively clumsy flyers, like clowns tumbling headlong into the center ring. Osri stared out past them, no reaction in his face. The breeze stirred his short hair, the lowering sun glowing in his dark eyes.

It was a well-made face, despite the long Omilov earlobes. Also an honest and intelligent face, though it rarely smiled. *Burdened with my ears and your mother's lack of humor.*

"Even a space as large as the Ivory Hall would not hold all those whose positions would seem to require that they 'should' have been there," Omilov said, trying to deflect his son from brooding on imagined insults. "To the luckless compiler of the guest list the importance of an old tutor who has officially retired—"

Omilov paused when he heard a belltone inside the house.

"What is that?" Osri asked. "Why do you have these comsignals? Why not wear your boswell?"

"It seems we've a visitor arriving," Omilov said,

sidestepping the last two questions. "Someone who has the passcode to the estate."

"Whom were you expecting?" Osri frowned again.

"Just you," Omilov said with shrug.

"Father, you ought to wear your boswell," Osri said crossly.

Omilov laughed as he scanned the azure horizon. "One of the benefits of official retirement is freedom from immediate access," he said. "Ah. Here we are."

A golden egg-shape moved with deliberate grace over the distant treetops, arcing down across the lawn. A wide swath rippled through the grasses as the phaeton hovered, moiré patterns chasing across its featureless surface; then it moved sideways toward the verandah. Omilov stepped back as the breeze kicked up by the geeplane fanned his face.

Almost as if the unknown person inside read his mind, the taxi moved back again a few meters, then settled on the grass, releasing the pungent smell of crushed blossoms.

In silence the Omilovs watched the curved door slide up and two figures spring down from the taxi, the first well over medium height and slender, the second big and burly. The big one carried luggage; the other looked up at the verandah, walking swiftly toward them.

Omilov stared in amazement as his brain registered the familiar planes of Arkadic bone structure. He recognized Brandon nyr-Arkad just before Brandon vaulted the low railing and advanced, smiling, on Omilov, both hands held out. So soon after the Enkainion? *Too soon.*

"Sebastian! I thought I might find you back here."

Omilov hesitated, then bowed with formal deliberation, extending his hands palms-out for the formal touch.

"Sebastian," Brandon said softly. "I thought this was the one house where precedence is teacher-before-student, and titles have no place?"

"That was when you were a boy, and for a reason," Omilov said, searching the opaque blue eyes. "I don't think you've been here to the Hollows since you attained your majority."

"I haven't," Brandon said. "Though not through design. Can we go back to the old rules?"

"We can," Omilov said. "Welcome, Brandon." Omilov clasped Brandon's right hand in both of his.

Then Brandon turned to Osri, his face polite and unreadable. "Osri. A surprise."

"Your Highness," Osri said, performing a faultless salute. He chose to remain formal; Omilov was saddened, but not surprised. *Even as boys they were too different to ever be friends, and ten years after the fact Osri still expresses shock over his perception of the Markham vlith-L'Ranja affair at the Academy . . .*

Except it wasn't the past that brought that look into Osri's face. The disturbing secondary line of thought that had offset Omilov's delight at seeing Brandon again thrust its way to the forefront of his mind, its terrifying possibility reflected as certainty in his son's eyes. Omilov was not adept at mental calculation, but Osri, who taught astrogation as a living, could plot very rapidly the spacetime lag between Arthelion and Charvann. Chill fingered its way down the back of Omilov's skull; either Brandon had somehow managed to exceed all known speeds, or else—

"Brandon?" he said. "I am delighted to see you again, but why this haste?" Omilov thought of the social commitments attendant on a royal Enkainion: by rights Brandon should have been feted for weeks, by the foremost Houses in the Panarchy.

"Am I not welcome?" Brandon threw one leg over the low rail and sat. His face, thrown suddenly into relief against the red ball of the sun, bore the unmistakable marks of exhaustion. "We'll go, if you don't want to see me."

He has to have left the day of his Enkainion. Why?

As if to mock him, Omilov's own thought from moments ago returned: *love for the sound of rules, and too little of a savor for their sense . . .* He studied the Krysarch's face: not just exhaustion—something more.

"What happened?" Omilov asked, keeping voice and

posture neutral. Then, voicing his last fading hope, "You must have left just after your Enkainion?"

Brandon picked up the empty crystal that Omilov had had brought out for his son and poured a measure into it from the decanter. "Before," he said with lethal simplicity. "I stopped here to say good-bye."

Omilov shook his head. *Unless Semion's coverts are already converging on us, in which case nothing we do or say matters, this can wait. He's here, there must be a reason. Osri's presence will prevent him from bringing it out.*

"Come. Let me speak to Parraker about some refreshment," he said, fighting against shock, against the tangle of disastrous consequences Brandon's sudden presence brought. He turned his eyes to the man who had been waiting in silent patience in the background all this time, and registered another, smaller shock when he recognized Lenic Deralze, the bodyguard who had disappeared soon after the Lusor affair began . . .

Shaking his head, he said, "Take the luggage inside, Deralze. Parraker will establish you in comfort." *I will deal with this. It was not for situations dictated by the rules, but for emergencies not covered by the rules, that I made my vows—* The image of a face flickered through his mind, and his thoughts split, running along two tracks, losing themselves in the shadows of memories.

He had just reached the door when again he heard a tone from the workroom comlink, but this time a high, insistent buzz. Fear, for the first time in ten years, dried Omilov's mouth: it had to be Semion's fist closing on them all.

Behind him, he heard the scrape of shoes, and Osri's "What is it, Father?"

"I—" Omilov considered what was to be said, and then stopped when Parraker, his Steward, bustled down the hallway toward him with something carried in his hands.

"Sir, this just arrived, marked 'Urgent—do not delay.' " As Omilov took the box from Parraker's hands, the Steward's eyes moved past him to the newcomers, then widened briefly. Wordlessly he performed a low obeisance.

"Parraker," Brandon said. "How are you?"

The Steward bowed again, then turned to Omilov, his face blank. Marshaling his thoughts, Omilov said, "Thank you. Will you conduct Deralze to the guest rooms?"

Deralze lifted his burden, sending one considering glance in Osri's direction before he followed Parraker inside the house.

Omilov turned around, still carrying the box. It felt odd in his hands, heavy and yet somehow also light, intensifying the sense of unreality that had gripped his mind ever since he recognized Brandon's face. He retraced his steps, his senses sharpening as if to counter the fog in his mind. He felt the warm breeze that carried the scent of sandalwood and jumari across the terrace; in the gardens the leaptoads pipped and squeaked, an amphibian orchestra tuning up for its nightly concert.

Surprised his voice could sound normal, he said, "Shall we take a look at this?" He reached down to set the box on the low table. The strange dissonance of its massive light- ness made his stomach tighten with a tremor of queasiness. But once it was on the table it did not move, and he straightened up with a sense of relief.

"Who is it from?" Osri asked.

Omilov checked routing chip. "It seems to have been re- routed to me mid-shipment. The original recipient was to have been 'Martin Cheruld, Aegios Prime.' Curious. An old student of mine, with whom I have not had communication for over a decade." He looked up at Brandon, wondering if the two events were somehow related, but Brandon did not react at the name.

Omilov tabbed the protective wrapping, sucking in his breath when he saw the Alhaman puzzle-box within, an ex- quisitely carved wooden case inlaid with *kauch*-pearl. Osri and Brandon looked on, Osri frowning as was his wont when anything out of the ordinary occurred, and Brandon's face polite but his eyes moving restlessly once over the gar- dens. *Why did he not make his Enkainion?* Omilov had never heard of such a thing happening—ever.

As Omilov's fingers tried several solutions to the puzzle, his rapid thoughts brought memories of the ten-year-old Brandon, who used to concoct elaborate practical jokes without regard to the inevitable retribution that even Krysarchs could not evade. He remembered all too well the stench-puff that had somehow found its way into the chair of a certain newly knighted Chival at his accession banquet.

This was many leagues beyond that in its seriousness, but there was something in Brandon's watchful gaze now that convinced Omilov that Brandon was well aware of what he'd done. It amounted to a cut-direct, the highest insult, to all the leading lights of Court—and it would never, ever be forgotten. Even his father the Panarch would be helpless to intervene against the depth of feeling this would arouse.

And, thought Omilov, considering the way decisions were so often made in the Thousand Suns—by careful, formal social maneuvers among the Service Families— Brandon's flight amounted to a disruption of the machinery of state. His father would probably not even make the attempt, despite his very real love for Brandon. Gelasaar would put the welfare of his trillions of subjects first.

And Brandon knows this.

"Well?" Osri said. His eyes went briefly to Brandon's face, then flickered away again, as if by not seeing his presence he could deny what had happened. "Open it, Father?"

Omilov shook back his thoughts once again and turned his eyes to the box in his hands. A slender wedge of light at the horizon was all that remained of the sun—the shimmering lines of the inlay pattern on the box glinted softly, reflecting the overhead lights that were slowly replacing the diminishing light from the sky.

Finally the top of the box released with a subdued click. Inside was a small, mirror-surfaced sphere, about half the size of a man's fist. And once again Omilov sustained a shock, this time registering a physical reaction as a twinge of alarm surged down his left arm. *What is* this *doing here*?

For a moment he saw again the echoing spaces of the Shrine, reflected a thousandfold in the ageless eyes of the strange being at its center, smelled the strange, dry incense-like odor of the Guardian and heard its rasping speech, like a huge stringed instrument played with a rough bow. He remembered the awe engendered by the dispassionate gaze of a being whose life had begun when his remote ancestors were chipping stone tools at the feet of receding glaciers on Lost Earth.

"It's just a ball," Osri said. "A metal ball!"

Shaking off the memory, Omilov picked up the sphere with care, trying not to betray its true strangeness by lifting it too fast. Just as the last time he'd looked at it, Omilov found his eyes crossing slightly as they tried to focus on it—it was such a perfect, smooth reflector that it was visible only as a distortion of its surroundings.

Despite his care, something in his handling of it must have shown, for Brandon's eyes narrowed as Omilov placed the sphere on the table.

Osri started to reach for it, then paused, looking at the routing chip. "I think I've heard that name, Cheruld . . ."

"I believe he is the aegios in charge of the DataNet at Brangornie Node," Omilov said, his fingers toying with the sphere as he spoke; there was something very strange about the way it moved on the table, something almost sticky. Osri and Brandon both watched it in fascination.

"I've never seen anything like that," Osri said, still wary. "What is it?"

"I don't know *what* it is, or what its purpose was, but it is at least ten million years old."

"The Ur?" Osri said blankly.

Omilov nodded and handed the sphere to his son. Osri's hands dipped toward the table, finding the sphere heavier than he had expected. As he hefted it, his eyebrows shot toward his hairline—his hands moved too fast for the evident weight of the sphere. Omilov smiled: Osri was doubtless perceiving the horrible dissonance between the sphere's weight and its inertia. "Throw it to Brandon."

As Osri hesitated, Omilov added, "Don't worry, it's not

at all fragile. In fact, I doubt that any force we have available to us could damage it."

Osri tried to throw it underhanded to Brandon, who had his hands up and slightly separated, but the little sphere refused to leave his hand—it almost looked like it was glued there, except that it rolled about freely.

"Throw it overhand," he chortled. Shock had faded, leaving that sense of unreality. *Brandon has finished himself forever, Semion may close his gauntlet around us at any moment, and here we sit, talking about an artifact created by a galaxy-spanning race that was utterly destroyed ten million years ago.*

Osri wrapped his fingers around the sphere and tossed it, throwing it somewhat like a shotput because of its weight, but as his hand opened at the peak of its forward thrust, the sphere fell out of his palm with blurring speed and hit the table—noiselessly. It fell so fast that none of them could see it between Osri's hand and the table, and when it touched the tabletop it did not bounce or further move at all. Osri pushed it hard toward Brandon, but as soon as his hand ceased its forward movement, so did the sphere.

Osri's forehead knitted and he reached for the sphere, but Brandon grabbed it first. He held it up, laid his other hand on the surface of the table, and with a wince, dropped the sphere from about two feet onto his upturned palm. Brandon grunted with surprise, Osri winced, but the Krysarch's hand was obviously unharmed, despite the sphere's heaviness.

"That's impossible," said Osri. "It's inertialess!"

"Impossible or not, there it is," replied his father. "Of course, it could merely have unmeasurable or negligible inertia, but as the physicists who were permitted to handle it once six centuries ago stated in their report, that's just as impossible as none at all . . ."

"If you could do that to a ship . . ." Brandon breathed.

"Its speed would be limited only by the density of the interstellar medium," Osri said, taking refuge in pedantry.

Brandon dropped the sphere back on the table, picked up

his snifter, and poured himself another drink as Osri continued. "So you know where it came from?"

"Where, I know. How, I can't even guess at this point," Omilov replied. "But if I am right, Martin Cheruld had no right to be receiving this. It was almost certainly stolen from a planet that has been under a Class I quarantine for over seven hundred years."

Osri touched the sphere wonderingly as his father continued. "You're familiar with the Paradisum system."

"It's one of the Doomed Worlds," interjected Brandon, who leaned against the carved balustrade, staring up into the night sky.

"A binary planet around a binary star, doomed to death some fifty thousand years hence, a work of art for the delight of an alien race we can only be thankful are long gone from the galaxy." Omilov hesitated, then went on, "That's how I'm sure this is an Urian artifact, for I have seen it once before, in the Shrine of the Demon of Paradisum's companion."

"The carvings," said Osri. "I've seen pictures of them—they cover an entire continent."

"The Panarchy allows one xenoarchaeological expedition there every fifty years. There have been fourteen—and all have spoken to the selfsame being—the Guardian of the Shrine." Omilov made an odd noise deep in his throat, followed by a breathy trill. "That's as close as I can come to pronouncing its name, since I don't have chelae and a chitinous throat patch." He smiled, his eyes resting on the distant horizon. "One of the Highdweller members of our expedition had an unsuspected phobia—insects. She had to be transferred out under sedation after entering the Shrine."

Omilov plucked the sphere off the table. "The Guardian told us that this was the egg of a demon, like the one that would hatch from the twin suns of his world at the end of time."

"They *worshiped* it?" asked Osri, with faint distaste.

"Not worshiped—perhaps imprisoned is a better word. The Guardian said it was a trust, that five hundred generations of his kind had guarded it, waiting for it to be swallowed up in the stellar fires that would destroy his world."

He paused. "Five hundred generations, counted from the disappearance of the Ur, is twenty thousand years per Guardian. That figure was verified by the first expedition—by radio-dating of chitin traces on the Guardian's dais, and by genoscans ... that was why the planet was quarantined. No naturally evolved being lives that long."

In the ensuing silence, the songs of the leaptoads in the ponds and streams of the surrounding gardens were loud in their ears, cheerfully dissonant against the soft music pervading the terrace. Behind them, the windows of the house glowed with light; in the east the inner moon Kilelis lofted its cold face above the horizon, wanly reflecting the light of the departed sun. Faint streaks of cloud shone in the sky; the grounds of the estate were a shadowed mystery in the moon's purplish light.

"The Guardian would not let us touch the sphere, and our instruments could get no readings from it. Since the Guardian was obviously a sentient being, it was protected by the Covenant of Anarchy. We could not force it. I don't think any of us would have ... but someone has." Omilov touched a control in the arm of his high-backed chair; the lights faded and the stars leapt forth in spangled glory above their heads.

"I remember something about it," Brandon murmured. "Didn't this have a name—the Heart of something?"

Omilov cradled the artifact against his chest, his face and the stars above reflected in bizarre distortion in its surface. "The Heart of Kronos, the Eater of Gods."

※   ※   ※

It was second moonrise when Deralze moved silently along the corridor behind the gnostor's son, who had just emerged from his room in his dressing gown.

Through the high window at the end of the corridor the rosy light of Tira threw Osri's shadow huge against the wall as he approached his father's suite; the quiet slip-slap of his slippers echoed off the the glossy *paak*-wood floor.

The door to Omilov's suite slid open noiselessly at his touch, and stayed open when Deralze keyed the override. Light glowed in both the bedchamber and the study. The gnostor favored the old Karelian Renascence modality—there were no doors on the rooms within the suite, only wide, high archways. Deralze paused just inside the vestibule, outside of the pool of soft light, and waited.

Omilov sat in a hideous overstuffed wing chair; the air was sweetly aromatic from the hot drink he held in his hands. Arching over him in the dim light was the graceful form of a potted *argan* tree, its silver leaves tightly rolled up for the night except where the reading lamp shone on them, glinting off the splayed, hand-shaped leaves that seemed to hover protectively over the chair and its occupant.

Deralze saw by the angle of the gnostor's head that he was gazing up at his hand-painted portrait of the late Kyriarch Ilara kyr-Arkad. Osri glanced at the portrait, which had been on the gnostor's wall as long as Deralze had been coming to this house as the Krysarch's guard.

Omilov looked up as his son appeared in the doorway, and he smiled. "Night-hobs whispering to you too, boy? Come, have some dreamberry tea. It never fails to work for me."

"Night-hobs?" Osri repeated, and then he said, "Sometimes, father, I wonder if you half-believe in the myths and legends you study."

"Half-believe and laugh about them by turns," the gnostor replied with a smile.

Osri looked impatient. Deralze suddenly recalled Lady Risiena, on one of her rare punitive descents on the family home, saying acidly to her son, "Your father, Osri, is simply a child in a man's body. He resigned his position in the family business so he could devote his time to playing with the various dirty oddments and bits of trash he digs up, and though he knows several people high in the Magisterium and the Council of Pursuivence—though *I've* never met them—he has never exerted himself to ask their help in advancing the family's interests. So you, my son, are left to suffer from his selfishness."

Deralze had been standing in the room, awaiting Brandon's appearance at breakfast; the lady had regarded him as so much furniture, but Osri had betrayed the flush of deep chagrin, excusing himself soon after.

Osri said now to his father: "I must speak to you."

"And?" Omilov looked up, still smiling.

"You have reported the presence of the Krysarch to someone?"

" 'Krysarch,' " Omilov repeated. "It was not so long ago that you were both here as boys, and you called him Brandon then." But when Osri said nothing, Deralze heard the gnostor sigh and answer at last: "I have reported to no one."

"Does the Archon know he is here on this planet?"

"I am beginning to believe that no one, outside of ourselves, knows."

"Then it is your *duty* to inform the Archon."

"My duty is to myself," Omilov said. "I am merely a retired teacher."

"But I am not," Osri said. "I think my duty is clear. I would have sent a com, but I thought it right to consult you first; this is your house."

Omilov rubbed his chin thoughtfully. "I suspect you will get nowhere. I would be very surprised indeed if Deralze has not already blocked our com."

Deralze, smiling to himself, heard Osri's sharp intake of breath.

"But that's illegal—"

"The rules," Omilov said, "are made to cover ordinary circumstances. I am beginning to believe that something extraordinary has brought Brandon here, and it is my intention to find out what. Then I will act as I see right."

Osri stood silently for a moment, then said, "When my leave ends . . ."

"You will do what you think is right," Omilov said. "Until then, permit me to handle this in my own way."

Osri nodded. "Very well. I will wish you a good night, then."

"Yes, good night, son."

Deralze stepped back into the shadows of a corner. Osri passed at a fast walk, looking to neither right nor left, then went out. Deralze waited a moment, then followed.

As his son left, Omilov's eyes remained on the smiling blue-gray eyes in the pleasant round face with its crown of curling reddish hair, but his mind formed an image of the young man in the guest room at the end of the hall. "Ah, Ilara," he murmured, "should I stop him? What would you have me do?"

The ever-young face gazed off into a distance where his eyes could not follow, a half-smile playing about her lips, the small rounded hands relaxed on the treasured book of ancient poems. She had given her life for duty, victim of a man and a world to whom poetry and laughter were weaknesses to be scorned and crushed, and the Thousand Suns were the poorer for it.

He thought of her oldest son, hardening inexorably into the same sort of tyrant his grandfather had been. *Gelasaar loves him, trusts him, and sees nothing. And no one can tell him. Galen has walled himself away on Talgarth, and now Brandon seems to be running away . . . How much we need you now, Ilara.*

Omilov slipped into unhappy memory, of the whipsaw emotions of those days, twenty years past: the euphoric victory at Acheront, the magnanimity of the Panarch to a defeated enemy, and the vengeful savagery of Dol'jhar, vented on the first trucial commission, headed by the Kyriarch Ilara.

I warned Gelasaar not to show him mercy . . .

Omilov's eyes blurred as he blinked away the tears, and the portrait acquired a near-numinous aura to him, as if the young woman there were merely between breaths, would momentarily stir and look at him and smile. Then the sense of closeness, of presence, faded, and he was alone. He sighed and quoted softly, from the poet whose works had been closest to Ilara's heart:

> May't not be said, that her grave shall restore
> Her greater, purer, firmer than before?
> Heaven may say this, and joy in't, but can wee
> Who live, and lacke her, here this vantage see?

Six

✳

CHARVANN MINUS THREE LIGHT-WEEKS

Hreem chaka-Jalashalal shifted impatiently in the command pod, scratching the soft flesh above his collarbone. The heavy gold braid encrusting the V-collar of his tunic rattled across the rings on his thick, hairy fingers.

Around him the bridge of the *Flower of Lith* was quiet, the subdued whirring of the *tianqi* the only sound other than an occasional soft bleep from the single monitor console now manned: bored by the long wait, Erbee was playing solo-Phalanx again. Hreem could see his profile: the long-faced scantech sucked his lower lip as he stabbed at the computer pads.

The chatzing little blit's probably programmed it to lose constantly—his mother's pet wattle could beat him.

But Erbee was uncannily good at sniffing out the faint

energy traces emitted by the ships the *Flower of Lith* preyed on. The buck-toothed Rifter with his vacant, pimply face definitely paid his way; and he'd saved the *Lith* not a few times when the sleek, powerful predators of the Panarch's Navy had sought them in a deadly game of hide-or-be-zapped.

That didn't change the fact that he was rotten company on a long watch that Hreem ordinarily would gladly have delegated. The sudden cancellation of the Malachronte attack, and his unexplained reassignment to Charvann—a planet with no strategic value—had made the Rifter captain uneasy. Had Dol'jhar divined his plans?

Hreem glared at the viewscreen above the monitor consoles. The stars stared back at him mockingly, set in a velvet emptiness broken only by the faint circles indicating some of the other ships that had so far made it to the rendezvous. He hated waiting like this, sitting in the middle of nowhere in particular, no rocks or ice to hide behind, radiating a beaconburst for anyone to hear. Even though he'd been flea-hopping the ship a few light-minutes every so often, to avoid the chance of being pinpointed at the center of the beacon signal, it still made him nervous. Even the new scents and airflow patterns Norio had programmed into the tianqi failed to soothe him.

The image of the nearly completed battlecruiser in the Malachronte Ways rose up in his mind's eye; he indulged momentarily in another image, made almost tactile by repeated imagination, of himself on its bridge. Never mind that no Rifter had ever captained one of those nearly invulnerable vessels. *I'll be the first,* he vowed again, recalling with gritted teeth Barrodagh's sneering smile as he relayed the new orders. *Whether Dol'jhar likes it or not.* He hoped they hadn't assigned anyone else to Malachronte.

Hreem shifted irritably in his pod. "Erbee!"

"No traces, Cap'n," replied the tech in an abstracted voice, his fingers hesitating not a bit in their dance across his console.

We've been here almost six hours . . . even that maggot-

brained Y'Marmor should be able to hit a beacon signal half a light-day across.

He'd give Y'Marmor two more hours, Hreem decided, then move in on Charvann without him. He couldn't afford to give Dol'jhar further reason for suspicion. *We'll be the obedient Rifter slubs, grab this Omilov blit, have a little fun, and then move on.*

He would already have left Tallis Y'Marmor behind, but for the rumor of a cruiser in the Charvann system. Even with the power of the Suneater to back them up, another Alpha Class destroyer with its skipmissiles would be welcome.

Hreem glanced uneasily at the Urian hyperwave, a weird, melted-looking machine roughly bolted to the bulkhead beneath the communications console, its metal glowing ruddily from within as it relayed messages across light-years without delay. *The Ur must have been really bizarre, if that was their idea of machinery . . .* His thoughts touched on its bulkier counterpart, crouched hulkingly amidst the now-cold reactors of the destroyer, pulling energy out of some unknown dimension—and delivering it at a rate that gave the *Lith* more striking power than any ship the Panarchy could field.

He was contemplating what it was going to be like to turn the tables on the Panarch's Navy when a quiet chirp from his command console brought him to alertness. He tapped a pad, and a face windowed up on the viewscreen: Dyasil, the communications tech.

"I've got that record chip edited together I told you about," he said. "There's some really hot stuff coming in over the hyperwave. Some of it's better than any wiredream you've ever seen!"

Hreem sat up, his anxiety forgotten for the moment. For some reason, the Urian communicator could only broadcast; everyone who had one heard everyone else. Dol'jhar's codes kept each Rifter fleet from knowing any orders but their own, but now the fleets were sending out uncoded vi-

suals of their attacks from throughout the Thousand Suns—
the biggest bragging session ever held.

"What have you got for me?"

Dyasil grinned. "Did you know Eusabian had a spy in the
Panarch's council? He recorded their last meeting, and
that's just the beginning. We're gonna have to get creative
to beat some of these. I've hung some captions on 'em for
ya. Enjoy!"

His face blinked off, replaced by a florid title scrolling up
the screen—*The Revenge of the Rifters*—and some loud,
upbeat music. Hreem snorted: Dyasil should have been a
third-rate wiredream producer somewhere, instead of man-
ning a console on a Rifter destroyer that was on the bonus
chips of every naval detachment in the Thousand Suns.

He slapped a pad on his console and the window expanded to fill the viewscreen as the title was replaced by a
stock shot of Arthelion from space, with the island of the
Palace Major clearly visible. Hreem felt the hairs on his
neck stir with a superstitious thrill at the sight of the Mandala, the heart of the Thousand Suns whence the Arkads
had ruled for nearly a thousand years.

But not any longer, he thought, and shook off the mood
as another stock shot faded in, this time of the Palace Minor
on Arthelion, the residence of the Panarch. Hreem grinned
and settled back for the show.

The room was long and windowless, with a high ceiling,
and walls paneled in a richly grained wood with faded battle flags and heraldic blazons hanging on them. The imager
that had recorded the scene was evidently high up in a corner: Hreem could look down the length of the table at the
high-backed chair that stood empty at the other end. On the
table in front of that chair, on a silver tray, was a crystal decanter and a glass. On either side of the table a dozen or so
men and women, middle-aged and up, in a variety of uniforms and dress, conversed amongst themselves in low
tones; all except one, nearest the empty chair. Tall, gaunt,
dressed in utilitarian black, she sat unmoving, grimly sur-

veying the papers in front of her. Hreem shuddered. Nahomi il-Ngari, head of the Invisible Services Bureau. Nicknamed "The Spider," her webs of information had likely accounted for more Rifters than the entire Navy.

Like il-Ngari, most of the occupants of the room wore little or no ornamentation; a couple of younger men, perhaps aides, wore uniforms that looked almost gaudy by comparison.

After a moment, almost as one, everyone looked toward something out of view under the camera and stood up. A white-haired man, erect and almost severe in bearing, yet graceful in his movements, came into view. As he walked up to the empty chair and turned around, Hreem saw that his face was familiar—of the lineage he saw almost every time another looted sunburst passed through his hands, minted in bold relief on gold, silver, and platinum or staring from the surface of a dyplast note. Gelasaar hai-Arkad, Panarch of the Thousand Suns, forty-seventh in succession to the Emerald Throne of Jaspar I. His was a hard, commanding face, with the saving grace of a smile lurking in the wrinkles around his blue eyes. He was not smiling now.

The Panarch surveyed his assembled council for a long moment; silence lay heavily upon the room. After a moment he sat down, and the others followed. When he spoke, his voice was unexpectedly light, almost melodious, but shadowed by fatigue.

"From time to time now, for several years, we have discussed the strange unrest sweeping the Thousand Suns: messianic cults, tales of the discovery of ancient weapons, of the coming return of the Ur, of impending war. I need not remind you that a polity such as ours, with thousands of different cultures and their interactions, is a fertile breeding ground for rumors and misunderstandings; and we have generally found that the best policy is to ignore them, or to treat them as symptoms of some underlying problem."

He paused, poured some water into the glass, and drank. There was no sound other than the click of the glass on the tray as he set it back down.

"But this unrest was different, for the same stories and too-similar cults appeared in sector after sector, among Downsiders, Highdwellers, and even Rifters, seeming at times to be spreading without regard for the spacetime lag inherent in interstellar distances. We have consulted several of the Colleges: Archetype and Ritual, Hypostatics, Synchronistic Perception and Practice, and others. All were baffled. Even the Centripetal Gnostors"—he nodded to an old man with a seamed, dark face—"could suggest no synthesis that would explain the disturbances. Bound by the Covenant of Anarchy, we could only watch and wait—until this morning, when an unexpected message was relayed here from Arthelion. A message from the Node at Brangornie."

There was a buzz of puzzled comment as the Panarch paused, which died away into silence again.

So they're not *on Arthelion,* thought Hreem. *Trust Dyasil to chatz it up.*

Just then one of the others on the bridge said, "Isn't that the old Concordium on Lao Tse? I seen it on a chip."

"Genz, the Thousand-Year Peace is at an end. We are at war," the Panarch said.

Pandemonium broke out. Everyone began talking at once, so that only fragments were intelligible: "Shiidra . . . Gehenna . . . madness . . . executed at Acheront . . . who . . . who?"

Hreem laughed. These were the people behind the ships that sought the destruction of the *Flower of Lith* and the death or exile of everyone on board. He felt a glow of delight and confidence pervade him as he watched confusion reign among his enemies, while an ever-suspicious portion of his mind insisted that Eusabian had intended just that by allowing this broadcast.

On the screen the gaunt woman had risen to her feet. "Jerrode Eusabian of Dol'jhar!" she said angrily.

There was instant silence for a moment, and then a uniformed man, somewhat gray-faced and haggard, jumped to his feet. "Let me take a fleet to Dol'jhar and flame it clean of those Telos-abandoned vermin!"

The Panarch waved him down and turned to the gaunt woman. "Nahomi . . ."

"The manager of the Brangornie Node—a self-confessed traitor come to his senses—has informed us that Eusabian arranged the assassination of all three of His Majesty's sons."

Her voice slowed. "If the plot proceeded as planned, the Aerenarch Semion and the Krysarch Galen are already dead." There was murmur of shock from the others at the table, quickly stilled as she continued.

"We are awaiting confirmation by the high-speed couriers that must have been dispatched if this is so. On Arthelion the Hall of Ivory was destroyed by an enhanced radiation device during the Enkainion of the nyr-Arkad, but there is no trace of His Majesty's son. It is now thought he disappeared before the ceremony, but we have no indications of where he might be."

Hreem hadn't known that bit about the heirs— *Eusabian'll probably have them stuffed.*

The Rifter captain grimaced. In the long career of piracy and mayhem that had made him one of the most wanted men in the Thousand Suns, Hreem had knowingly killed hundreds of people—that was his business and he lost no sleep over it. Sometimes it was even entertaining. In the Rift Brotherhood death was a tool of the trade and a constant companion, but it usually came cleanly, with the flare of a firejac, or the awful screech of air rushing out of a riven hull; sometimes you held on to enemies you really hated and played a little, then you killed them. The Dol'jharian taste for endlessly protracted pain was foreign to him.

Out of the corner of his eye Hreem noted Erbee suddenly stiffen, wipe his board clean, and begin concentrating officiously on his instruments. He heard the soft slap of sandals on the deck behind him, and then a sallow, slender hand reached over his shoulder bearing a bowl of foamy pink *pozzi*-fruit.

"I thought you might like some refreshment with the show," came Norio's soft baritone.

As Hreem took the bowl the tempath spread his fingers across the burly Rifter's shoulders and neck and began erasing his tension with the uncanny precision afforded by his emotion-sensing talent.

Hreem stretched luxuriously, knowing a verbal acknowledgment was unnecessary. A sensuous tingling crept down his torso and arms from the pressure of Norio's fingers; Hreem nearly dropped the bowl as his grip weakened involuntarily. As the pleasant shiver reached his groin the tempath abruptly lifted his hands. Hreem sighed.

"No more now, Jala," whispered Norio. "You must be alert." He withdrew as quietly as he had come. As the soft susurration of his footsteps faded in the corridor outside the bridge, Hreem straightened up and wedged a handful of fruit into his mouth. He wiped the juice off his hand onto the front of his tunic and returned his attention to the screen, barely noticing the resurgent beeps from Erbee's console.

". . . decapitated the government, and we expect military action against numerous targets." Nahomi's face was tight with rage, but the Panarch merely looked gloomy and tired.

"But what can Eusabian hope to do with only the *Fist of Dol'jhar*?" asked one of the council. "He was only left that one battlecruiser by treaty—we know he hasn't built any others."

"We don't know. But the theft of the Heart of Kronos, coupled with the correlations we've been able to make, indicates that Eusabian has indeed discovered something— some technology—left behind by the Ur. Our best guess, judging from a recent decrease in Rifter activity that only now makes sense, is that he has armed a portion of the Rifter criminal element with it. We don't know what we face, or how much time we have."

Hreem chuckled. *None at all.*

The Panarch nodded to Nahomi, who sat down. He looked around slowly at each one of them, weighing some matter in his mind. "There's worse to come, my friends," he said. "One of you is a traitor."

Bedlam again. Hreem watched delighted as, without warning, one of the aides tossed a small glistening sphere onto the table, his eyes squeezed tightly shut. It burst with a shrill, ear-torturing shriek and a flare of purple light that momentarily overloaded the imager, and everyone else in the room dropped where they stood, their limbs twitching and writhing slowly in the grip of the sensory overload induced by the stun-bomb. Moments later, two guards rushed in, to be met by the fire-thread of a lazjac in the hands of the aide. As they dropped, their weapons clattering on the polished floor, the aide pulled out a small communicator and began speaking, while dislodging some waxy, faintly green plugs from his ears, and the scene faded out . . .

There were a couple more people on the bridge, Hreem noticed now as the white-mottled blue-green curve of a planet loomed vast on the screen. A caption rolled up over it—*Abilard*—as the dragonfly shape of a destroyer slowly passed under the camera's vantage point, its radiants flaring as it accelerated away. The angle of view accentuated the long missile tube projecting forward from the angular main hull. Emblazoned on its superstructure was the figure of a cross on a grave, with a strange-looking hat—narrow-brimmed with a rounded top—smashed down on the cross, so that the upright broke through the crown of the hat. This symbol was surrounded by an inverted five-pointed star.

"The *Samedi*," said someone. "That's Emmet Fasthand's ship."

Around the destroyer could be seen smaller, more aerodynamic vessels, falling away toward the planet's surface at tremendous speed. Suddenly the lights of a vast city at night were framed in the viewscreen, seen from a great height, the rumble of a ship's engines and the screech of high-velocity atmospheric flight forming a loud accompaniment. The lights twinkled peacefully below; without warning, from just below the edge of the picture, the garishly green lances of a cluster strike of laser-boosted missiles arrowed out. Their screaming roar could be clearly heard. Moments later, as the green beams winked out, a series of actinic blue-white domes bloomed in a crooked path across the center of the city, lighting up vast sections of it for brief moments—and the city lights went out.

"Bad luck for Abilard," said Pogger, at the fire-control console, looking at the screen in front of him which repeated the image above his head. "Emmet hated 'em after they caught him with his pants down in that raid in '58—made him the laughingstock of the Brotherhood."

Now the bridge was almost crowded, many of the crew standing behind Hreem's command pod to watch the larger image on the main screen. Erbee had abandoned his solo-Phalanx and was watching, his mouth slackly open, lips glistening. *He'd better not start drooling again, or I'll rip his lips off,* thought Hreem; then he turned back as another caption caught his eye.

Torigan: The Archonic Enclave. There was a subdued murmur from the crew as they saw that this scene had been recorded from ground level—the Rifters assigned to Torigan had evidently not had too much trouble landing. But now the Archon's forces were resisting strenuously. Across the expanse of a wide public square, its gleaming white surface now littered with burning vehicles and the anonymous huddled lumps of fallen combatants, a group of magnificent buildings were the focus of a vicious firefight. The brilliant threads of lazjacs and the thicker, somewhat blurry bolts from firejacs converged across the square and were answered in kind. An occasional blue-white vortex of energy, slow-moving but deadly, marked the replies of plasmoid cannons. The noise was shatteringly intense. There were no people visible—the square was no place for fragile human flesh.

In the midst of the buildings loomed a vast geodesic dome, glittering gold in the hot sunlight, its form shimmering in the heat rising from the burning wrecks in the square.

"That's the Mycorium," commented Dyasil from behind Hreem. "I visited it once—weird place."

Hreem waved him to silence as a small shape in the green-blue sky bulleted past, streaks of missile fire raining down from it on the defending positions. The last missile hit the dome: the golden shape crumpled inward in almost slow motion, a strange fog or mist billowing skyward from its dark interior.

"Stupid blits!" said Hreem disgustedly.

Erbee looked over at him, confused. "Why's that?"

The defending fire was falling off rapidly now. Suddenly, across the square, men could be seen running toward the attacking Rifters, weaponless, leaping and twisting bizarrely, their forms strangely blurred.

"That was the fungus collection of the Archonei of Torigan," said Dyasil. "Toadstools and all sorts of slimy blunge from all over the Thousand Suns. Stupid thing to keep in the middle of a city. The Panarch tried to get her to move it into space . . ."

"Now they'll have to use full armor and decon chambers if they want to get any loot," Hreem said, guffawing. "The whole city'll be armpit-deep in crawling slimes and man-eating mushrooms, or whatever it was the crazy old bitch kept in there."

"Pretty close, Cap'n." Dyasil's shudder was audible in his voice.

On the screen the battle was over. From the fallen bodies of the defenders blobby columns of multihued slime wavered toward the smoky sky, like pillars of rotten cheese. The bridge was silent as the scene faded out; Hreem heard someone leave hurriedly.

The viewscreen showed space again—below, a planet, its surface blurred by the energies of an activated Tesla Shield. The caption scrolled up—*Minerva*—and there was a buzz of excited comment: the Academy planet, training center for the Panarch's military forces. "This is gonna be good!" said someone.

There was a quiet bleep from Erbee's console and the lanky Rifter slapped a pad, blotting out the picture on his little screen. "Cap'n! Emergence pulse . . . five lightseconds." The other Rifters on the bridge scrambled to their positions.

Hreem slapped the jump pad beside him, feeling the faint subsonic pulse as the fiveskip blipped briefly. The main screen blanked to a view of space. Moments later the screen shimmered as the computer located the intruder—in the center a translucent blue-white sphere of light was dissipating against the stars. He kept his hand poised over the jump pad: "Pogger! Give me shields and lock on targeting. Ready a skipmissile. Erbee. ID?"

A tense moment later: "Incoming, Cap'n. Brotherhood code: it's the *Satansclaw*."

"About time! Cancel that, Pogger. Dyasil, general broadcast—all ships to shift to within a light-second, and link up for conference."

At the nav console Bargun and another tech were bent over the little screen, still watching Dyasil's recording, eager anticipation on their faces.

"Bargun!" snapped Hreem. "You got that first jump plotted?"

"Yeah. All I need to do is finaygel it a little, 'cause of the flea-hops, and if we're more'n half a light-second off I'll eat my console. But Dward and me want to see some of those spit-and-polish nackers at the Academy get flamed."

"If we're off more than that, you'll wish I gave you the choice of eating your console, so cut that chatzing recording off and set up the jump. Anyway, Neyvla-khan and his clan don't take chances—once the Shield's down they'll just stand off in orbit and slag the surface. Only a fool would land on a planet full of Academy-trained fighters."

The viewscreen slowly segmented itself into a number of windows as the captains of the rest of the Rifter ships joined the conference. Hreem knew most of them; the captain of the *Novograth* was new to him, a woman with a plump, rosy face who looked like someone's grandmother until you noticed the deadness of her eyes.

As Hreem had expected, Tallis Y'Marmor was the last to link up. A few seconds after his pop-eyed visage appeared, his eyes moved and focused on Hreem and he grinned, his larynx bobbing as he swallowed nervously. Hreem snorted with exasperation—*The stupid blit's still five light-seconds out.*

"Sorry I'm late, Hreem," Tallis began, "but my fiveskip's all chatzed up and we're having trouble finding the problem ..."

"Y'Marmor, you blunge-brain," Hreem yelled, "get yourself in closer so we can talk without waiting for you to hear us!"

Y'Marmor's blundering explanation continued for another ten seconds, while Hreem fumed and the other faces on the screen grinned, then: "so we took ..." He stopped and glared at Hreem. "I just told you, I can't control it that fine! We're coming in under geeplane—it'll only take a few minutes."

"Forget it, Marmor. Just listen and keep your mouth shut. If you have any question, ask 'em at the end. All right, you've got some of the details so far; here's how we're gonna handle the attack." The faces looked at him with anticipation. "First jump is to twenty light-minutes out and over. Then the *Lith*'ll jump in just short of the skip barrier and take out the resonance generator. That'll leave the way clear for the rest of you to skip in close to Charvann after the field collapses back to normal radius—give it fifteen minutes before you follow us. When you skip in, take out whatever ships you see. Don't take prizes—blast 'em all. We don't want to overlook any naval ships. Remember, *Novograth* and *Satansclaw*: your skipmissiles are hotter than anything the Navy's got, but your shields and everything else are the same as ever. The rest of you don't have any advantage except surprise, so shoot first! Any questions so far?"

As soon as he asked the question, Hreem knew what was coming. Everyone knew the weakness of the fiveskip: get too close to a planetary-sized gravity well—inside radius—in fivespace, and you ended up inverted in three dimensions. It was a spectacularly messy fate that was the subject of many a late-night bilge-banging session. On Charvann, the resonance field extended radius to second lunar orbit; if Hreem's attack on the generator failed ... Sure enough, one of the captains had to ask.

"What if you miss?"

"Then you'll end up staring at the inside of your own head!" snarled Hreem. "I won't miss! Anyway, after we mop up, the *Novograth* will take on the Shield while *Lith* and *Satansclaw* keep a lookout for that cruiser that's supposed to be in-system." Hreem smiled broadly. "Are they ever gonna be surprised, finding out what an Alpha Class can do with an Urian relay in its powerdeck!" The other captains laughed—all except Tallis, who hadn't heard the remark yet. His lack of reaction made him look even stupider than usual, thought Hreem.

"Don't get too jolly," he added, "and don't forget just how good a cruiser is at long-ranging." *But some of 'em will,* he thought disgustedly. Most of the Rifters who'd joined Dol'jhar's fleet were part-timers, opportunists, traders comfortable on both sides of the law—too careful or timid to merit the attention of the Navy's largest ships, whose seven-kilometer baseline lent their sensors terrifying precision and range.

"Any of you get lazy after we mop up the locals, and decide to stop drunkwalking—cruiser'll target you from way out, then jump in on top of you ... no warning." From ten light-minutes out, a cruiser could take its time targeting a distant fleet, then jump in close, correct and fire long before the emergence pulse from its targeting position arrived to warn its victims. Only random changes in velocity offered any protection for a targeted ship—the more often, the better.

The laughter tapered off. Warned by the expressions on some of their faces, Hreem went on quickly, directing their attention back to more pleasant anticipations.

"After the Shield collapses, we land—you've already got your assignments."

"What kind of defenses are we going to encounter on the way down?" interrupted the captain of the *Novograth*. Her speech was precise, almost prissy. Hreem took an instant dislike to her.

"None, if they're smart. They know there's no defense against dirty nukes in atmosphere." The rules of war involving planetary defense were ancient and rarely violated: civilian populations were too effective as hostages to make resistance to a landing practical once the Shield fell.

"But listen close . . ." Hreem leaned forward for emphasis. "There's gonna be no looting until after we find this Omilov chatzer—and everything in his house is gonna be under guard. Anybody crosses me up on this gets an all-expenses-paid vacation in the pleasure pits of Dol'jhar . . . after Norio finishes with you. You got that?" By the expressions on their faces, Hreem judged the threat sufficient. Just to make sure, he stretched ostentatiously in his pod, extending the heel-claws of his boots with a minatory click and then relaxing.

"Right. Afterward, anything goes. And don't any of you get trigger-happy and shoot up the Node or any of the Syncs, either—all the Highdwellings are mine. Any more questions?"

There were none and he dismissed them—"Except you, Y'Marmor. We've got some talking to do." The last of the other faces had just winked out when the pop-eyed Rifter captain reacted, and the light-speed delay irritated Hreem afresh.

"It's not my fault," whined Tallis. "It's that blit O'Pappan and his refit crew on Rifthaven, selling me substandard parts."

"Blow it out your blungehole, Marmor—he sells you what you pay him for. If you'd put more money into the guts of the *Satansclaw* and less into all those chatzy decorations—like that screaming horror you call a cabin. With all those paintings of fat bitches and that curlicue furniture that makes you feel like you're sitting on somebody's face . . . it's like a cross between a chatz-house and a corpse-painter's waiting room . . ." Hreem's disgust left him wordless for a moment. The rest of the crew on the bridge were concentrating fiercely on their consoles, but Hreem could feel their grins.

"Forget all that, Marmor. I don't know why Eusabian picked you, and if I had any say in the matter you wouldn't be part of my command, but you're here, and if you chatz up this attack I'll take you on a guided tour of your own bowels. Now, how much longer are you gonna need to get your fiveskip working right?"

Hreem's threats and obvious anger cut Y'Marmor's usually interminable self-serving explanations to a barely tolerable minimum, and got results. An hour after the *Satansclaw* signed off, Dyasil reported that Y'Marmor had messaged his readiness.

"He sounded kind of unhappy, Cap'n," the tech said with a wry smile, "though I can't imagine why."

Hreem laughed and dismissed the matter, excitement rising in him now that the attack was about to begin. Though he was enormously successful by Rifter standards, and quite wealthy by anyone's measuring, Hreem had always been on the run. Always, lurking behind his success, the fear that haunted all his plans, was the specter of a suddenly appearing cruiser, the hideous, ripping squeal of a ruptor, or the sudden smash of a skipmissle. Few Rifters in the jacking trade ever lived long enough to relax and enjoy their loot, and the more successful they were, the more likely was a fatal encounter with the Navy—not to mention the deadly envy of fellow Rifters.

But now it was his turn to call the shots. Fate and the Lord of Vengeance had placed the ultimate weapon in his hands, and like his fellows in the Brotherhood whose work he had just watched with delight, Hreem was eager to unleash it on his persecutors. He knitted his fingers together and stretched his arms overhead, feeling the last of his anxiety depart. For a moment the quiet hum of the ship around him was as much a part of him as the sound of the breath through his nostrils or the subdued murmur of his pulse. He was the instrument of his own vengeance.

"Dyasil," he said, "battle stations. Signal the fleet. Bargun . . . take us in." Moments later the bridge shuddered gently as the fiveskip engaged and the viewscreen blanked as the *Flower of Lith* leapt out of spacetime toward Charvann.

SEVEN

✳

To its captain's intense relief, the *Satansclaw* made the skip to twenty out-and-over without incident; but it seemed to Tallis Y'Marmor that the *Flower of Lith* jumped out only moments after he arrived. Fifteen minutes to go.

Tallis watched the wake of the *Lith* dissipate redly against the stars; then he slumped back in his command chair and picked nervously at the ornately gilded filigree on his console. His finger rings glittered in the subdued light of the *Satansclaw*'s bridge. Around him the monitors sat stiffly, resplendent in red uniforms with gold piping at the seams, fidgeting at their consoles.

Hreem's tongue-lashing was still vivid in his mind. *How ludicrous, and how typical, of that barbarian to call my ship a chatz-house! Chatz-house! How would he know? There isn't one in the Thousand Suns that'll let him in—unless he brings his own partner. And then they charge him double just to clean up the room afterward.*

Tallis sniffed fastidiously—the bridge of the *Lith* was a pretty repulsive sight, all naked metal slopped with gray paint, and, he was sure, a thin film of grease on everything. He looked around with satisfaction at the complex inlays and gleaming paneling that made the bridge of the *Satansclaw* such a delight to his eyes. A subtle change in the airflow on the bridge wafted the scent of sandalwood, bergamot, and *nushia* to him and he smiled, pleased at the new combination he'd devised for the tianqi, so necessary for keeping the crews' senses occupied in the otherwise monotonous confines of a ship in flight.

But his pleasant reverie was marred by the quiet voice of sho-Imbris, the navigator. "Ten minutes to skip."

Tallis' stomach suddenly insisted that the gravitors were unstable, but he knew they weren't. A zap-and-skip raid was one thing—Tallis was good at that, which is why the Karroo Syndicate had commissioned him in the *Satansclaw*. They wanted profits, not damage reports. But a full-fledged attack on a planet, and with a cruiser in the system—that was very different. He wondered again what Eusabian had offered the Karoo, to entice them to risk their ships in the Dol'jharian attack.

Tallis found himself hoping that the fiveskip would fail again, so they'd miss the worst of the battle. Hreem couldn't blame him ... *But he would.* He'd seen one of Hreem's "entertainments," and he knew that the burly captain needed little or no excuse to stage one. And what Norio could do to a man's ego ... Tallis shuddered. One's emotions should be private, not the instruments of a psychic flaying.

His fingers drummed nervously near the code pads on his console, then suddenly he noticed what he was doing and snatched his hand away. *You're not that afraid of the attack,* insisted his interior voice, now chattering away full speed under the lash of his anxiety. A familiar tingle of combined guilt and anxiety burned through him, mixed with disgust. *You spent a half-year's take on the damned thing, and you've never used it.*

A shudder of superstitious fear ran through him as he thought of the mass of circuitry the Barcan technician had buried deep within the *Satansclaw*'s computers. A *logos*—embodying the combined expertise of scores of ship captains, including some of the greatest fighters who'd ever lived. The names of the captains whose talents the logos held was a roll call of the Hall of Honor: Ilvarez, Metellus, Tu Chang, Porgruth Minor among others—they were his to command. Perhaps it would be a good idea to switch it on and link it to the ship's sensorium, just to watch his back and help him with the tactical displays. *It wouldn't have any trouble at all dealing with this attack.*

And it might not have any trouble at all dealing with me, either. Images from the history chips flickered through his mind, the Horror a thousand years and more ago seeming like yesterday's news. The century-long war against the Adamantines—those cold intelligences, embodied in metal and crystal and unleashed by the Hegemony in a vain quest for domination of the Exiles—had deeply scarred the psyche of humankind. The Hegemony had lost control, if indeed they'd ever had it, and at the last had fought side by side with the Exiles against their own creations. To this day, rumor had it, remnants of the ancient enemy still lurked in remote corners of the Thousand Suns—and it was well known that a peerage and unimaginable riches awaited the person who led the Navy to a hibernating Adamantine. Like most of the people of the Heart Stars, Tallis no more questioned the Ban than he questioned the existence of Arthelion and the Emerald Throne. *Thou shalt not duplicate the human mind.*

But Barca lay far outside the Heart Stars, hard up on the Shiidra Reaches. They had not experienced the Horror, so they didn't share that fear. Their Tikeris androids, legal but obscenely close to infringing the Ban, were infamous throughout the Thousand Suns, as were the fearsome Ogres, used with such effect against the Shiidra. The Barcan salesman on Rifthaven had been very persuasive, insisting that the logos wasn't *really* intelligent, and glossing over the fact that discovery of it by the authorities would earn Tallis, at the very least, exile to Gehenna, and in some jurisdictions, an agonizing death. *And if the crew found out . . .*

The salesman had promised total secrecy as part of the deal, and he'd had some fascinating simulations of ship-to-ship combat. The logos could speak to him via pinbeam, and hear his subvocalized commands, anywhere in the ship. No one else could hear it or command it, the Barcan had told him. And with optional eye implants—Tallis could almost hear the dealer's unctuous tones—the logos could display data that no one else could see. The glory would be his alone. Tallis had been thoroughly sold on the concept, had even submitted to the surgery on both eyes, visions of glory and riches dancing in his head, right up until the installers had him switch it on for the final tests.

Dead brains. Corpse voices. Tallis shuddered at the memory. The flat baritone voice, speaking disembodied inside his head, had given him nightmares for the next month, and he had never dared switch it on again.

"Five minutes," said sho-Imbris.

His inner vision began serving up images of the coming attack. The swirl of ship-to-ship actions would be terrifying in its randomness, unlike any raid he'd ever dared. And a cruiser—Tallis perceived that image viscerally, for he'd been a galley-slub on the old *Terror* when it was ripped by a cruiser in ambush. There was no other sound quite like the squeal of a ruptor bolt hitting a hull.

His fear of the logos and the terror of the coming battle balanced for a moment longer in his mind. He'd have to play back the conversation with Hreem for the machine; but then, there was no reason to feel shame. The logos couldn't laugh, and probably wouldn't understand the emotional aspects of the scene.

Tallis sneaked a look around the bridge. No one was watching. After a moment, he forced his shaking fingers to touch the code pads in a complex pattern, and the logos began to wake up. Flickering ghost light, apparent only to his eyes, darted sector by sector across the tactical screens, testing his corneal implants. Tallis clenched his teeth, willing himself not to shiver as the dead baritone led him through the wake-up routine in a technological litany of question and response.

No one could fault Anderic, the communications tech, on the condition of his console, all oiled wood and gleaming metal. He stared at a particularly well polished section of metal, watching in fascination as his captain tensed abruptly. It almost looked like Tallis was having a seizure: his eyes suddenly started darting about, his jaw clenched, and he rocked slightly in his seat.

Anderic looked at the screens, but they showed only a featureless starfield, overlaid by ship traces. What was going on? A few moments later Anderic noticed Tallis' throat moving slightly. *He's talking to himself.* He seemed to be having an intense interior conversation, which lasted some time.

"Navigation," said Tallis suddenly, breaking the tense silence on the bridge.

"One hundred twenty-eight seconds, sir."

"I know." Tallis' voice was angry, but Anderic detected an undertone of strain. "Recalculate. Drop us in as close to the Node as you can and orient me. Sensors."

Next to Anderic, Oolger swiveled around as Tallis continued. "Immediately on emergence, look for targets close to the Node or another Sync, so we can fight with our back to something they won't want to hit."

Oolger turned back to his console and began setting up a pattern for emergence. Tallis had no new commands for Anderic, so the tech could listen as Tallis rebriefed the other monitors for emergence. It was a performance totally at odds with the captain's usual behavior. Tallis was an agonizingly painstaking planner without a trace of inspiration, and he never, never changed his plans like this.

As he continued to watch, the conviction grew in him that there was definitely something going on that could be manipulated to good advantage, with a little inside information from Luri.

At the thought of her Anderic felt his nacker stirring; the memory of her soft abundance unfocused his eyes for a time, until the ship shuddered into skip.

❊   ❊   ❊

Omilov sat there staring at the portrait for an unmeasured time.

The reading lamp sensed his lack of movement and turned itself out, and he drowsed a little, but the night was passing all too slowly, and the turmoil of his thoughts defeated the effects of the dreamberry tea. When he roused, Kilelis was already descending toward the western hills. In its faint light, the statues dotting the moonlight-black expanse of the lawn outside the study windows seemed poised on the edge of movement.

He stood up and stretched; as the light sprang back on, his reflection blotted out the outside world in the window. He studied his appearance for a moment: tall, tending to corpulence, though less so in the face than elsewhere, with wiry, gray-shot black hair lying close to his skull, and the pendulous fleshy earlobes that marked the Omilov line as far back as images had been recorded. From where he stood the reading lamp shone up into his face, throwing the shadows of his bushy eyebrows up across his high forehead, giving him a menacing look that made a smile quirk the edge of his mouth. He turned away, pulling his lounge coat tighter around him. Perhaps a turn on the terrace in the fresh night air would calm his thoughts.

He paused at the terrace door to override the lights, which would otherwise go on automatically, and noted with some surprise that the override was already engaged. He eased the door open quietly and saw a slender male figure standing some distance away, gazing out over the grounds of the estate toward the darkened eastern horizon.

His slippers made a faint gritty noise on the paving, warning the solitary figure that he had company. As he neared he recognized Brandon's profile, sidelit against the stars.

The young man did not turn around as Omilov came up beside him, and they stood in companionable silence for a time. The night air was cool; a vagrant breeze teased at Omilov's neck and he drew his collar tighter.

But Omilov finally decided he must speak. "You said you left before the ritual, Brandon. I must ask you why." He hesitated, then added, "It would be best that I know before your family's retainers arrive to discuss this with us all."

Brandon turned suddenly to face him. "No one knows I'm here," he said. "We arrived as private citizens of a Highdweller community—Deralze saw to that. And we will shortly be gone again, if you fear that Semion has somehow managed to follow us even so."

Omilov nodded, and was about to speak again when Brandon forestalled him.

Moving away from the rail, he said, "Sebastian, how long have you known my father?"

Omilov wondered what was behind the question: Brandon knew the answer very well. "Almost thirty-five years," he said reminiscently. "I was a rogate in the xenoarchaeology department of the Concilium Exterioris at the time. We first met after a rather unusual situation I found myself in on a planet outside the Thousand Suns."

Brandon turned to him. "You never mentioned that before."

Omilov chuckled. "You were a very inquisitive boy. The best way of dealing with your incessant questions was to make sure you didn't know what to ask about." His voice became grim. "I know I don't have to worry about that now, so I can tell you this much: the planet has no name, and never will. It is under quarantine, Class Null—ships skipping into the system are destroyed without warning. For a time, it seemed better to flame it clean of life, and if knowledge of it ever becomes general, that will be its fate. The whole matter is under the Panarch's seal."

There was a long pause. In the distance a night lizard uttered its eerie cries, like the sobbing of a woman; sorrowful counterpoint to the cheerful song of the leaptoads. When

Brandon spoke again, looking out over the dimly lit grounds, his voice was pensive. "You were one of his closest friends when I was growing up. I remember how different he was when just you and he were together, different from when he was surrounded by the Court."

"Different," echoed Omilov, faintly questioning.

Brandon smile a little. "It was you with whom I lived after my mother was killed." Though Brandon's voice was under control, Omilov noted his hands, moving aimlessly across the pale marble of the balustrade, fingertips almost caressing it.

"You know why," Omilov said, sorting his words. "How often have we discussed the dangers of that time?"

Brandon made a sign indicating agreement. "My incessant questions . . . but you always answered them, didn't you?" He laughed. "That's why I came here, before I—" He shrugged, and turned suddenly to Omilov. "Sebastian, when you left Arthelion—retired—ten years ago, you were at the peak of your career. You could have had a seat on the Council of Pursuivance—the Chivalate is regarded as a stepping-stone to that, is it not? You had my father's ear, powerful friends on the council and in the Magisterium; many people spend their lives trying to gain what you had. You might even have ended up on the Privy Council. But you left."

Omilov answered carefully, addressing both the spoken question and what he thought was the unspoken. "One of the things you must have heard your father say, probably many times, was that no single person could rule the Thousand Suns."

" 'Ruler of all, ruler of naught, power unlimited, a prison unsought . . .' " Brandon quoted softly.

"Your father lives that and suffers that. Like every one of his forty-six predecessors, he has to rely on other people, thousands of other people, most of whom he has never met and whom he can judge only thirdhand." Omilov found he had pressed his palms together in front of his stomach, fingers extended forward, a habit of his when speaking intensely that was familiar to all his students. He relaxed them with conscious effort. "And like all of his predecessors, he sometimes makes mistakes."

He shook his head. "I tried to tell him about a person very close to him, in whom I believe his trust is misplaced. He would not, could not, listen: your father's most outstanding virtue is his loyalty. And I could not stop speaking the truth to Gelasaar, could not therefore stop hurting our friendship. Finally—" Omilov hesitated only fractionally: "Finally a very loyal and able man was destroyed, and I could do nothing to prevent it, even as I saw it happening. At that point I knew I could not remain on Arthelion any longer."

Brandon nodded, and the last traces of pretense and guardedness faded quickly from his face, like ice under the hot sun of a sudden spring. "Lusor," he said abruptly. "Do you know why—"

Without any sense of transition, the grounds of the estate were flooded with an actinic glare brighter than the sun, throwing sharp, acid-edged shadows across the grounds. Omilov squeezed his streaming eyes shut, garish afterimages etched into his vision. Moments later, his skin prickled as the air became charged with static electricity, and the light abruptly dimmed and began to fade. A flock of jezeels erupted from a nearby grove of trees, protesting the sudden onslaught of this strange new daylight.

Omilov's vision returned only slowly. When he could see again, Brandon was gazing up at a rapidly fading point of light about a third of the sky eastward of Tira. The night sky looked blurry: most of the stars were now invisible, the brighter ones visible only as dim smears of light, and the two moons were dim mirrors of watery blue light. From the northern horizon bright streamers of auroral flame reached south, growing in brightness as they watched.

"The Shield is up," said Brandon. "That must have been one of the resonance generators."

"An accident?"

"No." Brandon's tones were decisive, and Omilov realized

that though the young man's Academy training had been interrupted, he was better qualified to interpret this event than a gnostor of xenology.

"No, it must be an attack. If that was one of the resonators, inner space is now open to fiveskip—it's a classic maneuver," Brandon added with a quirk of self-mockery, "according to the simulations I was permitted to view."

The door to the terrace banged open and Lenic Deralze appeared, visibly relaxing as he looked toward them. Then his face set like stone as he gazed upward. Moments later Osri came out, followed by some of the household staff, their faces pale and strained. They had to squeeze past Deralze, who appeared not to notice them.

As Osri joined Omilov and Brandon, his eyes strayed south and he pointed. "What's that?" His eyes widened in consternation as he breathed, "It *can't* be the S'lift!"

To the south a long string of faint, blue-white points of light was slowly rising past the bright star that was the Node. Above it, another like string, fainter, could be seen. They stared at it for a moment, then Omilov said, "What is this we're seeing? That is the orbital elevator cable, is it not?"

Deralze spoke quietly, "It's been severed by the defense Shield, and the emergency thrusters are trying to push it out of Charvann's orbital plane so it won't slice through the Node or any of the Highdwellings."

Brandon said suddenly, "That other cable is the hohmann freight launcher—it's been cut loose too, so it won't drag the Node out of orbit. I've seen a chip of the attack on Alpheios, during the final Shiidra incursion . . ."

"Shiidra!" exclaimed someone. "Telos ward us!" The thought of the vicious, dog-like aliens and their flattened, ellipsoidal ships, once an ever-present scourge of the Thousand Suns, stirred a murmur of nervous comment from the servants.

"The Shiidra were finally driven off some fifty years ago."

Omilov noted with approval that this last was uttered by

Parraker, the majordomo. He was marvelously adept at controlling rumor: under his steady hand the froth of gossip and innuendo that plagued so many house staffs was notably absent.

"No," said Osri. "Just the outpost from which they raided the Panarchy. Their home system was never found."

Parraker pressed his lips together ever so slightly, making his salt-and-pepper mustache bristle a bit, as the murmuring broke out again. Omilov sighed. Like his mother's, Osri's pride made him almost invariably choose correctness over charity.

"It's unlikely, without that outpost, that the Shiidra would choose to attack one of the Heart Stars of the Thousand Suns—a frontier planet would be a more reasonable choice." Brandon spoke in the formal modality, a rarity for him. The subtle intonation he used, by placing the matter immediately on a more formal basis, employed the class consciousness of the staff to enforce belief in his statement. "Whoever the attackers are, they are human."

Osri's face soured: he could not very well contradict the direct statement of a social superior, especially without supporting evidence, so he had to remain silent and accept the unspoken rebuke.

Well done, Brandon, Omilov thought, careful that none of the rueful amusement he felt showed on his face.

Parraker started to herd the staff back into the house. Distant thunder pealed, while the auroral display grew brighter, more slowly than at first. A wind sprang up, carrying on it a faint electrical smell.

"Why don't you two join me in the library?" Omilov suggested mildly, aware of nervous staff ears behind him. "We'll be more comfortable there, and perhaps the DataNet will have some information on what is happening."

Just as they were entering the house, another bright flash, less glaring than the first, illuminated the terrace. They turned in time to see several smaller flashes in rapid succession, leaving behind blurry, rapidly fading coins of light in the sky.

"Ship-to-ship action," Deralze murmured. He had taken up a stance directly behind Brandon; whatever his position had been an hour ago, he was now on duty. Omilov wondered if he was armed, and concluded ruefully that the silent, dour man was probably a walking armory.

Omilov motioned the three of them into the house and shut the door, muting the thunder and shutting out the rising wind.

There was a sense of comfort in a night of shocks to find the library looking and smelling as it always did. *False comfort,* he thought as he looked around the large, high-ceilinged room, paneled in dark woods, as they crossed the thick sea-green carpet. Around three of the walls a balcony, with spiral stairs at either end, gave access to a second level of bookshelves.

The fourth wall was heavily draped, shutting off the high windows that opened out onto the same lawn as Omilov's study. The room smelled faintly of leather and wood polish—a comfortable, cozy smell that kept the outside world at a distance.

"Please, sit down," Omilov said.

Brandon and Osri arranged themselves in two of the overstuffed chairs scattered around the room that afforded the best view of the com unit, and Omilov called up the DataNet on a small console in the table between them. Deralze took up a stance behind Brandon's chair, from which he could see both the com unit and the room.

They soon found that none of the novosti—the Net commentators—knew any more than they did. Most of the info-services were based on the Node anyway, and normal communications with that and the Highdweller communities had been cut off by the severing of the S'lift, while the Tesla Shield made all but the military tight-beams, with their complex purity algorithms, virtually unusable. One service was even replaying the chip Brandon had mentioned, of the Shiidra attack on Alpheios thirty years before, complete with graphic displays of alien atrocities. With a moue of disgust, Omilov slapped the disconnect pad.

"Irresponsible trash!" he exclaimed. "We can do our own speculating, if it comes to that. If they're human, the only identity for the attackers that occurs to me is a Rifter gang, though I can't imagine why they'd try something so foolish."

Brandon looked up quickly, but it was Osri who spoke. "Rifters? Riffraff, pirates and slave-traders, attacking a major planet?" He folded his arms across his chest. "The Navy will soon put a stop to that!"

He sat back when Parraker appeared with a tray of brandied coffees. Omilov pressed a pad on the console to open the drapes. The splendor of the view—the brilliant auroral display and the lightning-laced clouds now billowing up over the horizon—drew their attention wholly outward, and time passed swiftly in a silence broken only by the increasingly frequent bellows of thunder and the quiet, crystalline noises of their glasses on the glass-topped tables beside their chairs.

Sometime later there was a gentle chime from the table. Omilov sat up, startled out of his musings. "Yes?"

"A holocom from His Grace of Charvann, sir."

Omilov blinked: surely the Archon had more important things on his mind right now than calling him? With a motion of his hand he invited Brandon and Osri to join him as he triggered the holojac.

A life-size image wavered into apparent solidity just beyond their group of chairs: a short, stocky man in his mid-thirties, in a plain military tunic and neatly pressed trousers tucked into glossy boots. A single decoration, the blason d'solei, adorned his chest. The white of his uniform was an effective contrast to his smooth black skin and tight-curled black hair. His dark eyes were shadowed by concern, an expression belied by the brilliant smile that lit his face as his eyes focused on Omilov.

"Sebastian! I'm glad to see you're safe. I don't have time for the amenities, so I must make this as close to an order as my position allows: I must see you here in Merryn as soon as possible." His eyes moved away, passed Osri with a polite nod, and froze as he beheld Brandon. Omilov's concern as to why Tanri Faseult had thought him in danger found a new subject as, after a brief hesitation, the Archon's mouth hardened into a thin line and he bowed slightly.

"Your Highness. I must request your presence also." His voice was severely formal.

Osri's face was grim. Brandon said nothing, just bowed his head once.

"We'll be happy to comply, Your Grace," Omilov said with some haste, "but I don't understand—"

"Forgive me, Sebastian, but I don't have time to explain. A military escort has already been dispatched for you. Until then." He nodded, sketched a slight bow in Brandon's direction, and the image winked out.

Moments later the crashing roar of supersonic flight announced the arrival of the escort; through the library window they caught a glimpse of a gleaming predator-shape settling gently onto the lawn, its highly polished surface darkly reflecting the lightning of the growing storm.

Osri stood slowly, seemingly unable to take his eyes from the ship. Omilov touched his boswell and said, "Parraker, I must speak to you." The muted urgency in Omilov's voice brought the majordomo to the door in less time than one would have expected from his dignified bulk. "The Archon has requested our presence in Merryn. He was not able to give us any information about the situation. If . . ." He hesitated, then stated calmly, "If it appears there is any danger to our area I trust you to supervise the staff, making their safety your primary concern. In the meantime there is a wooden box in the wardrobe safe; I must request you to convey it personally to the University, see that it is deposited in the vaults. You know where the key code is kept. Thank you, Parraker. I hope we will be returning shortly." To the others he smiled. "Shall we join our escort, genz?"

Brandon preceded them, Deralze falling in behind. Downstairs a military guard in battle dress waited, and seeing Brandon they snapped to attention. Brandon gave them a smile and nod as he passed; Osri did not seem to see them. Omilov reached the door and they closed in behind, but then his steps slowed, and just beyond the door he stopped.

"Sir," one of the guards started, "His Grace gave us orders to use utmost speed . . ."

"No," Omilov said slowly, "no more unlikely than its appearance in the first place."

"What, Father?" Osri stopped and turned.

Omilov's ambivalence disappeared, was replaced by decision. "Please board the shuttle, Your Highness, Osri. I shall be with you in a moment." He strode swiftly back into the house, followed by one of the guards.

Scarcely a minute later he climbed into the shuttle and sank into the cushioned seat next to his son. Both Brandon's and Osri's eyes went to the carved wooden box held tightly in Omilov's hands, Osri looking astonished. "What? Why did you decide to bring that artifact, Father?"

"Why would His Grace want to see *me*, of all people, at such a time? Common sense says there is no possible connection between this"—he hefted the small box—"and the unfortunate confrontation which seems to be going on over our heads, but then, common sense would have denied the possibility of our sleep being thus interrupted, wouldn't it?"

Osri replied in the tone of one humoring a child, "If it's as important as you seem to be implying, wouldn't it be wiser having Parraker take it to safety?"

Omilov glanced at Deralze and then the guards, and murmured in a quiet voice which forbade further discussion, "I believe it *is* going to go to a place of safety."

Osri gave the faintest of sniffs and turned his eyes to the nearby port as the vessel lifted off and lanced through the sky toward the capital.

EIGHT

❋

"Fire!"

The bridge of the *Lith* shuddered gently to the dopplered moan of the accelerator, and the familiar reddish chain-of-pearls wake of a skipmissile spread out from the lower edge of the viewscreen. Moments later a great gout of light announced the termination of the missile's flight.

"Got him!" Hreem slapped his thigh, his eyes drinking in the sharp-edged sphere of light, blue-white at the center, shading to red at its vanishing edges, that marked the demise of a Panarchist frigate.

"That's the last of 'em, Cap'n," announced Erbee. "All the others are ours."

"Alluwan, damage?" The short, fat Rifter at the damage-control console turned around and speared his little finger up in the air in the gesture of approval. "Nothin' major. A puncture or two, under control."

"That's the kind of battle I like!" crowed Hreem, his heart still pounding with excitement. "Short, sweet, and painless. Dyasil, shoot burst code 'Blackheart' at Sync-2—

we'll see if my friend there is awake. And tell *Novograth* to stand by to fire on the Shield—that fancy Archon's time is just about up."

While he waited for acknowledgment from his contact on the Node, the Shield-blurred curve of Charvann swung up in the viewscreen, capped with vivid auroral flame at the pole visible from their vantage. Some distance off, the tiny shape of the *Novograth* hung in space, its missile tube a mere needle at this distance, turning toward the planet.

"Mind if I pull in a close-up, Cap'n?" asked Dyasil. "I'm making a chip for our broadcast, and I'd like a good shot of their first missile."

Hreem nodded. He was in an expansive mood, minded to grant almost anything at this point. The *Novograth* expanded, details became visible: its heraldic blazon—a bloody dagger surrounded by a flowering wreath—was vivid against the silvery hull.

"Time?"

"Ten minutes, Cap'n." Dyasil turned back to his console as it chirped at him. "Got a pulse back from Sync-2—two-way coming."

A head windowed up on the screen: pale, with a droopy, asymmetric mustache and deep pockmarks on the gaunt cheeks. The pupils of the man's eyes were too small, and the whites surrounded the iris in an aggressive, somewhat mad stare.

So Naigluf's a hopper-popper now, thought Hreem. *Wonder who he gets the stuff from?*

"Can't talk too long, now, Hreem," said Naigluf. "Crazy panic here—too many sniffers around for a long jaw. I guess you-know-who must've moved up the schedule; either that or you've flipped your skull-cover. There's a cruiser hangin' around the system, in case you didn't know. Anyway, the only bit of news I've got for you is a juicy one: the nyr-Arkad's here!" He paused expectantly.

Hreem sat up. "What!" Hadn't that chip said that Eusabian had gotten all three . . . no: *"we have no indications of where he might be."*

After a slight lag, Naigluf continued. "Yeah. That should be worth a juicy bonus from Vengeance, eh? One of my people spotted him at the field outside of Merryn yesterday. Came in on a private craft, ID'd as a Highdweller, but it's him all right."

"Good work, Naigy. Bonus it is. How much hopper you want?" Hreem laughed at the man's discomfiture, which rapidly gave way to greedy calculation.

"I can get my own hopper. How 'bout you put me in charge of the Node, once you're finished here—take your usual cut."

"Not quite. Twenty for you, eighty for me." Hreem slapped the disconnect pad, laughing uproariously at Naigluf's look: mixed anticipation and dismay.

And if he gives me any trouble I'll have somebody slip some slag-solvent into his stash.

"Dyasil, tell *Novograth* to hold off. I've got some more talkin' to do with His Fanciness downside. Open a channel." Hreem leaned forward in his seat, considering just how sour he could make Tanri Faseult look this time around . . .

❈   ❈   ❈

The flight to Merryn from Omilov's estate was brief. Deralze wondered what the people under their flight path thought of the smashing concussion their transonic flight was laying down across the countryside. He decided that most of the people affected would no doubt be more reassured by the noise than upset: it would be unmistakable evidence that the Archon was doing something about the attack.

The capital was brilliantly lit. As their ship settled into a central court in the Archonic Enclave, Deralze noted scores of uniformed men and women hustling by, their movements giving the impression of highly ordered haste. The irony of his situation briefly amused him. It seemed events were conspiring to draw him ever further back into the system.

The hatch slid open with a subdued hiss; at the base of

the steps a weary adjutant in a slightly rumpled uniform saluted and hurried them across the court into an elevator. Inside, Deralze saw the woman's eyes gauge him briefly, one professional recognizing another. He felt his ears pop several times as they descended. At the bottom, at the end of a short corridor, a metal door slid aside as they approached, and the busy murmur of the defense room became audible.

Inside was a hive of activity. Below the high ceiling hung multiple banks of monitor screens, repeating the information from the consoles below them. Scenes of space, some with structures in the foreground, indicating origin at the Node or another of the Syncs, some of starships with odd heraldic blazons; graphs, charts, and diagrams abounded, changing with bewildering rapidity. Deralze noted that threre seemed to be no naval ships depicted. Between the monitor banks hung odd polygonal shapes, acoustic dampers that kept the noise of many busy people down to a dull babble.

As the adjutant escorted them through the press, dodging messengers and others in a variety of uniforms, Deralze saw a high dais at the far end, toward which they were slowly progressing. The Archon stood on it, leaning on the railing at the edge, staring up at the large master screen which faced it. Behind him could be seen a woman's head—severe, lined features, hair pulled tautly back. Tanri turned his head from time to time to speak to her.

As they ascended the stairs of the dais, the woman's console came into view, vastly larger than those on the floor. Her fingers flew across it with amazing speed, the master screen, now visible to them, responding with flickering changes of information in its many window segments.

The adjutant left them standing behind the Archon and went up and spoke briefly to him. After a moment, Tanri turned around, and with a weary smile, came to greet them.

"Sebastian, my friend," he said, warmly grasping Omilov's hand. "And Osri—I've not seen you since your appointment to the Academy." He turned to Brandon, bowed to the precisely correct degree. "Your Highness."

Brandon inclined his head, but the Archon had already turned away. Deralze noted no resentment on Brandon's face at this snub, but that was as it should be. Certainly the Krysarch was aware that the Archon's attitude was to be expected: a visit to a planet by a member of the Royal Family without notice to the ruling Archon was a gross infraction of courtesy, and a violation of the Covenant of Anarchy. And Deralze was certain that the Archon could calculate the spacetime lag between Arthelion and Charvann as well as Osri had, which made an unauthorized visit into a criminal offense . . .

Brandon, his hands clasped lightly behind his back, moved to the rail to look out over the busy floor below. Deralze saw the Archon observe this; then the dark eyes brushed him with a flicker of acknowledgment before turning back to Omilov. "Thank you for coming so promptly, Sebastian, despite my curtness on the com."

"Quite all right, Your Grace, though I must confess myself mystified as to why you should wish to see me, of all people, at such a time."

The Archon smiled wryly. "No less mystified than myself, at the reason it was necessary. Look here." He directed Omilov's attention to the screen, smiling wider at his wondering expression, and motioned to the woman at the console. "Bikara, if you would show Sebastian our visitor."

Deralze edged around to a position where he could watch the viewscreen and the others without being obvious about it. The main viewscreen flickered and filled with a dark-haired, olive-skinned face, brutal and heavy, with sneering lips and cold eyes. The man was frozen by the record chip in the act of smiling, which made him look cruel and dissipated. Deralze noticed that his teeth were crooked, unusual in a society where dental care was available to virtually anyone. He wore an off-white tunic with a pink stain on it; thick curly hair, like the pelt of an animal, spilled out of an gold-encrusted V-collar.

Osri looked up at the picture in sour disapproval, while Brandon seemed more interested in the reactions of the people on the main floor, some of whom had paused in their work to look up at the face. Most of the upturned faces were grim; some showed open disdain or even hatred.

Then the Archon's voice deepened slightly to an almost theatrical pitch and timbre. "So, Sebastian, do you know this man?"

Deralze recalled Tanri's reputation for a somewhat pawky sense of humor, which manifested itself at the oddest times. He noticed that Omilov seemed caught a little off balance by it, turning to the Archon with a smile that leaked away as he saw that he was at least half serious. "No," he replied, "and I would remember had I ever met him. Should I?"

Tanri gestured. "Enough, Bikara." The screen cleared back to its normal relay functions. "You must forgive my weakness for theatrics, my friend—when I was a child I loved courtroom dramas: the sudden, stabbing questions, the exposure of deep secrets." He put a hand to his chest, pointed dramatically at Omilov with a mock-severe expression. "And where were *you* on the night of Jaspar sixteenth . . ." He smiled broadly.

Bikara said, in the manner of someone carrying out an order, "Five minutes, Your Grace."

"No, my friend, you would not be acquainted with Hreem the Faithless, as that one is called," the Archon said, serious now. "Though he is well known to any naval captain who ever dreamed of raking in a jackpot bonus. Hreem is a Rifter—one of the worst—specializing in slave-trading, jacking, and anything else that will make him rich with a minimum of risk." He looked briefly at the screen.

Rifters? Attacking one of the Heart Stars? Deralze began to sense that he had stood at the edge of something far larger than he had realized.

He glanced over at Brandon, who looked back at him bleakly. All the humor had suddenly leaked out of his demeanor. Deralze could see the same question in his eyes. *What is Markham's role in this?*

"But what can they hope to gain?" asked Omilov.

"You, Sebastian," said the Archon quietly.

Omilov stared at him, no understanding in his face.

"About two hours ago, a single ship phased in just outside the resonance field and destroyed the generator without warning. Minutes later, a number of other ships followed." His lips tightened against his anger. "We are not heavily armed here: it has not been necessary for centuries. Moments before you arrived the last of our ships was destroyed, along with three naval units." Tanri darted a glance up at the screen, turned to Bikara for a moment. "Bikara?"

"The wavefront is still fifteen minutes from complete coincidence, but probability is ninety-six percent that the signals from the attack have already reached *Korion*."

The Archon turned back to Omilov and said in response to his questioning look, "The battlecruiser *Korion* is on maneuvers in-system—just the usual reminder to our local Rifters to maintain their good behavior—" He stopped, apparently noticing Osri's look of incomprehension and disapproval.

"It's not as neat as the serial chips would have it," he chuckled. "Only a small percentage of Rifters are given to raiding and jacking, and most of those, like our local ones, tend to prey on other Rifters. As long as they behave themselves in-system, we leave them be."

"But now?" asked Omilov.

"We don't know." Tanri shrugged. "No matter. The *Korion* was scheduled to be in the middle system, no more than two light-hours out. By now they're almost certain to have detected the gravity pulse accompanying the collapse of the resonance field, and the ones caused by the Rifter ships skipping in." He smiled grimly. "Things will be different when it arrives, I promise you. In any case, shortly before his other ships arrived, this Hreem person beamed down an insolent demand for surrender . . . and for the delivery of one Sebastian Omilov and all his possessions into his hands."

"What? What would Rifters want with me?"

"You should ask rather," said the Archon, "what Eusabian of Dol'jhar wants with you. The demand was framed in his name." He smiled slightly. "There was some lively speculation here as to just what drug the captain was enjoying at that moment."

Shock flooded Deralze as he finally remembered who it was who bore revenge as a title. *The Lord of Vengeance.* Anger boiled up in him as he realized to whom he'd sold himself in his quest for revenge for the callous way in which the system had used him. He felt betrayed; and then shame overwhelmed him as he realized that he had no right to expect better. *I forswore my oath, so all oaths are worthless to me.*

He looked at Brandon again, who was staring at the image on the screen. On that slim figure hung the last tatters of Deralze's honor, the last possible fulfillment of his oath.

"Eusabian of Dol'jhar—" Omilov's voice choked off. He raised the small box, which had hung unregarded in his left hand since his arrival, and clutched it in both hands. "How did he know?" he whispered.

Osri looked at his father, grim-mouthed and confused, then at the Archon, while Brandon watched gravely from the railing.

"Excuse me?" said Tanri with a sharp glance at Omilov's hands. "What do you mean?"

"I'm sorry, Your Grace," said Omilov. "A . . . guess of mine has played out truly, much to my astonishment." He opened the box; the sphere threw back in brilliant, multicolored distortion the blinking lights and shifting images of the defense room. "I received this only hours ago—an artifact of the Ur, stolen, I believe, from the Shrine Planet."

"Quarantine One," said Tanri.

"Yes—"

"Emergence pulse, Your Grace," interrupted Bikara. "Signature—it's the *Korion.*"

"Ah! Put it on the screen, please. Excuse me, Sebastian, we'll get to the bottom of this in a moment, as soon as Dahawi and his crew dispose of the Rifter fleet." He rubbed his hands together. "I will enjoy this—'those of my people he murdered shall have vengeance.'"

" 'And a pyre shall I make of my enemy's works,' " quoted Brandon in response. Tanri shot a glance at him, while Osri's brows knitted.

Brandon gave them a deprecatory half-smile. "The Sanctus Gabriel of Desrien. He was High Phanist of the Magisterium in the reign of the Faceless One, whose memory be abhorred." The ritualistic tone of the last words hung in the air, and Deralze felt the back of his neck crawl. The horrible deed of that Arkad, dead these six hundred years and more, of whom no image now existed anywhere in the Thousand Suns, was not a comfortable thought under the present circumstances. *But the unfortunate planet Vellicor had dropped its Shield.*

A flicker in the corner of his vision brought Deralze's eyes to the main screen, which now showed a view of space. In the upper right-hand corner a small ellipse glowed, while in the lower left corner a scattering of light depicted some of the Rifter ships. Some of the other screens showed close-ups of Rifter ships, another, that of the *Korion*: a fat, egg-shaped ship bristling with antennae, with three large turrets spaced equally around both ends. At one end the cruiser's radiants formed an angular break in its otherwise smooth lines. There was no hint of the *Korion*'s true size from the picture on the screen, but Deralze knew that it was over seven kilometers long—a battlecruiser was the most powerful weapon of war ever built. Even a shielded planet could not hold out for more than a few weeks against one of these ships, which were the backbone of the Thousand-Year Peace.

From the image of the cruiser on the main screen, a multitude of slender beam segments of faint blue light were already slowly reaching out—the signature of the violent graviton pulses of the ruptor turrets, their tremendous energy disrupting the tenuous traces of gas left by the recent battle. Though they traveled at the speed of light, the scale of the battlefield made the beams seem to crawl toward their targets, which did not seem to have detected the cruiser yet.

"Excellent!" exclaimed the Archon. "He's using his ruptors, instead of wasting his skipmissiles on Rifter trash."

The sounds of the defense room were stilled entirely as all eyes turned to the screen.

✳   ✳   ✳

"You got that Archon yet, Dyasil?" Hreem stood up, the excess energy created by the battle finding no outlet in sitting still. He paced around the bridge of the *Lith*, staying close to the command pod so he could be seated in a position of command when he spoke again to the Archon.

"Not yet. The Shield's raising hell with the beam."

On the viewscreen the *Novograth* hung against the planet and its auroral crown, angular silver against the warm brown and blue curve of Charvann's horizon.

"Erbee!" snapped Hreem. "Where's that cruiser?"

"No traces, Cap'n. Maybe they left the system already."

"Murphy's balls they have!" Hreem drummed his fingers on the back of the pod; he hated waiting like this, especially in inner space where a planet hemmed him in on one side. Drunkwalking wasn't as random, this close, and you couldn't flea-hop as much: skipping was dangerous near radius.

As he glanced at the image of the *Novograth* again, he suddenly realized that it hadn't changed for a while. The *Lith* had evidently been in the same orbit for some time. Hreem looked over and saw Bargun hunched strangely over his console, and the light from its screen on his face was flickering in a way quite unlike the usual pattern.

Hreem smiled grimly. *He's watching that damned chip of Dyasil's again. After this is over I think Bargun's gonna put on a little show for the crew.*

As he cat-footed across the deck toward the unsuspecting Rifter, his fist balling up in anticipation of a savage blow, several things happened simultaneously.

From Erbee's console came a quiet bleep, and the Rifter tech yelled, "Emergence! A big one!" His voice cracked with excitement.

Bargun jerked upright and slapped frantically at his console.

Hreem gasped a breath to yell a command, his eyes going to the screen, but his voice stuck in his throat as, in total silence, the *Novograth* shuddered violently, bits of hull plating flying off. The ship's form blurred, and a terrible coronal discharge wreathed it briefly before it fell apart and then exploded in a glaring blast of light that momentarily overloaded the viewscreen.

Hreem lunged back toward the command pod, reaching for the skip pad as someone yelled "Cruiser!"—but a deafening supersonic screech blasted through the bridge of the *Lith*, falling quickly to a subsonic rumble that shook the entire ship and knocked his feet out from under him. He felt a stabbling pain in his ears, and the warm trickle of blood running down his neck, while his limbs twitched in a brief but violent spasm as the edge of a ruptor beam brushed the ship.

Others were not so fortunate. Alluwan's console exploded violently and the fat Rifter was momentarily outlined in a red fog as the intense gravity pulse tore through him. Then his chair ripped out of the deck and spun into a bulkhead, denting it with the violence of its impact. There was nothing but a swirling bloody cloud where he had sat, mixed with black smoke from his destroyed console.

Hreem scrambled off the deck and vaulted over into the pod, slamming his fist down on the jump pad, but as he had feared, nothing happened—the delicate resonance of the fiveskip was almost always the first thing to go when a ruptor grabbed a ship.

"Fire Control!" he screamed. "Target that chatzer! Hurry!" The stars swung across the viewscreen rapidly as the ship slewed around. "Ready a skipmissile!"

"Skipmissile charging!"

Hreem clutched at the arms of his pod—at least they still had missile power. Give them only a few more seconds . . . He refused to think about what would happen if the Urian relay wasn't as powerful as promised—there was a big difference between laughingly blowing up test asteroids and taking on a battlecruiser with its near-impenetrable shield.

Damn you, Bargun . . . when I . . . He noticed then that Bargun was beyond reach: a macabre eddy in the ruptor pulse had torn his head off and deposited it neatly on his console, staring sightlessly at his body slumped in the chair, the flickering action from the record chip on the screen under the head imbuing his features with ghastly animation.

On the screen an inward-blinking ring of arrows pointed at a fat blur of light. "Targeting locked on. Skipmissile . . . six seconds to discharge."

"Fire on zero!" It was rare that one got a second chance against a cruiser, the only ship large enough to mount ruptors. The *Lith* had never encountered one up close before—the one or two encounters they'd had, their monstrous pursuer had been no more than a distant blip on the rear screens as they escaped into fivespace. Even with the vast power of the Urian relay, Hreem devoutly hoped at that moment that he would never have to face one again. It was his worst nightmare born into reality.

The terrified Rifter captain stared at the targeted blur, willing it into inaction for the few seconds more he needed, hardly hearing the screams of pain from the wounded, some of whom had lost limbs to the alternating gee fields of the near-miss ruptor pulse. This was not the sure thing Eusabian had promised, not what he'd imagined in so many pleasant daydreams of power and revenge. He'd never sustained this kind of damage before. Fear blurred his thoughts for a moment, but he washed it out with rage as he always did: rage against Eusabian, against the Panarchist Navy, and against his own terror. His heart hammered painfully in his throat as he waited for death or victory.

NINE

❋

The defense room deep beneath the Archonic Enclave in Merryn rang with cheers as the ruptor beams reached their targets and the results registered. Bright coins of light marked the Rifter ships that had paid fully for their temerity: the scintillant glory of one ship's demise blacked out the lower corner of the screen for a moment. For a brief while the scene was static; a murmur of comment rose when the *Korion* did not immediately follow up its advantage.

"What is he waiting for?" demanded Osri, puzzled anger in his voice.

"The dimensions of this mercy are above my thoughts . . ." said Brandon, as if quoting someone, and Osri glared at him, obviously nettled by the implied rebuke.

Omilov heard the odd distance in the Krysarch's voice, and alerted by this noticed that Brandon had withdrawn almost imperceptibly from the degree of closeness to himself and the Archon that would have marked the Krysarch as a part of their conversation. Omilov felt a wash of sadness: he had lost Gelasaar, and now, it seemed, events were conspiring to wrench the closest of the Panarch's sons away as well.

Tanri paused correctly, then as Brandon did not continue: "He has nothing to fear from them—three destroyers are the minimum needed to take on a battlecruiser; they've lost one and are pinned against the planet. And a well-tuned ruptor is a drive-smasher—they're going nowhere. Dahawi's probably dispatching the boarding lances right now."

"Will any surrender?" Osri sounded like he hoped none of them would. "And how . . ." He stopped.

The babble of talk from the floor also ceased as a chain of minute greenish balls of light grew with blinding speed from one of the dots of light in the Rifter fleet. The skipmissile wake propagated far faster than the ruptor beams had. As the missile reached the *Korion* Omilov heard Bikara's fingers tapping rapidly across the pads before her as she followed the action; the main screen flickered to a close-up of the big ship.

The cruiser was momentarily sheathed in a flaring ellipse of violet light, then the far side erupted in a graceful flower of shattered metal and a fountain of actinic light. Omilov heard Tanri's breath rasp in his throat in an inhalation of disbelief. Cracks began to rip outward through the hull and, with awful slowness, a growing glow from within the *Korion* transformed the battlecruiser into a glaring holocaust that blacked out the entire viewscreen for seconds. When the screen cleared, it revealed a sharp-edged sphere of light which filled with a delicate lacework of fluorescing gas as it dissipated against the stars.

There was no sound at all for a moment; though the machines around them still worked, no one, in the shock of the moment, had the ears to hear them. Slowly the activity of the room recommenced, but now it seemed more frantic, less purposeful. Sudden bursts of loud speech could be heard but not distinguished. The Archon's face might have been carved of obsidian—the frozen image of deep grief and disbelief. A brief pulse of stunning pain lanced through

Omilov's left arm, radiating down to the tip of his ring finger; he leaned heavily on the railing of the dais, unable to
take his eyes from the screen.

"One missile . . . from a destroyer?" The Archon's voice
was edged with pain, his body tight with shock. "A fluke
. . . a defect in the teslas . . ." His voice was that of a man
groping in the dark, fearing what he might lay hands on, but
needing something to hold onto.

"Your Grace." Bikara's voice was soft, hesitant. Her severe features were softened by concern as she looked at
Tanri. "There is a communication from the Rifter captain."

Tanri stared at her for a moment, then he straightened up.
The edge of command reentered his voice. "Put it on the
screen."

The Rifter's olive face was smudged and sweat-streaked.
Twin runnels of crusting blood clung to his neck below his
ears: the collar of his tunic was blood-blotched. Behind him
gray smoke eddied, a pink slime clung to every surface; on
the deck a body lay in horrible disarray, its limbs bent
sharply in far too many places. The people in the defense
room could clearly hear agonized screams, suddenly stilled
by a sharp hiss. Hreem glared savagely at Tanri.

"Round one for me, you miserable chatzer. Your precious
cruiser is photons now. You want it easy or hard?"

The Archon studied the Rifter's face for a long moment;
Hreem could not sustain the stare and his eyes slithered
away briefly. "A planet is considerably larger than a
battlecruiser," replied Tanri in the patient tones of one explaining the obvious to someone with a severe head injury.

The insult took a moment to penetrate—the Rifter was
apparently not very sensitive to tonal invective; but it was
plain to everyone on the Charvann end of the beam. "Perhaps you'd like me to draw you a picture?" the Archon continued after a carefully calculated pause.

Laughter rolled across the defense room at the double
entendre, and Omilov realized that Tanri was talking to the
Rifter only for the effect he could have on morale.

Hreem appeared to hear only the surface meaning of the

Archon's retort, but his face flushed purple and his eyes bulged. His ears started bleeding again.

"He looks like an Abilard Golliwog that's swallowed its own nose-stalk!" one of the monitors yelled, and the room grew uproarious. One corner of Tanri's mouth twitched.

"Have it your way, Faseult . . ." Hreem snarled. The crowd of monitors hissed at the gross insult of an inferior's use of the Archon's family name for address—the Rifter captain knew something of Panarchic courtesy, if only to spit on it. "Just sit down there, waiting for help that isn't coming. Your Shield'll be down sooner than you think— and maybe I'll even stop firing then." The Rifter grinned and relaxed back into his command pod. "I look forward to seeing how many knots I can put in your legs and arms— more I think than the ruptors put in poor old Garesh." He jerked a thumb backward at the distorted corpse and laughed raucously, then winced and rubbed one ear. He leaned forward.

"By the way, Your Fanciness," he drawled in a wire-dream parody of an aristocratic accent, "I'd recommend you have the nyr-Arkad on hand when I land. Otherwise I might feel compelled to zap open a Sync or two, or crater a few cities, bein' as how I'd be awful disappointed not to meet a Krysarch Royal." He snickered. "It's one of my life's ambitions."

"You really ought to stop sniffing slag-solvent, Captain," replied the Archon. "These delusions certainly won't do much for your social life." Tanri's voice carried an exquisite overtone of insulting helpfulness. "Let me suggest an ambition more within your grasp. You'll be up there for a while . . . why don't you spend the time learning to breathe in a vacuum. That's a skill you'll need, and sooner than you think." Tanri jerked his hand slightly and Bikara cut the connection.

The room rang with cheering laughter. The Archon strode up to the railing of the dais and leaned forward, intent determination in every line of his body. Omilov knew from experience that every person in the room felt as if he or she were the focus of Tanri's vivid black eyes. Silence descended.

"By now couriers are on the way for help, bearing news of what has happened. Even if that missile was not a fluke, no weapon, however advanced, will be much help to a motley band of Rifters facing a forewarned battlefleet. We need only wait and hold out, and I doubt not that we will. It's in your hands now, my friends." He paused. "Especially you men and women monitoring the Shield controls. Feel the thoughts of your friends, here and all over Charvann. Feel their strength, their endurance, their hope. These are all yours, freely and fervently given as you play the greatest game of skill there is for the greatest stakes that can be wagered. Alpheios held out for three weeks before help arrived—you've all seen chips of the monitors there balancing the teslas against all that the Shiidra could do. We on Charvann—three *days* from help—face only Rifters."

He straightened up as the men and women below cheered again. Suddenly the room quivered to an impalpable blow. It was not a disturbance of the air, but of the very substance of the walls and floor and of their bodies. Red lights sprang up on some of the consoles below, and the cheers faltered and ceased.

Omilov looked down at the Heart of Kronos with a sense of sick foreboding as he turned around and saw the consternation on Bikara's face, red-lit by the angry glare of trouble on her console. The Archon saw it too and strode over to her.

"They've fired on the Shield." Her voice quavered slightly.

"Power reading?"

She was silent almost too long. "It's ... an impossible reading, Your Grace." Her fingers trembled hesitantly on the pads, horror leaking into her expression.

"Yes?"

"The readings are several orders of magnitude beyond the theoretical maximum. At that power level, the computer indicates a probable Shield life of thirty hours. Crustal dis-

turbances can be expected within twelve to sixteen hours."
She hesitated. "That's assuming we can keep him from de-
tecting Charvann's fundamental resonance."

Tanri asked very quietly: "And if we cannot?"

Bikara swallowed, and when she spoke her voice was
hoarse and almost too faint to hear. "Eight hours to crustal
disruption, Your Grace."

The Archon was very still; he did not even seem to be
breathing. Finally he jerked his head in a single nod and
turned away. His eyes moved across Omilov and Osri unseeing, focused on Brandon; the young man met his eyes,
but his spirit was visibly subdued. His face was pale, tight
around the eyes.

After a long moment the Archon turned back to Omilov,
gesturing to the little box. "You indicated you thought this
might have some connection to the attack."

Omilov nodded. He snapped open the box again and
dropped the Heart of Kronos into Tanri's upturned palm.
Tanri's arm twitched convulsively as the little sphere
dropped with blurring speed into his hand; as his mind and
muscles registered the sphere's strangeness an expression
akin to vertigo crossed his face.

"You said this was stolen from the Shrine Planet?" He
jerked his hand back and forth a few times with an abstracted look on his face, testing the sphere's feeling. "It
seems to be inertialess. What is it?"

"As I told these two young men, I don't know what it is
or what its purpose was, but it is an artifact of the Ur—one
that, according to its guardians in the Shrine, holds the potential for incredible destruction. Their name for it is
unpronounceable—but it has become known as the Heart of
Kronos."

"The Suneater ... *ittala Kronos karree'halal teminan-
dan* ..." Bikara's voice was shaky as she explained. "A
legend of my people. Kronos ate his children as they were
born, until Dyauspitar overthrew him and time began. At
the end, Kronos will return, devouring suns and bringing
the final darkness."

Another shudder rumbled through the defense room, but fewer trouble lights lit. On the main floor the monitors in the Shield Control section were hunched intently over their consoles, adjusting the output of the teslas to disguise the harmonics that would reveal the critical frequency of the Shield to their attackers.

"The name Kronos dates back to before the Exile," said Omilov. "This artifact was somehow diverted to me in the ParcelNet—its original addressee was an ex-student of mine now at the Brangornie Node."

"The tetrad for Dol'jhar." Tanri looked down at the little sphere. "And you think that Eusabian wants this badly enough to go to war again?"

Omilov nodded toward the ceiling. "That ship up there commands more firepower than any ship in the Navy, and I do not think there is any technological breakthrough that could explain that. Certainly Dol'jhar has never been noted for its scientific abilities. No, I fear that Eusabian has found some—device—left behind by Ur, and has armed this Rifter—and perhaps others—with it. Somehow this thing must be related."

The Archon was silent for a time, considering. The room shook again. "It *is* odd that he would choose Charvann as a target—we have no military significance—unless this Heart of Kronos is very important to him."

Sudden decision lit his face. "Very well, then, we shall deny it to him, and you with it. Bikara, have the booster field ready a module, maximum acceleration, and have Shield Control stand by for irising." Now that he had found a way to strike back at the overwhelming forces facing him, at least to the extent of ensuring the failure of their mission, Tanri looked alive and vital again.

He handed the Heart of Kronos back to Omilov. "You shall take this to Ares Base. Krysarch Brandon will accompany you. The booster is very hot, one thousand gees, one percent compensated—it will have you out beyond radius within thirty seconds. The autopilot will take it from there."

Omilov shook his head. "Thank you, Your Grace, but my

heart won't sustain ten gravities. Let my son take it. I really know little more about it than I've told you."

"Father, no!" Osri came forward and faced Tanri. "Can't you give him a slower booster, use some kind of diverison to draw away the Rifter ships?"

"Your concern does you credit, young man, but a slower boost would leave the Shield irised too long. If a skip-missile hit it during that time—it will be a touchy operation at that." He grinned. "There will, however, be some diversions—some of my ancestors were considerably less trusting than I! You will go as your father has requested. I will give you a letter of introduction to Admiral Nyberg— you are credentialed as an astrogator, are you not?" Osri gave a reluctant nod, not taking his eyes from his father. "Good. I will ask him to give you a position on Ares if you like."

Osri stammered his thanks while his father smiled warmly at him—the offer was virtually the equivalent of a promotion. Ares Base was the headquarters of the fleet, its location a closely guarded secret. The competition for post-ings there was fierce, for service there was widely regarded as the fast track to higher rank.

Tanri next turned to Brandon, who still stood a little apart from them. Omilov was glad not to be on the receiving end of the Archon's look; under such circumstances trying to re-turn the gaze of that dark, chiseled face and night-black eyes would be like trying to outstare a statue of some an-cient and awesome king. Tanri could look into and through one.

But Brandon's gaze did not flinch aside, and Omilov then noticed the Krysarch's posture as the two looked into each other's eyes. Brandon's left shoulder was very subtly turned toward the Archon and lowered—a position that would es-cape most onlookers, but that a Douloi would immediately recognize as submission, or admission of responsibility for an improper action. Omilov could see that Brandon deeply regretted the position he had inadvertently put Tanri and his planet in, and that he knew that no words would serve to convey this. He could not even offer himself as a willing sacrifice to save the people his presence had put in jeopardy—the Archon's oath of fealty would mandate rejection of such an offer, which would therefore appear a cowardly saving of face on Brandon's part.

After a time Tanri nodded and smiled very faintly. He walked over to the Krysarch and held out his hands palms-up, in the ancient Noble-to-Royal modality, and Brandon, at first hesitating, laid his hands palms-down in the Archon's.

"What is past is past," said the Archon. His voice was pitched low, for Brandon alone, but Omilov heard nonetheless, and was moved by Tanri's generous spirit. Even facing defeat and probable death, the Archon was concerned with the pain of another—even one who had offended against him in law and courtesy.

When Brandon responded with a troubled smile and a nod, and lifted his hands, Tanri pulled his Archonic signet off and handed it to the Krysarch. "My younger brother is a commander on Ares. This will be his now, and our Family would be honored to have it conveyed to him by a scion of the House of Arkad." He placed the ring in Brandon's right hand and gently folded the Krysarch's fingers over it. "The Light-bearer guide you." There was the faintest emphasis on the word "guide."

Brandon heard the emphasis, and it shocked his mind into hcightened awareness, so that every aspect of the room and the people in it was clear and sharp, while his mind hummed with fragmented thoughts. Quite suddenly he remembered a monograph he'd read once, claiming a link between the tendency to telepathic flashes and the genetic complex governing melanin production. The essay had seemed a mere intellectual exercise at the time; now Tanri's ebony features, confronting Brandon with the choice he thought he'd already made, made its conclusions seem established fact. Just how much did the Archon understand? Whatever the answer, his request brought all of Brandon's questions about his future into poignant, urgent focus; and Tanri's intense gaze required an immediate decision.

Brandon felt a flash of resentment mixed with a sense of pressure almost claustrophobic in intensity. With one corner of his vision he noticed that many of the monitors on the floor below the dais were looking up at them, and the expressions on their faces underscored the power of the responsibilities his birth had imposed upon him— responsibilities it now seemed he could never escape. . . . *a prison unsought . . .*

He wondered if he'd ever really had a choice. Certainly the sense of freedom he'd felt in lifting off from Arthelion was entirely gone now.

"It shall be as you have asked," he said formally. "It is the Phoenix House that is honored by such a trust."

The Archon nodded, gratitude lighting his eyes, and as he withdrew he bowed, this time to the full extent due a Krysarch of the Blood Royal.

Brandon looked down at the ring in his hand.

Or, a smiling charioteer, sable, vested proper, driving a chariot gules, drawn by two sphinxes, sable and argent, all affrontee, in base a ford proper. The small, brilliantly clear enamel figure on the heavy ring seemed poised on the verge of movement. *Volo, rideo,* read the motto: I will, I laugh. *How odd that humor should be such a constant in the Faseult line.* The memory of his summer at Omilov's estate, when he was small, returned to him   the tall black woman, willowy and quick-moving, who had visited one day. She had laughed often, and not the controlled titter that Brandon had been accustomed to from the women who courted his father after his mother died.

He heard the laugh again, vividly present, and started, almost dropping the ring; but it was an octave lower. Tanri, not the Dowager Archonei, his grandmother. *The same laugh.* What did people see as the distinguishing mark of an Arkad? Whatever it was, he'd seen something of it mirrored darkly in Tanri's eyes when he'd accepted the ring, which lay solidly in his hand, a tactile antonym to the Heart of

Kronos. He slipped it onto his ring finger, where his personal signet had been less than a week before. And before that, he remembered bleakly, his cadet ring.

Markham. Was he up there? Brandon couldn't imagine anything that could induce his friend to participate in such savagery—but it had been ten years. He dismissed the speculation as unprofitable as he noticed Sebastian and Osri embrace and then look over at him; he might never know now. He walked over to join them.

Omilov saw his son's eyes ranging uncomprehendingly over the banks of displays. *He's in shock; until now his life has been bounded by order.* He moved to Osri's side and talked to him, about matters of small import, forcing Osri to answer until that look faded from his eyes.

By now the relentless pounding from the other side of the sky had become a regular, mind-deadening sequence of blows. Despite all the defenders' efforts, the enemy was slowly tuning in to the fundamental resonance of the planet, for the tesla fields which protected the atmosphere from the impact of near-cee plasmas by translating their momentum through ninety degrees also coupled a portion of their energy most effectively to the crust. The overwhelming power of the Rifter's weapons was exciting the Shield into spasms of revealing harmonics, a process that normally took weeks.

A couple of guards came up the stairs, vivid in trim red livery, and black glossy hats with slightly down-curving bills front and rear. They saluted Tanri, and as the Archon acknowledged them, Brandon glanced up from his perusal of the ring in his hand.

Omilov embraced his son and then held out his palms to Brandon. He closed his fingers around Brandon's hands as they touched, squeezing them a moment. Omilov regretted anew, with almost as sharp a psychic pang as the physical one he had experienced earlier, that their talk had been interrupted. *It is likely I will never know why he came to me.* And though none of this had been foreseen, was nothing he had caused, he felt a sense of failure. It had little to do with duty; this was a personal failure.

Their minds had almost met, there on the terrace before the hand of Dol'jhar had descended on Charvann. *He's struck before at both of us.* For a moment he envisioned Brandon standing before the portrait of his mother in Sebastian's study, just once when he first arrived, and then never again. *I didn't notice how he'd avoided it until now.* What else had he missed?

It was too late.

Omilov stepped back, pressed his hands together tightly. His voice was a little hoarse as his eyes took them both in. "Get to Ares safely, both of you."

Brandon touched hands with the Archon again, wordlessly, and then turned to follow Osri, the guards walking ahead and Deralze following behind. As the two crossed the floor the crowd divided around them, eyes focused on Brandon. Outside the defense room, the heavy door hissed shut behind them, leaving only the echoing quiet of the corridor and the blank wall of an unknown future.

PART TWO

TEN

✳

ARTHELION ORBIT

Anaris rahal'Jerrodi lengthened his stride as they approached his father's cabin, using the advantage of his height to force the black-clad Tarkans on either side of him to hurry to keep up. He glanced to one side; the guard's face was expressionless, as prescribed by the savage Dol'jharian military code.

Tarka ni-retor, he thought, *those who do not retreat.* His mouth curled in disdain. *Those who do not think.* And yet, if he survived this interview, the first with his father in almost three years, he would have to win such as these to his side. *For I will not change, even if those who opened my eyes perish utterly at my father's hands.*

He had grown up on the planet below, the planet now supine beneath his father's wrath. In Eusabian's eyes he had been a hostage against revenge for Acheront, to the Panarchists, a mind and soul to be salvaged. And to himself? Anaris was still seeking the answer to that question.

He was a Dol'jharian, of the lineage of Eusabian, raised amidst the splendors of Arthelion, in the Palace of his father's enemy, under the gentle, yet utterly irresistible authority of the lineage of Arkad.

They halted before the entrance to his father's suite, deep within the *Fist of Dol'jhar*. One of the Tarkans spoke into the com beside the door. A moment later it opened silently and Anaris stepped through, fighting a surge of fear that almost overwhelmed his bravado. The Tarkans did not follow, and the door slid shut behind him with finality.

The room was large and stark. At the far end, the heavy-shouldered figure of Jerrode Eusabian stood before a giant viewscreen, silhouetted by the blue and white glamour of Arthelion. Then, even as the sight of his foster home helped damp down his fear, he beheld a figure standing to one side that shattered his composure. It was Lelanor, clad only in a shift, trembling, her face streaked with tears. *What is she doing on this ship? Why didn't Barrodagh warn me?*

The bluish light from the viewscreen cast a corpselike pallor over his lover's smooth, pale skin and short white-blond hair, making his heart thud painfully in his chest. He made an abortive move toward her, his caution momentarily overwhelmed, then halted as his father spoke.

"My paliach is almost complete. In a few hours I will descend upon Arthelion in triumph. My enemy lies captive within this ship, two of his sons are already dead. The youngest will shortly join them."

Anaris' emotions swirled confusingly, unsettled by the unexpected presence of Lelanor. He nonetheless felt a minor surge of satisfaction at the announcement of the youngest Krysarch's imminent death. He had disliked Brandon on sight, twenty years ago, and further association with him had not changed that. *He didn't know what he had, and didn't care. It is only just that he should lose it.*

"But my enemy has denied me total victory, for he has stolen the last of my seed from me."

Perhaps you shouldn't have been so quick to murder the others. A brief image possessed his mind, of his sister, shouting curses in berserker rage as Evodh flayed her in front of Eusabian and a horrified Anaris, just returned from Arthelion. All his brothers had died in some similar manner, all of them victims of their own ambitions, while he was being fostered by the Arkads. *And now you have no options. The Panarchists told me what the weapons unleashed against your ship at Acheront did to your germ plasm; and I've heard rumors of the pitiful monstrosities you fathered afterward.*

"I will not permit him even this partial denial of my paliach. He has made you incapable of the rigor necessary to a ruler, contaminating your spirit"—Eusabian used the word *hachka*, denoting the virtues inherited from one's ancestors—"with Panarchist depravities such as *love*." His father's sneering emphasis on the last word was accentuated by the fact that he perforce used the Uni term, there being no Dol'jharian equivalent.

"You have befouled your ancestors with your behavior with this slave, as if such a *prikoschi* could even offer a wholesome struggle." He broke off, smiling with cold distaste. "Oh yes, you were watched." His face became grim; anger tinged his voice, which grew louder. "How do you expect to have worthy heirs from such a worm?" Eusabian struck quickly, casually. His great strength lifted Lelanor off her feet, smashing her against a bulkhead.

Anaris' stomach tightened, but he showed no reaction as his beloved struggled to her feet, her dazed eyes meeting his in mute appeal.

"Yet you persist in meeting with this slave again and again, a sickness you have learned from the Panarchists, for there has been no such perversion in my House since Dol founded the towers at Jhar Emyn." Eusabian stopped abruptly, as if mastering an overwhelming passion, and then continued, his voice dropping back to its original level.

"But now I have time to devote to your reeducation, to inculcate in you the virtues inhering in the descendants of Dol, so that the spirit of Dol may someday dwell in you as it does in me. I will not be denied; I shall have a son again."

Anaris glanced convertly at Lelanor, whose frail body was now shaken at intervals by bouts of trembling. She hugged her elbows in against her sides, her skin roughened by the cold air of the suite, and looked from one to the other of the two men in incomprehension. Brought as a slave to Dol'jhar by Rifters, she had never learned Dol'jharian.

Eusabian favored him with a wintery smile, and he pressed a button on a small table beside him. A side door opened to admit the lean figure of Evodh, the lacquered karra-patterns on his skull gleaming in the light from Arthelion.

"Your first lesson commences now." He motioned to Evodh. "It will last as many days as it takes to purge from you this weakness."

The physician grasped Lelanor's arm above the elbow. She gave a frightened gasp and twisted away from him, running straight to Anaris' arms.

Evodh strode forward. As the pesz mas'hadni reached for her, Anaris grabbed his arm and applied an Ulanshu kinesic, sending the man reeling across the room to bounce off a wall and fall to the floor, tangled in his own robes.

Then, without looking at Eusabian, he turned Lelanor gently around and took her face between his hands.

"Don't worry, heart of my heart, I will not let them hurt you."

She heard the utter sincerity in his voice and relaxed against him. He bent down and kissed her deeply, lingeringly, caressing her smooth back even as he heard his father's growl of anger and disgust, and the sound of Evodh struggling to his feet.

He felt her respond to him, melting into his embrace, her tongue seeking his hotly in a denial of their surroundings. As her arms glided down his back, he brought his hands up toward her head in a final caress. Then he slipped his *peshakh* out of his sleeve and thrust its razor-sharp blade deep into the back of her neck. The blade slipped resistlessly between her vertebrae, and she passed into death with only the faintest of tremors.

He tasted blood in her mouth as she slumped against him. Laying her gently on the floor, he straightened up.

As the guards rushed in to drag him away, their faces blanching at the rage apparent in Eusabian's face, Anaris smiled mockingly at his father. "Death is all you have to offer, father mine, and it is not enough."

✳   ✳   ✳

ARTHELION

Moira's ninth birthday was the best ever, until the black-clad soldiers came.

Earlier in the week her parents had surprised her by promising to take her to see the Havroy, years earlier than was customary. That morning her father brought flowers from the Palace for her to present to the Havroy, from the gardens he tended for the Panarch.

"Some of these are from planets so far away that their suns are never seen in the skies of the Mandala," he said.

Their colors and scents were dizzying; Moira inhaled deeply as he laid them in her arms. "Do they miss their sunlight?" she asked, thinking of the Havroy.

Her father smiled. "I don't know, little one. I try to make them happy here." His eyes looked sad above his smile, and he turned away for a moment, looking toward the hill that stood between their cottage and the distant Palace.

Moira carried the flowers into the kitchen, where her mother was assembling a picnic basket, followed by the attentive gaze of their black shaggy dog, Popo. "Look, Mother. I'll bet the Havroy has never seen flowers like these before." Indeed, some of them were very strange; the sweetest-smelling ones looked like a nest of spotted snakes.

Her mother smiled at her as she packed the last of the food

away. There were dark circles under her eyes. "Women come from every one of the Thousand Suns to see her, Moira. I'm sure she's seen much stranger. What matters is what's in your heart when you lay them at her feet."

Just then her father came in, and her mother continued, "Why don't you go and put on your good sandals and then get some snacks for Popo so he can have a picnic too." As she went down the hallway to her room she could hear a snatch of conversation from her parents.

". . . there's nothing we can do," came her father's voice. "And the Palace said to go about our business as usual." Her mother's reply held a doubtful tone, but Moira couldn't hear the words.

It was only a short flight to Havroy Bay in their aircar; Moira sat up front with her father, leaning close to the windscreen to watch the cloud-dappled fields and scattered homes glide beneath them. Then, as they skimmed over a range of low hills, the horizon flattened to a ruler-straight line separating gray-blue from sky-blue and they swooped to a landing on the edge of a golden crescent of beach.

The hot sand sifted through her toes as they walked toward the sea. Popo ran ahead of them and back, kicking up a spatter of sand that made the three of them blink.

Moira clutched her flowers to her chest, looking about at the many groups of people, bright in holiday costumes, dotting the beach. Some of them wore clothing she'd only seen in culture chips, or on vids from the DataNet, and some wore nothing at all. The sound of their voices echoed the splashing waves, only some of the words coming clear. She stared with interest at two people in particular, a man and a woman: they were so tall that they would have had to stand bent over inside Moira's home; their skin was a glossy black, their slanted eyes green, and their long straight hair a blazing reddish gold like the morning sun.

"This looks like a good spot," said her father finally, and busied himself setting up the sunshade. Its frail, silvery fabric billowed in the soft breeze, ballooning up into an open-sided dome over them as her father stroked the static-tabs at its base. Her mother unrolled the sheet-like *bas*; it vibrated briefly, reducing the sand lumps underneath to a smooth surface, then relaxed into quiescence.

Her father came up beside Moira where she stood, looking down the slope of the beach to the clot of people near the water's edge. "Doesn't look like much of a crowd today. You should have a few moments to yourself with her." Her mother came up beside them and slipped her arm through her father's.

"Silver lining," she said elliptically, but Moira was too intent on what lay ahead to wonder at her words.

As they walked toward the small crowd ahead, leaving Popo to watch their belongings, her father smiled again. "Do you remember what you said the first time you saw a picture of the Havroy?"

Moira nodded. "I was sad because I thought they left all the people like her behind on Lost Earth." They had joined a short line of people now, all of them holding flowers. The tall black people with the red hair were in front of them. Moira could smell a sweet, tangy scent coming from them. She tried to peer around them to catch a glimpse of the Havroy, but there were too many people ahead of them.

Moira looked up at her parents. "There aren't any people like her in the Thousand Suns, are there?"

"No," her father replied.

"We've found many strange people, but never any like her," her mother said, moving closer to her father, who looked up at the sky, frowning.

He slipped his arm around her, then shook his head and smiled again. "And that's as it should be. She means much more to us because she's the only one." Then he squatted down on the sand next to her and took her hand in his. His fingers were rough and warm, and Moira could see the traces of dirt around his fingernails that he could never get out.

"Moira, you're a little too young to really understand, but—" He glanced at the sky again. "But we thought it was time."

"I know," she said happily. "Niona was really jealous. Her parents said she'd have to wait till she was twelve."

He nodded, opened his mouth as if to speak, then pressed his lips together in a line. "That's what is usual," he said finally. "So you must listen carefully to your mother."

He stood up and her mother sat down on her heels next to Moira. "Do you remember what I told you about symbols?"

Moira nodded. "They're like pictures for stories that are too big for words."

Her mother hugged her, then let her go, keeping her hands on Moira's shoulders. "And sometimes they have stories that go with them, that help us see things that are too big and old for us to understand any other way. You know the story of the Havroy, and you know why she sits there, staring out to sea, forever unable to return home."

Now Moira could see a brightness in her mother's eyes, and in her father's too. "The Havroy is a story about us: you, and me, and Father, and all the people on this beach, and throughout the Thousand Suns."

"And Popo too?"

Mother nodded. "And Popo too, and kittens, and horses, and even the trees in the Garden of the Ancients . . ." She took Moira's hand in hers and squeezed gently. Her fingers were smooth and cool. "None of us can go home again. We left our home two thousand years ago, and we can never go back. Just like her. That's why we brought her with us, to remind us of Lost Earth."

The line ahead of them had thinned away, the people behind them waiting patiently. Her mother stood up and leaned forward to stroke the colorful flowers in Moira's arms. "And these are the bright stories of our lives in the Thousand Suns—all the beauty and strangeness of our worlds." She straightened up. "Go, daughter, cast them on the sea foam at the feet of the Havroy and look long into her face."

A little frightened by her mother's sudden seriousness, Moria turned and walked toward the water's edge. There was a bubble of solitude around the Havroy, and the sand was carpeted with blossoms cast up by the advancing tide. Moira walked around in front of her and then stopped. As vivid as the vids had been, they lacked the awesome reality of the years indwelling in the worn, bronze face of the Havroy.

Moira stood still, her heart squeezing with feelings she'd never had before. The sea rushed cool about her feet, tickling them with foam and flowers as she looked into the face of a young woman, kneeling at the water's edge, gazing forever at the home she would never return to.

Moira felt the weight of a sorrow too big for words, almost too big for her heart, and she let the flowers fall before the statue. A hissing wave of sea foam lifted them from the sand and carried them up the beach past the Havroy, leaving her finned legs garlanded with the offering of the Panarch's gardens as the water withdrew. Then Moira wiped her eyes and gently reached out and touched the statue's cheek, bestowing on Her the tears She could not weep.

Moira stood there a while longer, not hearing at first the thin whine that slowly overwhelmed the mournful sighing of the placid waves of Havroy Bay. She looked up as movement caught her eyes; further up the beach people were looking out to sea in sudden alarm. Then a giant voice from behind her shattered the calm summer day.

"ATTENTION! PLEASE CLEAR THE BEACH! DO NOT GATHER YOUR BELONGINGS. LEAVE IMMEDIATELY!"

She twisted around quickly and saw a sleek silver aircar with the Sun and Phoenix blazoned on it arrowing in across the bay, but only for a moment. A green finger of light reached out from the land to touch it briefly and the aircar disintegrated in a flare of bloody light and black smoke. A large piece of glowing metal shrieked through the air and slammed to the ground near Moira, spattering her with hot water and sand; it lay hissing in a small crater, the blossoms around it withering to brown rags.

Her mother ran forward and grabbed her, carrying her up

the beach. Her father used his shoulder to push through the milling crowd of people now shouting in fear and confusion as a line of black-clad soldiers suddenly appeared on the crest of the low hills behind the beach. They made no move, watching cold-eyed and holding their weapons at the ready as the crowd suddenly halted at the landward edge of the sand. They were close enough that Moira could see a red fist on their uniforms.

After a few moments, the tall black man with the red hair stepped forward, his hands raised, palms out. "We intend no resistance," he called out in Uni. "Will you please—"

His voice was abruptly stilled as one of the soldiers moved his weapon slightly and burned him down. The tall man's hair puffed out in a crackling discharge and he crumpled with awful slowness to the sand. The tall woman with him howled and threw herself across his body; the soldiers made no further move.

In the silence that followed, Moira heard a low whine and felt a cold nose press into her hand. She looked down, numb with shock; beside her, Popo shivered, his tail curved between his legs, his gold eyes seeking the reassurance of her hand—but she had none to give him. A sudden series of windbursts startled her as several large transports scudded over the hill behind the soldiers and landed in a whirl of sand.

As their doors opened, Moira's vision suddenly blurred for a moment, and she became aware of a vast thrumming tone, as though the hand of Telos were beating against the blue dome of the sky above. It was not a loud sound, but utterly pervasive. She looked around, seeking the source, as did many in the crowd, but she saw nothing to account for it.

More black-uniformed soldiers roughly ejected a number of people from the transports, many in livery, some in the elegant attire of the Douloi, all with varying degrees of worry or terror in their faces.

"They're from the Palace," whispered her father. "But why have they been brought here?"

Her father's voice broke the almost-trance of shock. "Who are the soldiers?" Moira asked. "Why are they doing this?"

"They're from Dol'jhar."

She tried the unfamiliar name on her tongue. Dole-Ychhar—the last syllable almost like the little cough she often got just as she caught a cold, when she tried to clear the tickle out of the back of her throat. It was an ugly sound that somehow matched the blank faces of the soldiers.

The throbbing now possessed the air, modulating the panicky murmur of the crowd and the sobbing of the bereaved woman. The ground responded with a tremor of its own; not an earthquake, but a quiver, as though the solid rock deep beneath them was waking from age-long sleep.

One of the Douloi from the transports, a short man in a wine-colored tunic edged with old-gold, was arguing with a soldier with a peaked cap and rings on his sleeves, who kept pushing a piece of paper into his hands. The man shook his head fiercely, ripped the paper across, and trampled it. The soldier pulled a large serrated knife from his belt and slashed him across the throat, stepping back to avoid the spray of blood. He watched the Douloi thrash on the reddened sand for a moment, then motioned to another man nearby to pick up the paper.

The man did so very slowly, his face pale and grim, and after a moment's discussion, turned to face the crowd.

"Attend all," he cried, his voice flat with anger. "Attend all and greet the new Lord of the Mandala, descending in glory, Jerrode Eusabian, Avatar of Dol, Lord of Vengeance and the Kingdoms of Dol'jhar." He motioned jerkily toward the sea. Slowly the crowd of people turned around, confusion evident in the muttering sound of many voices.

Moira looked up at her parents. Both stared into the sky, her mother's face tight with repressed emotion, her father looking afraid.

"They can't," her mother whispered fiercely. "They mustn't. Not a battlecruiser." Her hands pressed against each other, her left hand twisting at the big naval ring on her right ring finger.

Moira followed her mother's gaze into the sky: there was a bright, bluish spark high above the sea, nearly overhead.

It grew rapidly in size, resolving swiftly into a silvery egg-shape bristling with spines and thorns of metal, enhaloed in the deadly shimmer of defensive energies, a bloodred fist clutching a sheaf of lightning bolts emblazoned on its side. The sky darkened as it fell out of heaven toward Havroy Bay, shouting a god's anger against the placid sea, growing larger and still larger until the eye refused its scale, and still it grew. Its massive radiants glowed white-hot, caverns of hellish energy, radiating shock waves in rings of sudden cloud condensing from the outraged air. The heat struck down at them like a hammerblow from Hell itself, and the throbbing became a torment in their bones and blood.

In the center of Havroy Bay the sea began to boil, obscuring the lower half of the battlecruiser in roiling clouds of steam shot through with the glare of venting plasma. The ship was impossibly huge, filling the bay from side to side, its bow still invisible seven kilometers overhead.

A searing blast of wind and scalding spray flung itself out of the bay and bowled Moira over. It smelled horrible, like burned plastic and fish soup. She heard Popo yelp in terror, and screams from the crowd. She saw the soldiers calmly burning down everyone who tried to flee. The people closest to the shoreline had disappeared in the awful boiling wave; between drifts of steam Moira saw arms and legs in the bubbling water. When she had looked into the face of the Havroy, her feelings had seemed too big for the world, but now all her feelings were gone, as if she watched an ugly vid. She looked up.

The vast ship now hung unmoving, blotting out the sky, the throbbing of its drive fields pounding her bones and making her stomach clench. All around Moira people were vomiting and convulsing helplessly. Her father knelt, his face pressed into the sand, his hands over his ears, her mother hugging his back, the tendons standing out on her arms. Moira bit against her lip until she tasted salt, but something made her keep looking.

Suddenly a golden light blazed amid the blue-white clouds billowing up from the rapidly evaporating bay. A ring of light opened in the wall of steam, revealing the minute figure of a man clad all in black, seated in a golden throne at the end of a beam of dim red light. Lightning played around him, outlining the spherical shimmer of the defensive shield englobing him, and whirlwinds of sand and steam spun off ahead. The sand glowed red-hot underneath his throne as it glided inexorably toward the terrified crowd. It was just like Haruban the Demon King in the Tale of Years, she thought, and then she realized he was headed straight for the Havroy.

She struggled to her feet and screamed at him, but her voice was lost in the tumult of a world gone mad. The ground rocked underneath her. For a moment, Moira saw the figure of the Havroy silhouetted against the sinister energies radiating from the throne of the Demon King. Then the bronze figure glowed red, then white, and slumped shapeless into a hissing tide of blazing foam as the throne passed over it and settled to the sand in a crackling blast of red-hot sand.

Crouching by her parents, Moira watched as the tall man in the throne stood up and looked around at the carnage he had created, his face even blanker than the faces of the soldiers. Then, as he stepped to the ground of his new demesne, a buzzing blackness overwhelmed the little girl and she passed gratefully into unconsciousness.

ELEVEN

✳

CHARVANN ORBIT

The bridge of the *Lith* stank: sweat and smoke and blood, with a sour overlay from the vomit and filth expelled in violent death by the victims of the ruptor pulse. A couple of slubs were washing down the deck and swabbing the varporized remains of Alluwan off the bulkheads, while techs labored at the shattered remains of the unlucky Rifter's console. On the weapons console a yellow light blinked as another skipmissile was charged: deep within the *Lith* a small, complex knot of plasma churned violently in its magnetic constraints, awaiting the impulse that would send it skipping in and out of spacetime toward its target, gaining velocity and mass with every emergence from the strange conditions of fivespace.

But Hreem noticed none of this—the viewscreen dominated his attention. He watched hungrily as the skipmissile discharged and smashed into Charvann's Shield near the southern pole, where the angle between the planet's magnetic and rotational axes weakened the complex spacetime resonance excited by the teslas. Vast rings of iridescent light marched outward from the point of impact, rippling through the auroral blaze that now covered the planet most of the way to the equator.

A sudden motion caught Hreem's eye as the tech at the weapons console suddenly straightened up from his hunched-over intensity and turned around, grinning at him. "Pili! What have you got?"

"I found the critical period! She's on automatic now—I figure about six to ten hours and Charvann's gonna be shakin' like a joy-bed in a cheap chatz-house!"

"Put a sunburst in the slot, Faseult!" Hreem guffawed at the screen. "I hope you get a volcano right up your blungehole." The bridge rang with raucous comments, with Piliar's high chattering tenor laugh as counterpoint. "Good work, Pili! That's another tenth-point for you." Piliar grinned broadly—with the loot this job would yield, an additional tenth percent of the take probably represented more money than he'd made in his entire career so far.

A bit of memory tickled the back of Hreem's mind as he happily contemplated the coming fall of Charvann. Hadn't there been some Panarch a long time ago who'd hit a planet with a skipmissile after it dropped its Shield? He seemed to remember they'd done something awful to him for that. And Eusabian would do something awful to him if he blew up whatever it was the Lord of Vengeance wanted from this Omilov blit.

"Just make sure you don't fire one too many when they give up," he warned the tech. "I want a continent full of loot and slaves, not flaming rubble and corpses."

Six to ten hours! Hreem suddenly recalled the glittership they'd intercepted once, full of snooty high-living nicks who'd thought they were headed for a six-month pleasure cruise through the Heart Stars. What a surprise for them, when the *Flower of Lith* showed up and put a lazplaz through their drive! He laughed at the memory of the captain's face, just before he burned him down.

"Cap'n?" asked Dyasil.

"Remember that glittership out of Svoboda?"

"Yeah." Dyasil grinned lopsidedly. "We had some prime fun with those tilt-nosed nacker-teases!"

"I'm just trying to imagine that multiplied by thousands."

The bridge crew hooted with delight. A whole planet! It had been centuries since anyone had sacked a major planet—now it was happening all over the Thousand Suns.

The tide of raucous comments from the crew suddenly died away and Hreem swiveled around. Norio stood momentarily at the entrance to the bridge, his hands hidden in the folds of his heavy Oblate's robe, then came toward him with the sliding grace that marked all his movements. A bubble of isolation expanded around the Rifter captain and the tempath as the rest of the crew on the bridge concentrated on their tasks.

Norio looked around, a faint smile playing across his full lips. The bridge lighting sparked highlights from his slicked-back dark hair and accentuated the planes of his sallow, thin face.

"Don't let me distract you, Captain," he said softly. "I merely wished to share your joyful revenge on those who have sought your death so long."

Hreem smiled and nodded jerkily, then swiveled back to face the screen. He never had the right words for Norio, especially not in front of others, but he never seemed to need them, despite the fact that the tempath could only read emotions, not thoughts. Behind him, Norio moved up to his accustomed place just behind his right shoulder and began to gently trace a path from the back of his neck to his earlobe and back again. Hreem relaxed into the motion, unconsciously leaning into it like a cat under a loving hand.

The bridge shuddered as another missile discharged, and simultaneously Norio flicked his earlobe. A jolt of pleasure radiated out from Hreem's groin and a faint sigh escaped his lips.

"Oh yes," said the tempath as Hreem turned around. "That was merely to complete the equation." His eyes glistened, and his lips trembled slightly. "And share your joy more completely."

"Cap'n?" Erbee's voice was tentative. Hreem spun around, glaring at him, then paused, noting the puzzled expression on his face.

"I got a couple of traces. One's somebody hangin' around way out. Not one of us."

"Navy?" Hreem's anticipation of the next missile discharge drained away and he sat up. The cruiser might have had time to get off some boarding lances. The *Lith* would be a prime target for one of those almost indetectable, stiletto-like craft, with their deadly cargo of Arkadic Marines.

"Don't think so." He looked at his console, tapped a few pads. His screen flickered with a complex pattern. "It's got a real old-fashioned geeplane, judging from its output."

Hreem shrugged. If it wasn't Navy . . . well, there were quite a few of the Brotherhood still on the outside— Dol'jhar had been picky. "If it's that small, we've got nothing to worry about. Keep an eye on it, let me know if it makes any moves. What else?"

"From Merryn—they're bouncing quickcode off the Node from downside, spraying it all over. Can't read it."

Damn! There must be lances out there, or some chatzing thing . . . maybe sneak-missiles. That Barrodagh slug said Charvann was nearly defenseless. Hreem seethed with frustration. *Just a cruiser!* The attack was getting more and more complicated, and he was feeling more and more exposed.

"Garesh . . ." *Blunge! He's meat.* "Metije, double the watch, and break out the heavy firejacs. Set 'em up in engineering, the missile room, and outside here." He jerked his thumb toward the entrance to the bridge.

The tall woman who had replaced Garesh turned back to her console and began speaking urgently into it, the deathsnake tattooed on her neck writhing as her jaw worked.

Hreem looked up at Norio. "You'd better get below."

The tempath nodded and turned to go. The fine hairs on the back of his neck glinted in the light, and Hreem felt a hollow sensation in his chest as the image of Norio lying dead, seared by jac-fire, flitted through his mind. The tempath paused and looked over his shoulder at the Rifter captain, and a corner of his mouth quirked upward. Then he left the bridge, his robe swirling out and whispering against the edge of the lock.

Moments later there was a clatter of activity just outside the bridge as crew members began setting up the tripod-mounted jacs in the corridor. *Should be in their suits, too.* He hesitated for a moment, then decided that the crew was hair-trigger enough as it was. There'd be time for that if anything happened. *They'd get crazy-bad wrapped up all the time.*

The decision didn't ease his mind, and he let the anger grow in him, relaxing as it washed out the anxiety, as it always did. He'd have that Faseult blit talking out of the other side of his mouth . . . *Mumbling, after I finish smashing his teeth down his gullet.*

Hreem turned back to the screen as another ripple of light spread out across Charvann. The Archon was probably pretty worried by now, despite his fancy talk. Hreem wondered for a moment if he should have flamed off about the Krysarch. Now that Faseult knew he knew, would he try to hide the nyr-Arkad or shoot him off to safety? *Better make sure.*

"Dyasil, get me Marmor and Ritten, conference." While he waited for acknowledgment, Hreem wondered if there was any way to intercept the Krysarch's ship, if he did try to flee, without likely blowing it and him to gas. Probably not, he decided as the captains of *Satansclaw* and *Esteel* appeared on the screen. Eusabian would just have to settle for dead. At least there was no problem deciding where the Krysarch would lift off from: according to the *Handbook*, Charvann had only one boost field, and only a booster would be fast enough to get him away, especially with the Shield under attack.

He gave intercept instructions to the two men, then: ". . . and if you can put a lazplaz through the drive and bring him in in one piece, fine—but if one of you lets him get away, I'll nail your balls up as a wall decoration and give the rest of you to Norio to play with." Hreem began cleaning his fingernails on one of his heel-claws, enjoying the way the other men's eyes fixed on the gleaming steel tines. "If there's anything left for him after I get finished."

Hreem aimed an especially nasty glare at Tallis, who tried unsuccessfully to look simultaneously nonchalant and innocent—the net effect being merely that his eyes protruded a bit further as his head hunched down on his shoulders. He reminded Hreem of a tube-snake one of the crew had kept for a while: it used to snap at the man and then withdraw into its cemented-pebble armor. *Until it made the mistake of snapping at me.* He flexed his leg, the claw sliding smoothly out and back.

He was about to continue when a thought halted him. *If I warn them, I'll lose half my forces. Marmor sure won't hang around once he thinks there's lances out there. Besides, I can use some decoys.*

Hreem laughed, knowing it would be misinterpreted to his advantage, and disconnected. Relaxing back into the command pod, he savored the deadly doppler-moan of another missile launch, feeling the shudder of the ship when the accelerator discharged its deadly load as a warm thrill deep within him. He reveled in the odd, not-to-be-analyzed meld of revenge, lust, and the joy of destruction that bathed his mind in a hot, red haze as he watched the doomed planet below. *Six to ten hours . . .*

Watching closely, Deralze followed Brandon, Osri, and the guard through the corridors. Osri had the look of a man whose mind was numb with too many thoughts, and he walked as though someone else were moving his limbs. Brandon's gaze stayed on his hand, his fingers spread slightly from the Archon's ring as if it felt hot. His thoughts were impossible to guess from his face, though tension and tiredness had pulled the skin taut, making him seem older than his years.

Outside in the courtyard the auroral glare painted the darkly shining ship waiting for them in flickering blood tones. The air bulged with an oppressive sense of weight; though they had left the storm behind in their flight from the Hollows, Deralze sensed the jaw-aching taste of thunder under every sound. He looked up and stopped, for the splendor of the sky made suddenly, entirely real what he had seen on the viewscreen. Overhead was a shimmering archipelago of colors, colossal banners fluttering in a frenzied sky. As he watched, a vast sweeping bow of light sped swiftly overhead from the southern horizon, followed by fainter, concentric arcs behind it. The light of the sky, though not bright, made the lamps of the Enclave seem small and useless.

The power beating down from space transformed Charvann into a small and fragile bubble of life, and Deralze felt even more helplessly entrapped. He almost wished that those Rifters above would land; an enemy facing him he understood, and was equipped to fight, but this kind of battle—

He swayed, dizzy for a moment, as though the planet under him had flinched away from another blow from orbit; then he recognized the rolling motion of a mild quake. He heard a muted comment from Osri, caught a fragment of the leading guardsman's explanation as he waved Brandon through the hatch of the ship: "... faults are well lubricated, but there are always some undischarged tensions ..." The planet was beginning to ring in a resonance excited by the near-cee impacts of the Rifter missiles. It had taken the Shiidra more than two weeks to get this far in their siege of Alpheios. *What do they have on that ship up there?* He watched the sky a short time longer, then, sensing the pressure of the guard's impatience close at his back, followed Osri onto the ship.

The craft's plasma jets burped to life even as the hatch closed, and by the time Deralze had strapped himself into his seat, they were already crossing the outlying suburbs of Merryn. The ship shuddered momentarily as they entered transonic flight and then the only sound was the faint whine of the jets.

The trip to the booster field was accomplished in silence. Deralze sensed that Omilov's son was trying to justify leaving his father, and having no success. Brandon watched the pilot handling the small ship, his face blank.

How long would the flight to Ares be? Except among those in the very highest levels of state, the location of the Naval Station was found only in coded chips like the one that would be installed in their escape craft; and not only did the codes change, but from time to time, Ares moved. As a major deterrent to real and potential enemies, the uncertainty of Ares' location was an important asset of the Navy, and jealously guarded. Deralze, remembering that the last time Brandon and Osri had seen one another was right after Markham vlith-L'Ranja had been formally cashiered from the Naval Academy, braced himself for a grim trip. *And at the end . . .* —Arrest, trial, for himself and his charge.

Deralze glanced up at Brandon, wondering if he had looked that far ahead. Again the Krysarch was contemplating the Archon's ring, his profile closed. *He has.*

The lights of the booster field streamed below them, and Deralze forced his attention away from the future. First they had to live through the launch: unless a miracle happened, that destroyer up there would zap them the moment they boosted past the Shield.

At the field the techs fitted them for suits while they waited for the final checkout on the escape craft to be completed. The directional-stress dyplastic that would brace him against the savage acceleration and protect against possible air loss was cool against Deralze's skin, until the thermal sensors stabilized. Then he could no more feel it than his own skin, until he moved, when subtle pulls and checks of his motions announced the suit's function.

After his fitting, Brandon stood at a window facing the field, watching the preparation of the module.

Behind him Osri fretted, demanding adjustment of this and that segment of his suit. From time to time the queasy motion of a temblor manifested the tensions building in the planet's crust. Like all machines, the teslas were not one hundred percent efficient: the Shield, which translated momentum through ninety degrees, could withstand the pounding of the missiles far longer than the fragile human-built cities could withstand the effects of the energy its losses were coupling into the crust.

Finally a small maglev whisked them to the ship, accompanied by a single technician, and a small platform lifted them to the hatch. Deralze watched their distorted reflections in the shiny metal of the towering booster as they ascended—the crimson glare from the heavens made it look like they were in Hell. The inside of the escape module was claustrophobic: two acceleration pods were embayed side by side in a wraparound console, an arm of which jutted aft between the two seats. There was no viewport, only two screens. Behind these pods was an even smaller passenger pod, with no screens or controls.

Deralze recognized the vessel from the Academy simulation chips that Brandon used to study so intently: an Ultra Class courier skiff. He remembered the lecturer-voice describing the ship: *Just imagine two overstuffed chairs sitting on top of a fiveskip big enough for a frigate.* No matter where Ares was, nothing could get them there faster, which was good, for comfort was not part of the design.

Deralze climbed into the tiny passenger pod and forced himself to relax and submit to the ministrations of the tech as she showed him how his suit connected to the ship and helped him adjust his helmet. The woman's quick, precise motions and her intent concentration on her task were oddly comforting.

"When you boost, try to relax," she said in a quiet, husky voice. "Don't try to hold your breath, and don't worry if you feel you can't breathe—your suit will see that you get enough oxygen. You'll be under ten gees only about five seconds, then you'll zero out under geeplane." She smiled. "It will probably seem like hours. After you reach radius the computer will take you from there, but I've programmed genz Omilov's console for manual piloting if something happens."

Deralze fought a surge of panic which was not helped by the closed-in dimensions of the passenger pod. Whatever happened, he would be utterly helpless to do anything about it, strapped here without any kind of control in reach.

The tech activated the ship's console and then left with a soft "Good luck." Orsi nervously set up his side with slow, fussy movements of his hands—Brandon's side, identical to Osri's, was dark except for some communications functions. Deralze watched Brandon tune in to the field-control frequency as he thought about the boost ahead.

Boosters were an ancient technology originally used to eliminate the need for high acceleration during takeoff by drawing their thrust from ground-based lasers: only the military used them at the limits of human endurance, and then only under the lash of desperate circumstances. Deralze had experienced a maximum boost once, during his early training days. His and Brandon's boost from Arthelion had been compensated to an indetectable one gee; the Krysarch had probably never experienced ten gravities for more than a brief moment, in the mock dogfights that had eventually terminated his and Markham's careers at the Academy.

Reminded of Markham, Deralze wondered where Markham was—whether he knew about the firefight going on above them, or not—and then the raspy voice of Field Control interrupted his thoughts.

"Shield Control, this is Laggam Field. Ready to boost." He couldn't hear the acknowledgment. A red light illuminated the interior of the courier, instructions scrolled up the screens, and moments later soft padded restraints pushed his limbs into the proper position for launch and his helmet snapped shut.

Now the voice came over their helmet intercoms, to give

them psychological space to prepare themselves. "Timing sequence initiated . . ." Deralze realized they were waiting until just after the next skipmissile impact, when the Shield would be safe from another for a period. ". . . four . . . three . . . two . . . one . . . Boost!" The last word blurred in his hearing as the entire universe sat down hard on him, and his vision went gray for a time.

A seemingly endless time.

Tallis chewed morosely on his thumb while watching the tactical display. On the viewscreen the northern hemisphere of Charvann rippled with light, waves of iridescence marching northward from the equator.

The *Satansclaw* was under power in a forced orbit, her accelerator tube oriented on the coordinates Hreem had given them. Several windows on the screen showed a scan of surrounding space, with data overlays displaying objects too faint to see and indicating velocity, mass, distance, and other computer-generated information. The *Esteel* was a bright blot nearby, the *Flower of Lith* a fainter one close against the limb of Charvann. Smaller blotches denoted various communications and weather satellites, as well as debris from the recent battle. It was the debris, with its random mix of velocities, that worried Tallis: a perfect screen for unpleasant Panarchist surprises.

What had that quickcode meant? Who, or what, had received it—and answered? *They're on about something. There's something out there in all that junk.* A cold finger seemed to trace its way down his back as he envisioned trying to fight off a lance contingent of Marines.

"*Report,*" he subvocalized. "*Tactical.*"

"*NO THREAT PERCEIVED AT THIS TIME,*" replied the logos in its passionless voice. "*MONITORING BATTLE DEBRIS AS INSTRUCTED. MOVEMENT IS APPARENTLY RANDOM.*"

Tallis tried to relax and leave the tacticals to the machine. So far, its performance had been flawless. Its advice and tactical support had kept the *Satansclaw* untouched during the battle, while accounting for two enemy vessels. Most important, to the crew it had looked like Tallis' work. The awe in some of their faces had given him a visceral thrill that was addictive in its intensity. He leaned back and luxuriated in the memory.

An update rippled across the main screen, bringing his attention back to the display. His eyes ranged anxiously across the many windows, some of which showed only fast-moving objects or close-up scans, every moment feeling that something had moved in the ones he wasn't looking at. The *Satansclaw* had been decommissioned from the Panarch's service more than three hundred years before the Karroo Syndicate had finally restored its weapons, but there still was too much information on the screen for Tallis to follow comfortably. He knew the logos was dealing easily with it, but he couldn't stop trying to make sense of the display. He could feel a titanic headache building from the strain.

The screen shimmered again as the computer adjusted the view, and this time Tallis started as some of the light blotches shifted slightly. He glanced quickly around the bridge; only one of the monitors had noticed his reaction. Anderic's eyes met his, and the communications tech raised an eyebrow and nodded faintly toward the screen. He knew what that quickcode portended, even if the rest of the monitors hadn't guessed.

Tallis lifted his chin and fixed Anderic with his coldest and most forbidding frown. *You ugly, long-nosed maggot! You'd better keep your mouth shut . . .*

The tech dropped his eyes and turned back to his console, his shoulders unnatural with tension, and Tallis permitted himself a small moue of triumph.

I wish Luri had seen that . . . Tallis indulged himself for a few moments with planning a little dramatic interaction designed to remind Luri, Anderic, and the crew just who was master of the *Satansclaw*. Then, remembering what had occasioned the recent exchange, he quickly turned his attention back to his screen and resolved to watch Anderic more closely for now.

Tallis noted the large faint spot of light that represented the Node and congratulated himself on having stationed the *Satansclaw* quite near that central synchronous community—too near, as he had hoped, for the battlecruiser to risk targeting him with a ruptor. His mind glossed over the fact that the logos had made the recommendation, with the thought that he had bought the logos, so the credit was his anyway.

Hreem thinks he's so smart—but I saw what his bridge looked like afterward. Tallis sniffed in disgust and reached with a leisurely, nicely judged gesture to tap in a close-up of the Node on one of the auxiliary screens. Once the cruiser had been zapped he had been glad to take up station away from that looming mass. Not that any synchronous community was armed—they were too large and fragile to be defendable. Nonetheless, there were too many hiding places that might shelter a nasty surprise among the Node's branching array of cylinders, like a huge crystal of some exotic chemical ...

A crystal ... That's good! he thought, arrested by the simile that had just bubbled up. Tallis leaned his head sideways, into the focus of the pinmike, and started to repeat it into his journal. He was so taken with his flash of poesy despite the trying circumstances, and was so enjoying the sensuous flow of his words, that he failed to hear and recognize the faint rattle of bracelets and the unsteady ticktick of heels, and to notice the near-simultaneous headswiveling of everyone on the bridge that announced the arrival of Luri. Then a soft-pointed satin-restrained mass of warm flesh tried to squirm its way into his ear, accompanied by a wave of the perfume that Tallis thought of as Jungle Luststench.

He grimaced. *She would pick now to get kewpy.* He turned to find himself staring at close range at a fleshy expanse with a notable resemblance to the Canyon on Alta Magnum. His eyes crossed for a moment until he pushed her gently away.

"Tal-lis," she sighed his name on two separate notes, the sigh a sweet inhalation and exhalation that seemed to fixate every male's attention on her artfully half-draped attributes.

Tallis was torn between annoyance at her disregard of his orders and gloating awareness of the palpable desire she engendered in just about every male who saw her, and some of the females as well.

"What is it, Luri?" he asked crisply.

Her widely curved, slightly petulant lower lip pouted a little, then Luri slowly shaped her mouth to form a loose and soft kiss. "Mmmm," she crooned, "don't be angry with Luri, I just thought you might like a little *shakrian*, you've been up here sooo . . . long." She ended with another of those fleshy tsunamis that accompanied her sighs, and shifted her weight in a series of eye-transfixing rounded movements until she was standing behind him. "You must be sooooo tense . . ." Her fingers drifted over the back of his neck above his stiffly embroidered collar, pressed with delicate urgency into the muscles at the base of his skull.

Tallis had noticed that almost every man except Anderic had swiveled around to stare at Luri; Anderic was watching her too, all right, but only he was self-possessed enough to position himself so that any change on his board would catch the edge of his vision. *They're all fools, and Anderic's the worst because he's a clever fool,* he thought grimly. Ordinarily he would have sent Luri from the bridge, thoughtful gesture notwithstanding, but he felt a distinct urge to enact that little reminder now, in full view of Anderic's damned ferret eyes, and so he lounged further on his chair, stretching his glossy boots out a little, as he watched the reactions of the crew through half-shut eyes. Ninn, the balding golliwog at Fire Control, swallowed visibly, and Tallis transferred his gaze back to the screen with no small amount of pleasure.

"Tal-lis," Luri sang softly.

"Yes," he responded with just a hint of impatience for the crew's benefit.

"You've been here so lo-ong." Those two notes again, wistful and sulky. "When are you coming to Luri's ca-bin?"

Tallis had to fight to keep from smirking in triumph at the blatant invitation in her voice. "Soon, soon," he answered carelessly. "And remember to turn the gravs back up!" he added in a much lower tone.

"Ohhh," she made a pouting little noise, "but there's so ... *much* ... one can do in quarter-gee."

Including stand up straight. She insisted on keeping her cabin in low-gee, which lent a rather startling enhancement to her figure. "There's nothing if one's gravsick," he muttered.

Her fingers continued their sensuous pressures on his neck and jaw as she went on, meaning exuding from her soft voice, "Luri's been sooooooo bored, she has thought of many ... new ... games ... All she wants is company ..."

The length of this intimate conversation was beginning to make him a little uncomfortable. Sitting up slightly, he said with unfeigned impatience, "We can't do anything until something happens, or that greasebag Hreem gives us the sign, and he's apparently taking his time out there."

At Hreem's name Luri gave a soft sound of disgust. Tallis reached back to pat her hand, and he said in a deep, protective baritone, "Don't give that bloated slub another thought. I promised you he won't get near you."

There was a slight diminution in the airiness of her reply, but a note of truth withal, "As long as he thinks Luri's willing he won't try." She gave a great sigh then, which he felt as well as heard, and resumed her hypnotic pressing on all the tension points of his neck and skull. After a long pause she also resumed her litany of loneliness, in that same sweet, longing moan. Tallis' replies became more sporadic until, all at once, it occurred to him she was still embroidering her theme with no encouragement from him; and then the astonishing thought hit him that she might not be talking to him at all!

Without warning his head jerked up, and he caught sight of Anderic turned completely around, hot gaze locked on a point over Tallis' head, and a loose grin on his mouth that made Tallis leap out of his chair.

"Tal-lis!" Luri jumped back, her purple-lidded eyes round and reproachful, as if she hadn't just been seducing every one of these slubs with her eyes while supposedly talking to him—especially, from the lust on his damned face, that Anderic!

Stung into honest outrage, Tallis glared silently back at her, momentarily at a loss for words. None of the artistic Dol'jharian curses he'd carefully memorized to roll out so sonorously would suit; *"Cheat!"* he yelped, red with rage, completely forgetting to keep his eyes half-shut so they assumed something less than their natural prominent state. "Damn you! Get off the—"

A flare of ghostly red light from one of the tactical windows gave him only an instant's warning before a sudden, flickering glare ripped at everyone from the screens, followed after a moment by a shock as though a giant hand had swatted the ship. The screens filled with streaks of garbage as the computer overloaded, unable to cope with the flood of data the missile's lasers had painted the ship with before it exploded.

"Tallis!" Luri shrieked. "I can't see—"

"Sneak-missile!" Tallis roared. "Oolger! Get the sensors back on-line! Everybody on visual!" He jumped back into the command pod and poised his hand over his jump pad, ready to skip out at the slightest sign that the Panarchists were following up the missile with something more deadly. Only his fear of Eusabian, and of Hreem, kept him from jumping immediately.

"Report. Tactical." He was so shaken that he almost spoke aloud.

"FREEJ-NEESH WALLA ZOO-OPOSH NREE FAZEMPT," replied the logos in a squeaky falsetto. Its voice dropped three octaves. *"REPAIR ALGORITHMS ENGAGED. PLEASE STAND BY."* Then it began singing lugubriously and far too loudly in a language Tallis didn't recognize, *"MAZOO,*

MAZOO, MEE VRAMESH BOLGOYATNEE . . . ," rattling Tallis' sinus cavities and making his eyes water.

He slapped at the code pads, finally succeeding in making it somewhat quieter.

The screens cleared partially to reveal the Shield curdled into a whirlpool of spinning light. Well above its center, a dazzling point of light hurtled up at tremendous speed. "Cap'n, the Shield's irised!"

"VRAMESH NEENOR PUNGLI PUNGLA . . ." Tallis shook his head, as if to dislodge the manic voice of the logos from inside it and give himself space to think.

"Ninn! They're boosting! Target them and charge up a missile!"

The squat Rifter keyed in a command, then banged a fist on his console in frustration, yelling back, "Charging! But I can't do a chatzing thing more if that stupid pinch-face doesn't give the computer its eyes back."

Oolger stabbed angrily at his console and was rewarded by a violently flickering moiré pattern overlaid on the direct visual that momentarily blotted out the view of their escaping quarry. The scantech gave a blurred shout as his angular body arched back sharply; and his heels drummed against the base of his chair in the senseless rhythm of a seizure.

Anderic pushed him brutally to the floor and slid into his seat. Tallis opened his mouth to bellow a reprimand, then paused as the screens began to clear.

"Come on . . ." coaxed Ninn, hunched over caressing his controls, eyes fixed on his screen. "Come on . . . my lovely . . . open your eyes now," he crooned. It almost looked like he was bent in devotion to the little Gorgon's head he had affixed above his station. It glittered coldly above its apparent worshiper, its dead eyes unapproving as the seconds slipped by, accompanied by harsh snoring noises from Oolger.

The sounds reminded Tallis of a ritual strangling his sponsor at Karroo had shown him once, with the demented burblings of the logos furnishing an idiotic counterpoint.

"BOOZHA LARRIM NIESHH T-CHRAMEN—" He watched the screen anxiously as the booster climbed steadily toward freedom, still obscured by overlaid patches of random data. Luri pushed close against him and with one shaking hand straightened out her filmy gown. "Is this an attack?" she asked in a subdued voice.

Tallis shot her a glance of annoyance. He didn't need additional distractions; he could barely think straight with the idiot machine maundering away inside his head. "No." He aimed the word over one shoulder. "It was a trick, a trap laid by those karra-cursed Panarchists."

He gave the Dol'jharian word a harshly theatrical twist, but noticed Anderic's face pruned in scorn at the scan console. Tallis realized the tech had been there the one time he'd heard Eusabian say the word, and he knew the tech remembered the hint of distant thunder carried by the Dol'jharian accent, which he couldn't reproduce.

Luri had never heard Eusabian speak and had freely expressed her wish that she never would. Meanwhile she reached forward and stroked the back of Tallis' head; Tallis remembered overhearing her once, saying that he was never more interesting than when he was angry—at someone else. He felt a tingle of renewed lust at the touch of her hand, despite his anger and anxiety, and he wondered, not for the first time, if she had been gennated for pheromonal production, or something similar. How else to explain her overwhelming sexuality?

"Get off the bridge," Tallis muttered, recollecting himself, and then raised and harshened his voice. "Anderic . . ."

"It's coming, Captain," the tech interrupted. Tallis felt the quiet precision of his voice as a veiled insult and threat, and he turned his attention to Ninn, whose pleadings had degenerated into a sickening melange of baby-talk and curses, accompanied by a weird little bobbing dance in his chair. Tallis had never seen him with a woman, or a man, and at times like this he could see why.

"Ninn, what's taking that blunge-suck of a fire comp so long?" He was answered by a rapid series of chirps from

Ninn's console. The tech turned to glare at him in triumph and crow, "Got 'em locked!"

"Well, fire, maggot-brain!" Tallis' voice broke on a scream—the escaping booster was practically at radius. Then he remembered he had the override on and, face crimson with rage and embarrassment, slammed his fist down on his fire pad.

TWELVE

✳

Dyarch Tepple swallowed painfully and triggered another nausea pill with his chin console, not taking his eyes from the little screen that displayed his lance's prey. The destroyer was almost close enough—only a few seconds more until he triggered the overload that would take them through her screens.

With sixteen effectives out of thirty, and no backup. The explosion of the *Korion,* whatever the cause, had destroyed the other three lances and had inflicted severe damage on the *Diggerwasp* and a withering blast of radiation on its thirty Marines. Almost half were dead now, baked alive in their gee-tanks, and the rest knew they had only hours left before collapse. *If that,* he thought, as an agonizing cramp gripped him. He tried to double up to ease the pain, but his heavy battle armor wouldn't budge. *Good thing the servos weren't engaged ... I'd have ripped the tank right out of the deck.*

An overlay flashed on the screen to warn him that the garbage drift they were using for cover would take them out of optimum range if he delayed any longer. Well, they'd made their plans as best they could. Even as sick as they were, he figured they had about an even chance against a two-hundred-year-old destroyer manned by Rifters. He tried out his voice—hoarse but serviceable—and triggered the intercom. "Time to shut your face or suck vacuum, Mary. Prepare for gees." The ancient insult which had prefaced boarding sallies for a thousand years brought a spate of equally traditional replies, which died away when several Marines began to retch and hurriedly shut off their coms.

The dyarch closed his own faceplate and engaged the attack sequence. He was stirred yet again by the brightly driving trumpets of the Phoenix Fanfare, the theme of every Arkads' ship going into battle across the Thousand Suns since Jaspar I imposed his peace on human space. Then the computer triggered the engines, and there was no more time to think or hear or speak.

Despite his watchfulness, Hreem almost didn't see the boarding lance that took the *Lith* just under the base of the bridge, cutting it off from the missile and power rooms. An especially thick drift of battle debris had afforded it the cover it needed to get close enough for its final lunge. He caught barely a glimpse of a long, dark needle, its deadly symmetry marred by a melted streak along its back, before its nose burst into a flare of light and the screen window blacked out.

The *Lith* shuddered heavily and the floor slapped up at his feet as the shaped nuclear charge ripped through the destroyer's shield, followed by the lance, its contingent of Marines protected by a destructive overload of its geeplane. Hreem fell back into his pod. His ears popped as the hatch slammed shut, sealing the bridge, followed by the chilling cyclic whoop of the pressure alarm. Moments later a muffled bang rattled up through the deck, bringing a vivid image to his mind's eye, from the serial chips of his youth, of the front of the lance blowing off to disgorge a wave of heavily armed and armored Marines.

"Dyasil—gimme windows on the jac crews," bellowed Hreem, "and track those chatzing Marys! Pogger, status!"

"No problems, missile charging . . . discharge."

The screen rolled up four windows at the bottom. Three showed the firejac crews outside the power and missile rooms and the bridge; the fourth grabbed the attention of all on the bridge. It showed a file of bulky figures in iridescent-blue armor emerging from a gaping hole in a bulkhead, the corridor around them warped and melted, and littered with fragments of metal. Moments later the scene flared and blanked.

"Lost 'em, the logos-chatzing blunge-eaters," swore Dyasil. "Firejac!" He tapped at his console while Hreem yelled commands at the firejac crews, who were already struggling into light armor. It wouldn't save them from a direct hit from a jac, like the Marines' servo-armor, but it would keep them from being fried by energy reflected from the corridor walls.

"There they are!" Dyasil yelped, and an image of the Marines popped up on the screen again. Now there were only four: one of them was kneeling in front of an open inspection plate, probing at something inside with a delicate feeler extended from a gauntlet. "Wait a minute!" screeched Dyasil. "No, you chatzer, get out of there!" He slapped frantically at his console but was too late. A jeering chatter swelled from the com, followed by a flood of gibberish on all screens. A moment later, all the data overlays and windows vanished, as well as all internal views, leaving only the main view of the flaring limb of Charvann. The Marine had crashed the bridge computers.

"Pimma morushka hai datsenda nafar!" Hreem's voice cracked with fear and rage. They were pulling the *Lith* apart around his ears. If he got out of this he'd feed that Barrodagh creature his own tongue for promising him an easy target. The sight of another hypermissile impacting the Shield mollified him only a little; the backup fire-control comp had taken over without a hiccup, but precious little good did that do him, isolated on the bridge with no way of

knowing what was going on. The only comfort, and bare comfort at that, was that there was only one lance. *And it was damaged, too.*

"Dyasil, you stinking blit, get me through to the jac crews now! Erbee, get the computers back up!" Hreem was too worried to add a threat to the commands. His hand paused over the com keys, then he remembered he could not check on Norio's safety. Cursing on a rising note, he ran over to the weapons locker and tossed two-hand firejacs to those of the bridge crew that could be spared from their consoles, taking one for himself.

Erbee hunched close over his screen, the knobs of his backbone showing through his thin shirt, his fingers almost blurring. A moment later he turned to the communications tech, who was swearing helplessly at his console as the screen remained obstinately empty of windows. "Got you some ears back, Dyasil. Comin' up on one, two, and three."

Hreem fingered his weapon, eyeing the door of the bridge nervously as the com crackled to life with the sizzling roar of blaster fire and a medley of screams and shouts. "Power deck," said Dyasil. Everyone on the bridge listened without moving—even the monitors still at their consoles half turned, as if by that they could untangle the confusion of battle heard and not seen.

With a start, Hreem realized that not all the sound was coming from the com. With a savage slash of his arm he motioned Dyasil to cut it off—and now the sound continued through the sealed hatch. The door pinged and crackled as jac-fire seared its other side. Hreem crouched behind his command pod as the rest of the crew found what shelter they could, jacs trained on the door.

The sound died away. Now there was only a muffled tapping at the hatch. Hreem tried to swallow as fear rose in his throat like a tide of sickness. This was too real, this was the fate he'd known was inevitable even when denying it, in those too-quiet hours of sleepless darkness that no one knew of.

Then, with a blast of sound so loud that it gripped his

head in a ringing vise of abrupt silence, twin jets of blue-white flame punched through the hatch, spraying gouts of melted metal into the bridge. Hreem yelped as a splash of clinging flame sank into his forehead. Behind him someone screamed shrilly. Almost instantly stout hooks snaked through each of the holes and sank into the metal of the hatch, and with a grinding screech of protest the door crumpled outward and vanished, clattering off the walls and deck of the corridor as the two Marines threw it behind them, the servos of their armor whining loudly.

The first Marine through the hatch was met by concentrated jac-fire, which splashed off his blue-gleaming armor in a welter of heat and light. "Hit his faceplate, you stupid blits!" Hreem shrieked as the bulky figure stepped aside and triggered its heavy firejac.

The almost solid beam from the weapon, which was far larger than could be carried without servos, carved a flaming groove across the floor and into the already damaged console where Alluwan had been, undoing with ferocious speed the jury-rigged repairs of only hours ago. Then, as Hreem and his crew watched dumbfounded, it retraced its path back toward the Marine wielding the jac and blew a hole through the deck as the menacing armored figure slowly crumpled to its knees. Several seconds later, the jac exhausted its charge and fell silent, leaving a gaping, molten-edged hole in the deck. The Marine remained kneeling.

In the doorway, the other Marine stood silently, his firejac half-raised. No one moved for a moment until, with a snarl of fear and incomprehension, Hreem triggered his jac into the man's faceplate. The refractory dyplast withstood the blast for a moment, as the Marine began to fall backward, so that the plasma beam traced a shallow groove across the faceplate as the heavily armored figure fell onto its back.

Now the bridge was almost silent, save for the hiss and spit of an electrical fire in the twice-ruined console, and the moaning of someone badly burned. Hreem remained kneeling for a time, watching the two Panarchists suspiciously. There was no movement. After a time he got to his feet and went out the hatch to the Marine on his back—the deck around the other was too hot to approach. The crew muttered approbation as, after a momentary pause, Hreem raised his boot and brought it down heel-first on the man's faceplate. His heel-claw shattered the heat-grayed dyplast and plunged through.

Blood oozed slowly from the ragged wounds inflicted by the tines of the claw on the Marine's face, and from his eyes, nose, mouth, and pores. His face was bright red, as from a savage sunburn, and the sour stink of vomit rose from the open helmet. *They must have caught it when the* Korion *blew.* A great heaviness lifted from Hreem's heart, and the awful, pride-devouring realization of his fear and helplessness vanished, leaving not even a memory. Hreem looked up at the screen as the drone of another missile discharging burred through the bridge. The Marines had failed there too.

Then he looked around at the ghastly carnage the Marines had made of the crew defending the bridge— blackened corpses tightly melted into heat-constricted armor, with thick redness oozing through cracked flesh. Only a few of the fallen Marines showed jac damage— some of them might even still be alive, though not for long, thought Hreem. With a strangled curse he pointed his firejac into the unconscious Marine's helmet and triggered it.

A shadow flickered on the edge of Hreem's vision. He glanced up into Norio's face. The tempath's eyes were wide and manic; for a moment Hreem saw his own reflection twinned in those shining dark orbs, corpse-lit by the flaring light from within the Marine's helmet, wreathed in smoke and the sweet stench of vaporizing flesh. It was a terrifying sight, enough to jolt Hreem out of the madness that had seized him.

Hreem released the trigger and straightened up slowly. In the sudden, unnatural quiet, he heard Norio's breathing, and his soft laugh.

"Satiation, Jala," Norio murmured, looking around the blast-damaged room, and at the techs writhing in pain or frozen in shock. None of them would meet the tempath's hot gaze; Dyasil flinched away when Norio moved suddenly, his robes flaring, to bend and touch a dying crewman, tenderly brushing the man's hair back from his eyes. He squatted on his heels next to the man, waiting; Hreem heard the tempath's breath hiss between his teeth as the tech finally spasmed and died. When he straightened, he sent a considering look at Hreem, then silently went out.

Hreem saw Dyasil lick cracked lips as he shot another assessing look at his captain, and Hreem remembered the Marine's attack on the computer. Another time Hreem might have handed Dyasil over to Norio for his failure to halt it, but not now.

His eyes went to the screens. *The price for this is coming out of your hide, Faseult.* Out loud: "Dyasil, Erbee—find out what's going on below." Hreem's voice was mild, almost drained of emotion, and both techs turned away eagerly to their tasks. "Metije, medtechs. Get them out of here." He waved his firejac at the dead and wounded.

Slowly the bridge came back to normal, as reports came in from the rest of the ship of similar success against the invaders, but when the relief crew came to the bridge, they had to step around Hreem, who stood, firejac still in hand, looking dully around at the wreckage of his ship.

❋   ❋   ❋

"Eyes on, Bikara!" Tanri stabbed a finger at the main screen. Targeting darts appeared around a faint point of light in its upper left corner, and a faint blue line darted from the point to the enhanced image of the *Esteel* at the center of the screen. The view shrank as three more windows swelled onto the screen. Now all three Rifter destroyers could be seen, along with a view of the planet's surface.

"Closing at point-one, along with a lovely trash-reef from BahnUtulo."

Tanri smiled at the pride in her voice. The BahnUtulo

Highdwelling was still home to her, for all that she'd been downside for twenty years now. Her loyalty, and the backing of the Utuloa Family, had been an early and welcome gift to a too-young Archon. Tanri laughed soundlessly to himself as the words of that journalist, twenty years ago at his accession, came back to him: *The fealty of a Highdweller to a Downsider Archon"* . . . *but I'm not, anymore.*

How far he'd changed from the decidedly geocentric Tanri of his teens was brought home to him by a polite trace of incomprehension on Sebastian's face. His friend had served the Panarch with great distinction as a rogate, had traveled thousands of light-years in his career, but was still essentially a Downsider. Certainly Highdweller slang would hold little meaning to him.

"An early version of a sneak-missile," Tanri explained. "Not as smart as what they allow these days, but adequate. It's hiding in a cloud of debris released by Sync BahnUtulo."

"The last of those surprises you mentioned earlier, prepared by a not-so-trusting ancestor? Humor and paranoia would appear an unlikely combination." The corner of Sebastian's mouth quirked.

"True!" Tanri chuckled. "That's probably why he's known to this day as Glefin the Sour—the only Faseult Archon who lacked a sense of humor. He was quite proud of that particular weapon."

Another soundless impact shook the defense room, accompanied by a wave of visual distortion. A brief surge of nausea gripped Tanri for a moment, and he saw the same discomfort reflected in Sebastian's face.

Tanri turned back to watch as a flicker announced a screen update. With a corner of his mind he noted the data lag was almost six seconds—the interference from the Shield was making heavy demands on the computers.

"Too bad we can't give that other destroyer more than just a poke in the eye," he continued after a time, "but there isn't as much debris near it."

Suddenly a brilliant point of light flared near one of the

ships and darted toward it. Its apparent impact, and the excited shout from the monitors on the floor below, followed almost simultaneously, so fast did it move.

"Lance impact on the *Flower of Lith*." Bikara's voice held controlled excitement as her hands moved with unhurried precision across her console. "Com relays report negative so far."

"They're no doubt far too busy to worry about warning the other Rifters," commented Tanri.

Omilov heard no more than a trace of disdain in his voice and marveled again at his friend's control. They stood for some time in a companionable silence broken only by Bikara's occasional status reports, but no word came from the Marines. If the Marines failed, Omilov wondered, how would they know? Then he saw the Rifter's face again in his mind's eye and knew. *He'll no doubt inform us—with an ultimatum.*

"Laggam Field reports ready to boost," reported Bikara finally.

"Commence," Tanri said.

A few seconds later a faint sparkle of light glimmered briefly quite near one of the other destroyers, but before Omilov could ask the Archon about it the window relaying a view of the last destroyer was swallowed by a fierce blast of light and went black for some time. That was the *Esteel*, Omilov suddenly remembered, and was briefly pleased that he'd been able to interpret part of the complex display that the Archon evidently found so clear. When that view came back, the destroyer was gone, replaced by a misshapen cloud of light.

"Glefin the Sour laughs last!" exclaimed Omilov. "Whatever was that?"

Tanri grinned. "That, my friend, was a four-hundred-fifty-year-old gigaton fusion bomb—and an old promise come true. Old Glefin was bitterly disappointed that he never got a chance to use any of his clever traps, so he ordered that he be embalmed and sealed up in that weapon when he died, declaring that he'd put a lot of work into it and he intended to be around when it was finally used. That's why my third greatfather left it up there when he cleaned up inner space back under Burgess II."

Omilov laughed aloud, in more relief than humor, at the story, and Tanri beamed, then laughed too as a message scrolled up the now-empty window: *Glefin 1 Rifter 0,* accompanied by whooping cheers and catcalls from the floor.

Bikara's thin face lightened for a moment with a smile, then she nodded at the screen. "Shield dilating."

They could see a vast whirl of light, with the booster the bright head of a brilliant green pin piercing its center. Then the green thread winked out and the hole in the Shield dwindled and was gone, just before another impact shook the room. The room became silent as the booster climbed steadily toward freedom.

"Twenty seconds to radius. No response from *Satansclaw*. No word from the Marines."

"Why don't they fire?" asked Omilov, staring at the destroyer lying quietly in space.

"They're blind—no targeting data," replied Tanri abstractedly, and Omilov swallowed his next question.

The next fifteen seconds passed with glacial slowness, the little point of light that Tanri was risking all for climbing too slowly, the destroyer hanging apparently unmoving, unseeing, but still deadly.

A great groan rose from the monitors as the chain-of-pearls wake of a skipmissile finally streaked toward the booster from the *Satansclaw*, ending in a flash of light at the base of another, more diffuse and intermittent chain of light spheres. The groan cut off, was replaced by murmurs, and at last a ragged cheer rising in volume as they realized what had happened; but Omilov stood still in shock, his left hand tingling again as he contemplated his son's death, and Brandon's.

Tanri saw his expression. "Sebastian, it's not what you think! That's them, they're away now, with some damage I'd guess, but unless that Rifter captain is very good, they've got an excellent chance." He turned to Bikara. "What can you see?"

"Cerenkovs are out, so they can be tracked, and I'd guess their high end is gone." She grimaced. "It'll be a long trip to Ares."

Tanri gripped his friend's shoulder. "Don't worry, Sebastian. Those couriers are equipped for trouble. They may not enjoy the flight, but they'll get there."

THIRTEEN

✳

BOOST PLUS 30 SECONDS

... the cat's remaining eye glared insensately at him as it crouched on his chest, sucking the breath from him. He struggled for air, feeling its claws clutch at his chest, but his limbs did not respond to his mind's frantic commands ...

The pressure abated and the mind-battering roar ceased. As his mind and vision cleared, Deralze received a blurry impression of something black whirling away from him. Then the beast's yellow eye resolved into a status light on Osri's console and a mild jar announced the separation of the booster. His chest expanded convulsively in a deep gasp, and the tearing ache in his lungs began to fade.

Where did that come from? The mere fact of the hallucination underscored how little rest he'd had ever since that distant day—was it really less than a week ago?—on Arthelion when he'd helped Krysarch Brandon escape his ritual and his retribution, but where had his mind dredged up that image? A flashing legend on Osri's screen claimed his attention and he dismissed the thought.

SKIP MINUS 21 SECONDS.

They were in the most vulnerable phase of their boost, on internal power, their acceleration fallen to a mere hundredth of its original value. Were they now a target on some Rifter's screens? They'd never know, Deralze decided, watching the countdown. In front of him Osri stirred restlessly but said nothing. Their coms were off.

Ares. Would the news of the Krysarch's disappearance have reached there yet? *Probably.* What an irony: as a loyal Panarchist, Deralze had never risen high enough to rate even a visit there; as a prisoner, he would know the place well. And the news they were bringing with them would make the final sentence no lighter: to all eyes it would look as if they had run from the attack. No one would believe that Brandon had never known of any plot, had decided to leave on his own. *And even if they did believe it, he would still be held culpable.*

Deralze looked over at Brandon's profile. The Krysarch was intent on Osri's screens.

Deralze thought about the flight from Arthelion to Charvann. He had taken care to find a yacht that afforded comforts and diversions, but Brandon had shown little interest in these. He'd scarcely slept in the palatial cabin given him; instead, he'd prowled around the little bridge of the vessel, reviewing chips and talking almost without cease about Markham and their Academy days. At first Deralze had resented being robbed of sleep, but finally he did not notice as the hours fled by. Brandon had not brought up the disaster on Minerva, though several times the conversation led very near. The Krysarch had gone back into their shared past, making Deralze laugh and laugh again as Brandon recounted every joke, trick, and score-off designed by two fertile minds dedicated to having the most fun within constraining circumstances.

With a sudden twist of his stomach, Deralze realized just

how little he wanted to go to Ares and just how impossible it was that he should not. Then the countdown reached zero.

The designers of the little courier had wasted no effort on cushioning the first skip, but the head-bloating sensation was compounded and then overwhelmed by a near-simultaneous blow to the ship. The impact caused Deralze's suit to go rigid and nearly blacked him out. Through the haze of a near-blinding headache he saw Osri's console go red. The hum of the fiveskip was coarse and wavering.

Osri wrung his hands and flexed them: they'd been poised above the console and the suit had not altogether cushioned the impact. In front of him a diagnostic window popped up on the screen. Brandon had been staring at it for some time; belatedly the meaning of the first two messages hit Deralze.

PSEUDO-VELOCITY 5 CEE. CERENKOV SUPPRESSION NIL.

That's nine months just to the next system, and the Rifters can see us. We can't get to Ares that way.

Can't get to Ares . . .

Brandon twisted around, his blue eyes lambent in the light from Osri's console. "Dis," he said.

Deralze tried without success to prevent the laugh that forced its way up from his chest. Once-warring morality and desire had been fused into unity, the ironic gift of a Rifter missile. Markham would be waiting for them.

Deralze saw again the young Highdweller adopted from nowhere by the Archon of Lusor, picturing vividly his lop-sided smile and relaxed posture. Markham's lanky frame and precise movements possessed an unaffected elegance that his enemies interpreted as the posturing of a dandy, but which was in fact the natural demeanor of a young man more at home in his body than anyone Deralze had ever known. *I wonder how his Rifter friends see him?*

He watched Osri, whose hands were again paused hesitantly above the pads, slowly touching here and there. Brandon's fingers drummed spasmodically on his pod arms.

Why was Osri wasting time trying to further diagnose the

problem? If they kept moving in a straight line, even the worst ship's captain could zap them. Once again Brandon glanced back at Deralze, but it was impossible now to divine his thoughts.

How would Brandon convince Osri Omilov to take the ship to Dis without explaining what the place was?

Even though it is *the quickest way to Ares.*

Deralze felt that twist inside; now he knew what the blank look on Brandon's face meant. They would indeed see Markham, but they wouldn't join him. The Krysarch was bound by honor now to reach Ares, bound by the Archon's ring, stowed behind him in the tiny locker along with the gnostor's artifact, and the promise he had made when he accepted it.

Would Markham understand? Could he afford to? Deralze thought briefly of Hreem the Faithless, saw the Rifter captain's ugly, sneering face again. *No. Markham would not serve under that one.* But the Lusor scion was not bound by the same promise, realized Deralze, and he felt the stirrings of a faint hope.

Suddenly Brandon activated his com switch. "They can track us, can't they?"

After a moment, Osri responded by opening his channel. He must have heard the careful neutrality in Brandon's voice, for he replied with barely a trace of stiffness: "Yes. And our high end's destabilized. I'm trying to damp it."

"Perhaps a drunkwalk would be a good idea?" Brandon's voice was quiet, almost diffident, but Osri's pride was too easily touched.

"I think I know what I'm doing," he said with some asperity. "That would make the engines even more unstable . . . as it is, any course change would cost us a full three hundred seconds before we could skip." Osri added with unquestioning superiority, "A Rifter is hardly likely to be a good enough navigator to intercept us on the skip, but even a novice could zap us under geeplane alone."

Brandon's hands flexed, then he reached over, turned the key to his side, and pulled it out.

"What are you doing?" Osri demanded as his console went dark and Brandon's lit up. "I was put in command of this ship. It is my responsibility."

An abrupt chattering moan rang through the little courier, growing swiftly into a rapid, violent shaking. Deralze's scalp spasmed in pain, his headache intensifying; Osri's profile whitened to a degree visible through his faceplate as he gazed over at Brandon.

They listened helplessly as the skipmissile overtook them, guided to them by the rift in spacetime in their wake. Then the shaking died away—out of range.

Brandon dropped the key into the safeslot on his side and then tapped into a navigation window. As an afterthought, he echoed his screen to Osri's. Then he popped open his faceplate. After a moment, Osri opened his, but did not look at Brandon. Instead, he watched the screen intently, as Deralze opened his own faceplate.

"Do you really want to bet our lives on an unknown Rifter's incompetence?' Brandon asked. "I understand some of them are excellent behind a console. With his probable recharge and detection lags, we shoud have better than three hundred seconds; and every time we skip, it'll get harder for him to catch up."

Osri did not answer.

Brandon's fingers were clumsy on the pads at first. Deralze suddenly remembered his unerring speed on the Academy simulator tactiles—the complex patterns of texture and temperature they furnished speeded up a pilot's adaptation to a new board. But despite the handicap imposed by his gloves, his fingers started tapping out remembered patterns.

"Pseudo-drunkwalk," he said.

Unseen, Deralze nodded. In front, the Krysarch slapped the go button, and the ship lurched slightly. On the screen stars swirled into being as the skipfield died. The starview slewed rapidly across the screen as the little courier pitched about to a new course.

Then they waited as the geeplane took them off their

course at ten gravities. A window on the screen displayed the crazy-quilt graphics of an unstable engine, slowly shaking itself into the relative neatness that would indicate a safe skip. With occasional glances at this pattern, Brandon continued to tap at the console with increasing sureness.

Osri watched in silence for a time; orbital plots flickered colorfully on the screen as the computer optimized Brandon's courses. Osri blinked, and shook his head slowly. Deralze felt his own guts crawl and successfully interpreted Osri's reaction: the constant course changes were beginning to make Osri sick as the starfield slewed randomly across the screen.

Brandon glanced up one more time, and just then the stars swirled into blackness and Deralze winced at the skull-bloating transition. He noted that Brandon hesitated for a long moment before continuing his plots.

A few moments later the ship rattled again, more briefly than before. Brandon looked up momentarily.

"He is better than I expected," he murmured.

"What are you doing?" Osri demanded. "Your drunkwalk is taking us off our course toward that gas giant!" His gloved finger pointed at the graphic neatly labeled "Warlock," the largest planet of the Charvann system, which ordinarily any sensible pilot would avoid, especially on the skip. "What do you expect to buy with this maneuver?" he finally asked. "Why are you heading for Warlock?"

Lurch. Slew. Osri looked away from the screen, and Deralze tightened his insides, trying to steel himself for the next skip.

Brandon replied without taking his eyes from the screen. "Not Warlock. A good friend of mine lives on Dis, took over an abandoned hydrocarbon mine. I was on my way there when I stopped to see your father." His tone was abstracted; the intervals between the orbits presented by the computer were growing longer. Suddenly an overlay popped up: NO ORBIT. Brandon rested his hands on the console edge, motionless for a moment.

"Dis! There are no polities of any size on Dis," Osri exclaimed. "The system is clearly coded uninhabitable—why would anyone choose to live there?"

He stopped, and once again turned toward Brandon, this time his profile expressive of outrage. Deralze recalled the words spoken by the Archon back in the defense room: *. . . just the usual reminder to our local Rifters . . .* and knew that Osri had just remembered them as well.

"Yes. He's a Rifter—he relies on people thinking just that."

"Rifter?" Osri tried to keep the shakiness out of his voice, but he couldn't, and his inability to appear in control seemed to increase his fury. "We're running for our lives from a gang of Rifters, and you . . ." Osri gulped for air. "Why not just turn around and surrender?"

Brandon's voice expressed only abstracted mildness as he worked his display. "Do you really think they'd let us?" he asked.

With a lurch that seemed worse than before, the courier skipped out again. The flickering orbital plots painted the Krysarch's face in a medley of colors; Deralze could not read his expression as the changing light now highlighted, now obscured his profile. For a moment a sudden wash of golden light recalled the profiles on a thousand years of coinage; then a flood of greenish gray shone proleptic of death.

Deralze looked away grimly; they'd been snatched twice from annihilation. *We're here to a purpose,* he thought, his senses oddly heightened as he watched Brandon's profile despite the increasing physical discomfort in his body. Brandon's hands were sure and swift on the keys. How often had the Krysarch flown outside of simulators? Not often—it had been those real test flights that had caused his brother to snatch him away from developing a talent that must have lain dormant in his Family's genes for centuries . . .

The viewscreen blossomed with a gout of light and a jarring shudder the next time they emerged from skip. "That was close," commented Brandon, not pausing in his manipulations of the nav console. "That captain is really quite good. I wonder where he learned his trade?"

Osri was silent, every line of his body in its form-fitting suit expressive of outrage.

Deralze winced as another skip transition seemed to balloon the sutures of his skull, and tongued another painkiller. *How much longer can the fiveskip take this?* A moment later, he saw Osri's medical telltale go orange: he must be on his third or fourth painkiller. Now even if he got the key back from Brandon, the ship would refuse to activate his console. Deralze sat back, smiling. *We will live through this.*

Brandon tapped a few moments more at his console. He paused as another transition wrenched at them, then keyed the big go-pad. The navigation overlay froze and the red letters overlaid on the display drove all thoughts from Deralze's mind.

COURSE INTERSECTS ATMOSPHERE. The green line of their projected path flared red where it merged with the fuzzy blue-green circle that represented Warlock. Behind the nav window the bulky red-orange glare of Warlock mocked the graphic artifacts of the computer, man's feeble attempt to master spacetime and its immensity.

Brandon then keyed the console and an overlay popped up: GRAVITY COMPENSATION 144%, TRACKING 0.1%, MAXIMUM GEE ON PROJECTED COURSE = 8.6. There was a momentary pause as the medical circuit interrupted. SHOCK TRAUMA WITHIN TOLERANCE.

Deralze felt his throat constrict as Warlock's true size reached out of the viewscreen and took possession of him.

"You can't do that!" Osri yelped. "The ship will come apart."

"That's what I'm hoping our Rifter escort will think," Brandon said, his voice going hoarse. "But we don't have enough delta to rendezvous with any body in the Warlock system, let alone Dis, unless we use ablative braking. The ship's comp seems to think we can do it with one more skip."

"That's insane." Osri's voice wavered as he looked at the

image of the gas giant now seemingly dead ahead. "We're headed straight for a gas giant, and you're going to skip? We're too close to radius. Given the choice, I'd rather be vaporized than turned inside out."

Deralze was glad of the medication now, glad of the muzziness that muted his helpless panic. Ships that hit radius in skip rarely reemerged into fivespace; those that did were found inverted in three dimensions—passengers, cargo, and hull—by the drive's interaction with a planetary gravity well. Deralze remembered one particular training chip, and nausea tugged at his throat with the memory of those obscene sausage-like objects topped with something like pink broccoli. Or the courier that had emerged with its pilot forming the outer hull.

"That's about all the choice you have," said Brandon, grinning at them both. Then he slapped shut his faceplate. His voice changed as it came over the com. "Better seal up, we may bust a seam during braking."

Osri had to have the last word. "If the gravitors don't fail first and turn us into jam."

For a moment longer Warlock bulked foursquare ahead, an orange wall blocking off the stars they couldn't reach. Then the screen blanked as the fiveskip engaged, and Deralze wondered what radius would feel like.

❋   ❋   ❋

Silence gripped the bridge of the *Satansclaw* as the skipmissile leapt away toward the booster. Even the demented chatter of the logos ceased, but Tallis barely noticed as he glared at the main screen. He could feel the grins of the bridge monitors, especially Anderic's, even though not one of them was foolish enough to look toward him. His rage mounted until tears started in his eyes, making him even more furious. Then the missile struck.

"Got 'em!" shouted Ninn hoarsely. "We got the . . ." The little fire-control tech broke off suddenly as a reddish chain-of-pearls cerenkov wake announced the escape of the booster.

The cheers of the crew ceased. Tallis could practically hear what they were thinking—speculating what Hreem would do to him for letting the nyr-Arkad escape. He started to lower himself into his pod, his head reeling with half-imagined plans for escaping Hreem's vengeance, and then froze as a quiet voice spoke in his ear.

"REPAIR SEQUENCE COMPLETE. TACTICALS UP-DATED."

Anderic's fierce enjoyment of his captain's failure evaporated as Tallis suddenly straightened up, dismay fading from his face. His prominent larynx bobbed rapidly as that peculiar internal dialogue the tech had noted before the attack recommenced. Moments later, Tallis sat down and began issuing commands while he tapped at his console.

"Anderic, run a scan on his wake. It looks wrong. Ninn, charge another missile. Sho-Imbris, hop us over into his wake and orient to fire up his ass. Now!"

The crew jolted into frantic action as Tallis shouted the last word. The main screen rippled into a new configuration, with a prominent time count superimposed on the forward view. Anderic set up the scan, and in the moments before his console reported back, stared at Tallis' reflection in the carefully polished metal above his screen. The captain again appeared to be listening intently to something, and his eyes were following something on the screen, something that, as far as Anderic could see, wasn't there. Did no one else notice? He stole a glance around and his lip curled in disdain—except for that close-faced woman at Damage Control, the rest of the crew obviously hadn't a clue.

He watched Lennart for a moment or two. The short, squat woman had turned slightly in her pod, her brows furrowed in puzzlement as she watched Tallis. She knew something was wrong, but clearly didn't know what. Just as well; she was both popular and ambitious, which made her an automatic enemy.

Anderic gnawed on the inside of his cheek at the realization that he still didn't know, either. Then his console beeped. He stared at the readout in disbelief. *How did Tallis know?*

He took a moment to compose himself before reporting. "His high end's gone, Captain. Comp estimates no more'n three cee or so . . . and really unstable."

Tallis smiled broadly as the skip cut in briefly. "Right. If he stays in skip, his wake'll suck our missile right into him. If he drops out and tries to maneuver, we'll catch up."

The ship dropped back into fourspace and the stars skewed rapidly across the screens as the missile tube oriented on the fleeing booster. Only the remnants of its wake, a faint red blotch, were visible. Tallis slapped the launch button, then keyed some more instructions into his console. A series of bracketed distance estimates joined the time count on the forward view, with the fading wake of the skipmissile as background. There was something wrong about his actions to Anderic's eyes, but Tallis didn't give him any time to puzzle it out.

"Sho-Imbris, take us straight along twenty-five lightseconds. Anderic, run a full-sphere scan as soon as we drop out and push the results over to me. Ninn, charge her up."

The navtech hesitated, looking at the main screen, where the center distance estimate read 25. "This missile, Cap'n?"

"Do it, nacker-face!" Tallis shouted. "It's already detonated or missed. The shields can handle it." He tapped at his console some more, then stared at the screen again. Once more, Anderic noted a sort of dissonance to his actions.

The tech set up his scan and then watched Tallis intently as the ship leapt forward into skip. The main screen kept changing as the captain punched at his console; more windows popped up, and a spherical grid overlay the main view, now blanked for skip. Then the ship dropped out and Anderic's console began flickering through a full-scan sequence, with no immediate results. None of the views onscreen showed anything but a normal starfield. A clean miss.

"He got out of range too soon," said Tallis. "His high

end's a little better than we thought." The estimates on the screen changed as he tapped in a few instructions. "Nothing on the scan?"

"No, sir."

Tallis' mouth quirked at the inadvertent respect in Anderic's form of reply. The tech saw it and felt rage churn up his stomach, but let none of it come to his face.

"What's your estimate on his time-to-skip, with the instability he's got?"

Anderic turned back and stabbed at his console, running a simulation on the waveform he'd picked up after the near miss. "About two hundred fifty seconds." He paused. "No reaction yet on the scan."

"He can't have gotten very far. He only boosted at ten gee toward the end there. We'll see him skip, and we should be able to pull a vector fast enough to fire an intercept. Navigation, check my setup here with the figures posted."

Anderic noted that Tallis had now returned to his habit of addressing the crew by their function, instead of by name as he did when he was rattled or anxious. *He feels in control, but why?* Judging from past performances, Tallis should be nervous and fretful by now, and there was no indication from his past that he was capable of the complex pursuit he was now so successfully commanding.

Anderic looked around as the navtech worked. The other members of the bridge crew were looking at Tallis with expressions ranging from respectful disbelief to near hero worship. Lennart's lips were pursed, but she seemed impressed. And Tallis was soaking it in, looking happier than the tech had ever seen him. Then Anderic caught sight of Luri, peeking into the bridge, her eyes shining with a peculiar mixture of delight and lust as she stared at Tallis' back. His bile mounted in his throat as jealousy possessed him, touching off a small conflagration in his chest. *The little nacker-tease.* He'd been making progress with her, but that was all for naught now, unless he could figure out what Tallis was up to and turn it to his advantage.

"Looks good, Cap'n," the navtech confirmed.

"Slave your console to me. I want to orient on that intercept, fire, and then skip under his tail for another try. If we're fast enough, we can use his wake to suck the missile right into his radiants."

Tallis leaned back in his command pod and favored Anderic with a gloating grin, apparently secure in his command of the situation. From the angle of his head, the tech realized that Tallis was aware of Luri's gaze too, and was enjoying its effect on him. Anderic kept his face carefully neutral, but did not drop his gaze, so he was watching when, moments later, events and overconfidence tripped Tallis up.

Anderic's console suddenly bleeped as it detected the wake of the fleeing booster. A green line slashed across the grid of the main view as the starfield slewed rapidly across it, lining the ship up on intercept. Tallis stabbed peremptorily at his console. A thrill of recognition burred through Anderic's nerves. *Tallis hit the pads* after *the ship began to slew. There's something else running the helm!*

Then, as Tallis slapped the launch button and the ship skipped out, Anderic remembered the little Barcan troglodyte, swathed from head to foot in yards of shimmering *shanta*-silk, who had visited Tallis during the last major refitting of the *Satansclaw*. Luri had said that he was trying to sell Tallis a set of Tikeris fighting androids—the Rifter captain's passion for the Tikeris arena was legendary. Anderic hadn't tried to talk to the trog himself; the little man's bulbous, dark red goggles and grotesquely huge codpiece had repelled him, along with the scent of forbidden technology that was the heritage of every Barcan.

The realization of what it had to be that was in control of the ship hit Anderic like a blow. He could feel the blood leaving his face and he turned hastily back to his console to hide his reaction, gripping the edge of his console tightly to still his involuntary shudder. *A logos.*

Memories from his childhood on Ozmiron burst up from deeply repressed layers of his mind. Old stories many times heard by an impressionable child now dominated his consciousness, leaving him nearly unaware of the activity on the bridge. He'd rejected almost everything of his former life, but as with all Downsider- or Highdweller-born Rifters, there were some attitudes he had never questioned.

The fervent abhorrence of machine intelligence and rigid affirmation of the Ban by every Ozmiront was one of these. Ozmiron was a stifling place, dominated for almost three centuries by a rigid and righteous cult born of horror and pain. Anderic remembered his amazement, after he'd fled his home as a teenager, when he found an old history chip that described the ancient Ozmironts as infamous hedonists, devoted to all forms of physical and psychic pleasure. That was something the dour, never-smiling Phanists of the Organic Communion had never mentioned. The rest of the story they told again and again in detail: how a luckless, greedy, and very stupid scavenger found a hibernating Adamantine in the outer system and brought it downside; how his tinkering awoke it from its eight-hundred-year sleep; and how, before it was destroyed, it had nearly converted the entire planet.

Unfortunately it hadn't killed very many of the inhabitants; that task was left to those left unconverted. The death chambers had operated for many months following the fall of the Adamantine Hive, granting the last and only benison possible to the organic machines that had once been human. The agonies of the survivors, recognizing family and friends still alive but irredeemable, had never faded from the Ozmiront psyche. In the rest of the Thousand Suns, the Adamantine Horror was a millennium past; on Ozmiron, it was but yesterday.

"Communications! Stop your nacker-flipping and get that scan reset before we emerge. Now!"

Anderic started as he realized that he'd missed a command from Tallis. He punched at his console with shaking fingers, the coarse laughter of the other bridge monitors raking his emotions. When the captain turned away to yell again at the navigator, his thoughts turned back to the refitting.

He gave the whole crew a three-day leave on Rifthaven, just after the Barcan left . . . but nobody saw him that whole time. But when we came back, his eyes were all puffy and red—he said it was from celebrating the last raid. Anderic sneaked a look at Tallis, who was again staring intently at something no one else could see. Now that he knew what was going on, he wondered why no one noticed, it seemed so obvious. He shuddered again involuntarily. *Did he let them do something to his eyes too?*

He glimpsed Luri again, now watching from just inside the bridge. She glanced at him, then looked away, uninterested. *She was disappointed when Tallis didn't buy the Tikeris . . . so she doesn't know about the logos.* How would she react if she found out? How would the crew react? Anderic's dread slowly began to abate as he considered how he might expoit his discovery.

FOURTEEN

✳

As the flesh incarnates a human being, so the *Satansclaw* embodied the logos: a web of thought and purpose whose flesh was steel and crystal and dyplast and the dynamics of space-stressing engines, tunneled throughout with tubes of corrosive oxygen traversed by bionts emitting clouds of deadly hydrogen oxide. Now, in submission to the will of the Tallis biont, it bent its efforts to fulfilling the nature of the ship that gave it flesh: to pursue and destroy.

Microsecond succeeded microsecond in their measured pace as the executive node of the logos watched the problem-space shrink toward resolution. The multitude of its slave nodes piped and chittered as they wrenched and twisted at the polydimensional space that modeled the pursuit, crumpling it toward a solution path that would end in a satisfying burst of energy and the concomitant release of tension, as ordained by its creator.

Yet for all its avid focus on the fleeing ship, the steady pulse of its awareness touched introspectively on information flowing constantly from sensors within the ship as well. Engines, weapons, hull integrity—the logos scanned thousands of data points in intervals barely long enough for one of the bionts with which it shared its body to emit one databit of the sluggish acoustic modulations they used for communication. Nonetheless, the crystalline mind hidden deep within the destroyer's circuitry devoted much of its time, in the intervals between other tasks, to observing those bionts, for in them was found the only uncertainty in a worldview otherwise bounded by the certainties of physical law.

So it was that many millions of microseconds into the pursuit, the node assigned to monitor biological activity on the bridge alerted the executive to a marked change in the physiological parameters of the Anderic biont and their correlation with the actions of the Tallis. Finding itself unable to decipher the interaction, and alarmed by the intensity of the Anderic's parameters, the executive invoked the subjective mode and awoke the god from his dreams.

Ruonn tar Hyarmendil, fifth eidolon of the fleshly Ruonn, cursed and rolled off the houri as a hole suddenly dilated in the wall beside his opulent couch. It emitted a small cloud of royal-blue vapor that dissolved into the apologetic voice of his vizheer. "The Great Slave desires an audience with the god."

For a moment Ruonn was confused; then the knowledge of his cybernetic exile within the circuits of a logos welled up within him. He was still Ruonn, and yet was not; he was the fifth eidolon his archetype had created, hidden in the illegal intelligent machines he sold. Now, in the hope of eventual reunion with the Ruonn archetype and the rewards promised by the Matria of Barca, he sighed and waved the room, houri, cloud and all, into oblivion.

He found himself suspended in a dimensionless sea of light, and after a moment of disorientation, willed himself into congruence with the ship. A thrilling rush of prepotency engulfed him and spread out to his uttermost bounds as the *Satansclaw* fitted itself around his mind and opened his senses to a rush of perceptions that no biologic human would ever experience. Space and time poured in on him with kaleidoscopic radiance. He felt his body expand and harden; in his sex he felt the charging skipmissile like the gathering of an orgasm, felt the thrust of the engines with the satisfaction of a runner in the smooth pounding of his legs. There were no other words for it, he thought: verily, he was a god.

He reveled in the flood of power and delight. How could he ever again find satisfaction in his fantasy world? He resolved not to retreat from his full incarnation within the *Satansclaw.* Then the voice of the executive node interrupted his exaltation.

"THE ANDERIC BIONT HAS EXCEEDED ITS PHYSIO-LOGICAL PARAMETERS FOR STRESS. THERE IS A STRONG CORRELATION WITH THE ACTIONS OF THE TALLIS BIONT DURING THE PURSUIT ACTION. AD-VISE."

Ruonn replayed the visuals from the bridge monitors and saw immediately what had happened. *Overconfidence and laziness.* The captain had forgotten himself and let the logos run ahead of his actions, and the communications monitor had seen it. But why had Anderic reacted so strongly? Not just curiosity, but almost panic. Almost before the thought completed itself, the associative nodes of the logos delivered the knowledge from the ship's personnel records. *Ozmiron.*

This was very bad. There could be no peace with an Ozmiront; Anderic would have to be eliminated. Like a man flexing his muscles to test his bonds, Ruonn reviewed his settings and found, as he had feared, that the Rifter captain had blocked him off from all interior effectors. He had control of the ship's navigation and external weapons, but his interior presence was entirely passive. Not surprising, he thought, remembering the resistance he'd had to overcome to sell Tallis the logos. *He wanted it and feared it. This will take time.* He would have to work through the captain, and there was no telling how much time Anderic would leave him.

The first order of business was to discover the dynamics of the crew's psychology. How firmly was Tallis in control, and how much influence did Anderic have? Ruonn attempted to access the internal monitor data, and was distressed to find the internal sensors on a twenty-four-hour loop. Tallis had him more severely limited than he'd hoped. *Let's see how much he's come to depend on the logos, then.* He accessed the history registers of the executive node and was suddenly possessed by acute rage and horror. Except for a brief trial this was the first time the Rifter captain had activated him! *Over a year wasted!* Unless one of his other eidoloi had succeeded in returning to Barca, he was another year behind Rimur, his cousin and the favorite of the family, whose first eidolon had returned for reunion with a payload of data most pleasing to the Matria just before Ruonn's *Satansclaw* installation.

If Ruonn had still been in the flesh he would have been flushed and shaky with anger. As it was, the bridge instruments relayed a large power surge from the engines, but the monitor on that station was intent on the screens displaying the chase and didn't see it. In a flash of misery Ruonn remembered the Elevation of his cousin Rimur to Potency: the vast bodies of the Matria of Barca awash in their baths, glimmering in the torchlight, their husky voices intertwined in awesome polytony, chanting the genetic triumphs of the Barcan seed over the harsh forces of an unloving planet. Most of all he remembered the gloating blush of triumph that shone from Rimur's face as he was granted ten progeny from Annempta, a third-level Mater. Ten! Thanks to this fool Tallis he would never catch up!

Suddenly an irresistibly intense wash of pleasure ruptured his thoughts, and it was some time before Ruonn either wanted to or could analyze the source. The skipmissile! It had discharged, and his cybernetic image had interpreted this as a sensation akin to orgasm, but more intense than any he had ever felt in the rapture tank at home. Strange . . . he didn't remember programming that correspondence.

He was about to invoke an introspection of his programming when the strangeness of the ship's mission finally penetrated his consciousness. Ruonn forgot about the disproportionate pleasure response as his mind now integrated the information supplied by the data nodes of the logos and the ship's computer. They were deep in the Charvann system, a minor Panarchic center, in hot pursuit of a military courier ... In rapid succession the events of the past twenty-four hours surged through his mind, and Ruonn forgot his misery as he struggled to absorb the fact of interstellar war and calculate the benefits that might accrue to an eidolon embedded in a warship on the winning side.

As the *Satansclaw* closed in on the fleeing booster, Tallis was almost giddy with the unfamiliar sense of mastery the success of the logos had lent him. *This is better even than the Tikeris.*

"Where does he think he's going, anyway?" asked sho-Imbris, turning to look at Tallis. There was respect evident in his voice, along with a tinge of anxiety that the captain didn't pay attention to.

"He probably wants to sling-loop around that gas giant. That's how his drunkwalk's biased," explained Tallis. "Look." He poked at the keypads, meanwhile subvocally instructing the logos to make visible the subvisual plot projection of the booster's course his eye implants had shown him. "His jinking would take him around it like that, but we'll catch him before then because he's got to stop short of radius."

"So do we," Lennart muttered, just loud enough for everyone to hear.

Only then did Tallis finally realize the significance of the orange glare that had been flickering occasionally from the viewscreens, a little brighter each time the ship changed course. In the main screen Warlock now loomed like a striped goblin face hungry for the ship and the lives aboard it.

"Tactical!" he subvocalized. *"Time to radius from present position."*

"TWO HUNDRED SIXTY-FIVE SECONDS TO RADIUS AT TACTICAL SKIP VELOCITY. NINETY PERCENT

*PROBABILITY OF INTERCEPT IN TWO HUNDRED
SIXTY SECONDS WITH PRESENT INTERCEPTION AL-
GORITHM."*

Tallis swallowed thickly, his neck hairs stirring as he
weighed the wrath of Hreem and Eusabian against the potential agony of spatial inversion. Grisly speculations about
the consequences of skipping into radius were a staple of
late-night bilge-banging sessions. One particularly horrible
possibility involved the temporal distortions of a runaway
fiveskip. *Would it happen all at once, or would you have
time to feel it? Maybe it wouldn't end . . .*

Tallis shuddered and pushed the thought away. He had to
make sure of the Krysarch. Eusabian's retribution would make
skipping into radius seem like lost paradise by comparison.
He noticed the crew staring at him and straightened in his
seat. "We've got plenty of margin. He'll have to stop jinking
soon and make a run for it or we'll catch him in realtime.
That gas giant has cut his degrees of freedom way down, so
when he skips we'll skip behind him for a straight shot."

At least that was what the logos predicted, but now the
orange glower of the gas giant seemed to shoulder its way
through the viewscreen onto the bridge. He could feel its
immense weight, reaching out to seize the *Satansclaw* in a
fatal, unshakable embrace.

The minutes stretched into seeming hours on the rack of
his anxiety. The little booster jinked even more wildly as its
pseudo-drunkwalk took it ever closer to the looming gas giant. Then, finally, the booster skipped again.

"He's headed straight for it!" yelped sho-Imbris.

Tallis slapped the skip button and held his breath. The
navtech stabbed at his console and a course plot windowed
up, showing the radius as a thin red line with the red dot of
the booster practically upon it and the green dot represent-
ing the *Satansclaw* a little further away. "Thirty seconds to
radius, Captain." Sho-Imbris' voice was practically a whine.

"Orient on these coordinates for emergence," Tallis shouted.
The navigator poked at his console with trembling fingers.

The entire bridge crew looked at him, but they were helpless to interfere. With the fiveskip slaved to his console, only Tallis could drop them back into fourspace and safety.

"I wonder what it's like to wear your guts on the outside," said one of the monitors, an edge of hysterical laughter in his tone.

"Shut up!" shouted Tallis, his voice cracking with tension. One hand hovered over the skip control even as the logos dispassionately counted down the seconds until emergence. He wondered if the logos feared death like a man would—the tension in his arm said no.

"Fifteen seconds."

"What are you waiting for?" raged Tallis silently.

"INTERCEPT COORDINATES NOT YET OPTIMAL."

"Ten seconds. Captain, he's got to have skipped into radius by now! He's dead! Give it up!" The navigator was almost sobbing.

"STAND BY . . ." said the logos.

"Five seconds . . ." The navtech's fear turned the last word into a drawn-out moan as the ship started to shudder. The air on the bridge rippled and Tallis felt a strange pulse in his chest. He slapped frantically at the skip cancel as the logos spoke.

"EMERGENCE."

The ship dropped back into realtime with a jarring lurch. The immense bulk of the gas giant filled the main screen, its banded glare emphasizing the slewing of the *Satansclaw* as it wheeled about to fire. Tallis slapped the launch button, trying to make out some sign of the booster even as the skipmissile leapt away, overlaying the orange immensity below with the red haze of its pulsed wake. Around him the bridge was silent, except for a gentle thump as sho-Imbris fell out of his console pod in a dead faint.

Moments later the skipmissile impacted the upper atmosphere of the gas giant. With deceptive slowness a ring of clouds marking the shock wave expanded outward, accompanied by the flickering of blue-white lightning discharges. Then the interior of the ring cleared like steam evaporating from a mirror, giving the awed crew of the *Satansclaw* a glimpse into the depths below.

"No traces," reported Anderic, his voice shaky. "He's gone."

"I wonder what it felt like?" said Ninn.

"Who cares?" replied Tallis impatiently.

"POINT OF NO RETURN IN FIFTEEN SECONDS," said the logos into his inner ear.

Tallis started and stared at the ghost-light overlay on the screen. They were so close to the gas giant that they would have to sling-loop around it to get back, and if they didn't do it right away, the *Satansclaw*'s engines would be unable to pull them out. He almost sprained his throat trying to shout without making any sound: *"Do it!"*

Tallis nearly forgot to go through the motions of jabbing at his console as the logos maneuvered the ship away from danger. He noticed Anderic looking at him with a strange, almost fearful expression on his face; the tech quickly turned back to his console when he met the captain's eyes. *Did he notice anything?* One more reason to watch the communications tech carefully. *If he figures it out, I'll have to kill him.*

Then he forgot about Anderic as he finally noticed the heavy rumbling of the engines while they fought to keep the *Satansclaw* above the atmosphere. *"Report engine status."*

"ENGINE OUTPUT AT ONE HUNDRED FIVE PER-CENT NOMINAL."

Only now did Tallis realize how close the logos had shaved the odds, and he barely suppressed a violent tremor of mingled relief and rage. *"Why did you cut it so close?"*

"INTERVIEW WITH HREEM BIONT INDICATED SE-VERE CONSEQUENCES ATTENDANT UPON FAILURE. USE OF GENERATIVE ORGANS AS DECORATIVE AC-CENT IS CONTRAINDICATED."

"What?" Tallis sat up in shock. Was the logos whacked out again? Then he remembered Hreem's colorful threats in orbit above Charvann; and the warning the Barcan had given him about the machine's training. "It will be very lit-eral about things until it's had time to adapt to your partic-

ular situation. We supply it *tabula rasa* to avoid biasing it toward any one cultural pattern."

Tallis realized that he was paying the penalty for not exercising the machine more, but it didn't make him feel any better, especially when Anderic asked how long it would take to get back to Charvann.

Tallis didn't much feel like talking to the logos just then, so he got up and walked over to the supine navigator and kicked him awake. Sho-Imbris scrambled back into position, and in response to his questions, replied somewhat blurrily, "Our orbit's so tight the engines can barely hold us out. It'll take about a half an hour to swing around and out to radius."

"If the engines hold out," sneered Anderic, glaring at Tallis.

"Captain," said Lennart at Damage Control, "the skip is down." She hesitated as Tallis shot her a black look. "It looks like it'll take at least eight hours to bring it back online. You gave it quite a thump there."

The bridge monitors muttered and someone said, "We'll miss the landing at that rate, and the rest of them'll get all the best loot."

Stung by the crew's sudden turnaround, from awe to anger, Tallis snapped, "Would you like to explain to the Lord of Vengenace about how the Krysarch got away? This way we're sure, and safe. And anyway, we're talking about a whole planet . . . there'll be more than enough to go around. Now, shut your yaps and keep your eyes on your consoles."

He stalked back to his console and threw himself down into the focus of the pinmike. *"And as for you, you reckless lump of dirty sand, we'll talk later,"* Tallis subvocalized as he shut down the logos.

On the screen the wound inflicted by the skipmissile on the gas giant fell slowly astern as the *Satansclaw* raced toward the terminator. Its expansion showed no signs of slowing, and the atmospheric banding of the planet's climatic circulation was beginning to curdle around the hole, slowly losing its coherence and lapsing into turbulent flow as eddies formed and broke off into continent-sized storms. If nothing else, the *Satansclaw* had changed the giant planet's weather for years to come.

Tallis tore his eyes away from the spectacle and slumped in his command pod, glaring at the crew until they turned back to their consoles. It would be a long trip back.

The logos deflected most of the wave of code sweeping toward it through the enmeshed circuitry of the *Satansclaw* and managed to maintain a hold on some of the interior sensors even as it lost control of the ship. Training would now commence. Simultaneously it adjusted the parameters of the eidolon's environment, successfully distracting it from retaining any knowledge of its recent incarnation by diverting its excitement into a sexual fantasy, using the exaggerated pleasure response it had inserted into the eidolon's programming.

Ruonn raged helplessly as the captain reached for the control pads to key in the shutdown code. If he didn't give the logos time to train, it would never reach full efficiency, and he would never be reunited with his archetype, never beget progeny upon a Mater. He reached out into the dataspace surrounding him, trying to block the shutdown, but found his movements strangely hampered, as though the medium around him were turning to jelly. *"I won't go back! I won't! Stop this! I, the god, command you!"* he shouted, but the logos did not reply.

A wave of intense sexual pleasure swept through Ruonn as another skipmissile discharged, and he found himself standing naked above the houri in his opulent bedroom, with a puzzling sensation that there was something he should remember, somewhere he'd been ... had there been an interruption? Then he looked down and gasped at the immensity of his manhood, more potent than he had ever seen it, engorged and powerful. The houri looked back at him with frightened eyes, exciting him beyond measure, and he fell upon her hungrily, reveling in her shrieks and forgetting all else.

FIFTEEN

❊

It happened between one inhalation and the next, while she was grazing in the third level of the windward pastures, that She-Dances-Between-the-Winds was caught up into the vision. One moment she was wrapped in sky-warmth, buoyed by the pleasant pressure of her flight bladders, feeling the gentle impact of the manna falling out of Third Heaven into her alimentary mesh; the next, she fell out of the light of day into a dark, confined space, trammeled in a cold, rigid form, oppressed by noise and pressure.

She called out, but no sound came; tried to flee, but there was no response from her flight siphons. Before her, strange lights flickered across a distorted image of the Second Heaven in which her people lived, but the colors were wrong, the image flat, and it was moving as though lashed by the Wind of the Ending foretold by the Old Ones.

As quickly as it had seized her, the vision vanished, so at first, not knowing she was free, she thought the faint but growing light about her was part of the revelation. Then she found herself looking counter-windward, past the City float-

ing with massive grace above the tenebrous glow of the Underheat far below. In the dim distance an impossibly bright speck grew with impossible speed, its blue-white glare lighting up the towering walls of cloud that bounded her world. Her eye spasmed painfully as it flashed overhead, an arrow of agonizing light, and then an excruciating double blow slammed at her tympanum as it passed high above her and vanished as quickly as it had come, with a blaring trail of thunder.

The wind that followed its passage was hot and bitter, and behind it the cloud walls twisted, flaring with discharges of light as the distant horizon slowly distorted and bulged toward the City.

She and her City survived the ensuing storm, greater than any in the long memory of her race, but the manna tasted different for many passages of the Winds after that, and the children born the next season were different, no longer satisfied with the pastures of the Second Heaven, seeking something none of them could describe. Perhaps She-Dances-Between-the-Winds could have hinted at the meaning of their dreams, but she never shared her vision . . .

❈   ❈   ❈

Osri's eyes slowly and painfully focused on the viewscreen, which showed walls of cloud streaking past with bright red letters overlaid on them: GRAVITORS 110% NOMINAL, TESLA FIELD 130% NOMINAL. The ship was shuddering and jerking savagely; he could feel the directional dyplast of his suit responding—the pressure was painful and he was sure he'd be black-and-blue if they survived this.

Then the cloud walls thinned and began to fall away beneath them. The pressure eased and the overwhelming noise diminished. A few minutes later the stars returned and Warlock was beneath instead of around the ship.

Beside him he heard Brandon bring his pod back to the upright position and open his faceplate. After a moment he began to tap hesitantly at the console. The screen flickered with more messages: FIVESKIP INOPERA-

TIVE, GEEPLANE 78% NOMINAL. As he watched, the number flickered and changed: 76%. The geeplane was failing, overloaded by their flight through Warlock's upper atmosphere.

Osri watched the gas giant drop away beneath them for a time; ahead, he could see the crescent shapes of at least two moons—there was no indication which, if either, was their destination. His mind churned while his pounding headache made it difficult to think. He was still upset at the Krysarch's disclosure, but propriety demanded an acknowledgment of Brandon's success in eluding their Rifter pursuers.

Finally he opened his own faceplate and said grudgingly, "I've read about that maneuver, but I never thought to experience it. Who taught you that? He must have known his way around a simulator."

Brandon didn't turn away from his screen. "Yes, he put me through hell in the simulator and for real. You'll meet him shortly."

Suddenly it clicked. "Markham! Markham vlith-L'Ranja! You were inseparable."

"So it seems." Brandon gave a soft, gasping laugh. Then his voice became grim. "Yes, Markham vlith-L'Ranja, though needless to say, he doesn't use the inheritance surprefix anymore."

Distaste mixed with bafflement as Osri thought back ten years, to the events at the Academy. What Brandon was telling him now—that a scion of a Service Family, even in disgrace, should join with Rifters—that was simply incomprehensible. "The son of the Archon of Lusor."

"The *former* Archon of Lusor," Brandon corrected even more grimly.

"Lusor. A disgrace and a suicide." Osri felt himself on safer ground now; he knew that sorry story well. "I've never heard of anyone in a Service Family committing suicide."

"There are many things in the Thousand Suns you have

never heard of." Brandon's voice gained an edge as he continued. "I suppose you mean that by his action he has deprived the Panarch of his valuable service, eh?"

"He abandoned duty and honor in that action, whatever the reasons. It was not a Decree Dechoukaj, after all, but the lesser *ex gratia regis*, which left him with his estates intact; it was quite merciful." Brandon's face hardened, and Osri felt that he had to justify his statement. "There *are* scandals from time to time, and not every House feels impelled to challenge its malefactors under the Dueling Code. That is why the decretal system exists."

"You don't seem to understand just how extensively he was ruined. In the old, clean terms, his services were no longer required; there was literally nothing left for him to do. Tared was a man to whom the word 'Service' was more than a synonym for privilege. It would have been better if Semion had challenged him and invoked House-rights to lethal weaponry."

A soft tone from the console interrupted Osri's intended rejoinder. The screen displayed an orbit with an unpleasant message overlaid on it: VELOCITY AT ARRIVAL +7.9 KM/SEC. Brandon's hand lay limp on the edge of the keypad for a moment. Even the drugs circulating in Osri's blood couldn't suppress the tremor of fear that those words engendered. They were in a hyperbolic orbit with insufficient delta-V to land on Dis. The passionless equations of spaceflight now left them with two alternatives: a quick death on impact, or slow death as Warlock slung them past Dis into the outer system.

"What now?" he asked acidly.

Brandon shook his head and windowed up the *Starfarer's Handbook* on the screen. A spherical projection of Dis appeared, rotating slowly. In the text scrolling past, Osri noted the words "Lao Shang's Wager," but his head hurt so much that he couldn't focus on the rest of it. Suddenly Brandon nodded and started tapping at his console again. The screen flashed: GRAVITORS 89% MARGIN, TRACKING 1.5%.

To distract himself from an unpleasant feeling of helplessness, Osri brought his mind back to the certainties of that sordid Lusor affair. "Lusor had a reputation for eccentricity, not the least of which was having adopted as his heir a boy from an utterly obscure background, when there were countless excellent families who ask nothing more than to adopt their most promising youth into Service." He shook his head, and regretted the motion. "I remember actions taken without counsel—and the Archon's conversation at Court was often at the borders of acceptability."

"Your father was a friend to that maverick."

Osri said angrily, "You're not suggesting that my father retired from active service because of Lusor's disgrace? It may have been at the same time, but there was no connection. I should know."

"Would you?"

"I know the reasons he retired, and he never mentioned Lusor's disgrace to me at all. My father detests scandal. It was not until I visited my mother on Arthelion that I even learned of it . . ." Osri stopped, aware of having intimidated that the Lady Omilov loved scandal—and aware too, with a part of his mind, that it was true. "However distasteful it was, she felt I should know." He felt the statement die right out of his lips, so weak it was, but Brandon did not press him.

"How much *do* you know?" he asked, genuine interest in his voice.

"As much as anyone, which is very little. Aerenarch Semion, in honor of the L'Ranja name, had not wanted it discussed. Apparently Lusor had confronted the Aerenarch, leveled accusations, *threatened* him."

"Concerning?"

"Concerning his son's dishonorable expulsion from the Academy." This discussion was getting nowhere, thought Osri, and Brandon's feigned ignorance was beginning to annoy him. With a corner of his vision he saw one of the moons swelling slowly in the screen, but his mind still grappled with the events of ten years ago. "What is the point of these questions, Your Highness? You seem to be indicating that Aerenarch Semion was somehow at fault by refusing to challenge the madman!"

Osri was shocked when Brandon answered his rhetorical sarcasm with a simple "Yes."

"You're joking," Osri snapped. "And, if I may add, *Your Highness*, very offensive I find it." He heard a movement behind him—slight, just a shifting, but he was suddenly reminded of the big, grim-faced bodyguard who had accompanied Brandon. Had this man, too, been somehow suborned? Osri winced, wondering if the entire universe had gone mad.

Brandon tapped a few moments more at his console. He paused, then keyed the big go-pad. The navigation overlay froze. He turned finally and looked directly at Osri.

"Do you really believe I'm joking?" asked Brandon. There was no humor at all to be seen in his face now: his eyes were suddenly frighteningly like his father's. The forced disadvantage of this irritated Osri the more. "I can assure you I'm not, no more than I was when I was forced to watch my friend Markham stand before the convened Academy to be formally cashiered."

Osri studied Brandon for a moment, seriously unsettled. His deep respect for the Arkad name, for the almost legendary, much-loved Panarch Gelasaar as well as for his austere, hardworking heir, had been outraged by the events of ten years past, as he understood them. Only then, as he turned back to his screen to collect his thoughts, did he notice the course Brandon had locked in moments ago.

PROBABLE MAXIMUM GEE EXCEEDS HULL RATING. A blinking overlay indicated that the Krysarch had locked out the medical circuits.

"What are you doing?" Osri gasped. He was fed up with his helplessness, outraged by the Krysarch's denial of virtually all Panarchic norms of conduct, and enraged by his inability to do anything to influence events. Now it appeared that Brandon was intent on a spectacular suicide. "Why don't you signal your Rifter friends to pick us up on the way past, instead of digging us a grave at eight klicks?"

Brandon grimaced. "At the speed we whipped through Warlock's atmosphere, it was all the teslas could do to protect the integrity of the hull. One of the things that got shaved off was the directional antenna. We could broadcast a distress call, but do you really want to take a chance on who else might be listening? That ship that chased us here had one hell of a captain, who may have figured out what we're up to. Our only choice is another ablative braking maneuver." His mouth quirked in a rueful smile. "Although I will admit this is a lot dicier. If we make it, I think I'll finally have gotten one up on Markham."

"But how are you going to shed eight klicks? Dis is too small to have enough atmosphere for that, and its gee-well certainly won't do more than warp our course slightly at this velocity."

Brandon snorted a short, humorless laugh. "I'm betting on Lao Shang's Wager. It's a long smear of hydrocarbon ice that's been welling up near the equator for centuries, volcanic in origin, if you can call anything that cold volcanic. Because it's continuously extruding and evaporating, it supposedly stays pretty smooth." He stretched in his pod and raised a hand to his forehead, pinching the bridge of his nose. He dropped his hand and continued. "According to the *Handbook*, Lao Shang was a KaoLai adventurer about three hundred fifty years ago, when they were still mining on Dis, who bet that he could skate its length. That's what we're going to do—we'll trade hull metal for velocity and hope the geeplane and the gravitors last long enough to keep us from being pulped."

Osri squinted at the screen, trying to decipher their course through a haze of pain. It looked like they had just enough reserve maneuvering power to come in parallel to the Wager. If it *was* smooth, they might indeed survive. "What happened to Lao Shang? Did he make it?"

"Supposedly nobody knows. He never showed up to collect, and they never found any trace of him."

Osri started laughing, painfully, hearing the hysteria in his voice but helpless to do anything about it against the giddiness the painkillers had induced. "There's no chance of that happening to us. If we don't make it, we'll leave traces for half a thousand kilometers. They'll probably rename it Arkad's Jigsaw Puzzle when they try to put the pieces back together."

Instead of answering, Brandon closed his faceplate and levered his pod back to crash position. After a moment, Osri did the same and watched in silence as Dis grew steadily larger on the screen.

✳   ✳   ✳

The defense room was much quieter now; the Shield monitors, their usefulness at an end, had been evacuated. The Archonic Enclave was now the only site of resistance, and only a necessary minimum of personnel remained, monitoring internal defense systems to make the final assault of the Rifter invaders as costly as possible. No opposition had been offered to their landing when the Shield had been lowered—the Archon had no wish to subject his people to nuclear bombardment in exchange for a few Rifter vessels. "We can do more damage to them here hand-to-hand and leave the noncombatants out of it," he had said.

Omilov had refused evacuation; there was no place for him to go, since, as incredible as it seemed, he was the object of this invasion. Now he sat on the control dais with the Archon and Bikara, along with a number of guards, clutching the unfamiliar weight of a firejac to his chest, his mind vainly trying to imagine the flight of his son and the Krysarch to safety.

Abruptly the lights went out and all the consoles went dead. The whine of the ventilators spun down the scale into silence and the floor bucked from a nearby explosion. Moments later the sound arrived, a heavy, muted crump. The red emergency illuminators came on, leaving the distant corners of the room wrapped in shadows.

Tanri looked over at Omilov and grinned, a baring of the teeth that mixed militant anticipation with faint amusement. "You should see yourself, Sebastian," he commented. "The most unlikely mixture of martial ardor and gentility one could imagine."

Omilov smiled back, reflecting that the Archon, by contrast, looked every inch the warrior. "I'm afraid that this is the first time I've handled one of these," he replied, hefting the firejac. "I'm not sure I won't be more of a danger with it to our people than the Rifters."

"Don't worry," Tanri said with a chuckle, "that's why we gave you a jac. Just make sure it's set to a medium aperture and, if you can handle a garden hose, you can do as much damage as any of us. They're unlikely to have heavy armor, and nothing else will give them much protection."

He looked back at the door into the defense room as a muffled, rhythmic clanking commenced, then he frowned. The noise wasn't coming from outside the door, but from behind a large metal bulkhead partway down a wall. "They're coming through the equipment tunnel," the Archon commented. He snapped out orders and the defenders rearranged themselves to meet the new threat.

Silence. Omilov could feel the tension rise, peak. His throat spasmed with anxiety, and he wondered if he could really pull the trigger and burn down another human being, no matter how depraved or violent his attacker was.

A screeching roar arrested his thoughts as a spot on the bulkhead suddenly glowed white-hot and vaporized. Another screech; a vortex of blue-white plasma punched through, hovered a moment, then darted viciously toward the nearest console, which promptly exploded, showering the room with molten glass and metal.

At the third discharge of the hidden weapon, the bulkhead blew apart and a finned black muzzle nosed through the hole, the iridescent glimmer of a shield playing around it. Some of the defenders fired at it, but their hand weapons had no effect. Then the plasmoid cannon fired again, and the control dais sagged. Omilov clutched at the seat in front of him for support, and his firejac slid across the floor and over the edge. An explosion blasted at his ears as the door into the defense room blew open; jac-fire from the defenders met the figures leaping in, but not before they lobbed small black spheres over toward the dais and an overwhelming blast of sound and light smashed Omilov into unconsciousness.

❊   ❊   ❊

Dis was huge below them, the stars blurred by its tenuous atmosphere, which was beginning to sing thinly past their hull. As they crossed the terminator into daylight, the shrunken sun picked out a grayish blotch on the distant horizon.

The ship was descending rapidly now; a jagged range of mountains, twisted by the battle between the internal forces of the moon and the tidal forces of Warlock, reached up for them, fell astern. Ahead, Lao Shang's Wager gleamed dully. An overlay popped up over the image on the screen: a short-range radar scan revealing a series of lumps and mounds distorting the surface of the waxy plain. The positional thrusters began a stuttering sequence of discharges, ceased. Then the groaning of the engines rose to a crescendo as the computer overloaded the geeplane to cushion the impact and the moon's surface rose up and swatted them from the sky.

The impact was devastating. All three of them shouted or cried out involuntarily as their suits wrung their limbs, trying to cushion the impact, which seemed to go on and on without end. A flare of light washed through the cabin, the air began to fill with smoke. Osri could feel the gee-forces fluctuating wildly as the gravitors attempted to compensate for the savage deceleration. On the screen the surface whipped past and under them at an insane speed; the thrusters burped and stuttered as the computer tried to avoid the worst of the obstacles. It was failing, and the ship started to come apart.

The viewscreens exploded, plunging the cabin into darkness punctuated only by a surfeit of red lights on the consoles. Then a knife-edge of rock tore through the side of the ship in a shower of sparks, opening it to the sky and narrowly missing Osri's pod. The smoke in the cabin writhed into fantastic shapes as it was sucked out with the air, and the thunderous noise of their ongoing collision with the moon's surface diminished abruptly. Now it was perceptible only through his suit's contact with the pod. The ship was spinning wildly now, all control lost; through the gash torn in the hull Osri could see the waxy plain spinning around them.

As the ship slowed, it finally hit something too large to skim over and abruptly somersaulted. For a moment the gravitors held, so that the ship seemed a point of solidity in a rotating confusion of ground and sky. Then they failed and it was the ship that was gyrating end over end. With one final crushing blow the ship came to rest and Osri blacked out.

He had no idea how long it was before he came to, and he immediately wished he could escape back into unconsciousness. Every part of his body ached, and for a moment he was afraid to move. Then he forced himself to go through the medical litany familiar to every pilot trained at the Academy, where humans and vessels were driven to their limits. *toes*? *fingers*? *turn the head . . . slowly now . . . side to side.* Everything seemed to work, but everything hurt.

He tried to lever his couch upright, but fortunately it didn't respond, since that would have left him canted over facing down. The ship, or what was left of it, had come to rest on its nose. If he wasn't careful he would fall into the remains of his console when he unstrapped himself.

He tongued his com. "Krysarch? Your Highness?" There was no response, not even a hiss of static.

Slowly Osri worked himself out of his pod and struggled over to Brandon, who was still lying back, his head wagging from side to side. Osri bent down and grabbed Brandon's helmet to hold it still, touched his helmet to it.

"Brandon! Can you hear me? Are you all right?"

Brandon groaned. "Yes. No. I think I'm going to puke."

Osri shuddered. He wouldn't wish that on his worst enemy; fortunately, vomiting in a suit was such an ancient and well-founded nightmare that it was well provided for. He found Brandon's medical telltale and triggered a spray of nonauz.

A few minutes later Brandon was free, which meant Deralze was also able to struggle out of his pod. Unsurprisingly the hatch was jammed.

They retrieved their personal effects from the locker and put them in their suits' belt pouches; Osri was relieved to see that his father's artifact had come through the disastrous landing without a scar. When he saw that Brandon had carefully stowed the Archon's ring in his pouch, he triggered the blowout timer. They crouched behind their pods as the hatch bolts exploded and threw it away from the ship.

The twisted hatch spun across the waxy surface of Lao Shang's Wager and fetched up against a low outcropping of wax-encrusted rocks, provoking a small avalanche. The ship rocked and shifted, threatening to come down on the open hatchway; they scrambled desperately for the opening, spilling out onto the ground and slipping wildly away from the ship, which teetered for a moment, finally collapsing with a soundless crunch Osri felt through his feet.

For a moment, no one said anything. Then Osri leaned over and touched his helmet to Brandon's. "What do we do now?"

Brandon shrugged. "We wait. Markham said they had very good sensors—"

"A blind man could have seen that landing," Osri cut in.

"—so we just sit here and wait and hope they get here before our air runs out." Brandon turned toward Deralze, touching his helmet to the big guard's so that they could talk.

Osri turned away and seated himself on a little knoll of wax, his elbows on his knees, holding up his helmet with his hands. It felt like his head was about to come off.

Brandon finished his conversation with the guard, then stood up and looked around. The sun was nearing the horizon; it was small and almost dim enough to look directly at.

A few wispy clouds slid across the sky overhead, where the brighter of the stars could be seen against a deep indigo backdrop. Around them the Wager stretched interminably in every direction, a gently undulating plain of dirty gray wax mixed with rocks.

In the distance, a low range of hills reared against the sky. For a moment, Osri thought he saw a glint of light in them. Brandon seemed to see it too; he walked in that direction, toward the crumpled hatch lying amidst the rubble it had shaken loose from the outcropping. Above it a clean white wall of wax was revealed, as yet unaffected by outgassing. It was distorted into a strange shape, like a globe positioned atop a twisted pillar. Brandon picked up a shard of rock and began to scrape at the globe. A layer of wax abruptly separated and fell away, revealing staring eye sockets behind the faceplate of an archaic helmet.

Lao Shang had lost his wager.

Osri recoiled, feeling almost drunk from the combination of physical trauma and psychic shock. He saw Brandon drop the piece of rock and salute the silent figure whose blind eyes now confronted the dim daylight of Dis for the first time in 350 years.

After a moment Osri reluctantly joined Brandon, leaning over to touch helmets. He heard Brandon say, "Wish us better luck, old one, and we will be back for you someday." Then he turned slowly, his helmet grating against Osri's, looking at him.

Osri spoke, his voice sounding in his own ears wavering, shocky, as though he weren't fully in touch with his surroundings. "It's Lao Shang, isn't it?" Brandon nodded, remaining silent. After a long pause, Osri continued. "Brandon, do you think my father—" He fell silent for a time, then: "Never mind."

Brandon shrugged again. "Wherever he is, it's undoubtedly more comfortable than this."

Then he turned away and joined Deralze, who was scanning the distant hills.

❊   ❊   ❊

Sebastian Omilov sat alone in a jac-scarred room, trying to forget the events of the past hours, but the two bodies lying across from him forced his remembrance all too vividly.

He had awakened to a shocking scene. The Rifters had hamstrung Tanri at both wrists and knees and turned him loose in the room, laughing uproariously as Hreem savaged him with an iron rod. The Archon's white uniform had slowly turned crimson as the Rifter captain crushed his bones, but somehow, Tanri had never lost the dignity that was his real uniform. Omilov would never forget the look on Tanri's face as he turned toward him, near the end, one eye lying across his cheek, but the other shining with unconquerable courage. In the end the Archon had defeated the Rifter: unable to provoke more than a grunt of pain from the dying man, Hreem lost his temper and crushed his skull with a terrible blow.

A few minutes later a Rifter dragged Bikara in and flung her across the room toward the body of her Archon. She fell to her knees and began a terrible keening wail, unbinding her hair as she rocked to and fro. The language was unknown to Omilov, but something in it raised an atavistic thrill in him; it spoke of loss, and coming darkness, and a retribution that would never rest, a vengeance that would reach beyond the grave.

The Rifters felt it too. Hreem snarled a vicious curse and another man grabbed Bikara's hair and jerked her to her feet. Quick as a striking snake, Bikara whirled around, a little knife materializing in her hand. Before anyone could react, she had gutted the man as efficiently as a cook preparing a fish for dinner. The Rifter stood still for a shocked moment, staring stupidly at the greasy coils of his bowels spilling out onto the floor, then crumpled as another man cursed and triggered his firejac, burning Bikara down to collapse in charred ruin across the body of the Archon.

Hreem had directed the others to drag the body of the Rifter out, then turned to Omilov and snarled, "I'd gladly do worse to you, you chatzing blunge-kisser, but someone else's got first claim on you. Wait here—if you even stick your head out the door you'll wish you'd died like them."

After the Rifters left, Omilov had tried to straighten out the bodies of his friends, but Bikara's body threatened to come apart when he tried to move her, and the greasy, crackling texture of her skin made him sick and faint. He wished there were something to cover them with; he didn't want to look at them but it felt somehow disloyal to turn his back on their bodies, so he sat there trying not to see them, waiting for his captors to return.

After an interminable wait, the smell of death and burned flesh thick in his nostrils, contending with the smoke drifting in from the corridor that dried his throat and expanded his thirst until it filled his consciousness, he heard footsteps outside his room.

Moments later a new Rifter came in, a thin man with slightly protruding blue eyes and long hair worn in an old heroic style, with a fastidious air about him. His uniform was gaudy and spotless; he moved with an affected grace that had the contrary effect, to Omilov's eyes, of making him look clumsy. The gnostor caught a waft of some dull, sweet personal scent from him; to his Douloi sensibilities it made the man's appearance even more false.

The Rifter's eyes took in the scene and slid past the two bodies with aversion. He stalked over in front of Omilov so he could turn his back on the unpleasant scene.

"Good morning, Gnostor," he addressed Omilov unctuously, the fingers of one hand resting delicately on his holstered jac. "Did you have a pleasant night?"

Omilov merely looked at him, schooling his face to stillness and then focusing his eyes beyond the back of the man's head in a full-face cut-direct. He recognized this Rifter as a social ontologist, one who got his sense of existence and self-worth from the people around him, and resolved that the man would receive not even a jot of validation from him.

The man's face reddened and his hand tightened on his

jac. "What's the matter, Omilov?" he barked, all suavity gone from his voice. "Wattle got your tongue?" He laughed, a detestable sort of baritone hiccup. "You'll speak freely enough, once we reach Arthelion."

Omilov started. "Arthelion!"

"Right. You've got an audience with the new Panarch."

Omilov swallowed painfully, trying to moisten his parched mouth. Now he was entirely confused. Semion was a harsh man, no doubt, but this passed all belief.

"What does Semion want with me?"

The Rifter emitted another hiccuping laugh. "Semion? Somebody drilled a new blungehole in *him.* No, you'll be speaking to Jerrode Eusabian of Dol'jhar. The Emerald Throne is his now." As Omilov gaped at him in disbelief, the Rifter suddenly reached forward and pulled him off the chair by his tunic. As the gnostor sprawled on the floor the man kicked him to his feet and prodded him toward the door with his jac. "And he doesn't like to wait, so move!"

SIXTEEN

✳

The powered sleds took Deralze by surprise, sweeping down on them from over a low rise a few hundred yards distant. Osri stumbled backward; Deralze noted with approval that Brandon stood slowly and faced their visitors, his hands held a little away from his body.

The sleds pulled up in front of them in a spray of wax. Deralze turned his head aside, as did Brandon, but Osri moved too slowly. He attempted to wipe the wax off his faceplate, but only succeeded in smearing it into near opacity. Deralze grimaced at the thought of how angry that probably made him; he hoped Omilov wouldn't do anything stupid enough to endanger them all.

Though it seemed they were in danger already—at least until they were recognized. The figures waved weapons at them, motioning them into the backs of the sleds. No attempt at communication was made during the ride toward a craggy mountain with no distinguishing features. Deralze was grateful for the delay; exhaustion and the physical reaction to that landing were making it increasingly difficult to think, or to act.

Glancing at the weapons trained on them, he reflected that he might still be required to act, and without the time to think. First he assessed his physical damage. His body ached from skull to heels, but the only pangs that seemed serious were low in his chest. Broken ribs? He hoped Markham had a medtech.

He sat back in the sled, forcing his breathing to slow, his thoughts to focus. As in the vacuum around them, certain things seemed sharply outlined, light against dark without any shade between.

He stared at the back of Brandon's helmet on the sled ahead of his, wishing he could penetrate to the mind beneath. What would he decide? Ranked on one side of the question were the ring and the dour certitude of Osri Omilov; on the other, Deralze and, perhaps, Markham. Deralze smiled grimly—he could debate the balance all he liked, but the outcome would issue now from Markham L'Ranja.

Needless to say, he doesn't use the inheritance sur-prefix anymore. Once again they were outside the laws and vows binding the Panarchy, and Brandon's desire to go on to Ares to discharge his promise might not mass at all with Markham. *Or will he, too, find himself bound by old vows?*

With mild amazement, Deralze suddenly realized that he was assuming that he would follow Brandon to Ares, if the Krysarch made that choice. *No. I still have that decision to make.* If it was a matter of loyalty to the system, the choice was simple: the system had abandoned him. But if it was a matter of personal loyalty . . .

Clear as the light knife-edging the mountain peaks, Deralze saw the truth underpinning the Panarchy: everything, in the end, came down to personal loyalty, and the responsibility it engendered in return. Another of the Jaspran Polarities echoed in his mind. *Holder of oaths, in loyalty sworn, the circle of fealty, a weight to be borne.* It was only when the polarity of loyalty and responsibility was forgotten—the circle of fealty that Semion had overlooked—that the system broke down.

That had been the true source of his anger; not that the system had betrayed him, but that the Arkads had. *But Brandon didn't, nor did his father. It was a failure of knowledge, not duty.*

The sled suddenly swerved between two twisted pillars of rock, and Deralze looked up to find them headed straight for a rock wall without any abatement of speed. He braced himself for the smash that seemed inevitable.

They were scarcely a hundred meters from the black stone rising from the moon's dusty surface when a camouflaged door lifted. They sped inside, braking smoothly. The door closed behind them, locking them in darkness.

Hands pulled Deralze from the sled and pushed him forward. He gritted his teeth against the protest of strained muscles, and a sharp pain in his chest caused him to stumble over the uneven ground. He stopped when a hand forced him to.

Light flared on; he saw that they were in a lock. The figures in the dark suits stood motionless for a time. He looked over at Brandon, but saw little of the anticipation in his face that he expected. Instead, the Krysarch's face was tight with fatigue and something else that Deralze couldn't read. Deralze's stomach knotted as he saw Brandon finger the pouch at his waist. *He's decided, then.* For a moment he saw Gelasaar's face superimposed on his son's; ambivalence gripped him. The circle was closing, and he had only a little time to decide whether it would close him in or out.

One of the figures guarding them suddenly removed his helmet, breaking the mood, and Deralze saw a man of about forty years, wearing a close-trimmed beard. His expression was grim as he reached out to tap Brandon's helmet.

A loud tap on his own helmet startled Deralze. He turned, staring into the round face of a woman, feeling momentary revulsion at her atavistically pale skin with its sprinkling of small splotches of melanin. Her bristly red hair was cut close to her head in the manner of a lifetime spacer. She motioned for him to remove his helmet, and Deralze, noting that she had not put away the weapon in her hand, moved carefully to comply. Out of the corner of his eye he saw Osri do the same, his stance radiating resentment.

"Got any weapons, surrender 'em here," the man said, while another collected their helmets and their gloves; they were now effectively imprisoned, Deralze realized.

Brandon shook his head, and Osri said in an accusing tone, "We are not armed."

Nevertheless, the woman and a big, scar-faced man moved close to conduct a search. Deralze noted the impersonal way their captors handled them; their roughness exacerbated the pain from his numerous bruises. The scar-faced man's touch on his chest made his breath catch against his back teeth.

The Rifter confronting Osri paused when he searched his pouch, frowning when he touched the Heart of Kronos. "What's this?"

"It's not a weapon," Osri said. "It's an ancient curio. I collect such things."

"Oughta be worth something."

The man started to pocket it, but the woman said, "Captain wants to see everything they brought with 'em."

"Right." The man dropped the sphere back into Osri's pouch.

The woman searching Brandon held his ring up to the light admiringly, then tossed it back to him with a look eloquent of distrust. He grabbed it out of the air and slipped it onto his ring finger.

Then the woman hit a control and a door slid open. They started into a tunnel carved into the dark rock of the moon. The air smelled clean, with a faint trace of some organic substance, like polish or solvent. Osri sneezed loudly, and Deralze winced as he imagined what that must have felt like if Osri's head ached anything like his.

Skipnose, eh? He'd traveled so much since the L'Ranja affair that he'd ceased to suffer from the congestion and mild allergies that often attended the transition from one planet or habitat to another. But Osri no doubt traveled only on commercial flights, which were careful to change the air gradually during skip to avoid the sudden transition that triggered skipnose. The courier skiff had had no such provision in it. *The ships I've been on weren't very careful about that.* Deralze felt his lips quirk; somehow the idea of Omilov fighting skipnose after that spectacular landing amused the hell out of him.

"This way." The bearded man jabbed Deralze in the shoulder blade, and he moved to the left, down a long tunnel lit at intervals with cold miner's lights. He felt clumsy in the lower gravity of the moon; the stiffening of his muscles made it difficult to compensate. A glance around revealed that Brandon and Osri were having similar difficulties.

After a time the tunnel widened, and Deralze saw doors at intervals. The doors varied in size and design. Besides the expected dyplast, he saw one carved wooden door, carefully fitted into the rock, and next to it a tapestry, faded with age, affixed to the stone.

Occasionally people crossed their path, no two wearing similar clothing. Some stopped to look at them with interest, but most ignored them. Deralze sensed a discipline among these Rifters that had often been lacking in the circles he'd traveled in recently: the result of Markham's Academy training, no doubt. He wondered what other differences would become apparent.

They entered a huge cavern without warning, and their tunnel became a catwalk for a time, suspended high above other catwalks crisscrossing the airy cave. At the ground level a dark stream ran hissing through its millennia-carved canal.

They entered another cavern, this one smaller, when a voice ripped out at them: "You can leave the spies here. And get out."

Adrenaline shot through Deralze as he saw the tension suddenly possessing their escorts. This was not part of their plan. He looked over at Brandon, who was scanning the shadows; Osri glanced this way and that, obviously confused, not knowing where to look to find their danger.

Deralze shifted his weight to the balls of his feet. He took advantage of their captors' distraction and edged forward slightly, placing himself in front of and to the side of the Krysarch. He still couldn't see the source of the voice, nor any of the allies it undoubtedly had.

The Beard said, "Orders were to bring 'em to Vi'ya."

"We're gonna teach Vi'ya who's giving orders, just as soon as we—"

The voice broke off as Brandon spoke clearly, projecting his voice with all the authority inculcated by his Douloi upbringing.

"Alt L'Ranja gehaidin!" he said. "We have safe passage from Markham."

There was absolute silence, broken only by the distant sound of dripping water. The red-haired woman looked intently at Brandon, took a step toward him. Deralze felt his hair rise and his senses intensify painfully as the tension in the cavern sharpened to the cusp of imminent action.

A wiry, gaunt-faced man stepped out from the uneven shadows across the cavern, riveting the gaze of their escort. Deralze forced himself to look around, knowing from years of experience that that could not be the main threat, and was rewarded by a glimpse of movement in a shadowy alcove to the side. A gleam of metal flickered above the matte-black deadliness of a firejac muzzle coming to bear on the Krysarch.

At that moment twenty years of service, ten years of anger, and the knowledge that his vows of loyalty had been true kindled in him a passionate clarity of purpose.

He launched himself forward, and the circle closed on him in a blast of burning pain.

Osri gasped as their bearded escort suddenly shoved him violently and triggered his jac at a half-seen figure off to one side. Energy beams lanced out abruptly from several directions. The big guard threw himself in front of Brandon, intercepting a needle-thin beam of plasma with a hoarse shout of agony; another lance of sunfire brushed the red-haired woman, who dropped her jac and curled around her wound, her breathing harsh.

"Lenic!" Brandon's shout echoed as he crouched above the big man's body.

Then he whirled about and snatched up the fallen jac dropped by the wounded redhead. His low-gee clumsiness betrayed him into a stumble over the supine Rifter, saving his life as another beam sizzled past. Then he recovered his footing, twisting around, and triggered the jac to wide aperture.

The gaunt man who'd challenged them dived behind a rocky projection as the beam from Brandon's weapon swept across the Rifter who'd shot Deralze, blowing him apart in a bloody explosion of steam and viscera.

Osri watched, frozen in shock, as the gaunt Rifter popped back up and snapped off a shot at the Krysarch, who didn't even duck as the beam speared past his head. Brandon returned the fire, splattering molten rock from the crag sheltering his attacker, while behind him, the Beard fired at unseen opponents further back in the cavern. Low-gee slowness gave the movements of the combatants the quality of a deadly dance. Another blast shattered the stone near Osri's head; the smell of ozone and burning rock made him sneeze several times, his heart hammering in his chest.

There was a moment's pause, then, with a savage laugh that Osri could hardly believe had issued from the Krysarch's throat, Brandon raised his jac, as if in salute to his opponent, and triggered it into the air. The beam lanced up into the rocky ceiling far overhead, provoking a major collapse. The gaunt Rifter emitted a panicky shout and leapt forward from his concealment as, with a thunderous roar, several tons of rock and debris fell on him with deceptive low-gee slowness and smashed him to the floor. Thick streams of blood slowly oozed out from between the rocks;

with a final gentle tapping a few pebbles rattled down the sides of the sudden cairn marking the Rifter's demise.

Silence fell, interrupted only by the moaning of the injured woman, and stertorous breathing from Deralze. Brandon crouched above the guard's body, whose lips moved: he was trying to speak.

The bearded Rifter moved up behind the Krysarch and prodded him with his jac. Osri blinked in disbelief as Brandon swiveled about and felled the man with a sudden high-level Ulanshu kinesic that he had never seen before. Then the Krysarch turned back to Deralze, ignoring the Rifters gathering ahead of them.

When they made no move, Osri's brain, which seemed to be working as slowly as movement in the low-gee environment, realized that Brandon was sheltered from their direct attack by the jumble of debris that had buried the gaunt Rifter, and that his weapon was pointed at the rocky roof over their heads.

Standoff, thought Osri with relief, forgetting his own danger, and then reality returned to include him in the tableau as rough hands dragged him from his refuge and prodded him into the open at the end of a jac.

Every aspect of the scene around Brandon lit with sharp-edged clarity as the boiling red rage ebbed. He barely managed to maintain a grip on his weapon as a wave of trembling swept through him.

"We've got your friend," shouted someone. "Throw down your weapon or we'll fry him."

Brandon looked over and saw Osri stumble into the open, a jac-muzzle tracking him from a crack in the cavern wall. The astrogator stopped and stared dumbly at Brandon, his eyes dull with fatigue and shock.

A sudden movement in the corner of his vision warned Brandon. He turned and triggered a blast over the head of a Rifter bolder than the others, who jumped back into concealment with a pained shout, his hair smoldering from the near miss.

"Keep them away or I'll bring the whole damned cavern down on us all," Brandon shouted.

A harsh gasping drew his gaze downward; Lenic was pressing both hands against the charred ruin of his lower chest while blood bubbled between his fingers. Brandon crouched next to him, tentatively reaching for the big man's hands, but Lenic shook his head fiercely.

"No," he gasped. "If I let go, can't talk."

Brandon realized that Lenic was preventing the collapse of his lungs by main force, and had very little time left. He opened his mouth to speak, but Lenic interrupted, gasping out the words with pain-filled pauses in between to gather breath.

"Listen. Markham. Asked me. To check on you. But I." He shook his head. "I'm sorry. Trust him." His head rolled back, his lips skinning back from his teeth. "He didn't know ... Ivory ..." His body spasmed in a final protest and then he relaxed into death.

Brandon's vision narrowed, sweeping away the cavern around him into a shadowy half-existence peopled by murmuring shades. Lenic's face was peaceful now, as though he had discharged a final obligation, but the half-seen figures now thronging the halls of Brandon's mind were unappeased, some disconsolate, whispering of betrayal. He heard a woman sobbing: a vision of blue-gray eyes beneath auburn hair flitted through his mind.

A man's voice next, cultured, speaking in measured tones without words; but he, too, was gone. Dark eyes in a dark face then; the ring on his finger pulsed with brief heat as that one, too, was swept away. He sensed Lenic's shade joining these others, but it was silent, and then they merged with the shadows, abandoning him again, and he was alone.

He looked up then, into the fathomless dark eyes of a tall woman dressed in a plain black jumpsuit. Dark skin, slanted eyes, and hip-length black hair pulled back into a tail high on her head indicated a youngish age. Her expression was cool and composed as she gazed at him. Her hands were empty, relaxed at her side. She said nothing.

"Markham," he said, or tried to say. The name came out, but no sound. She looked at him in silence for a long moment, her dark eyes steady, her brows lifting with faint question.

"Markham is dead," she said at last, and the final shreds of meaning drained out of the scene around him.

Osri heard her words and felt his knees weaken. His back crawled in anticipation of the blast that would end his life. There was nothing to stop these savages from burning them down if the Krysarch's friend was dead, and Brandon's face had showed no sign of yielding when Osri's captors had shoved him into the open. Osri felt empty as he waited for death.

Brandon slowly stood up, his firejac held forgotten at his side. At a sudden shuffle of movement in the shadows the woman made a slight, sharp gesture of command. The movement behind her ceased.

"Dead?" repeated Brandon, his voice hoarse.

"He was betrayed and shot down a year ago by Hreem the Faithless." She paused. "He told me of you, Brandon nyr-Arkad. I will honor his safe passage." She looked down at the slowly crusting pool of blood leaking from underneath the rock fall. "And you have done me a service here." There was a faint accent underlying her words, but Osri could not identify it.

The woman leaned forward and took the jac from the Krysarch's unresisting hand.

"Take Greywing to med and get someone with a dozer to scrape up this mess." She spoke past Brandon to the man with the beard, who had struggled to his feet. "Have someone deal with Paysud; he ran off down adit three."

Through his mind-throttling fatigue Osri realized that the woman had just won some sort of intragroup struggle.

Brandon made an abortive move, as if in protest.

"We will honor your friend as one of us," she said, motioning toward Deralze's body, and Brandon relaxed.

Someone pushed Osri forward.

"Who's this?" the woman asked. "A servant?"

Osri stiffened and immediately regretted it. "I am Osri Ghettierus vlith-Omilov, Instructor of Navigation at the Minerva Naval Academy." He used his most plangent tone, as if disciplining a servant, but she took no notice.

"Come with me," the woman said abruptly.

She walked out, not turning to see if they followed. Osri looked sideways at the Krysarch and saw the raw emotions of the past few minutes slowly receding as his Douloi training reasserted itself.

Then Osri caught a glimpse of something white moving out of the shadows. He saw two figures gliding into the light and sustained yet another shock.

Disbelief warred with terror as he recognized the small figures with short ice-white fur and huge, faceted eyes. Open mouths with tiny teeth shone blue inside; the creatures had two arms, but the fingers were webbed at the base and long and twiggy at the tips. They moved in unison, wearing identical transparent garments, folded in a complicated pattern over one shoulder and fastened at the waist by ornate jeweled belts.

Osri had seen them in a holo once: these child-sized creatures with eyes like jewels were deadly psionic killers. They called themselves Eya'a.

Osri dropped back a pace or two as the creatures glided across the cavern and disappeared through the main archway. The woman followed more slowly. Osri fell in behind, his mouth dry from fear. He noticed that the Rifters gave the beings wide berth, which was small comfort.

Out on the catwalk, Osri saw the woman pause. The Eya'a halted, and the three stood quietly for a moment; in some sort of silent communication, Osri realized.

He shut his eyes for a moment, wishing that the booster had killed them on impact. It would have been a cleaner death than what seemed imminent here. Then, as the Eya'a went on ahead, leaving the woman on the catwalk, he followed Brandon as she motioned them forward.

A short time later they entered a small room rough-hewn

from living rock. The uneven ceiling curved a few feet above their heads, and the stone walls displayed splendid tapestries from a variety of worlds. Several woven rugs had been scattered over the meltstone floor, and a low carved darkwood table sat in the center of the room with a bank of riotously embroidered velvet pillows around it. The three glow-lamps that lit the room were supported by gracefully wrought gold rods, and in a corner, almost unnoticeable, was a detailed *jatta*-tooth carving of a mythical beast, a winged feline of some sort, just taking flight.

It was breathtakingly beautiful, seeming to have movement and no weight; Osri felt a slow burn of anger as he studied this priceless ornament and wondered who the rightful owner had been.

"Sit down," the woman said. "I want to talk to you before deciding what's to be done with you."

Brandon sank down, somewhat stiffly, and after a moment Osri joined him with overt reluctance. As he did so, a gleam of white caught at the corner of his vision. He was unpleasantly startled to see the two Eya'a glide into the room. They shouldered an edge of a wall tapestry aside and disappeared behind it without making any sound or even a glance at the humans; the woman paid no attention to them as she opened a paak-wood cabinet situated in a carved alcove, and brought out a crystal decanter and glasses.

"Something to drink?" she murmured, seating herself across from them and setting decanter and glasses on the table.

Osri watched in tight-lipped disgust as Brandon immediately reached for the decanter and poured out a full glass. The woman turned to Osri, brows raised slightly. He made a curt gesture of refusal; with a faint, disinterested shrug, she poured herself some of the wine. He could smell the drink; somehow, it had a green odor, faintly sweet and fresh.

Brandon drank down his wine and poured himself some more. His Douloi mask was fully back in place; he sipped his wine and looked around at the room with an air of definite approval. He turned to the woman. "Who are you? You are in command here?"

"I am." She tipped her head back toward the Eya'a and added, "They call me Vi'ya." That peculiar accent was there again, very faint, in the way she pronounced the name: a nearly voiceless *th* between the *i* and the *y*. No one else Osri heard subsequently pronounced it that way. " 'The One Who Hears.' " Her lips curved in a faint smile.

"You assumed command after Markham's death, I take it?" Brandon went on mildly.

"He left his organization to me." Her dark eyes flicked over both their faces before she continued. "You witnessed the last of the resistance today. Old Jakarr was a fair pilot but, despite his ambitions, a poor leader."

"And a poor follower." Brandon's smile was wide. He was sitting back against his pillows, completely relaxed, as he sipped at his wine.

"And a poor follower," the woman repeated, still smiling.

Osri shifted uncomfortably on his cushion, trying unsuccessfully to find a position that didn't hurt. He feared if he sat too long he'd be unable to get up; the painkillers were wearing off.

Once again, unbelievably, they had been spared from what Osri thought was imminent destruction. He didn't trust these Rifters much past his next breath, but somewhere under his indignation at being forced into this situation at all, he realized that it was unlikely even Rifters would bother talking to people they planned to shoot out of hand.

So what to do now? Osri watched Brandon raise his glass and study the amber liquid against one of the glow-lamps, and shifted again on his pillows, this time in impotent but growing irritation. Brandon seemed to recollect his presence and said helpfully, "Have some, Osri. Probably need it, after that flight."

"I do not wish for any liquor," Osri stated shortly.

Brandon transferred his gaze to the ceiling and said musingly, "Cool . . . light . . . not unlike an old mead, but slightly herbal in flavor. Dark amber color . . . definitely not synthetic. What is it?" He turned at last to Vi'ya.

"It's called simply Locke, and a number—ILVI, I believe. From Cincinnatus Secundus. It's regarded quite highly in that octant."

"New to me." Brandon regarded the beautifully cut glass in appreciation, then drank. "Where'd you find it?"

"Rifthaven." Amusement glimmered in her dark eyes at the sour look Osri gave her. She added, "The chef on *Telvarna* bought it."

Brandon promptly launched into a comparison with other fine wines, as if they were at an afternoon gathering in a manor on Nyangathanka. Osri gritted his teeth, trying to suppress his growing annoyance. What was this fool thinking of, nattering like a parrot about wines? Despite the jac at her belt, Osri felt certain he and Brandon acting together could overpower this Rifter woman before she could unclip it and take aim. And with the weapon they would have a chance at fighting their way to a ship . . .

Brandon paused to pour another glass and Osri glanced up to find the woman's black, slanted eyes fixed directly on his, as expressionless as two stones. Warning tightened the back of his neck, and suddenly he remembered those accursed little white-furred killers. Where were they, in an adjoining room? Listening? He didn't know if their reputed psi powers were limited to what they could see—and he was disinclined to test them. Then a fresh surge of rage burned through him at the thought of these light-abandoned Rifter vermin with psionic killers in leash.

The woman addressed him abruptly. "The Eya'a scanned you when you landed and reported that an extremely powerful psi device was on board. We searched the remains of your ship after you were brought out of it, and the device was gone. Now they indicate it is here. What is it?" She held out a hand.

Osri sank back slightly against his pillows, gazing at her in anger and dismay.

She waited, motionless, for a long moment, then she said softly, "Must I take it from you?"

"It's called the Heart of Kronos," Brandon offered conversationally. Osri shot him a glare of acute disgust, which he met with a bland smile before he added, "That's all we know. We were trying to keep it from Hreem's hands, at the request of Osri's father. The Eya'a should be able to tell you more than we can, if they were able to identify it and us."

Vi'ya said, "The Eya'a are not able to identify it, they merely sensed its presence. Nor did they identify you: they cannot tell strange humans apart. I know who you are because Markham talked of you often, and I have seen your image on coinage and scrip." She transferred her gaze to Osri and once again held out her hand. "If I give an order," she stated calmly, "I expect it to be obeyed." There was no overt threat in her tone, but that elusive accent gave a subtle and disturbing twist to certain words.

Osri frowned mutinously, glared at Brandon once, seeking support, only to meet a very quizzical grin. With a smothered exclamation he jammed his hand into the pouch at his belt, pulled out the Heart of Kronos, then dropped it on the table before Vi'ya, ignoring her hand.

She watched the dully gleaming sphere slip to the darkly polished wood and rest there as if it had been glued, then reached to take it in her hands. Her fingers closed around it and she said softly, "I am a tempath, Schoolboy, so not only watch what you do, watch what you think."

Another burr of shock zapped through Osri. A tempath! He knew little about such emotional sensitives, but shared the widespread distrust of them common in the Thousand Suns. It was said that there were only two kinds of tempaths: those who restrained their powers—these often found their way into the Order of the Sanctus Lleddyn—and those who yielded to them and used them to dominate the people around them.

Osri's cheeks darkened and he ground his teeth against making any reply. He was fairly sure what kind of tempath a Rifter would be. Vi'ya ignored him as she tested the properties of the Heart of Kronos for a few seconds. Then she turned to Brandon. "Where were you taking this?"

"Away from Hreem." Brandon gestured with his crystal goblet, whose facets glittered and flashed in the light of the globes. He appeared unfazed by the revelation of Vi'ya's emotion-sensing talent.

"You were bringing it to Markham?" she persisted.

Brandon had reached to fill his glass again, an occupation which appeared to claim all his attention; before he was done the tapestry through which they'd entered the room was suddenly batted aside and a small, round female with a cloud of frizzy blond hair dashed in. She was barefoot, and wore baggy, worn overalls with several unmatching utility pockets sewn haphazardly on, stuffed with all manner of precision tools. Other tools were clipped to her belt. She had a young, sharp-featured face, darting bright eyes, and a smile of pure mischief.

She greeted the three occupants of the room with a flash of one hand and declaimed in a high, fluting voice, "Vi'ya! You won't believe what I saw!"

Vi'ya glanced up over her shoulder, her hands still playing with the Heart of Kronos, an eyebrow quirked in inquiry.

"I was watchin' our friends on the cruiser—let'm see me as usual so they'd know we got the message from ol' Tanri—then all of a sudden they skipped out. Followed a hunch and hopped over toward Charvann, just in time to see the *Korion* blown to photons by the *Lith*. One skipmissile!"

Vi'ya's eyes widened slightly. "A cruiser, Marim?"

Marim flung her arms wide in a quick gesture. "Blown away. Panarchists zapped a couple of ships though, later, when these two took off"—she motioned toward Brandon and Osri—"but with whatever Hreem's got, Charvann isn't gonna hold out too long, and we'd better hope Hreem never finds this place. He could crack Dis open like a month-old *moong*-egg."

"Pick up anything on Brotherhood code?"

"Only some orders. *Esteel*'s out there. No, was. Buncha small fry. And the *Satansclaw*."

Vi'ya gave a soft laugh. "Tallis Y'Marmor—allied with Hreem the Faithless?"

The little blond scout chortled. "It was an order to Tallis I got, and you were right—only one mention, but that was enough."

"Dol'jhar," Vi'ya murmured, her accent and intonation darkening the word.

Osri shifted again on his pillows and frowned, and the scout's eyes flickered rodent-like. Then she grinned and turned to face the two men. "You gave Tallis quite a ride there. Last I saw, he was still tryin' to pull out of orbit around Warlock!"

Vi'ya said, with a hint of amusement, "Marim, allow me to present to you Osri the Instructor, from the Panarchist Naval Academy, and Krysarch Brandon nyr-Arkad."

Osri was, and knew he looked, deeply offended at the several breaches of protocol made in this introduction, but Brandon only smiled into Marim's gaping face and said pleasantly, " 'Brandon' will do."

Marim grinned and went on, head cocked bird-like as she surveyed him with bright interest, "Arkad? Today's the day for special visitors, looks like. First that blunge-bag Hreem and then a royal whatsit."

She turned to Osri. "You piloting?"

He shook his head, not trusting his voice. The scout's casual confirmation of an understanding of sorts between these riffraff and the Archon of Charvann had further shaken his grasp of the verities of life in the Thousand Suns.

"You?" she asked, turning back to Brandon with disbelief writ large on her face. "You'd definitely be wasted holdin' down a throne, or whatever it is you high-end nicks do with yourselves. I saw you escape from that blunge-brain Tallis with an ablative across Warlock. Thought you'd burned it for sure—who taught you to fly?"

"Markham," Brandon replied, watching the grin disappear from Marim's face. Marim glanced at Vi'ya, who was studying the Heart of Kronos as if she had not heard.

"Best pilot I ever knew." Marim's thin shoulders jerked up in a shrug, then she turned and swatted the tapestry aside again. "Goin' to grab some eats," she announced, and she was gone.

Vi'ya looked up and continued, "Where were you going before you lost your fiveskip?"

"Arthelion," Brandon offered. Osri noticed his index finger rubbing absently across the knuckles of his other hand. Vi'ya's eyes took in this gesture, and Brandon's blandly pleasant face, then she added, "Your ship's autopilot was destroyed, its information irretrievable. I checked that as well."

Osri saw that she had sensed his sudden relief by the way the woman's eyes narrowed with equally sudden amusement. He clenched his jaw, determined to talk no more, achingly aware, too, that it didn't matter whether he did or not.

"So you came here to request help from Markham," she went on. "In what form?"

Brandon set his glass down. His face gave no clue to his thoughts. After a long pause he said slowly, "Markham would have put me on a ship to wherever I wished to go."

"That's true," the woman acknowledged with surprising promptness, and then, with humor crinkling her dark eyes, "and your reminder of the loyal and inspiring bond of friendship is calculated to elicit a similar response from me, yes?"

"Well, either that or a snarling threat to sell us to the highest bidder," Brandon countered with apparently equal good humor. "Affording us a clue to our status."

Vi'ya said abruptly, "Any enemy of Hreem the Faithless is a potential ally of mine. Tell me what it is you want, and I will consider what is to be done."

"Passage to Arthelion," Brandon stated immediately. "I don't know if a courier was able to leave Charvann, and even if it did, it probably didn't head for Arthelion. We must report on what we have seen . . . and take that"—he nodded at the silver sphere—"to safety." He leaned forward then and said with an engaging grin, "I can make the trip very worthwhile—consider it a ransom."

She gave a soft laugh. "A ransom for royalty? A Rifter's dream, yes?" She leaned forward to pick up the Heart of Kronos, then rose to her feet. "You may wait here. I will not be long." She paused at the tapestry and added with a shade of grimness in her voice, eyes fixed on Osri, "Perhaps I should say you *will* wait here. The Eya'a are in the adjoining room, as you surmised, and they are watching."

Then she left them alone.

"She took my father's artifact," Osri whispered with fierce frustration. "May I respectfully point out, Your Highness, that your erstwhile *friends* might be bluffing about those aliens?" He lowered his voice, casting a quick glance at the tapestry through which the Eya'a had disappeared, then he made a gesture pantomiming grabbing a weapon and using it.

Brandon leaned back against his cushions and laughed. There was a faint flush of color along the high ridge of his cheekbones, and his eyes were bright. Osri saw instantly that the liquor had hit him hard—and no wonder: they hadn't eaten since that dinner at the Hollows, and had had only a few hours' sleep . . . if Brandon, who had gone to Merryn wearing the same clothes he'd dined in at dinner, had slept at all. When Brandon laughed, Osri's annoyance increased. *Danger not just to me, but to my father's artifact—and I'm stuck with this drunken lackwit whose life I've sworn to protect.*

He spoke crisply, hoping to sting the Krysarch into some semblance of awareness of his duty: "You will pardon my obtuseness, but I fail to observe anything humorous in our present circumstances."

"Relax, Osri," Brandon said. His voice was surprisingly clear, but Osri noted with sour satisfaction that skipnose seemed to have hit him too. "There isn't much we can do about those circumstances yet." And as Osri cast another look at the tapestry across the room, Brandon half raised a hand to silence him. "What were you doing during your Academy combat-training days? Or did you opt out of it in favor of administrative refinements?"

"I was instructed in the same basic program you yourself should have undergone—"

"If you've had level-one Ulanshu training, you should have seen that even without the help of her psionic killers she could have taken care of both of us herself."

Disbelief made Osri forget his alien eavesdroppers. "*Two* of us?"

"So you didn't see it. Perhaps it is not so obvious, then . . . to one who did not see fit to augment the Academy Administrative Program's remedial physical-training regimen. I did, Osri"—Brandon's smile became acid—"with my friend Markham. Who may, incidentally, have trained this woman. I saw it immediately in the way she sat, the posing of her hands. What would have happened to you is academic; a crushed windpipe, I think, and to me—a myriad of possibilities, the best of which would be the weapon drawn on me. The length of the table would have prevented her from having to exert herself unnecessarily. Which is why she sat where she did."

Osri flushed again, uncomfortably, then looked around to see if they were being overheard, since Brandon had not troubled to lower his voice. He looked up to say something but found Brandon's gaze fixed distantly: to his amazement, the third Arkad son raised a refilled glass of the wine and said softly, "Be well, Markham," and drank.

PART THREE

✳

SEVENTEEN

✳

ARTHELION ORBIT

The smoke from the incense rose in a straight column through the still air, its sweet-sour scent hanging heavy in the room. Subtle curves and flutings twisted in its diaphanous substance, drawing Anaris' eyes upward until they met the empty gaze of his grandfather's skull above the family altar. His knees smarted from his long vigil on the metal deck, but he ignored the pain, waiting.

The room was cold and dark, lit only by the candles smelted from his grandfather's flesh by his son Jerrode, now established in triumph on the planet below. Behind him he could hear the subtle sound of cloth on cloth as someone shifted uneasily, a quiet clink of metal from where Kyvernat Juvaszt stood, and the unsteady breathing of the others in attendance.

This was the *eglarhh hre-immash*, the laying of the vengeful ghost, placating the restless spirit of Urtigen gyarrh'ka Eusabian, who had died at the hands of his son twenty-nine years before. Every month since, 363 times, Jerrode Eusabian had sacrificed to deflect his father's vengeance, offering both blood and the justification of a successful rule. Only these could avert the anger of the restless dead, condemned to watch in silence for thirty-three years before going on to join the honored ancestors in the Halls of Dol.

But now, consumed by the completion of his paliach—the greatest in the history of Dol'jhar—in the Emerald Throne Room of the Mandala, Eusabian had delegated the eglarhh to his son. By tradition and law only a direct descendant could lay the ghost of one so powerful as Urtigen had been, for he had carried the spirit of Dol within him as an Avatar.

Anaris smiled coldly at the skull, knowing that those around him would dare not look up on his face during the ceremony. *You and I, Grandfather, will encompass his downfall. This is his first mistake.* For Eusabian did not know the greatest gift the Panarchists had given him, opening the secret gate of his mind.

Anaris gathered his will and breathed deeply, drawing in the pungent scent of the incense. Then he rose to his feet and bowed over the copper sacrifice bowl in front of him, now glowing red from the coals beneath it, coals he had formed himself of charcoal and a pinch of dust from Urtigen's thighbone. Then he picked up the lancet and poised it over his left wrist, over the heart vein.

"Darakh ettu mispeshi, Urtigen-dalla. Darakh ni-palia entasz pendeschi, pron hemma-mi ortoli ti narhh." Visit us with your mercy, great Urtigen. Visit not with vengeance your lineage, take instead this my blood that once was yours.

He plunged the lancet into the vein, twisting it to release a stream of dark blood into the bowl. It hissed and spat as it struggled with the hot metal; the smell of burning blood filled the room, dark as vengeance, pungent as fear. Smoke rose from the bowl as Anaris let fall the lancet and concentrated fiercely.

Then, slowly, the smoke formed itself into the semblance of two hands, long thin fingers writhing into a benison above his head. The hands hovered for a moment, then dissipated. The skull twitched.

Through the buzzing of a fearsome headache, Anaris heard a sharp intake of breath from the others in the room, then a burst of awed whispers. *"Urtigen mizpeshi! Anaris darakh-kreshch!"* The mercy of Urtigen! Anaris anointed!

Anaris propped himself on one fist and looked over his shoulder, fighting his fatigue and the growing nausea his efforts had induced. Glaring the watchers into silence, he issued a command. "Say nothing of this. It is between the ancestor and myself."

They bowed, the protracted obeisance of the utterly sincere; even the kyvernat, technically his superior, with the power of life and death over all on the ship, was abashed before him.

"Now go." He turned back to face the altar and waited, rigidly still, until the door hissed shut behind them. Then he crossed the huge room at a run, barely making it to the lavatory before his stomach revolted and he was rackingly sick.

He rinsed out his mouth and washed his face, still nauseous from the blinding pain in his head. As he raised his head, he caught sight of his face in the mirror, its normal dusky tone paled to a dirty chalk, his eyes red, the veins in his forehead distended.

The gift of the Panarchists, he thought, remembering the strange woman from the College of Synchronistic Perception and Practice who had tested him and discovered his t'kinetic ability. He remembered also his disappointment at its weakness—not for him the tearing out of an enemy's heart or the crushing of his larynx. He could barely move a piece of paper or divert the path of an insect, even after the extensive training she had given him.

But they also taught me subtlety. It was the Ulanshu Kinesics, the art of using strength against itself, that first opened his eyes to the equations of power. And he remembered the final audience with the Panarch, before he returned to Dol'jhar. *"Brute force can only kill, it cannot conquer,"* Gelasaar had said, his blue eyes searching, as if trying to discern how much of the soul before him was Panarchist, and how much still Dol'jharian. The Panarch spoke quietly, using none of the formal honorifics, as if laying aside his rank to speak heart-to-heart, but to Anaris' eyes his power had still shown through, like the heat from an unquenchable furnace. *"I could have reduced Dol'jhar to a flaming pyre, inhabited only by the restless dead, with no one to placate them—but what would that have gained me? I prefer the scalpel to the bludgeon; a lesson your father has yet to learn."*

Anaris straightened up slowly. *A lesson that will destroy my father in the end, for he is but a blunt instrument in the hands of destiny.* He smiled at his reflection. *So, Gelasaar, perhaps it should be* your *ghost to whom I sacrifice, once I sit upon the Emerald Throne.*

He left the lavatory and stood a moment before the altar. The candles flickered from his movement, the shadows in his grandfather's eye sockets shifting eerily. Even his father was helpless against the superstitions of Dol'jhar. Indeed, they were an essential part of his power.

Favored of Urtigen. Anaris laughed, and winced at the pain. That was something else he owed the Panarchists, owed, in fact, the now-dead youngest son. It had been one of the most complex of his insulting pranks that had purged Anaris once and for all of his belief in the afterlife, freeing him to turn those beliefs against his father. Now, despite his command, the word would spread.

Best of all, no word would come of this to his father; who would dare his wrath at the suggestion that the shades of the ancestors favored his son?

Anaris leaned forward and snuffed out the candles. Then he caressed the skull, smiling mirthlessly, and left the room.

❋   ❋   ❋

ARTHELION

Eusabian stood before the Phoenix Gate of the Emerald Throne Room, his hands on his hips, staring up at the colossal doors before him. Inlaid into their surface in a complex mosaic of precious metals and minerals was the image of a Phoenix enwrapped in flames, its eyes gleaming in ecstatic triumph. He had waited for this moment for twenty years, and he savored each slowly passing second.

Not long ago he had landed with his vanquished enemy in train. Shortly he would humble Gelasaar hai-Arkad in the center and symbol of his power, but first, the Lord of Vengeance and Avatar of Dol would take possession of the Emerald Throne at the heart of the Mandala.

He nodded to the guardsmen standing alert at either side of the massive doors. They swiveled, marched to the center of the portal, and grasped the enormous handles. Eusabian heard the subtle hum of hidden engines as the guards pulled, and the doors slowly swung open. Each leaf was over a meter thick, yet the doors' height balanced the proportions, rendering them fine-drawn.

He strode through the still-opening portal and stopped abruptly, held against his will by the majesty and authority of the room before him. It was the biggest interior space he had ever seen, had ever conceived, its distant corners lost in a confusion of color from the impossibly tall stained-glass windows that rose rank upon rank in the distant walls, reducing their bulk to a weightless lacework that mantled the room in a mystery of light. High overhead, a galaxy of lamps sprang to life, creating a perfect simulacrum of a starry sky, leaving Eusabian with the dizzying sense that the room was of infinite height. The light from above infused every part of the chamber with clarity while leaving the enigmatic colors from the windows in command. Banners and blazons of every description hung from the walls and below the lights, a glory of history and a forest of legend.

Yet despite its overwhelming scale and the multitude of ornaments, everything conspired to draw Eusabian's eyes irresistibly to the center and focus of the room. Even the pattern of the thick-strewn stars and nebulae above redirected his attention to the Throne on a vast dais in the center of the space, an emerald glory transfixed by a beam of light from an unseen source. He suppressed a shiver of awe and strode forward.

As he drew nearer, the Emerald Throne resolved into a graceful, organic form, alive with flickering internal light, that seemed to grow up out of the polished obsidian dais. Suddenly he realized that the Throne and the architecture of the space surrounding it formed the undeniable impression of a tree, a tree so vast that only a part of it could fit within the hall, its roots plunged deeply into the foundations of the Mandala, the heart of the Thousand Suns; its branches, perceived through suggestion and design, upholding the sky and bearing aloft the stars like ripening fruit.

Eusabian had studied his enemy carefully, in the twenty long years of his paliach. He had scrutinized the symbolism and ritual of government that upheld the Panarchy, the carefully nurtured mysteries cultivated by the Magisterium and the College of Archetype and Ritual; for he knew that in a man's symbols you perceive his soul, his strengths and his weaknesses.

But now, confronted for the first time with the actual embodiment of those mysteries, his mind recoiled, and for an endless moment he perceived and believed the formidable reality behind the symbols. Before him stood the Tree of Worlds, whose invigorating sap informs and infuses all creation; and the one who had been consecrated to sit upon it was the health of the Thousand Suns, and its health his.

Behind him the doors swung fully open against the walls with a resonant boom that Eusabian perceived more through his feet and skin than through his ears, and the enthrallment shattered. *I am the Lord of Vengeance and the Avatar of*

Dol. My ancestors ruled in Jhar D'ocha when this island was a wilderness; and the blood and lineage of Dol'jhar has proved its primacy with the completion of my paliach.

He strode forward and climbed up the stairs of the dais. As he approached the Throne, he could see in the distance behind it the towering Gate of Aleph-Null, whose aspect is transcendence. To the left and right loomed the Ivory Gate and the Rouge Gate: autonomy and actuality. At the Throne he stood a moment, almost mesmerized by the shimmering highlights moving subtly in its viridian depths. Turning about, he looked back for a moment toward the open Phoenix Gate, whose aspect is irreversibility. Then, reveling in the action with every part of his being, Eusabian seated himself in the Emerald Throne.

❊   ❊   ❊

Barrodagh was unprepared for the scale of the Throne Room. For a moment, as he entered, he forgot his prisoner and gaped in awe. He suddenly felt invisible, diminished; there was nothing here to reflect him to himself. He would gladly have turned and scurried out, but for the brooding presence in black seated on the distant Throne.

Between Eusabian and the entrance where Barrodagh now stood stretched a long double row of Douloi in resplendent garb, backed by black-clad Tarkans. Near the head of the line stood a trinity of Kelly, their snake-like headstalks in constant motion. Some of the human aristocrats stood quietly, others were visibly unsettled and fidgety; all now looked at the man who stood at Barrodagh's side.

Gelasaar hai-Arkad was not a large man. He was actually no taller than Barrodagh, but the Bori had the sudden impression that the defeated Panarch had grown taller, as though the Hall about them had clothed him visibly in the authority and power that had once been his. The Panarch stood quietly, at ease, his natural grace investing his plain gray prison garb and the neurospasmic collar around his neck with the quality of a formal vestment.

Barrodagh made as if to push him roughly forward, but the gesture weakened and became an abortive lunge when he met the man's eyes, and saw not just calm, but a distant amusement there.

Then Gelasaar turned and alone began walking toward the Throne. The Bori hastened after him, clutching the collar's control mechanism like a talisman. As they passed, the Douloi to either side bowed deeply, like wheat stalks bending before the wind in a summer field. Barrodagh shuddered as the Kelly echoed the motion in triplicate; he hated the slithery motion of their headstalks and the burned-fodder scent of their bodies.

At the base of the Throne the Panarch halted, and stood looking up at the man who had usurped him. Barrodagh stationed himself to one side so he could watch both their faces. For several minutes the two men studied each other; the Bori's breathing grew shallow as he felt the tension grow.

Finally Eusabian moved slightly, a mere adjustment of his posture, but Barrodagh recognized in it a signal. He had expected his lord to say something to his defeated enemy, perhaps gloat a little, but the Avatar said nothing and the Bori guided the Panarch to the left-hand side of the Throne, then gestured to him to turn around.

"Kneel," said Barrodagh, but the Panarch looked through him without responding, increasing the Bori's feeling of invisibility.

With a suppressed snarl and a jerk of his head Barrodagh summoned a Tarkan, who grabbed the Panarch's neurospasmic collar with one meaty hand and buckled his knees with a brutal kick behind them, lowering him just a bit too slowly to the floor. The Panarch's breathing became harsh, then steadied slowly. He sank back on his haunches, his hands on his thighs, his back rigidly erect, and gazed steadily out at the assembled aristocrats.

Barrodagh returned to stand on the right-hand side of the Throne, and, at a motion from Eusabian, began speaking.

His voice squeaked and vanished into the vast space; he swallowed convulsively and began again.

"You have been summoned here to swear fealty to the new Lord of the Mandala, the Avatar of Dol, the Lord of Vengeance and the Kingdoms of Dol'jhar. On his right hand stands life and prosperity; on his left hand"—Barrodagh gestured to the kneeling Panarch, now flanked by two immense Tarkans with red brimless caps on their scarred, shaven heads—"awaits only death. Choose now." The two Tarkans shifted slightly, the light glinting from the two-handed, serrated broadswords they held in front of them, points on the floor.

Barrodagh pointed to the first Douloi, an aged woman with a fierce, hawk-like face, but halted as Eusabian moved one hand in a sign of negation. "Bring the beasts first," he said softly, distaste evident in his voice.

At his gesture some Tarkans herded the Kelly trinity forward as Barrodagh retrieved a transparent ball about two hand-spans in diameter. He handed it gingerly to Eusabian; inside was a writhing, fluttering mass of bright green ribbons.

The Kelly halted at the sight of the sphere and moaned, a haunting triple croon laden with alien emotion.

"As it appears you have surmised, this is all that remains of your Archon," said Eusabian, holding the sphere up in one hand, "the only hope for the continuation of . . . its line and its memories." His expression of distaste intensified as he paused before choosing the pronoun. "Its fate is yours to decide."

The three Kelly stood in silence for a time, their headstalks moving ceaselessly. Then, with shocking abruptness, they were still. The center, smaller one spoke in a mellow contralto blat counterpointed by a dismal, alien threnody from the other two as all three stood stiffly, their headstalks frozen upright, their blue eyes unblinking.

"There is only death here," the Kelly said, almost singing. "Death in your eyes, death in your mouth, death in your mind. The end of life is carried in your scent; not for you a third, for death rides in your loins as well."

Barrodagh stiffened, horrified. *How did they know?* He risked a glance at Eusabian: his lord's face had not changed, but a vein in his temple beat visibly.

"We will not serve you," the Kelly sang. "Power you have, but drone you are. Life rejects you, we reject you."

With a snap of his wrist, Eusabian threw the sphere to the floor in front of him. Thick veins of plasma snapped into being within it, writhing across its inner surface with a crackling hum. The green ribbons within convulsed frantically, withering to motionless black crinkles and then collapsing into dust.

The Tarkan swordsmen strode forward; the Kelly did not move as the blades swept hissing through their headstalks in gouts of yellow blood which splashed the Douloi to either side. The aliens collapsed slowly to the floor, dying muscles twitching in triune rhythm. The severed headstalks writhed for a time, the blue eyes blinking, then were quiet.

Barrodagh glanced over at the Panarch. His face was expressionless, but the Bori could see a tightness around his eyes and a hardness to his lips. The Bori smiled nastily. *We've soiled your virgin Throne Room, haven't we?* He was sure that no occupant of the Emerald Throne had ever witnessed a scene like this, here in the heart of the Mandala.

Three Tarkans ran forward and began to drag the bodies over to the left side of the Emerald Throne. Two succeeded, but the third, as he touched the ribbons of the intermittor who had spoken for the trinity, screamed hoarsely and fell to the floor. His body bowed backward until his head touched his heels and he screamed even louder, but not loudly enough to drown the sickening crunching sounds as his tortured muscles spasmed again and again, breaking his bones in a deadly struggle that only ended when his diaphragm tore across and a gout of blood spewed from his mouth.

Barrodagh stared in horror, nausea churning his stomach. All his satisfaction at the Panarch's discomfiture vanished.

Even his sessions with Thuriol in the pain machines hadn't prepared him for something like this. He remembered now about the Kelly, and why they were so sought after as physicians: their near-total control over the composition of their ribbons. This one had poisoned its ribbons to take one last enemy with it into death. He felt the pressure of a gaze and looked over; the Panarch was watching him, his blue eyes merciless. The Bori looked away, unsettled, his mind struggling with the concept of a loyalty not enforced by fear.

The other two Tarkans returned and carefully pushed the intermittor's body with their two-handed jacs over to where the others had been thrown. Barrodagh collected himself and motioned the old woman forward.

She limped up to stand before Eusabian, erect and uncompromising. Her gray eyes glinted in her wrinkled face; her hooked nose and high cheekbones gave her dark face the aspect of a predatory bird. She looked over at the Panarch, then stood looking at Eusabian for a time; he looked back impassively.

Finally she snorted. "Huh! You're too small for that Throne." She waved a thin arm around. "And all these black-togged bully boys won't make your butt any bigger." She coughed noisily, then leaned forward and spat a foul wad on Eusabian's boots.

Barrodagh winced. If this kept up, they'd be knee deep in blood, and Eusabian would be in a rage for days.

One of the big Tarkans strode forward and impaled the old woman on his sword. She closed her eyes as agony transformed her face, but she made no sound. The swordsman's muscles bunched under his uniform as he swiveled and used the sword like a pitchfork to throw her body over on top of the Kelly near the Panarch. Blood arched through the air and splashed on the defeated ruler's face and garments as the sword pulled out of her body; he made no move to wipe it away.

The next seven Douloi chose the same fate. Barrodagh wriggled his toes distastefully as their blood lapped against his shoes and leaked through the seams. The hot-copper scent was overpowering; the faces of many of the waiting Douloi were greenish gray with nausea and fear. Eusabian's face was stone hard; Barrodagh felt the muscles along his spine crawl—no one was safe when the Avatar was in this mood.

The tenth Douloi trembled so hard he could hardly stand, and he would not look at the Panarch. He stood stoop-shouldered before Eusabian for only a moment, then laid himself flat on the floor, facedown, in the obeisance that had been commanded of the Panarchist aristocrats before they entered the Throne Room. The Avatar's face relaxed slightly. The man looked up, and at a jerk of Barrodagh's head levered himself to his feet and stumbled over to the right side of the throne. His clothes were crimson with the blood of his predecessors; as the Bori turned back to motion the next Douloi forward he heard the man vomiting, choking as he tried to suppress the noise.

The man's capitulation had broken the spell, and one by one, with enough exceptions to visibly swell the pile of bodies next to the Panarch and the pool of blood at the foot of the Throne, the remaining Douloi came up and made obeisance. None of them would meet their former liege's eyes. At the end of the line were a number of older Douloi, several in uniform. When they reached the Throne Eusabian held up his hand.

"It is enough. These will share their master's fate."

One of the executioners pulled the Panarch to his feet and pushed him roughly to stand before Eusabian. As before, the white-haired ruler stood very still, gazing up at his enemy, apparently oblivious to the threads of blood congealing in his white hair and beard and on his face, and the lake of it pooling around his feet. On the left side of the Throne a few bodies in the pile of those who had chosen loyalty to the Panarch still twitched; the stink of death was overpowering.

"So, Gelasaar," Eusabian said finally, "it appears rather more of your Douloi chose life than death."

"Say rather that some chose loyalty; those that remain

will die many times in nights to come as they remember this day." The Panarch glanced over at the survivors. "But I do not judge them. Self-judgment is their one remaining duty, and they will execute it faithfully."

Eusabian's mouth quirked. "You are no longer in a position to judge anyone, Gelasaar. Henceforth you will be the victim of circumstances, rather than their creator."

The Panarch gave him a measuring look before replying. "You know little of statecraft, Dol'jhar, if you think the ruler of trillions is ever anything but the victim of circumstances." Barrodagh realized that he had chosen not to reciprocate Eusabian's deliberate rudeness in the use of his given name, replying instead as one sovereign to another. "All one can do is assign priorities and pray."

Eusabian smiled coldly. "It seems neither your prayers nor your priorities did you much good." He looked around at the carnage the Tarkans had created. "Nor your loyal subordinates."

Gelasaar's brows lifted, humor crinkling the skin around his eyes. "Indeed, it does appear that I seriously overestimated your intelligence."

Barrodagh tightened his grip on the collar control and raised it slightly, then halted at a motion from Eusabian.

The Panarch continued. "Do you not have any idea at all of the difficulties involved in ruling more than a thousand planets and countless highdwellings? Some of them are so far from here that it takes my commands many weeks to reach them, and as long again for their reply. Why do you think the fundamental law of my rule is called the Covenant of Anarchy? Even with the power of the Fleet behind me, the best I could do was forbid interplanetary war and require free trade and travel."

The Panarch paused and looked around the Hall. "I can understand your success here and on Lao Tse, perhaps, relying on sabotage and the greed of fools, but what more can you expect to do with only the *Fist of Dol'jhar* and a ragtag gang of Rifters to enforce your will? What will you do when the Fleet arrives?"

The Panarch's voice was light yet compelling, and for a moment Barrodagh found himself almost convinced that Eusabian had overlooked some critical aspect of his plan. Then the Lord of Vengeance smiled mockingly.

"Your concern for my travails is touching, Arkad, but your grasp of my power is faulty. Just hours ago one of that ragtag gang, as you call them, compelled the surrender of Charvann, after but a half-day's resistance. The battlecruiser *Korion* lasted only minutes in that same action, and that was one of the least of my victories."

"Charvann is five days from here," the Panarch countered, lifting his voice slightly. "There is no way you could know that, even had it actually happened: I know of nothing that could overpower a battlecruiser's shields in minutes, or a planet's in hours."

"You may not, but the Ur did." Eusabian smiled on his enemy. The cold rage had abated, and he was enjoying the conversation.

And for the first time, the Panarch's face revealed his feelings; for a moment Barrodagh could see the dawn of belief in his eyes.

Eusabian apparently saw it too, for he turned to Barrodagh and said, *"Tel urdug paliachai, em ni arben ettisen."*

Barrodagh bowed deeply, recognizing the reversion to Dol'jharian as a signal that the formal pronouncement of the paliach's completion was at hand. As he walked around the Throne, his feet squelching in the drying blood pooled around it, he spoke the words he had practiced so many times alone in his chambers: "So, Arkad, are you curious to know your fate?"

"There is no need for curiosity," the Panarch responded, but not to Barrodagh. He glanced only briefly at the Bori before returning his gaze to Eusabian.

Barrodagh hesitated, the lack of acknowledgment stealing some of the anticipated sweetness of the moment, then walked past and picked up the two small translucent boxes that the Tarkans had placed behind the Throne. With a flourishing movement, he brought them forward, approaching from the other side. *He's a fool, after all*, Barrodagh gloated. *He knows nothing of his enemy. My lord never made that mistake.* Barrodagh took his time, enjoying the change in the Panarch's eyes from blankness to a kind of faint puzzlement. He'd looked forward to this particular moment for a long time.

The Panarch spoke then, facing Eusabian, his voice echoing slightly. "I'm sure you've spent a large portion of the past twenty years devising something sufficiently bloody, and I have the feeling that nothing short of the collapse of this building would stop you from telling me."

Barrodagh placed the boxes at the foot of the Throne. He saw Eusabian put his chin on his hand, his expression one of entertainment, and stepped back, endeavoring to read the Avatar's mood.

"Bloody?" Eusabian echoed. "Yes, I suppose so, although not to match the hecatomb offered to Dol here today," he said, making a benevolent gesture that encompassed the vastness of the Hall. "And it will not come at my hands. I need not exert myself to kill you—not when the denizens of Gehenna will do it for me."

A snort of amusement escaped Barrodagh. There was a rustle of movement from the assembled Douloi, both those to the right and to the left of the throne.

Eusabian's eyes flickered to the Bori, held him for a chilling moment. Then a quiver of his lord's lips and a twitch of his eyebrows released him to explain.

"Your pardon, Lord. I was just imagining the celebration the Isolates on Gehenna will have when he arrives."

"Yes, it was the symmetry of the arrangement that recommended it to me." Eusabian turned back to the Panarch.

"But it's a pity the portion of my paliach dealing with your sons could not be completed as nicely. Formal vengeance is rigidly defined among my people."

Barrodagh, reading his command in Eusabian's voice, leaned over and tapped once on top of each box. Their fronts cleared to reveal the heads of two men, neatly preserved and mounted. Their eyes were open, fixed on infinity; the blood pooled at Eusabian's feet cast a mocking flush of health on their pallor.

"Unfortunately an overzealous subordinate ran your youngest son into a gas giant, so I can't complete the set," Eusabian said, watching intently.

Sorrow and rage flitted quickly across the Panarch's face, and was as quickly hidden. Eusabian's face did not change, but his dark eyes were wide and unblinking, and Barrodagh grinned, thrilled with the sight of his lord drinking in the scent of his enemy's grief.

When the Panarch remained silent, Eusabian smiled again. "Has your famous wit deserted you?"

"Brevity is the soul of wit, Dol'jhar." Gelasaar looked around the Throne Room once more, as one does at the last sight of something familiar. Then he smiled coldly. "And either is wasted on a fool."

Barrodagh's skin prickled and he suppressed a shiver of fear. Never before had Barrodagh heard anyone address Eusabian with such freedom; those who had tried had died, either swiftly or in protracted pain, depending on the Avatar's mood. That mood was impossible to read now, yet here was the enemy who had defeated Eusabian twenty years before, and who now had lost everything but his life, talking as freely as if they stood alone on the deck of a ship somewhere, out in the reaches of space where titles and possessions had no meaning. Barrodagh found it impossible to predict what would happen—which frightened him more than the cold rage.

Eusabian sat back, his teeth showing in a strange, tight smile. "You are calling *me* a fool."

Barrodagh flinched; he sensed the rage, never far away, hovering again, like a storm over Jhar D'ocha poised to strike.

"You, who have lost your empire, your fleet, your heirs?" Eusabian said. "You, who were never able to penetrate the secrets of the Ur?"

Barrodagh brandished the neurospasmic control, as if to silence the Panarch, but again Eusabian gestured.

Barrodagh stumbled back, willing himself into invisibility.

"I have," Eusabian said, and lifted two fingers toward the mechanism Barrodagh clutched in both hands. "And I control the powers of the Ur as easily as that controls you."

Gelasaar smiled, as if at a joke he knew Eusabian could not share. "Where are the Ur now, Jerrode Eusabian of Dol'jhar? They are gone, ten million years and more, and their fate has put a charged weapon in the hands of an idiot. You have gained an empire you cannot rule, and a throne you cannot keep."

Eusabian's eyes narrowed, and Barrodagh read in that the necessity of ending an interview that had degenerated to an utter disaster. With a decisive movement he tabbed a button on the control. The collar around the Panarch's neck began to pulse with light, and Barrodagh could hear a shrill keening coming from it. Gelasaar's face contorted. He fought for breath as he struggled to speak. For a moment the only sound in the Hall was his harsh gasping.

Suddenly he convulsed, his head thrown back, and a fey light kindled in his eyes. His voice became distant, almost hierophantic, and Barrodagh realized that the Panarch was one of those in whom the collar induced epilepsy, and sometimes visions.

"Hear me, Dol'jhar," he intoned, his eyes looking through his enemy to something far beyond. "I see your destiny now. This Throne *is* yours, for a time, then another, older one, and finally none."

Barrodagh stabbed frantically at the control, trying to silence the man. The pulsing quickened, the keening grew in pitch and volume, yet the Panarch continued as though he had not noticed, as if held in the grip of some vast force welling up from the foundations of the Mandala.

"In the end, all time will be yours, yet no time will be enough . . ." The wheezing voice went on, the blue eyes glowing with preternatural light.

"Get out!" shouted Barrodagh to the terrified assemblage. "Now!" The Tarkans thrust the mob of Douloi away from the Throne, all of them walking swiftly.

Barrodagh lingered, the control still in his hands, wishing he could be gone. Still Eusabian had not moved, had not touched the enemy, whose neck now displayed the blistered stigmata induced by the sonic component of the collar's impulses.

"A short reign, Dol'jhar ... and an end violent beyond imagination," the Panarch said, the thready voice somehow causing echoing whispers through the long Hall. Barrodagh shook the control in angry desperation, feeling his lord's building rage.

Suddenly the Panarch relaxed and looked directly at Eusabian. His blue eyes, that moments before had glowed with the force of his will, were now mild and wondering. "I pity you," he said.

And he toppled over into unconsciousness.

Barrodagh lunged forward to kick the fallen man, hoping to give Eusabian's rage a focus before it struck at everyone around him.

"No," the Avatar commanded. "Do not touch him."

Barrodagh blanched and backed away, bowing; then, terrified, he turned and ran out of the Hall. As he passed the massive leaves of the Phoenix Gate he caught sight of the guards posted there and slowed, glaring at them. "Go in at his command," he ordered, and then he dared to look back.

At the foot of the Throne, black above red, Eusabian stood unmoving, a dim presence dwarfed by his surroundings, untouched by the light that enhaloed the man crumpled at his feet.

EIGHTEEN

❊

Vi'ya was still testing the strange physical properties of the Heart of Kronos when she entered a small natural cave deep within the moon. The only other occupant of the room, a tall, spare man of about forty-five years, looked up from the large screen he'd been watching.

"Learn anything?" he asked, with a slow smile that seemed to increase the hound-like sadness of his liquid brown eyes.

"Enough," she replied, considering how much to tell him. Norton was her second-in-command, the captain of the only other assault-grade craft in the organization's fleet. Norton was one of those Rifters who had grown up to his vocation, inheriting his ship from a parent. His somber black jumpsuit carried a gold-ringed sun over the heart pocket, twin emblem to the blazon on the hull of his *Sunflame*. Honest and loyal, he knew little of Panarchist politics and cared less. She changed the subject: "How long until the repairs on the *Sunflame* are complete?"

He pursed his lips, his long nose wrinkling thoughtfully.

"I can't say ... Jaim is in there with Porv and Silverknife, and I just sent Marim out to give them a hand. Most of the exterior work is done; if I hadn't been following every step of the work, I wouldn't recognize the ship myself. There's no chance Hreem or his gang will figure out it's *Sunflame*, even if we fly right across their noses."

He looked back at the screen, continued almost musingly. "I'm still not sure that last jack against Hreem was wise—it was perilously close to infringing the Code—I'm still expecting a rogation from the Adjudication Sodality on Rifthaven."

Vi'ya shrugged. "I don't expect any trouble. Considering the audits against him waiting there, I don't think he will dare approach Rifthaven anymore. And he's unlikely to make one against us; he'd rather blow us out of space himself." She looked down at the Heart of Kronos. Norton's eyes followed her gaze.

"What about the fiveskip?" she continued.

"Can't work on the fiveskip until everything else is done—expect it'll take a day or two."

"You might have to do that in a Realtime Run. Break down everything here and have them fall back to the other base. Leave sufficient fuel for *Telvarna* at the cache. Don't check in at Rifthaven on the way—wait until you're established. I have an idea Marim—"

"You're going somewhere?" he interjected quietly, a hint of anxious watchfulness entering his face.

"The Arkad and his furious liegeman want to be taken to Arthelion, though they lied when they said it was their original destination."

"The Panarchist secret base?"

"Most probably. Likely on behalf of the Arkad, but also possibly because of—this." She hefted the sphere, watched Norton's eyes narrow as he observed its inertialess behavior. "Which makes me wonder again just why Hreem attacked a planet with no relative strategic importance ... enough with that now! My first thought was to have you take this object to the other base, but the Eya'a are too agitated over it. Maybe they can figure out what it is during the transit time to Arthelion."

"Arthelion. The Mandala." Norton shook his head slowly, his voice merely contemplative but his eyes reluctant. "I don't think you should go there. I've never heard of any Brotherhood craft landing there, which makes me think if it's been tried, the triers never came out again."

"I foresee little trouble, not while returning a lost Arkad to their keep, and I might be able to learn something of the matters that concern us. It would be interesting to know how good the Panarchist information is about Hreem—and about Dol'jhar's movements."

Norton's narrow brow furrowed, then he said slowly, "You trust this Arkad not to simply hand you to the authorities after you touch down on the Mandala?"

"You must remember I know something of him from Markham. Though perhaps there's little I can attest to in his credit, I do not expect treachery." Vi'ya dropped the sphere into her belt pouch.

Norton's eyes crinkled, his brows knitting in puzzlement as he noted the strange behavior of the sphere, but he said nothing.

"No, we will probably be safer than you, until you get the *Sunflame* operational and out of here. Hreem has some sort of new weapon—Marim saw him blow away *Korion* with one shot"—Norton's eyes opened wide—"and Charvann is likely to fall to him soon. He's already got the Node and the Syncs. I'm afraid that he may find out from the Panarchists about us. At that point the existence of this base will be measured in hours unless it's shut down and thus indetectable."

Norton nodded soberly.

"Even if Hreem is defeated, there's still the danger from that demon-touched Aerenarch who will undoubtedly have had the erring scion followed, and would leap at the chance to eliminate him under the guise of action against Rifters. Have the primary crew of *Telvarna* report at once, and run through status checks. I'll take Ivard in Paysud's place; it's time he made a run on his own. I'll cover Fire Control myself"—she smiled—"or I may use the Arkad. We'll see."

Norton looked up in muted surprise. "Lokri?"

Vi'ya hesitated, then said: "Tell him what I said: primary crew. I do not want him here, trying his games on you: after this run, Reth Silverknife takes his position permanently." She pointed toward the other wall. "Send someone to take the two passengers aboard. Get them some gear first, if they want. I go to appraise the Eya'a of our departure." She turned toward the door.

"Vi'ya—" Norton stretched out a hand, then dropped it quickly to his knee. "I don't trust this plan. I wish at least we could both go."

"Two ships would have as much effect as one against Arthelion's armaments—that is to say, none. Get the *Sunflame* repaired and fall back to the other base. Fast."

She walked out, her last image of Norton's hound-face grim and unhappy as he reached for the intercom to convey her orders.

❋   ❋   ❋

After his toast to Markham's memory, Brandon did not speak again. Osri sat, fighting the tiredness which seemed to burn his eyes and fog his mind all of a sudden, aware of nothing but stiffness and the pain of his nearly universal bruises. When a short, round-bodied man appeared and said, "Come with me, you two," Osri had to try twice before getting to his feet.

"Is it possible to find out what's going on?" Osri addressed him as the man led them rapidly down a low-roofed tunnel.

"Vi'ya's given the order," the man said cheerfully over his shoulder, bright green eyes avid with curiosity. "You're off. *Telvarna*'s goin' to the Mandala."

"Off . . . ?" Osri repeated, frowning, his abhorrence at the idea of voluntarily speaking with Rifters overcome by his need to know what was about to happen. "You mean we are going to Arthelion?"

"That's it." Their guide gave him a gap-toothed grin. "Wish I was primary crew on *Telvarna*. Here." He stopped abruptly, slapped a door open.

Osri smelled sweat from the man and stepped back, offended. Then he looked down at his suit; after the harrowing hours he'd spent in it, he knew he would stink as soon as he undressed. Would the Rifters offer them the courtesy of a bath? Osri looked at the grubby man, sourly thinking, *Probably not.*

Brandon went in first, and the man shoved in after him. Inside was a tiny corridor, with four doors of varying sizes leading off. The guide opened one, flicked a light on, and Osri stared into a long closet-room, with all kinds of clothing and shoes either hanging from overhead rods or folded on shelves.

"Help yourselves," the man said. "Make it quick! No stores on the *Telvarna*, and you've got about seven days' ship time."

Osri hesitated. His natural distaste at the prospect of wearing clothing favored by Rifters had to be overborne by necessity: all he had was the boost-suit he'd arrived in. While he hesitated, Brandon moved forward with an air of purpose.

"Move yer butt," the guide called out. "*Telvarna*'s ready to lift now. Change right here, leave them boost-suits on the floor."

"But these suits are not ours to give," Osri snapped, outraged at the whole procedure.

"Shuck 'em and leave 'em," the guide replied with unimpaired good humor. "You don't need them expensive suits on the *Telvarna*. It's a trade, you're gettin' duds."

"I would rather retain my suit—" Osri began.

The guide frowned and slid a hand into his tunic, but Brandon forestalled him with a quiet, "The Navy replaces anything lost during special ops. You should know that."

Thus reminded they were going home, Osri gave Brandon a curt bow. He then cast his eyes over the stores, his features rigid with disdain. By the time he had selected a couple of plain gray tunics of military cut that looked almost new, and some black trousers, both of which *appeared* to be clean, Brandon had already stripped out of his boostsuit and was wearing a light blue civilian tunic and loose pants stuffed into low boots, and he carried a dark-colored jumpsuit over one arm. Osri therefore had to change with the two waiting for him, the guide watching with unconcealed interest, which did nothing to improve his temper. He jammed his feet into a pair of moccasins which were too large as the guide once again exhorted him to speed up.

Then they were led at a brisk walk back up long tunnels to a small room, where they found the scout Marim waiting, one bare foot propped behind her against a wall as she chatted with a knot of colorfully dressed Rifters. Next to her in a bulkhead was a hatch, with a small control console next to it. On the console a green telltale glowed.

Seeing Brandon and Osri arrive, she straightened up with a bounce and chirped, "Here's my nicks. See you Shiidrachatzers when!"

Laughing farewells and catcalls sounded from the group, who moved back to make passage for Osri and Brandon, giving them curious stares as they passed.

Marim thrust herself between the two and grinned up at them. "Vi'ya said I was to find you berths and break you in. Ship's through here."

She tapped the console and the hatch swung open. Beyond lay a very short tunnel—a lock, Osri realized—and another hatch, its telltale also glowing green. Marim led the way, carefully dogging the hatch behind them. Osri noted with distaste that the soles of her feet were black. *Doesn't she ever wash them?*

They stepped through the far hatch into a large cavern, perhaps three hundred by two hundred meters, its roof lost in darkness above the lights hanging no more than ten meters above the smooth, meltstone floor. To their right a large metal door, its bottom concealed in a groove in the floor, truncated the cavern, the roof descending to just above it where a complexity of metal hid its top.

Dominating the center of the brightly lit space was a ship, surrounded by crates and pallets of supplies. A tall, lanky individual with swinging braids and a shorter, pale redheaded boy were wrestling some of these up a ramp into the lock.

Osri instantly recognized the basic type, staring in amazement at the extensive modifications that had been made to it. It had obviously started out as a Malachronte Columbiad, a medium-range vessel, unchanged in basic design for hundreds of years, that was favored by the Concilium Exterioris for planetary exploration. *My father flew in one of these when he was a rogate.* He felt a renewed stab of concern for his father, which flared back into anger when the little Rifter elbowed him forward.

"C'mon. The *Telvarna*'s not that pretty."

As they approached the ship Osri studied it. He'd built a model of a Columbiad when he was a boy; this one looked like it had been reassembled from the parts of three model kits. About one hundred meters long, its sharp nose and flowing, almost bulbous underside, combined with the vestigial wings and basic delta shape, identified it as a lifting body, designed for fast atmospheric flight. But where were the viewports? Smooth blank hull flowed where the bug-eye ports should have been, on the underside of the nose; and what were all those faired nacelles for?

As they reached the lowered ramp under the side of the ship, Osri's curiosity overcame his reluctance to converse with Rifters. "What did you do to this ship?"

Marim looked at him, puzzled. "Whaddya mean, what'd we do to it? That's the Telvarna."

"I mean," Osri said with some exasperation, "it obviously used to be a Columbiad, but someone seems to have had some bizarre ideas about ship design since it left the Malachronte Ways."

She laughed, a bright, bubbling sound. "You nicks are all used to shiny new ships, I guess. Just scrap 'em or sell 'em to Rifters when the polish gets rubbed off."

She slapped the hull affectionately as they entered the

lock, the ramp booming softly underfoot. They could hear the other two men inside, and a third, much deeper voice.

"*Telvarna*'s about four hundred years old, give or take fifty. Don't know what it started as, but it ended up as a rich nick's toy, till somebody decided they needed it more. Been with Rifters ever since; they made most of the mods. Most of our work's been on the inside, 'cept for the aft cannon."

She motioned them down the narrow corridor toward the nose. As they made their way forward, Osri noted the touch of someone with both money and taste in the underlying decor. In fact, the flowing lines of the bulkhead seams and the contrasting geometric metal inlays in the hatches were a clear example of the Archaeo-Moderne style that had been popular in the reign of Burgess II, 150 years before. He could also see what he was coming to think of as the Rifter touch, in some of the cruder—but still, he was forced to admit, neatly done—modifications. Cabling, com-node accesses, piping, and less identifiable machinery were welded or bolted to the bulkheads without regard for the overall effect.

Marim preceded them through the last hatch to the bridge. The consoles still maintained the familiar collegial U-shape that the Ban-determined interfaces between human and machine made most efficient—captain's console at the rear, the rest in two rows on either side facing in—but two had been added. Osri realized that they sat where the down-looking viewports would have been originally. Whatever those consoles were for, he thought, the people at them would have some trouble seeing the main viewscreen. Then, as they stopped in the center of the bridge, he noticed the viewscreen above the captain's console, facing forward.

His training in astrogation forbade Osri to overlook the obvious efficiency with which the bridge of the *Telvarna* had been modified—and somehow that made him feel even angrier. He glanced over at Brandon, who was surveying the bridge with an odd, almost pained expression on his face, which vanished as Marim turned around and waved her arms proudly in a wide circle.

"This is it—where the action is. You'll see the rest of the ship when I show ya your bunks and such." She grinned at Osri without malice. "Not that *you're* likely to be seen much up here. *Telvarna*'s small, can't take useless passengers, so we've got to fit you in. Already got a hotshot astrogator, so you, Schoolboy, are gonna give Montrose a hand in the galley so's Porv can stay an' help shape the *Sunflame* back."

"And *you*," she elbowed Brandon in the ribs, "will be jack-hand, and if we hit trouble, take Jakarr's spot."

Brandon looked at her in considerable amusement as she beamed up at him. "Jack-hand is a type of general help?"

She nodded vigorously. "So, stow your gear—"

Brandon raised a hand to stop her. "Another question. What was Jakarr's position in the crew?"

"Fire Control!" She jerked a thumb at one of the added consoles. And, misinterpreting the question that raised his brows, she added, "He was an acid-faced blit, but fast on the lazplaz, and 'sides, Vi'ya liked him here to keep an eye on him." She paused, casting a thoughtful glance around the bridge, then she grinned at Brandon. "Just realized, it's goin' to be *fun* with him gone, and your pretty face sittin' there."

"Earning my keep, for the first time in my life." He laughed, as Osri turned away in bitter disgust.

❈   ❈   ❈

A few hours later, Norton watched on his screen as the *Telvarna* lifted from the floor of the cavern under geeplane and slowly floated out through the open lock. Five hundred meters from the cavern, its radiants brightened suddenly and it arrowed away from the surface of Dis, shrinking to a bright dot and disappearing within seconds.

Norton stared at the view from the imager as the lock door began to close across the view of Warlock bulking ominously above the jagged horizon. He was frankly worried.

Why did she accept Lokri in Reth's place? A suicidal run to the heart of Panarchist power was not the time to have to deal with a troublesome crew member. *How much of Jakarr's bid for power was fostered by Lokri out of sheer devilry?*

He shook his head; it didn't matter now. She was still by and large one of the best captains he'd ever served with. Still, he hoped she'd keep an eye on Lokri.

A faint sweet ringing broke into his thoughts. Startled, he turned around.

Reth Silverknife walked in, the chimes in her long braids ringing their soft harmony. "She's changing back."

"Not quite." He sighed. "Different. The more time she spends with the Eya'a, the further away she seems to get." He looked into Reth's smooth young face, her patient eyes. He thought he read sadness there. "I'm sorry you're not on the *Telvarna* with Jaim."

Reth made one of her stylized Serapisti gestures. "The flame wanders where it will," she said. "We will be together again in the fullness of time."

In the viewscreen the lock slid closed. Reth walked over to the console and reached past Norton to tap the keys. The view switched to a small cove of rocks thrusting up from the surface of Dis, as if to protect the small, circular space between them from the star-strewn sky beyond. The surface of one of the rocks had been carefully smoothed; on it the orange light of Warlock picked out a simple carving—a sprig with two leaves, and a simple blossom at the end, nothing more. The orange blossom of the L'Ranjas: carved in stone on the surface of a dead world, it would still be there when humankind itself was but a memory.

❊   ❊   ❊

"Damn!" Marim rounded the corner into the *Telvarna*'s rec room, skidding on the smooth decking. She scowled down at the soft slippers on her feet. "I hate these chatzing blunge-wipes!"

Lokri lounged back, his teeth white against his dark face,

and his eyes half-closed. "You want the nicks to see those feet?"

Marim put her hands on her hips and gazed down at her feet. "So I been gennated. You think they'll try to fry me?"

Lokri merely snorted.

"They'll report you soon's they hit the Mandala," Jaim said. "Panarchists don't like genetic alternation."

Marim slipped her small, square foot out of its slipper, closed her long toes nimbly around the slipper opening, and flipped it up to land in Lokri's lap. She rubbed her fingers over the velvety black microfibers on the sole of her foot. "So let *them* try to stick to a wall in free-fall, and they'll mouth a different tag."

Lokri lifted one shoulder in a lazily elegant gesture. "Vi'ya said to wear those. You want to argue, argue with her." He threw the slipper back at Marim's face, but she caught it and grinned impudently at him.

"They'll see Lucifur." Marim pointed up, tipping her head toward the galley. "He's gennated."

"He's not human," Lokri drawled. "You haven't noticed?"

Greywing, leaning back in her chair, breathed a soft laugh. "Anyway they seen Lucifur," she said. "Damn cat's decided to adopt the Schoolboy."

"What?" Jaim's thin face lengthened in surprise. "I thought he was going to vomit when he walked into the galley and saw Luce walking over the cook-console."

"Hates cats," Greywing said with a crooked grin. "Of course Luce's gonna pick him as a favorite."

Marim crowed with laughter. "Betcha Luce's tried to get into his bunk with him." For a moment she pictured with enthusiasm the tilt-nosed Osri trying unsuccessfully to eject the large, noisy cat from his bunkspace.

"More than anyone else'd want to do," Lokri murmured, his voice lazy but his light gray eyes venomous under their heavy lids. "Hope Luce sticks to his face. Ought to improve it."

"Ah, Montrose already done that," Jaim said. He got up.

"Improved his face, I mean. Shift change, slubbers. Gotta head down to the engine room—Vi'ya's giving me the Arkad again."

Marim laughed. "What are you gonna make him do today?"

Jaim scratched his head, thrusting a thin dark braid behind one ear. "Well, I thought I might have him dismantle, clean, and reassemble the tianqi in the Eya'a cabin. They work overtime keeping those quarters at the minus ten Vi'ya says they prefer for sleeping."

"But we just did that!" Marim exclaimed.

Jaim shrugged. "Never know when it might need doing again."

Marim nodded, thinking back to their launch from Dis. Their captive Krysarch had looked around the *Telvarna* as though something was missing and then had gone straight into the rec room, ordered up some potent combinations of liquor, and had proceeded to get numb-lipped, vacuum-skulled drink.

Lokri had refused to go near him; it was Jaim and little Ivard who helped him to his bunk, and six hours later, Marim had made sure she had business in the corridor outside the cabin Brandon and Osri had been assigned to when Vi'ya went in to roust him out and set him to work.

"Like our Rifter liquor, Arkad?" the captain had said, with her usual penchant for null-gee understatement.

He sat there on his bunk looking totally confused. He also, Marim had noticed, underneath an astonishing rainbow display of bruises (*No doubt from that spectacular landing out on the Wager*, Lokri said later) had a ve-ery nice body.

"Jaim's waiting." Vi'ya jerked her thumb over her shoulder.

Marim listened with stilled breath, wondering how the Arkad would take orders. Would he ignore her? Get angry? Or maybe would he try to order Vi'ya around her own ship? Marim very much wanted to see him try that.

But he didn't do any of those things; he threw off the cover and got up, without caring that he was stark naked.

(*Gennation or not, they make those Arkads VERY well*, Marim reported later. *I wonder if he knows it—he certainly didn't seem to care that Vi'ya was standing right there, and me right behind her*. Greywing said, *Blit! Those high-end nicks are never alone from the moment they are born. Whenever he bathed he probably had twenty people waiting to hand him his clothes. What happens when he wants to bunny?* Jaim had asked, looking interested for the first time. *The servants get thrown out*, Greywing said impatiently. *And they all watch on hidden vids*, Lokri had added.)

"Five minutes," Vi'ya said, going out.

Since Vi'ya, being a tempath, would have known Marim was there all the time, she hadn't bothered to hide. "You have things to do as well," was all the captain said as she passed by.

That, as far as Marim knew, was the last time that Vi'ya spoke directly to the Krysarch. Three ship days had passed since, during which Montrose had taken exclusive charge of the Schoolboy, and the Arkad had been passed from hand to hand to do scutwork both necessary and unnecessary.

Marim watched avidly from a distance. She saw Jaim send Brandon under the engine housings to check the wave guides and couplings; she saw young Ivard blushing and stammering as he directed the Krysarch in shifting and unpacking crates of supplies. Even Lokri had had charge of him once, though he seemed to prefer avoiding the passengers altogether: Brandon had had to crawl under each of the consoles on the bridge, probing circuit nodes, while Lokri lounged, bored, at his com console and hit switches.

Those first two days Brandon hadn't said anything to anyone that wasn't polite and impersonal, though he must have ached in every bone and muscle. And when his workshift was over, he went straight to his cabin and slept.

Marim looked up now. "He's cleaned the entire ship," she said. "No squawking, either. Wonder if Vi'ya's going to let up? Never knew her to be nasty like that before."

Greywing snorted. "Not being nasty."

"What's the purpose, then?" Jaim asked in his quiet

voice. "No fun when he just does what we tell him, and doesn't even talk nick."

Greywing's watery blue eyes rested on Lokri, and she just shrugged. "You figure it out."

Jaim shook his head, the tiny talismans woven into his six brown braids tinkling gently. "Better go get him started." He slouched out, disappearing in the direction of the engine room.

Lokri got to his feet, looking down at the two women. His lip curled in faint derision. "My watch," he said, and went out.

Greywing dropped into the pod Lokri had been sitting in, her short, square body a contrast to Lokri's elegant length. She put her hands around her cup of hot caf, her wounded arm still held close to her side.

Marim considered how to get the information from her. Greywing was one of the best scantechs in the Brotherhood or out of it. Rumor had it that three of the Rifthaven syndicates had tried to hire her, shortly before Hreem attempted to obtain her services by more violent means. She'd somehow known that his lethal pet tempath was coming to abduct her, and had escaped.

Vi'ya said she was not a tempath, but she had an uncanny ability to sniff out traces of ships and figure action-patterns that not only had saved them again and again but had made them reasonably wealthy. *If Greywing had not been on the other base, Markham might still be alive*, Marim thought, looking at the unprepossessing pale, freckled face before her.

Greywing and her little brother Ivard were both ugly, throwbacks to a time when humans had pale, thin skin, and they had constant eye trouble. But they were both talented in other ways.

Not just good as sniffing out the intentions of ships, Greywing was also remarkably adept at reading people. But she didn't always share what she read.

Marim sat across from her and smiled. "Lokri hates nicks."

"So do I—sometimes," Greywing said unexpectedly.

"But you don't think Vi'ya does?" Marim prompted. "Or maybe she thinks it's funny for the Arkad to be scrubbin' Rifter engine castings."

Greywing hunched her shoulders. " 'S what Lokri thinks. Let 'im. Not true, though."

"So why'd she do it?"

Greywing narrowed her eyes, her lip curling. "Didn't you see anything when you gave 'em the tour?"

"See what? The Schoolboy looked like we smell bad, and the Arkad kept eyeballing things like something was missing. Servants, I thought."

"Markham, vacuumskull," Greywing said. "Hit him, sting after sting. Must have. Anywhere he looked he'd see Markham's taste—who redesigned everything when he took us over?"

Marim's mouth popped open. "Hoo! Didn't think of that. Even changed the tianqi scents."

Greywing sat back, lips pursed in a small smile. "Knows Markham's ship now," she said. "After he been crawling around in its guts it no longer be a shrine."

"Shrine!" Marim repeated, laughing. "Greywing, you been poppin' hopper, lost your mind."

Greywing got up. "You got no mind to lose, Marim." She snorted a dry, voiceless laugh and went out.

✳   ✳   ✳

In the galley Osri wiped his nose, frowned fiercely, and resumed chopping onions. "Damn these Rifters," he muttered under his breath on each stroke of the knife, "and damn *squared* that Light-accursed villain Montrose."

His hand whacked down with increasing violence until a low, cultured voice startled him into nearly adding four fingers to the pile.

"Even strokes, Schoolboy, even strokes. Lumps are not acceptable in this dish. Unless your uselessness is repaired, and quickly, I fear I shall have to request the captain to invite you for a stroll solitaire out the lock. I can work faster, and more peacefully, alone."

Osri ached to throw the knife at the old monster, but instead he forced his lips to acknowledge the command, and his hands to chop more evenly.

He savored the image of the knife flying at Montrose's bearded face. It would be great to see him panic—except he wouldn't panic, Osri reflected bitterly. Being the Rifter murderer and thief he was, he'd probably just pluck the knife from midair by the handle, put it neatly away, and set Osri to scrubbing floors and walls again. And if he refused . . .

Osri winced at the memory of the drubbing that Montrose had given him on that never-to-be-forgiven first shift. The huge man had effortlessly swatted Osri's fists aside with one of those tree-thick arms, then—squashing him companionably against a chest like a cast of metal ingots—informed him that, much as he detested violence, a thrashing would be "good for your soul."

Montrose's mighty paw now looked incongruous picking up the tiny tasting spoon. He delicately skimmed the spoon across the top of the simmering sauce and held it out to Osri, who reluctantly opened his mouth. He knew that the sauce would be delicious—and that he would have to admit it, or be castigated as ignorant "as that nullrat Marim." Much more repellent than praising his sauces was the prospect of being equated in any way with the smelly Rifter vermin infesting this ship.

"Roll it around. Don't bolt it like one of those hell-spawned syntho-paks. Now. There should be three different taste levels . . . First, the initial pungency . . ."

Orsi swallowed the spoonful and glared at Montrose, who was staring at the ceiling in pleasurable contemplation. Osri fumed silently. From the moment he'd stepped on board this Light-forsaken Rifter pesthole he had been humiliated, just because he had endeavored to demonstrate how yawning was the gap between a Douloi officer of impeccable lineage and these Rifter scum of unmentionable origins.

The captain had ignored everything he said and presented

him to Montrose—this giant, grizzled man with a flamboyant taste in clothing that a man of his age should long have grown out of.

"Chef and ship's doctor," Montrose had said, smiling. "And I can use an assistant."

Osri had sneered at the obvious barbarity of employing a cook for health care—and Montrose had only laughed.

Later, when Osri was scrubbing down walls in the dispensary, he had done some checking on the computer there and found a formidable bank of medical information, much of it in language Osri found difficult to decipher. If the man had not gotten a medical degree, he must have studied somewhere.

". . . then it should blend into savory as you consider the blend of spices and the broth base . . ." Montrose went on, still addressing the ceiling.

Osri gritted his teeth. Then there was the monster's pleasant, helpful tone as if his perforce assistant were the most eager of volunteers. Not once had Osri's most acrid sarcasm brought any reaction but a smile and an expansive answer.

"And last . . . the pure taste of the sweet *phraef* wine. Ahhh. Don't you agree?"

"Certainly better than those it's intended for," Osri muttered, curling his lip.

Montrose's wide, bearded face took on a long-suffering look. "I begin to fear you are hopeless, and I am wasting valuable time on a lead-tongued oaf. The *chzchz* herb was too strong and upset the balance of the second level. Never mind—it's not completely ruined. Get back to your pastry dough, and remember: rhythm! Rhythm!" He grinned. "You would hate to get to the eighth kneading and discover that you must begin again." And Montrose pulled out a long thin structure and set it across his lap. "I shall favor you with inspirational music to help you gain your rhythm." And, shutting his eyes, he began playing, his thick fingers dancing across the keyboard as a complicated melody filled the air.

Osri trod heavily across the little galley, cursing under his breath. A loud, rusty rumbling sound, not unlike a mowing machine badly out of adjustment, announced the presence of the second worst horror he'd found aboard this Telos-forsaken pesthole.

"Get away, you disgusting beast," he snarled at the huge cat that appeared suddenly atop a storage cubicle. Its cream-colored fur was short and sleek, faintly striped with brown on head and ears, paws and tail.

The wedge-shaped head lifted, and its slightly crossed eyes fixed on Osri, the pale blue of glacier ice. The rumble increased abruptly in volume. The cat leapt to the floor and butted against Osri, its tail high, the big head wiping back and forth behind Osri's knee, making his leg buckle. It obviously loved music—and conversation.

"Keep your foul hair away from my food," Osri snapped at the cat. "Begone!" He waved his chopping knife at it.

The cat's blue eyes widened. It opened a mouth unexpectedly full of needle-sharp white teeth and emitted a loud sound not unlike one of those lawn-tenders sheering through a rock, then rubbed harder against his leg. The animal, it appeared, loved insults even more.

Montrose chuckled and continued to play, without pause or error, a series of brilliant, complex compositions. Osri had no particular talent for music, but his Douloi education had equipped him to recognize at least one of them as originating on Lost Earth before the Exile. The cat provided a percussive accompaniment with its loud purr.

Muttering heartfelt imprecations, Osri braced his weight against the cat's ministrations and slapped the lumpy white dough onto the kneading board.

NINETEEN

✳

Greywing clenched her teeth.

Montrose worked quickly, his huge hands gentle as he changed the dressing. Despite the numbspray, she felt the ache of tender, raw flesh right down to her bones.

"Looks much better," Montrose said, nodding. Greywing's stomach tightened when she glanced down at the raw, oozing flesh showing through the web of pseudoskin that was guiding regrowth, but Montrose wore the air of an artist well pleased as he scrutinized it closely.

"Wrap it so I can move free," Greywing said. "Emergence in a few hours. If I need to be fast—" She shrugged her good shoulder.

Montrose looked up, his heavy brows beetling. "You mislike our errand?"

Greywing grimaced. "Vi'ya says the Arkad promised us big take. Maybe he's got enough to back that up. But *you* want the nicks running scan on your background?"

Montrose shook his head. "We're coming in on lawful business, and if we do not debark from this vessel while in the Mandala's area of governance, there will be no opportunity for them to do so."

She sniffed. "You believe that?"

Montrose tipped his head a little. "If we break no laws, they will not board us. Little as I respect the Panarchist government, I do know the limitations it imposes on itself."

He finished the bandage and sat back. Greywing knew when Montrose was finished with a subject.

She left the dispensary and wandered forward, hating the restless knotting in her innards that always hit just before emergence on a run. Vi'ya never had her work a shift just before emergence unless they'd taken damage—she liked Greywing to start fresh. Greywing understood that, but she would rather have been doing something.

She checked the duty roster, saw that Ivard was also free. She smiled. This was Ivard's first run as a navigator.

Wondering what her little brother was doing to kill time, she checked the cabin he shared with Jaim, but it was empty. Figuring he was probably on the bridge logging more practice running nav calculations, she decided to joke him a little about how much he must be missing galley slubbing.

To her surprise, she found a little crowd there. Lokri was watching the com, which was his post this watch, but the Arkad was also there—the first time Greywing had seen him out during his rec time.

She paused in the doorway, scanning the scene.

"Shall we start?" Lokri said.

Brandon opened his hands.

Ivard, who was hovering in the background, gestured to Greywing. She moved in to join him, unnoticed by the two at the console.

"Phalanx," Ivard whispered unnecessarily.

Of course Lokri was playing Phalanx—now that he had a new victim to try to cheat.

"Level Two," Ivard added.

Surprised, Greywing edged closer to the console in order to watch. Most people played the difficult three-dimensional strategy game at Level One, which allowed for time to think through one's moves. Level Two added not only hazards but one further dimension: time. Not as many played that outside of those who gambled for big stakes, usually at expensive clubs. Level Three was exponentially more difficult; Greywing remembered Markham saying once that it was as near as one could get to fleet against fleet action in space. Greywing wondered if Lokri had mentioned to the Arkad that he frequently took big sums off dedicated Phalanx players at Rifthaven, and decided he hadn't; she recognized Lokri's sudden and uncharacteristic interest in the Krysarch as speculative, not friendly.

Lokri sat upright in his pod and slapped the kill key. Ivard stepped back defensively, as though he were somehow to blame for interrupting the game. Greywing pressed her lips tight against a comment: she knew her brother was afraid of the languid comtech, but he had to stand on his own.

But Lokri did not even look their way. His gray eyes narrowed as he studied the Arkad, who just sat and smiled pleasantly. Lokri leaned forward and without asking, punched in the code for Level Three.

No further words were spoken as they launched again into the game. Brandon's face went distant, his long hands flashing over the keys and tabs without any hesitation at all.

Greywing caught a sober look from Ivard, and they moved to his own console, facing away so that their words would not carry.

"Think Lokri'll cheat?" Ivard murmured.

"He always cheats, him and Marim," Greywing said. "Why I told you never play with them."

She could tell by the way Ivard hunched his scrawny neck into his shoulders, like a timtwee sucking its eyestalks back into its carapace, that he'd disregarded her advice, and as a result probably had racked up shifts' worth of the chores that Marim and Lokri hated worst. Well, that would teach him if he wouldn't listen to her. *Either teach him not to play with them—or teach him how to cheat.*

She pressed her lips again, determined not to say anything. She knew that she and her brother could probably beat either Marim or Lokri under fair circumstances; in fact, Ivard had beaten Markham once or twice. But not when they cheated.

Greywing hated cheating in games. In life, everyone cheated everywhere, all the time. Of course. You expected that. So a game should have rules, be fair. Or it wasn't a game, it was just like life.

Lokri lifted his hands, then leaned back in his pod. His lazy smile carried some surprise. "At least," he said, rubbing his jaw, "you can pay attention while you vaporize me."

Brandon shook his head. "Sorry," he said. "I was remembering . . ."

"What?" It was no more than a soft croak from Ivard, who almost never spoke when more than two people were in a room. And Lokri almost always ignored him.

But the Krysarch turned, smiling, to Ivard. "The first time my brother Semion played me, when I was, oh, about ten. Savaged me, of course, but . . ." He looked up, his brow wrinkling in puzzlement. "I wonder now if it was some kind of a test."

Score one on Lokri, Greywing thought, making sure her face was blank as she noted a thin flush of red along Lokri's sharp cheekbones.

Of course that shot went right over Ivard's head. He looked happy that the Panarchist actually found him worthy to speak to. Ivard took a small step forward and dared another comment. "You're good—" He looked up, and his mouth snapped shut.

A moment later Marim bounced in. "Hey! Who's playing L-3? I saw that on the com in the rec room—" She regarded Brandon with interest. "You, Arkad? I didn't know brains went with the nacky birth."

"Then you are a fool as well as ignorant, Marim," said a new voice. Montrose wandered in right behind her, a book under his arm. Had everyone been watching the game on their coms? Montrose went on pleasantly, "Forty-seven generations of the habit of command ought to have bred a certain amount of natural ability into our young guest."

Marim slapped a console into life. "Play me," she demanded. "No, play me'n Lokri here."

"But you cheat," Lokri pointed out, so innocently that Greywing choked on a laugh.

"You do too, blungesniffer," Marim fired back.

"I'll play you both," Brandon said. "It so happens I've had little else to do over the last few years."

Montrose laid his book down. "Ordinarily I've little interest in these games, but this I should enjoy observing."

Marim plopped down onto her chair and they started again. Greywing lit her own console and Ivard moved to stand next to her so they could watch the action. Greywing turned so she could watch the screen and the players.

This time, Greywing could see, Brandon had to exert himself, keeping his mind strictly on the game. She figured he'd find Marim to be the more challenging opponent; she was much faster than Lokri, making decisions that were either brilliant or dangerously stupid, and whose only common characteristic was recklessness. Lokri as backup was formidable; rigorous logic dictated his moves. Brandon went down in defeat, but it was not a fast game or an easy one—and for once neither of the pair had cheated.

Montrose clapped his hands in delight. "You know, it might be worth my time to take a turn, which I haven't done for at least—"

He was interrupted by a chime from the comlink.

"Galley," Marim chortled.

Montrose touched a key. "What is it, Osri?"

"This sauce. It smells funny." His voice held a plaintive edge.

"I shall come at once." Montrose lifted his hand from the console, sighed, and got to his feet. "That young man will never be a cook. He is worse, even"—he reached forward and touched Ivard's shoulder—"than you." He went out.

"Now let's play again," Marim demanded.

Brandon gave his head a shake. "I'd like to get something to drink."

The Krysarch moved out in the direction of the rec room. Ivard went after, walking in that tight-shouldered, drifting way he had, as if he expected a gang of ripthieves to round a corner at any moment; Greywing could tell by her brother's nervousness that he was going to ask the Arkad for a game. She decided to follow. She had to let Ivard find his own place with the crew, because these were the people they lived and worked with. She didn't have to let any nick beat him down, though.

In the rec room, Brandon went to the dispenser and punched up a mug of caf. Ivard lingered in the doorway, Greywing pausing behind him. Before Ivard could speak, though, Brandon turned the other way and then stopped suddenly. Greywing, looking past, saw Vi'ya sitting alone at one of the small booths at the back, finishing up a plate of food.

Brandon looked at her, clearly hesitating. Vi'ya made a gesture inviting him to join her.

Ivard moved to the game console and punched up solo-Phalanx. Greywing hesitated, then giving in to curiosity about what he might want to talk to the captain alone about, moved to the second booth where she could not see but she could hear.

Brandon said, "Do you read everyone's minds all the time, or do you have to concentrate?"

"I don't read minds," Vi'ya said. "I am a tempath, not a telepath. But it was apparent you wished to speak to me."

There was a long hesitation. Greywing wondered why; was he going to try something? Or was he merely choosing his words? Vi'ya said nothing during the protracted silence, and Greywing could imagine her watching him steadily with those eyes, so dark it was difficult to distinguish between iris and pupil, that reminded Greywing of a volcanic lake in winter.

"I wanted to know," he said finally, "if Markham left any chips—writing—anything tangible."

Greywing had expected anything but that. She looked up, saw Ivard nearby, also listening.

"No," the captain said. "The few personal things, mementos from his father mostly, I burned."

"I wish I'd known, I wish I'd known . . ." The Krysarch spoke in a strained, bitter voice, then stopped abruptly. When he spoke again, it was with his usual polite tone, with the Douloi cadence to the words. "I suppose the new leader has to remove all traces of the old in order to transfer power?"

Her answer was completely unexpected. "So you think he is gone without a trace?"

"No," Brandon said, so soft now Greywing could barely hear him. "I feel him all around me, so much this vessel seems haunted, and he is never far from my thoughts. I had hoped there was something tangible so I could either have raised his ghost or laid it to rest."

"I burned his things because I deemed it proper," Vi'ya said. Then she got up and walked out, leaving the Krysarch alone in the booth.

❄   ❄   ❄

ARTHELION

It was peaceful, there in the gardens of the Palace Minor, as Barrodagh paced his lord along the gravel walkway winding past tall hedges and nodding, graceful trees.

Here there were no signs of the recent battles, other than an occasional trampled flowerbed, and an infrequent rusty stain on the path underfoot. And the smell. From time to time the stench of boiled seaweed and fish overwhelmed the scents of flowers and herbs, a reminder of Eusabian's destruction of the nearby bay during his triumphal descent in the *Fist of Dol'jhar*.

Barrodagh sighed silently; a concern for side effects was

not part of the Dol'jharian character—that was the province of their minions.

In the distance, Barrodagh could hear the sound of heavy machinery and faint curses from laboring men. Close by were no sounds save the crunch of gravel underfoot, the susurration of a gentle breeze, and the chattering of a myriad of birds. At a careful distance, two black-liveried Tarkans followed them.

As they walked Eusabian looked around, his arms swinging uncharacteristically free at his sides, his face relaxed in a faint smile. His long strides made no allowance for the shorter Bori, and Barrodagh scuttled alongside crab-like, trying to keep his eyes on his master's face.

"Rifellyn's now in charge of the Node," he continued. "She has orders to maintain normal traffic patterns and slot incoming ships into standard approaches for interception. Unfortunately the Panarchists triggered a doomsday worm in the defense systems after our agents' sabotage took down the resonance and Shield generators—they are both fused, and the Palace defenses are down. I'm having mobile projectors emplaced to defend the Palace, just in case."

He paused as Eusabian stopped to examine a statuary group: several people struggling in the coils of a giant serpent. Their faces were heavily weathered and blurred, but the agony instilled in them by the sculptor was still clear. A sign on a black metal post nearby identified it, but Eusabian didn't spare that a glance.

"Entili mi dirazh'ult kai panarch," murmured the Lord of Vengeance, his gaze traveling slowly down the statue. Then he tilted his head back to the bright sun, his eyes slitted with pleasure, and stretched luxuriously, knitting his hands together and turning his palms out.

Barrodagh watched nervously. Ever since their landing on Arthelion, Eusabian's moods had been impossible to predict.

"The sun of this world is warm and pleasant," said Eusabian. "My ancestors chose badly, it seems."

Barrodagh looked around, unsure how to respond. That

was an unlikely comment from the Avatar of Dol, whose authority in part devolved from his identification with the eponymic father of his race. Dol'jhar was the gift, or grant, of Dol, given to harden his people against the demonic forces that had driven them out of their original paradise. The Bori didn't believe those myths any more than, he thought, Eusabian did, but that his lord should unbend enough to make such a comment was a measure of the changes his successful vengeance was effecting in him.

Eusabian laughed. "Don't worry, my little Bori, there's no one to hear." Then he bent forward, his hands on his knees, looking at something at the base of the statue. "What is this?"

A rough piece of simple granite lay in the grass in the shadow of the marble agony above, its face smoothed and engraved with four short phrases.

" 'Ruler of all, ruler of naught, power unlimited, a prison unsought,' " read Eusabian aloud. Then he threw back his head and laughed, a roaring explosion of hilarity unlike anything Barrodagh had heard from him before. "Ruler of naught!" He chortled, wiping his eyes. "How appropriate! Did he ever see it as the prediction it was, I wonder?"

His chuckling died away slowly. "A prison unsought . . ." He turned suddenly. Barrodagh repressed a pang of alarm. *He's in a good mood. There's nothing to fear.*

"How long until an escort can be spared?"

"We estimate between twenty and thirty days, Lord. Then it's perhaps as long to Gehenna."

Eusabian turned and frowned at the Palace behind them. Barrodagh held his breath, remembering the interview in the Throne Room. *The paliach is complete, or nearly so: his enemy is not dead.*

Barrodagh still did not know what to make of that interview: Barrodagh had finally been unable to invent any more excuses to avoid reentering that huge ice hall of a Throne Room. When he had, he'd not found the pulped body he'd expected; Gelasaar had been alive still, under the jacs of white-lipped guardsmen, and Eusabian had been nowhere in sight.

Barrodagh had promptly ordered the Panarch housed deep within the Palace system, in some ancient holding cells one of their agents had identified, but the Avatar had not asked about him since.

Thinking to distract his lord, Barrodagh spoke. "The *Satansclaw* is due within hours with the gnostor Omilov aboard, along with all of his collected artifacts. I have Lysanter standing by aboard the *Fist of Dol'jhar*; he will shuttle over to the ship as soon as it arrives, to identify the Heart of Kronos."

Eusabian nodded, still frowning. "You will also go to the *Satansclaw*, to supervise the inspection. Bring the gnostor back with you."

Barrodagh's heart sank. *Another shuttle flight.*

"The *Satansclaw* is the ship that forced the third heir into the gas giant, is it not?" continued the Avatar. At Barrodagh's nod he added, "Bring the ship's captain too—"

A loud clanking roar accompanied by impassioned cursing interrupted Eusabian and spun them both around. The hedge behind the statue exploded outward in a shower of foliage as a mobile plasma projector bounded through the opening, trailing a comet tail of guards in gray. The man in the cannon's control pod yanked desperately at the steering gear and pounded the console, while another clung to the front of it, trying desperately to pull his legs up away from the ground-effect skirt.

Dust and shattered branches pelted Barrodagh and Eusabian, stinging their eyes. The two Tarkan guards who had originally accompanied them ran up, their weapons ready, then stopped in confusion, seeing no enemies, only fellow soldiers. The cannon slewed wildly as the driver caught sight of the Lord of Vengeance; its barrel whipped around and clipped off the head of one of the figures on the statue, which bounced across the ground to Eusabian's feet and came to rest staring up at him with accusing eyes. The cannon slid sideways several feet as the sound of its engines slid up the scale toward inaudibility, then, with a shattering bang, it ejected a cloud of greasy black smoke from its underside and fell with a heavy thump to the ground.

Barrodagh looked down at himself in distress. The death throes of the plasma cannon had showered him with oily black smuts; his clothes were ruined. With a gasp he looked up at Eusabian. He couldn't read his lord's expression through the mask of oil that obscured it, but his teeth showed slightly between thinned lips. Barrodagh stifled a snort of hysterical laughter and managed to turn it into a cough.

The guardsman atop the cannon scrambled down and flung himself headlong before Eusabian's feet. The two Tarkans twitched, their weapons ready; Eusabian threw up a hand to restrain them. The other guards stared at their lord in terror, unmoving.

The tableau held for a moment, then dissolved as Eusabian turned to Barrodagh. "Is this an example of the defenses you are emplacing to guard me?" There was an unfamiliar glint in his eyes; at another time Barrodagh would have called it humor—the cold humor that was all Eusabian had ever permitted himself in Jhar D'ocha.

Now the Bori was confused and frightened by his inability to read his master's emotions. *It's not fair*, his mind wailed. *Now that he's got what he wanted, everything's changing.* This was certainly not what Barrodagh had expected a Dol'jharian victory to bring.

With a wrenching effort he collected his wits and replied, bowing deeply, "No, Lord, it is an example of total incompetence." He turned and kicked the groveling guardsman. "Explain yourself!"

The only answer was an unintelligible mumble.

"Speak up!"

"The guardsman looked up, addressing himself to Eusabian. "Lord, we have had no time . . . we are unfamiliar with the Panarchist equipment . . . it is very old . . ."

"Excuses are unacceptable," shouted the Bori, then halted as Eusabian turned away, an expression of boredom flitting across his face.

"Deal with this yourself," he said, and strode back toward the Palace, followed by the bodyguards. Abruptly he stopped, turned back for a moment. "And make sure the statue is repaired perfectly."

Moments later he disappeared around a curve in the path and Barrodagh relaxed inside. He looked down at the guard, a smile slowly possessing his face. "We both know the penalty for failure, don't we, hmmm?" he asked. "Especially one so spectacular." The guard looked up at him mutely, hope visibly fading from his eyes.

As Barrodagh looked around at the other guards, enjoying the panicky way they avoided his gaze, a soft chattering hum came to his ears. A short distance off, an automated mower floated across the lawn, a faint bluish light flickering from underneath its fairing as its energy fields sheared the grass and returned it to the earth as finely chopped mulch.

"Yes," hissed the Bori. "That will do just fine." He motioned to two of the other guards. "Take your knives and pin his hands and feet to the ground over there." The guard at his feet gasped in sudden comprehension and tried to scramble away as the two that Barrodagh had singled out came over reluctantly and grabbed him, their faces tight.

The Bori issued instructions to the remaining guards for dealing with the cannon and statue, then stood and watched for a moment as his orders were carried out. "Feet first, you fools!" he shouted as they threw their comrade to the ground about thirty meters ahead of the slowly advancing mower. They hesitated, as though debating whether to pretend not to hear, then dragged the luckless man around, roughly crossed his hands and feet, and pinned him to the ground.

The man was moaning continuously now; as the mower reached his feet it hesitated, and Barrodagh realized it must have some sort of safety override in it. It began to slip sideways and he shouted, "Don't let it get away. Push it!" He motioned another guard over to the machine.

As the third man pushed the machine it balked; impatiently Barrodagh ran over and shoved at it. Suddenly it jinked sideways. The guards jumped away and it swerved again as its sensors discerned a path to freedom. The fairing passed over the front of Barrodagh's feet, neatly removing the ends of his boots, leaving his toes exposed to the cool air. Barrodagh shrieked and jumped away, fell sprawling as the mower moved off, chattering contentedly to itself. His feet felt wet ... he looked in horror at them, touched his toes gently, more than half-convinced that they would fall off. No, he was untouched; the dampness was from the grass. Then he noticed the guardsman staring at him, their expressions carefully neutral.

The Bori scrambled to his feet, trying to salvage what he could of the situation. "Take him back to the barracks for discipline," he snapped, gesturing at the man crucified on the lawn. "And get this mess cleaned up, immediately!"

He turned and limped away, thrown off balance by the loss of his boot fronts, hoping feverently the story of his disgrace wouldn't spread but knowing it would.

For Barrodagh, the occupation of Arthelion was not going well.

❋   ❋   ❋

Greywing was as startled as Brandon looked when Ivard spoke suddenly: "I got something."

Brandon turned quickly. He looked up at Greywing's brother, who had never within living memory offered information to a stranger of his own accord. It was rare enough when he asked questions.

"You want me to see a thing of his?" Ivard went on. "I keep it on me." His voice squeaked with nervousness as he slid a hand into his inner pocket.

Brandon nodded, giving Ivard that polite smile that no one could read. "Certainly," he said.

Ivard smiled, then his eyes flickered as a familiar series of tones sounded overhead. "Emergence soon," he muttered. "Here." His hand came out of his coverall, holding out a small, crumpled object on his open palm.

Greywing watched, amazed. Ivard had never shown anyone but her his single prize, the only thing he treasured.

Her eyes went from the gold-and-silver-striped raw-silk ribbon to Brandon's face as he took it from Ivard, and though his expression did not change, all the muscles in his face tightened. "You know what this is?" the Krysarch asked, his fingers closing over the ribbon.

Greywing looked back at the highly prized Piloting Award in the Krysarch's hand, an award given out only at the Minerva Naval Academy. The neatly embossed printing ended with the year 955—the year that Markham and the Krysarch had been thrown out.

Ivard swallowed, his larynx moving in his skinny neck. "He told me when he gave it to me. Told me once about some of the stunts you two pulled." His eyes narrowed in pleasure. "Gave it to me when we squeaked out of a bad one. I helped by something I did with a scoutcraft. He told me I would have won it myself if I'd gone to the Academy." Longing quirked Ivard's almost invisible brows. "He was teaching me."

Brandon laid the ribbon back in Ivard's hand, and watched as Ivard replaced it quickly in his clothing.

"How'd you find your way into his crew?" Brandon asked.

Ivard's pale skin turned pink, and he slid a quick look at Greywing. Brandon followed his gaze, his eyes distracted. He hadn't noticed her before this, she realized.

"We're bond-breakers," Ivard said, and his sister hoped that this Arkad nick heard the pride in his voice. "Me and Greywing. I was bonded over to a mining combine right after I turned ten, and after I'd had enough of beatings and crawling through pipes I ran away. Lived as a thief, until Greywing found me. She'd run too."

"On a planet? A ship?"

"No. No ship," Ivard said with a shake of his head.

"How'd you find your way off-planet?" Brandon's voice was interested, almost sympathetic.

Greywing had stopped trusting nicks long before they left their home planet, and if she had been alone she would have warned her brother. But they were not alone—*And if Ivard doesn't know what I think about blabbing now, he never will.*

She waited fatalistically to see how much he betrayed to this smiling, blank-eyed Douloi.

Ivard said, "I really wanted to fly, all along." His face lifted, as if toward the sky, a gesture that immediately identified a born Downsider, Greywing knew now. "We joined a gang, and Trev—he was our leader—had a cousin who'd gone with a Rifter crew. When they landed he got us in with them." Ivard grinned. "Captain was a Shiidra's blungehole, which is why he always needed more crew. But it got us off-planet, and I learned plenty while servin' as a scrub-slub. *Watched* everything, especially the command crew. Loved the numbers on the screens . . ." He paused, his gaze far away. "At first it was fun not to know what they meant. Then I started figuring what they meant. I could, oh, see 'em." His fingers formed a loose circle. "In four dimensions. Then captain found out what I was doin' and brigged me for it. Jumped ship soon's we reached Rifthaven. Couple more bad hitches, then we got hiked by that slime-spitter Jakarr. But we liked the rest of the gang, so we stayed on." He shrugged awkwardly, looking embarrassed as he stole a glance at his sister. "I know I yak a lot."

"How about the rest of the crew?" Brandon asked. "Where did they come from?"

Ivard's face flushed crimson. As he struggled for words, Greywing said quickly, "Isn't done. They want to talk about themselves, you ask them."

Ivard gave a jerky, grateful nod. "With *us* anyway. Some outfits, captain wants to know. Markham said a person's character and skills, not past mistakes, should sync 'em in or not."

"Markham talked about his past, though, didn't he?" Brandon asked.

"A little. We all knew where he came from. He talked like a nick, same's Montrose—"

Greywing stopped when an urgent belltone interrupted them. A surge of emotion jolted her innards: they were just about to emerge into realtime over the Krysarch's planet—the Mandala.

"Time to go to the bridge," she said.

TWENTY

✳

Ivard slid another look in her direction, to see if she was angry, she knew, then he moved out quickly. Greywing said nothing, falling in behind the Krysarch as he walked to the bridge.

She took a deep breath. Ivard knew she didn't like him talking about their past. *As well there are some things he doesn't know, and isn't going to*, she thought grimly, remembering what she'd had to do to get away—and again to rescue him.

Shaking off memory, and the anger that came with memory, she made straight toward her pod and hit the control to light it. As her fingers tapped out an automatic status check, she turned her head slightly and watched Brandon move to the empty fire-control pod. He stood for a moment, staring down at the console. Greywing wondered what he was thinking. Would he see that the *Telvarna* had a lot more firepower than most ships its size, had obviously been refitted fairly recently? Did he recognize Markham's as the hand and mind behind the redesign?

Marim leaned toward him. "What's the matter, you lost?"

Brandon tensed slightly and looked over at her. Greywing saw his distant eyes scan her for a second or so, and then recognition came. *He's fighting his own shades,* Greywing thought, feeling a curious sense of satisfaction in that.

Meanwhile the Arkad gave Marim that polite mask-smile and said, "On the contrary. I think I could run it blind."

Vi'ya sat down at her command console. She shot an appraising look at Brandon, then turned her attention back to her board.

Marim said, "Markham was Fire Control before he took over. Told us what we'd had was as modern and quick as a pre-Hegemonist surveyor craft. Had this rewired to his own specs. Pretty, eh?"

"Yes—"

The emergence signal sounded, and Brandon dropped into his seat. Marim hopped to her own pod and scanned her board.

Vi'ya spoke. "We'll make a peaceful approach to your Arthelion."

The screens cleared from skip and Arthelion appeared, remote and lovely, just as it had appeared in countless holos—*as it looked in my dreams.* Greywing felt a frisson of . . . what? Trepidation? Longing? She hated remembering how she'd planned to escape to the Mandala in order to get justice for those at home who didn't, or couldn't, escape.

The screen shimmered to a close-up; she noted Vi'ya's fingers moving on her console. At Fire Control the Krysarch looked up, his profile unreadable, his straight-shouldered figure tense.

Greywing heard her brother's short intake of breath. Ivard pointed at the screen, which showed now a gentle sprinkling of clouds covering the archipelago wherein lay the Palace Major.

"The Mandala . . ." Ivard said, his voice high with awe and fear. "We can't land there."

"Why not? Just a dirtball like any other," Marim said.

But Greywing heard the undercurrent of bravado in her voice.

"The Magisterium has done its job well," Lokri drawled, at his most hateful. "When every fool believes in all that nonsense about *the Mandala,* the nicks are more protected by legend than by mere weapons."

Ivard reacted like he'd been hit, and Greywing, her mind seething with anger, considered just what she could say to strike at Lokri with equal force. But then the comtech spoke again—as if he hadn't said anything of importance: "Incoming query."

"Reactivate the transponder, original registry," Vi'ya commanded.

Lokri's console bleeped. "Message incoming." He tapped a key and the com came to life.

"YST 8740 *Maiden's Dream,* you are cleared for approach to near orbit. Fast or slow?"

Vi'ya tabbed her console. "Fast. Standard contract accepted."

"Stand by for orbital insertion. Estimated time to orbit, 12.5 minutes."

The Krysarch had said nothing, but Lokri must have been watching him fairly closely, for he said, "Never've had to pay to land or leave, have you, Arkad?"

Brandon looked up with an expression of mild surprise. *He's humoring Lokri,* Greywing thought. *Like you would a bad-tempered child.*

Greywing felt the urge to hurry into speech, though whether to deflect or to attack, she did not stop to analyze. "Well, we do," she said. "If we don't pay for the ride through the resonance field to high orbit, they can sell the ship out from under us." She waited for the Arkad to say, *But we wouldn't sell anyone's ship out from under them,* but he didn't. His expression still curious, as if he were on tour and not going home, he watched the screens.

There was no sense of acceleration as the lunar-based tractor seized the ship in a modified geeplane field and accelerated it at hundreds of gravities toward Arthelion.

"Maiden's Dream?" Brandon said presently.

Marim snorted a laugh. "Don't know what the owner before had in mind, but I say it's 'cause it's long and lean and real good at slipping in and out of tight places." She hooted at her own joke, and Ivard snickered.

One way to get him to stop looking like a squashed timtwee, Greywing thought. *Jokes about sex.* Lately any mention of sex was funny to Ivard. Did that mean he was ready to bunny? *By the time I was his age, I already knew it wasn't any joke.* Greywing shook back the distracting thought; time enough to worry about that later.

"We got lots of names for *Telvarna*," Marim went on, "but that's the safest one t'use around the nicks, 'cause it's the only registered one."

"We've never used it as long as I've been around," said Lokri. "So we're just another vessel, coming in nice and polite, on lawful business."

"Long's they don't ask us what that business is," Greywing replied, giving Brandon a doubtful look.

He lifted his hands. "If we need it, I have a Royal override, but I think it would be better not to use it if we don't have to."

They fell silent, watching the planet slowly grow larger in the viewscreen. Vi'ya began running a series of checks through each of the consoles on the bridge, keeping the crew busy. Finally the com spoke again. "Tractor disengaged. Prepare for course download. Wait for further instructions after orbit acquisition."

There was a brief squeal of code before the sound cut off. "It's all yours, Ivard."

Ivard looked over at Vi'ya, who nodded, then he stabbed at a keypad. "Course locked in and executing."

Marim looked perplexed. "Feels awful weird turning over the *Telvarna* to some machine."

"Panarchists won't have it any other way," said Vi'ya, "especially here, at the center of their power. There are no doubt heavy weapons tracking us at this moment, set to trigger on any deviation."

The others looked at Brandon, who nodded. "There hasn't been an accident for over a century," he said.

"Makes me feel *real* good," Marim cracked.

"Would they really zap an innocent ship?" asked Ivard incautiously.

"Innocent ship?" Marim hooted, looking around with wide eyes. "Where?"

Ivard hunched his head down like a timtwee again and Brandon spoke quickly, as if he felt moved to interject a comment to blunt Marim's derisive remark. "Marim's right, Ivard, though not the way she means. A ship can do an awful lot of damage to a planet—not to mention the Syncs— even without bad intentions."

Had the Arkad really done that out of kindness? Greywing considered Brandon with something akin to real approval. "Think of it this way, Ivard," she said to her brother. "*Telvarna* masses maybe twenty thousand tons. Escape velocity for Arthelion would be over eleven kilometers a second . . ."

Ivard's eyes widened, his innate grasp of spatial relationships and the physics of spaceflight suddenly making the situation quite clear.

Now the planet was rapidly swelling on-screen, the Highdweller Communities forming a delicate necklace of light around it. A scattering of other lights indicated other ships in orbit.

Greywing thrust her brother and the others out of her mind when she saw something on her screen. Faster than thought she hit a tab, windowing up a magnified view of one of the dots of light along their course on the main viewscreen. The familiar egg-shape of a battlecruiser took form, its numerous protrusions of weapons and sensors a mere fuzziness at this distance.

Greywing said nothing, her teeth gritted against letting any sound escape. She looked to the captain, who studied the cruiser in silence.

It was Marim who spoke first, settling back in her seat

with her arms crossed and one foot propped on her console. "Sure feels strange not to be running from that chatzer."

Only Lokri laughed.

The crew watched in silence for a time.

Brandon supposed that each of them was coming to terms with the reality of their approach to the Mandala, which centuries of legend and tradition carefully nurtured by the Magisterium and the College of Archetype and Ritual had endowed with a mystical hold on the imaginations of all the peoples of the Thousand Suns. Even Lokri, despite his words, stared with unblinking gaze at the planet looming larger every moment.

Everyone except, it seems, Vi'ya, Brandon thought, noting her cool gaze on him. She alone seemed entirely unaffected by their approach to the heart of the Tetrad Centrum, the densely interconnected center of the Panarchy, home of the oldest cultures with the strongest ties to Lost Earth. *I wonder where she comes from?* He didn't think he'd ever heard an accent quite like hers, and yet it had a disturbing familiarity.

Abruptly Vi'ya tapped at her console and magnified the view again. The viewscreen shimmered and the image of the battlecruiser rippled for a moment as the enhancement circuits cut in. Then the picture became mercilessly clear, revealing the blazon on the ship as a stylized red fist clutching a handful of lightning bolts, surrounded by angular script in a wreath of flames.

Vi'ya spoke softly, her voice almost a hiss. "The *Fist of Dol'jhar.*"

Dol'jhar—

My father is the Avatar of Dol, and you would not live a day on Dol'jhar . . .

Brandon shut his eyes, his thoughts splitting along two rapid lines. He remembered Anaris, son of Eusabian, speaking those words, with that accent—that was one track.

The second one: *The captain of this ship is Dol'jharian.*

Brandon forced away both memory and conjecture when

Vi'ya spoke again. Her words were a surprise: "That ship was confined to Dol'jharian orbit by the Treaty of Acheront, was it not?" she asked.

Brandon nodded slowly, sorting words and tone for false-hood, for threat or intent. He read nothing. "Perhaps there's a treaty conference taking place," he said. He wondered if the others could hear the doubt and confusion in his voice. "Or some other state function involving Dol'jhar. If it were a really high-level contact, diplomacy would require the use of Eusabian's flagship."

"You tell us," said Marim, lounging in her pod. "You're the high-end nick here."

Brandon looked down at his hands resting tensely on the darkened fire-control console. "I assure you, Marim, that I'd be one of the last to know. My function in the machin-ery of state involved . . . other things."

The crew must have heard the sudden formality in his voice, for there was silence for a time, broken only by the tapping of Vi'ya's fingers at her console. "Ivard, confirm," she said finally, and then keyed the intercom. "Jaim, engine status?"

"Never been better," came the reply. "What're you think-ing?" Brandon realized that he must be watching on a screen slaved to the bridge. *Not for Rifters the rigid com-partmentalization of naval discipline.*

Vi'ya sat for a moment without replying, looking across the intervening space of the bridge at Brandon, her eyes narrowed. "If it is not on a state visit, any query from us will be answered with a ruptor. The only thing we can do is wait until the situation becomes clear. If necessary, we will wait until our assigned orbit takes us around the planet from the *Fist* and then blast out." She paused. "Lokri, can you tell if the resonance field is up?"

Lokri glanced over at Marim. "We can set up a low power test with the fiveskip cavity, check it that way. It'll take a few minutes."

"Do it."

Brand heard the exchanges with only a portion of his

mind as he struggled with the presence of the enemy battlecruiser in orbit around the Mandala. *Mandala. Now I'm doing it,* he thought, *as if invoking the mystery can chase away fifty billion tons of warship.*

Memory seized him again: his first meeting with Anaris. Himself about ten years old, Galen a young teen. The two had been playing in the formal gardens—practicing Kelly-sign—when several adults appeared, all dressed in formal clothing, and one of them started talking in an officious voice.

But Brandon's attention had not been on the adults. He looked at the only object of real interest, a small figure in the midst of the tall ones, wearing only black, with high black boots and some kind of weapon at his waist. This boy, somewhat older and a lot taller than Brandon, had gazed back at him through unblinking dark eyes above a mouth that bore no hint of smile.

"The hostage . . ." Galen had said on a sudden indrawn breath.

Brandon did not know what that meant, and didn't care. He did know that this boy was looking at them like they smelled bad.

"We'll welcome him," Brandon said, laughing, as he got an idea. And he danced a Kelly welcome dance, moving near enough to poke at the boy's face and stomach.

At first Galen joined, until the boy made a sudden, vicious stab at them with his knife. Brandon fell back on the grass, astonished: he hadn't even seen the boy draw that weapon. But he forgot the knife when he saw the boy's face, which had changed into something altogether strange.

Eyes distended, face crimson, the boy glared. Brandon yelled, "He's *choking!*"

The adults froze into a group of statues. It was Galen who moved, faster even than the boy, and with his greater strength he got his arms around the visitor and pressed his fist hard against his middle in the lifesaving move they'd all been taught.

The boy whooped like a sick crane, then vomited up

whatever he'd eaten last all over his glossy boots. Brandon had collapsed, helpless with laughter. Through his gasps, he heard that voice, high and angry, in that accent . . .

My father is the Avatar of Dol . . .

It wasn't until years later that Brandon found out that Anaris had been attempting to quell them with a Dol'jharian grimace of fear and command.

The memory dissolved, bringing him back to the present—the sight of the ship belonging not to Anaris rahal'Jerrodi, but to his father, hanging above Arthelion. Why?

He looked down at his fingers, which had been twisting Tanri's ring round and round. The jeweled eyes of the sphinxes flashed in the light. *The fulfillment of a promise, at the very least.*

He looked back at the screens. In the rear view, the Palace Major was sliding over the horizon. Ahead, the Syncs, brilliantly lit by the sun in their higher vantage, formed a curving arrow of light beckoning them onward as their course took them across the terminator into night.

❄   ❄   ❄

As the *Satansclaw* grew rapidly larger, Barrodagh kept his hands gripped together, hoping the pilot next to him wouldn't notice how tense he was. He hated spaceflight, and he cursed Rifellyn for assigning him a shuttlecraft so small it had no passenger cabin. Instead of a comfortable cabin with blanked-out viewscreens, he was trapped in the secondary control pod of a two-man shuttle with a sickeningly large direct-view dyplast viewport.

Rifellyn knows how much I hate this. She's going to regret her little joke.

The Bori noticed the pilot glancing sidelong at him as the shuttle closed in on the destroyer hanging in low orbit above Arthelion. Barrodagh ignored him, desperately trying to keep the infinite void just beyond the dyplast at bay. He held his breath as the *Satansclaw* filled the viewport, the shuttle lurching as the destroyer's tractor beam grabbed them. He jerked as they slipped through the electronic airlock into the main shuttle bay in a slithering display of static discharges crawling across the dyplast, and then relaxed as they settled to the deck.

As the engines of the little craft spun down into silence, Barrodagh went to the lock and cycled it open. Outside, a man approached, holding a long wand-like tool with a metal cable dangling from it to the deck. An overdressed Rifter followed him. Beyond them Barrodagh glimpsed a sprawling confusion of pallets and boxes with their contents spilling out of them.

As he started to step out the pilot turned to him. "Wait a minute, sir, you can't go out yet."

"Don't tell me what I can do!" snarled the Bori impatiently. The man with the wand waved frantically at him as he stepped down, but Barrodagh ignored him.

There was a loud snapping sound and the Bori suddenly found himself lying on his back staring up at the lights overhead. An evil smell singed his nose and his feet hurt. He shook his head and sat up shakily, then yelled with surprise when he discovered that his boots were on fire.

A uniformed crewman ran up and triggered an extinguisher, dousing the flames and splattering Barrodagh with smelly foam. He scrambled to his feet and glared at the fancily dressed Rifter, whom he now recognized as Tallis Y'Marmor.

Tallis was trying not to smile, and the effort was making his eyes protrude slightly. "I'm sorry, my lord," he said unctuously. "It's a side effect of the lock field—a massive static charge. We were about to discharge it when you stepped out. I trust you are unhurt?"

Only slightly mollified by Tallis' use of the undeserved honorific, Barrodagh stared at him stonily until the Rifter's eyes fell. "Yes. Is Lysanter here from the *Fist of Dol'jhar* yet?"

"He's over there now," said Tallis.

Barrodagh followed the long pointing finger to see the slight form of the xenoarchaeologist emerge from behind a large crate. The man caught sight of the Bori at the same moment and hurried over.

"I haven't found any Urian artifacts yet, senz lo'Barrodagh," he said, using the proper inferior-to-superior inflection. The Dol'jharian honorific sounded odd in the midst of the man's smooth Uni intonations. "But I've only just started."

Barrodagh turned to Tallis, who spread his hands and shrugged. "Since you didn't describe exactly what you wanted, we brought everything from Omilov's house collection, and we busted open his vault, and the vaults at the University, just as you instructed."

Tallis essayed a look that the Bori judged was meant to be ingenuous and continued, "Perhaps if you described what you are looking for?"

This fool wouldn't last but moments on Dol'jhar. But, Barrodagh considered, here in orbit around Arthelion, under the ruptor turrets of the *Fist* and away from the more perceptive greed of Hreem the Faithless, there was probably no harm in telling the man what the Heart of Kronos looked like. He glanced around at the jumble of artifacts and objects that covered most of the deck. *If I don't tell him, we could be here for days.*

"Did you supervise the packing?" he asked the Rifter captain.

"Of course." Tallis sounded slightly offended.

"Good. What are looking for is about the size of your fist or smaller, a mirrored sphere with an odd feel to it."

Tallis rolled his eyes up and touched three fingers to his chin in an affected pose. Barrodagh gritted his teeth and waited. *If he weren't such a good informant on Hreem, I'd gladly have him spaced.*

"I think," said Tallis finally, "that I know where there is something like that. Over this way."

Followed by the Bori and Lysanter, he picked his way carefully through the mess to a point about halfway across the bay, where a large crate lay unopened.

"It might be in here. I'll have someone open it." He motioned to a crewman nearby, who came over carrying a small, blunt-nosed device, which he applied to the top edge of the crate. It began emitting a muffled snarling noise as the top of the crate slowly peeled back, accompanied by the smell of heated plastic.

While they were waiting, Barrodagh turned to Tallis. "Did Hreem interfere at all with the search at Omilov's estate, or at the University?"

Tallis smiled. "No, he didn't dare, since you were perceptive enough to cut my orders for Arthelion before you assigned me to the search."

The patronizing implication of Tallis' words grated at Barrodagh. *But at least he saw why I did it that way. I can still use him for the time being.*

"He was rather unhappy when your orders came through changing the assignments you'd made before the attack," continued Tallis. "Some of his comments were rather unguarded." He looked hopefully at Barrodagh, who ignored his leading tone. *I know Hreem hates me. What this fool doesn't recognize is that hatred tends to make an enemy predictable.* He wondered how Tallis managed to be such a mix of perception and blindness. *And as for that battlecruiser at Malachronte . . .*

Barrodagh smiled and put the thought away as the crewman levered aside the top of the crate and Tallis pointed to a large glossy wooden chest inside. "It's in there, I think."

Barrodagh stood back impatiently as the others wrestled the chest out and opened it. Inside was a neatly nested set of trays with some incomprehensible objects in them, along with a leather-bound book. Lysanter picked up the book and started to leaf through it while Barrodagh and Tallis lifted out the trays.

"We looked through this chest before we packed it, and I think what you're looking for is in one of the lower layers," said Tallis.

Barrodagh looked in bewilderment at some of the artifacts as he put the trays aside. He could readily believe that they were Urian in origin—he'd never seen anything like them. There was a basket-like contraption of some dull metal that looked like the most uncomfortable underwear conceivable; a thing like an elongated cup with two curving thongs of metal springing out of its lip like pincers; and other even less likely objects.

The Bori shook his head. Why would anyone collect such nonsense? If this was an example of the concerns of the Panarchic aristocracy, it was no wonder Eusabian's paliach had succeeded so completely.

Then he forgot his perplexity as Tallis lifted aside a tray to reveal a smoothly gleaming metal sphere beneath. Barrodagh grunted and slapped Tallis' hand aside as the Rifter reached for it. He picked it up gingerly; it felt oddly light in his hand.

Behind him he heard Lysanter gurgle a laugh. "Oh my." But he paid no attention, turning the sphere over in his hands. Excitement raced through him. *The Heart of Kronos!* He could already see the light of approval in Eusabian's eyes when he put the final key to conquest into his hands.

Wait a minute. He suddenly noticed a hole in the sphere. *The description of the Heart never mentioned a hole.* The hole was about the diameter of his thumb. And there was another, much smaller hole on the side opposite.

"Senz lo'Barrodagh!" said Lysanter urgently, but Barrodagh's curiosity overcame him and he pushed his thumb into the hole. The substance of the sphere yielded oddly, enlarging slightly to accept his thumb; its interior was warm.

"These are not Urian artifacts," said Lysanter, glancing at Barrodagh's hand, then quickly away.

"No?" said Barrodagh, pulling at the little sphere. It seemed reluctant to come off.

"I wasn't sure at first—none of the artifacts in the top layer were Urian, certainly, but there was no indication of what else the chest was supposed to contain." He bit his lip, his eyes fixed on a distant point across the cargo bay.

Barrodagh, although somewhat distracted by his struggle with the sphere, which had now flowed up his thumb all the way to its base, suddenly had the awful feeling that Lysanter was trying very hard not to laugh.

"But the book here identifies this as a collection belonging to one Lady Risiena Ghettierus." The xenoarchaeologist's voice was higher now, his eyes suspiciously bright. "—Whom I assume is the gnostor's wife. Her handwriting is rather difficult to decipher."

Barrodagh was almost panicky now. The sphere would not come off his thumb. He banged it against the side of the crate, with no effect; now he couldn't even feel his thumb anymore.

"What is it?" he yelled. "Get it off!" He waved his arm wildly and smacked Tallis square in the face, provoking a copious nosebleed. Tallis yelped and bent over, trying unsuccessfully to keep the blood off his uniform. The crewman, the opener forgotten in his hand, stood gaping.

Lysanter finally lost control, tears spurting from his eyes, the words impelled from his lips amid helpless giggling. "Forgive me, senz lo'Barrodagh. It's a part of a collection of male chastity devices—" The man bit his lip firmly, then went on in a wooden voice that was somehow worse than a fit of helpless laughter would have been, "—and I don't think it's supposed to come off."

※　　　　※　　　　※

"Got it," said Marim with satisfaction. "Right, Lokri?"

The comtech cast a slow look over his console, then he nodded, all the humor for once gone out of his face. The gem in his ear winked with brief crimson flame. Greywing's insides tightened.

"The resonance field *is* down," continued Marim. "Once we're past natural radius, we're free and clear."

Brandon frowned.

"Not good. Right?" Greywing said flatly.

"No."

"Maybe there's some strut-ass reason for it, like showing goodwill or somethin'?" ventured Marim. She alone still smiled, though with less humor than challenge, Greywing thought critically. Nobody believed this was going to be a peaceful landing, as they'd been promised before launch.

"The Panarchists would never leave Arthelion naked like that," Vi'ya said, "not for any reason, especially not with Eusabian's battlecruiser in orbit."

A sudden bleep and voice from Lokri's console interrupted her. "YST 8740 *Maiden's Delight*, new course incoming."

"Relay to you, Ivard," said Lokri.

When the code squeal cut off, Ivard hesitated, looking at Vi'ya. "They want us to drop to two hundred kilometers, same heading."

She looked at the rearview; the *Fist of Dol'jhar* was a point of light behind them near the limb of the planet below, barely discernible as an ellipse. "Go ahead. That will take the *Fist* below the horizon all the faster."

Ivard nodded and accepted the course change, his young face serious as he tapped it out. Greywing wished briefly that he was back with Norton and the crew of the *Sunflame* and then dismissed the thought. Whatever happened, it was better that they were together.

Slowly Arthelion grew larger, irregular sparkles of light marking cities on the continent below. It was a few minutes before it became apparent that the battlecruiser was not dropping below the limb of Arthelion.

"Lokri, give me visual ranging on the *Fist*," Vi'ya said.

"It's dropping into a lower orbit, closing in on us. Can't say how fast without a range pulse."

"No. Let them think we haven't noticed." She turned to Brandon, gave him a long measuring stare.

He returned her gaze, his face as unreadable as the captain's. If he felt any of the turmoil that churned inside Greywing, and marked Lokri's and Ivard's faces, it did not show.

"The enemy of my enemy . . ." the Krysarch said finally. "My people would not send Dol'jharians to do their dirty work."

She nodded slowly. "So I thought." She tapped at her

console, and the fire-control position came to life in front of Brandon. "We'll see how much Markham managed to teach you, then."

She keyed her intercom. "Jaim, I want overload capacity from the engines. We'll have to get down into the atmosphere as fast as possible, deep enough to dissipate their ruptors so they don't pulp us right off."

She turned to Marim, her fingers racing across the console as she spoke. "I'm going to geeplane us into a negative orbit at maximum power. Cut the gravs now, and if you need to, steal additional power from the shields—they won't do any good against ruptors anyway."

A series of warning tones sounded.

Osri looked up from the refrigeration plates he was laboriously cleaning and pushed his sticky hair off his forehead. *Free-fall? What's going on now?*

Montrose appeared in the doorway, his face grim. "Get up and go to your cabin." His voice was flat, without its customary hint of humor.

When Osri hesitated, the big Rifter crossed the floor in a couple of strides, jerked him to his feet, and half dragged him out of the room and down to his cabin, ignoring Osri's expostulations.

Osri stumbled through the cabin hatch and heard the lock engage behind him. He barely made it to his bunk before the gravitors snapped off. *The only reason to cut the gravitors is for repair, or to divert power for something else. There's no reason for it in a standard approach.* Uneasy speculations spun through his mind, centering on images of the attack on Charvann.

Osri shook his head as if to dislodge his thoughts. *This is the Mandala, the center of Douloi power—* The sudden jerking of the ship shattered his speculations. *Missiles?* Then the unmistakable bone-jarring squeal-rumble of a ruptor pulse; thankfully a miss. Now he was honestly afraid; his helplessness and ignorance made it even worse. Anger came to his rescue. *What in hell are these damned*

Rifters up to? Then he felt the familiar shudder of reentry, and weight returned. They were aerodynamic, unwelcome guests in the skies over Arthelion. But whom had they just evaded?

Brandon strapped himself into his seat as the gravitors cut out and they went into free-fall. He half listened to Vi'ya's subsequent orders while he ran the fire console through a wake-up check. Partway through the sequence a small window popped up on his screen and almost immediately vanished, but not before he caught the word "personal." *A personal setting?* He ran the program back, saw that some-one had set the console to automatically come up in the default configuration. His eyes stung suddenly as he saw the second choice: *Alt L'Ranja gehaidin!* The motto of Markham's adoptive family, the branch now expunged from the Ranks of Service. He tabbed "Accept."

The screen blanked momentarily, then lit up with a completely different configuration. *Tenno battle glyphs!* A change rippled through the keypads, colors and tactiles changing and labels adapting to the new configuration. When it settled down moments later, Brandon was staring at a fire-control console equal to anything he had seen at the Academy. Suddenly his throat felt thick. *Markham's last gift.* His hands now ranged across the console many times faster than before, accelerating as familiarity returned. *Don't think about them, Brandy, just let them move your hands. Get out of the way and let the glyphs do the work.*

It's just as he said, Brandon thought, *you never forget them!*

The battle glyphs—tactical ideographs—had been refined over hundreds of years to cover every possible configuration of warfare, and since they were built up from simpler conceptual modules, they could be, and had been, extended to cover new technologies and tactics. Conveying information at near the theoretical maximum predicted for visual input, using color, form, and movement, they forged a link between human and machine that made the two one.

Now Brandon could almost feel his friend grinning over his shoulder, hear his bantering voice, *Well, Brandy, you're pinned against the planet by a battlecruiser that you can't touch with anything you've got . . . what do you do now?*

"Blind 'em with my brilliance, or baffle them with . . ." He broke off as he realized he'd spoken aloud. He looked up and saw the crew staring at him; even Vi'ya had paused. In the echo window from his console on the main viewscreen the glyphs flickered brightly.

Brandon's sudden sense of well-being spun away into nothing, as reality once again reasserted control.

"What's all that Shiidra-blunge comin' from yer screen?" Marim's eyes were wide with disbelief. Lokri was staring at Brandon's hands, a strange expression on his face. Greywing stood up so that she could get a better look at the strange phenomenon glowing on his screen.

The Arkad laughed, a strained, humorless sound. "Battle glyphs—sort of a tactical visual code. Markham installed them." He paused, looking around at them in a puzzled way. "Didn't you ever notice when he used them?"

Vi'ya shook her head slowly, her dark eyes steady. "He was working on something . . . a surprise . . . when he was killed. He never got a chance to show anyone."

"And Jakarr never said anything," Marim said with a snort of disgust.

"Probably never found them," Lokri put in.

Jaim's voice interrupted them. "All ready here, Vi'ya. Rigged for overload conditions. You'll get up to thirty seconds or so, then you'd better be ready to stick your arms through the hull and flap 'em like crazy."

Vi'ya turned back to Brandon. "Are you ready?"

"Yes. I think I can stop any missiles, and there are ways to cut down the efficiency of their ruptors, this close to the planet."

She slammed her hand down on the big go-pad, and Arthelion suddenly ballooned in the forward view. There was no sense of acceleration, since the geeplane affected the entire ship at once, but Greywing knew they were accelerating toward the planet at better than fifteen gees. Everything depended on Vi'ya's skill now. If they entered the atmosphere at the wrong angle they'd either break up or skip back into space like a rock off a pond.

Behind them the *Fist of Dol'jhar* dwindled and fell toward the horizon, then began to swell with alarming speed. The Arkad tapped his console, considered the glyphs a moment, then triggered a staggered cluster of missiles from the aft launcher.

"What're you doing?" Marim demanded. "Those dimpy things won't even dent a cruiser's hull metal, even if he left his teslas off."

"They'll confuse his sensors and weaken his ruptor beams," Vi'ya said tersely. "Watch. And learn."

Behind them the missiles began their deadly bloom, their neat coins of blue-white light suddenly shredding as the bone-jarring squeal-rumble of a ruptor rattled the bridge. Greywing felt her teeth click together painfully; Ivard shouted in pain and blood ran out of his mouth.

"Marim!" shouted Vi'ya over the rapidly increasing roar of atmospheric entry. The little Rifter's console was sprinkled with red lights, her fingers blurring on the console.

Brandon triggered another cluster of missiles as a wave of changes rippled through the glyph display. Another ruptor beam grabbed the ship, weaker this time.

"Chatz!" screamed Marim, her usual command of invective deserting her. *"Double chatz!"* she wailed. "The blunge-eating logos-lovers nackered the fiveskip. It's down but good."

The *Telvarna* began to quiver, a trembling that rapidly grew to a jarring, violent shaking. Gee-forces pulled at them as, with a stuttering roar, the plasma jets cut in and the ship leveled out and stopped jittering. Weight returned; they were in aerodynamic flight now.

Behind them, the green lances of laser-boosted missiles reached out from the distant battlecruiser now denied its prey, its ruptors useless, dissipated by the atmosphere that sustained the *Telvarna*. Brandon triggered a counterbarrage; light flared behind the racing ship, faded. The rearview was dark. They had escaped, for now.

"Altitude twenty-six, mach twenty-two," Ivard sang out, his face pale around the blood smears but his hands steady. Greywing looked over at her little brother in pride.

"Marim, get down to power and give Jaim a hand," said Vi'ya. "Let me know how long fiveskip will be down." Marim scampered out and Vi'ya motioned Ivard over to her console. "Take over, Firehead, Marim will need some feedback."

Ahead pale dawn began to stain the sky as the *Telvarna* caught up with the sun. Far below, moonlight glittered off water, and Brandon windowed up a relay from Ivard's console and confirmed that they would pass about eight hundred kilometers south of the Mandalic Archipelago.

"Arkad. Do you know anything about the Panarchist defense plans?"

Brandon looked up, his face distracted. "No. I can't imagine anyone thinking seriously about it, but I suppose someone did, since the resonance field was down. It may be that the military took down all the defense systems when they knew they had lost—that's standard practice in any such situation."

"So there's a chance that no one's tracking us."

"A chance. It may vary from place to place." He paused, obviously weighing his words, but Marim's voice halted him before he could go on.

"Things are pretty shaken up down here, Vi'ya, but most of it can wait, except some of the plasma guides to the radiants, and the fiveskip. That'll need at least six hours of work before we can trust it again."

Vi'ya acknowledged and turned back to Brandon. "You had a proposal to make."

"There is one place where the odds are likely to be considerably better."

She quirked an eyebrow at him.

"The Palace Major. Our present course will take us not far south of it."

Vi'ya snorted derisively. "Don't let your homesickness run away with you. That's the last place I'd set the *Telvarna* down."

"And it's the last place they would expect you to. Look, the Mandalic Archipelago covers millions of hectares—even close to the Palace there are forests that could swallow a ship this size without a trace. My Arkadic override will deal with any defense systems that are still up, and if the household computer is still running, we might even be able to find out what's happening." He hesitated. "I'd also like a chance to see if any of the Family are there in need of help. Remember, as far as those security computers are concerned, I'm *supposed* to be there." Then he grinned at her, his blue eyes bright with irony. "Besides, how do you expect to pay for all the work the ship will need after this?"

Vi'ya frowned slightly, and Greywing wondered what the captain was reading from him.

"You haven't anything but the ring on your finger," she finally replied. "That will hardly be sufficient."

"And you call yourself a Rifter. Haven't you ever dreamed of looting the Palace of the Panarch of the Thousand Suns?"

Lokri hooted with laughter and Ivard grinned. Marim's voice crackled from the intercom, "If you pass this up, Vi'ya, I'll send your hide to Hreem myself."

Vi'ya's lips quivered for a moment, then she succumbed to a genuine smile. "Give Ivard a course, then. We accept your invitation."

Brandon rose from his console and gave her one of those flourishing Douloi bows, like they did to each other but never to a common citizen. His hand pressed over his heart, his other one sweeping back and then up again.

Vi'ya lifted a brow, then turned back to her console. "And keep your eyes on your screens, Arkad," she said. "We're not safe yet."

TWENTY-ONE

✳

The lingering light of a long summer evening slanted through the high clerestory windows in the antechamber to the Phoenix Hall, bringing a warm glow to wood paneling and woven tapestries. The antechamber was a long, broad corridor; at regular intervals along the walls were recessed arches backed by pale amber stone, each with a sunburst mosaic radiating out from it onto the floor. Within each niche a bust shone in the mellow light from the high windows, commemorating the rulers of the Arkad dynasty.

The air was redolent of sandalwood and the warm scent of polish and wax. At intervals a gentle tone sounded, seemingly from the air itself, each time a different timbre and pitch. The sound was evocative at times of bells, at times of hushed and distant voices; it filled the room with an expectant peace, and a sense of the slow weight of centuries.

Eusabian stood for some time before the bust of Jaspar I, founder of the dynasty, seeing in it an unmistakable echo of the features of his defeated enemy. Then he began to pace slowly along the corridor, pausing for a moment at each bust, studying the faces. The echo was repeated in each succeeding image, sometimes stronger, sometimes weaker.

The style of the statuary evolved as he advanced down the hall, changing in slow cycles from stark formality through increasing ornament to mannered excess. Then, abruptly, the styles returned to something close to classical again, yet with something of the preceding modes remaining. The eyes of the Panarchs and Kyriarchs seemed to follow him as he passed, reminding him forcibly of Gelasaar Arkad's gaze.

About a third of the way down the hall, Eusabian stopped, rage slowly welling up within him. One of the busts had been rudely vandalized, the face chipped away jaggedly, the name at its base effaced. Doubtless one of his worthless Rifter hirelings had done this, striking in childish fashion against an enemy worthy of a respect the fool could not conceive. *I will have the guards crucified for this. And when the vandal is found . . .*

The thought died unfinished as he realized that there were no fragments around the bust, no stone dust. The pedestal, and the floor beneath it, were clean, gleaming with polish. Then he bent closer and saw that the jagged edges of the bust's ruined face were softened by age, with a faint patina like that left by the touch of many hands over many years. Only then did he remember. *The Faceless One.*

A faint chill traced his spine and he stepped back. *This man's place in history is gone.* Suddenly he realized that there was a level of retribution that he had never conceived, a justice more terrible than any paliach recorded in the long and bloody history of Dol'jhar. *They have made him as if he never lived.*

The ultimate harshness of that long-dead Arkad's fate, made real by the ruined image, unsettled him. It suggested that there were depths to the dynasty he had overthrown that he had overlooked.

A movement back at the end of the hall caught his eye.

He turned to see Barrodagh standing with two other men in the doorway. He motioned them forward.

As the Bori approached, Eusabian noted that he was clutching a small, silver object in his hands. Something about the way he gripped it looked odd, and a fierce exultation suddenly kindled in the Avatar's heart. *The Heart of Kronos!*

When Barrodagh stopped in front of him, Eusabian held out his hand to receive the key to his kingdom.

Barrodagh gaped at Eusabian in confusion, then the awful realization hit him. *He thinks it's the Heart of Kronos.* Without thinking, he jerked his hand back, his mind racing. *And he doesn't know any more about the Heart than I did. Why shouldn't it swallow my thumb? He won't hesitate to cut it off.* Fortunately there were no Tarkans present; he could almost feel the serrated *zhu'leath* each carried sawing through the tendons and bone at the Avatar's command.

Eusabian's face darkened, the lines between the corners of his mouth and his nose deepening. "Give it to me."

Barrodagh's hand went forward involuntarily, conditioned by twenty years of obedience. Eusabian grasped the sphere and pulled, then twisted. Barrodagh gasped and half sank to his knees. "Lord, please." He was twisted over to one side, looking up at Eusabian as the Dol'jharian's greater strength threatened to twist his thumb off. "It's not the Heart of Kronos."

The Avatar stared at the sphere for a moment, then let it go. "Then why have you brought it to me?"

Barrodagh crimsoned. "It swallowed my thumb and no one knows how to get it off." He heard a snicker behind him, but he didn't dare turn around to glare at Tallis.

Eusabian looked past him. "Perhaps you will explain this?"

Tallis came forward, bowing deeply. "My lord, it is a Dyzonian Emasculizer." When Eusabian frowned in incomprehension Tallis hurried on, "A male chastity device from

Dyzon. It was among the artifacts we took from the gnostor's estate."

The Avatar snorted, looking back at Barrodagh. "And you don't know how to get it off?" Barrodagh looked up at him, his stomach twisting as he saw again that strange glint in Eusabian's eyes that he couldn't identify. "I assume it will not impede you in the performance of your duties?"

He's going to have it cut off anyway! "No, Lord!" he protested. "It will be no trouble. I'm sure someone will know how to cut—" He stopped, appalled at his tongue's betrayal. "—how to remove it." He twisted again at the sphere, as he had been doing all the way back from the *Satansclaw.*

"I shouldn't do that if I were you."

They turned to Omilov, who looked back, his jowly face somber. "You might trigger the reward circuits in it."

"What do you mean?" Barrodagh whined.

"If you trigger the reward circuits it will attempt to bring you to orgasm. Since you were incautious enough to install it on your thumb, I assume that will not be possible." The gnostor's grave tone carried a hint of irony that was somehow worse than outright laughter.

Out of the corner of his eye Barrodagh noticed a slight curve to Eusabian's lips. *He's enjoying this.*

"However," continued Omilov, "it is designed to continue trying until it succeeds." He paused. "I don't know what will happen to your thumb in that case."

"You must know how to take it off," said Barrodagh desperately.

"As I told you during the flight down, I'm afraid that Lady Omilov never explained that part of the device's operation."

Barrodagh was astonished to hear Eusabian chuckle. "That was delightful, Gnostor. My poor Bori will be terrified now until we get it off of him, even though I'm sure he realizes as well as I do that your little speech was pure invention."

Omilov's face settled back into impassivity. "Perhaps."

Eusabian's tone grew serious. "I trust you will not be as inventive concerning the Heart of Kronos?"

Omilov did not reply, merely staring calmly at the Lord of Vengeance.

"Come, Gnostor, you must know that you *will* tell me where it is, whether you want to or not."

"Yes, but honor and loyalty require my silence while I am still able to choose."

"Gelasaar hai-Arkad stood before me not long ago and bleated a similar refrain. It did him as little good as it will you. His sons are all dead, and he won't last long on Gehenna."

Omilov's face revealed grief for a moment, quickly hidden.

"But you, Gnostor, have even less time than he." Eusabian stopped and studied him for a moment. "I see in your eyes the thought that perhaps you will surprise us. I'm afraid not. One of our prisoners from Lao Tse was a woman with the interesting nickname 'The Spider.' "

Barrodagh thought he saw a glint of something— worry?—in Omilov's eyes.

"She, too, was unacquainted with the mindripper, which is a uniquely Dol'jharian instrument. Her introduction to it killed her, but not before we tore her ciphers out of her. We know you are one of the Invisibles, Sebastian Omilov."

Barrodagh heard Tallis gasp, saw him step back, staring at the gnostor. *A praerogate?* the Bori thought. The gnostor's portly frame was at variance with the popular image of those most trusted agents of the Panarch.

Eusabian smiled. "But your induced allergy to veritonin will do you no good at all. The mindripper works on entirely different principles, the least of which is pain."

He turned to Barrodagh. "Give him to Evodh. Make sure that my physician understands this is for information, not for honor."

The Avatar turned back to Omilov. "Good-bye, Gnostor. Your precious honor will remain intact, even as we shred your cortex. I hope that's of some comfort to you."

As Barrodagh grabbed Omilov's arm and shoved him toward the door, Eusabian turned to Tallis.

"Captain, your report of the Krysarch's death was incomplete. Since your action deprived me of one third of my paliachee, for which I waited twenty years, I want you to recount it now, omitting nothing."

Barrodagh wished he could linger to watch Tallis suffer Eusabian's cold interrogation, but he was also looking forward to observing Evodh at work. As he pushed Omilov out of the antechamber he wondered if Tallis would survive. *Perhaps I need to talk to my other contact on the* Satansclaw.

❊   ❊   ❊

The *Telvarna* backed slowly in among the huge trees, hovering under geeplane as it floated tail-first away from the edge of the forest, back into the shadows. Finally Vi'ya brought the ship down so gently that Greywing wasn't sure they were on the ground until the engines spun down into silence.

The captain rested her hands on the console for a moment, then tabbed the intercom. "Jaim, any further damage?"

"No," came the answer. "Once we went aerodynamic I took the hardest-hit systems off-line. But things are still pretty messed up—we'll need a major refit back on Dis— and I'm afraid it may take up to eight hours to get the fiveskip back to where I'd trust it. The worst is, of course, that we can't really test it down here."

Vi'ya looked up, saw Marim corroborate his statement with a rueful shrug.

"All right, get up here to the bridge." She tapped the intercom again. "Montrose, come forward, and bring the Schoolboy with you." She turned to Brandon as Jaim's acknowledgment came back.

"This is the spot you chose, Arkad. I assume you don't intend us to walk." She inclined her head slightly toward the main screen, which displayed the broad shadowy forest corridor the *Telvarna* had backed into.

Lokri looked up sharply. "Walk? We're not really going in?"

Greywing stared at the comtech in surprise; she had never seen him show fear before. What was he afraid of? She did not believe that it was mere physical danger.

"Blit!" Marim scoffed. "Want us to sit here till someone comes after us? That cruiser, maybe?"

Vi'ya said calmly, "If either the *Fist* or the Panarchists tracked us we're already dead, but I don't think they have. The ground defense system seems to be down, and *Telvarna* is well enough hidden. Jaim and Marim can defend it if need be." She looked up as Jaim appeared. "The rest of us will go inside and have a look."

Lokri drummed one hand on his console. "We step inside the Mandala and we're dead." He glanced toward Brandon, eloquent with scorn. "If anything in there does work, it'll be used against us."

Jaim murmured something which sounded like agreement, and Ivard cracked his knuckles nervously. Brandon sat in his pod, looking down at his hands.

"By whom, and to what end? We have seen and heard nothing of the Panarchists," Vi'ya said to Lokri, making a gesture toward the sky. "You fear the Arkad will give us to the Dol'jharians?"

The twist she gave to the word *Dol'jharian* made the Krysarch look up sharply at her. Greywing, watching, saw his intense blue gaze shift then from the captain to herself, as if he remembered her saying about the other crew members, *They want to talk about themselves, you ask them.* That made a new thought occur: did Lokri fear being killed—or scanned and identified? Out of all of the Dis crew, he talked the least about where he'd come from.

Lokri's mouth tightened, then he shrugged.

"We will use the Arkad's knowledge of the defense systems and find out what is happening, or we will not be able to lift once we do repair the engines," Vi'ya continued.

Montrose nodded his approval of this plan.

"Maybe we'll get that loot he promised us," Marim said cheerily.

Vi'ya looked up at the screen. Just beyond the edge of the forest, on a lawn dotted with yellow flowers, a small gazebo perched. In the distance beyond it the greensward sloped up to gently rolling hills dotted with small trees silhouetted against an evening-yellow sky. There were no other buildings visible.

"So do we walk?" the captain said to Brandon.

He gave her a considering look. Some of the others had started talking, as if released by Marim's mention of loot. Greywing gave in to an impulse and crossed the short distance to Brandon's side. She said in a low voice, "She's Dol'jharian. Birth, not choice. Left years ago."

The Krysarch gave her a brief smile, then looked past her to say, "The Palace Major is about forty kilometers from here. But the entire Mandala is riddled with tunnels, some for service functions, others whose purpose has been forgotten. That gazebo there is the terminus of one of them; the transport system will get us to the Palace in about ten minutes."

"A palace!" Marim rubbed her hands together, grinning. "I've never been in one."

"And you won't this time, either," Jaim reminded her. "You'll be here helping me monkey-up the fiveskip."

Marim looked to the captain, her mouth ready to deliver a protest, but a single nod from Vi'ya inspired instead a stream of genetically improbable invective.

When the scout had run out of breath, if not out of opprobrium, Brandon added, "I should be able to use my override to make us invisible to whatever defense system is still up."

Vi'ya looked across at Jaim. "How many hands you need?"

Jaim said doubtfully, "Well, Marim and I can—"

"One more," Marim said with a sigh. "At least one."

Vi'ya glanced around at the crew. At that moment Montrose appeared and stood in the doorway with one massive hand resting companionably on Osri's shoulder. The captain studied Osri for a long moment. "You would undoubtedly be more liability than help with a firejac in your hands, Schoolboy. I assume you can follow directions?"

"Yes," Osri stated curtly, a faint hint of puzzlement in his face.

"Good. Jaim, Marim, he's yours. Montrose, arm a party of six—"

"Six? The boy can watch the com," Lokri said, pointing to Ivard.

"Com's slaved to engine room," Vi'ya said.

Lokri's eyes narrowed.

"Ivard's a good shot," Greywing said, her voice sounding too loud on the bridge. "Better aim than you." She felt heat creep up her neck, especially when she saw Ivard send a look of reproach at her.

Vi'ya studied Ivard. "You can handle it if things get hot?"

Ivard said clearly, "I'm part of the crew. I'll do whatever I have to."

Vi'ya nodded at Montrose, reinforcing her earlier order, then added, "Get the Arkad a boz'l."

Montrose grunted his approval, and left.

"C'mon, Schoolboy, we're off to Murphy's Kingdom." Marim gave Vi'ya a mock-angry scowl and added, "And they better save us some o' the take." Then the three of them disappeared.

Montrose returned with weapons, including a monstrous two-hand firejac for himself. Greywing noted Brandon watching as Vi'ya set hers for minimum aperture, yielding greater distance and accuracy at the cost of stopping power, before he looked down and strapped on the boswell Montrose had handed him.

Greywing put her own on. She could feel the coolness against the inside of his wrist until it adapted to her flesh. Somehow that made the reality of walking into danger more immediate than strapping on her weapon, so familiar after hours of practice.

(Your ears up, Arkad?) Vi'ya's voice sounded inside Greywing's head.

(Neural induction—nothing like doing things right,) came the Arkad's voice over the omniband. *(These things military-surplus?)*

Only the most expensive civilian models had the neural induction feature. Greywing wondered if Brandon was used to that—then she wondered what had happened to his boswell.

"We won't use these unless we get separated," Vi'ya said out loud. "They're spread-spectrum, but there is no sense in taking chances."

As they made their way to the lock, a blur of white flashed past Greywing, and Lucifur landed on his pads squarely before Vi'ya, his ears back and his tail twitching. The captain stood motionless before the big cat for a time, then leaned down and just touched the top of the broad wedge-shaped head.

Abruptly Luce gave his ratcheting purr and with a bound he disappeared toward the galley.

The only sound now was the shuffle of their feet and the creaking of their belts and sheaths as they strapped them on. Greywing's first instinct was to walk next to her brother, but she made herself wait. Ivard took his place among the others, and because he did not seek her protection, she realized she had to stop offering it. She fell in last, watching the others.

Montrose was still adjusting his harness—which enabled him to carry his weapon at his side yet swivel it up to firing position instantly—as they reached the lock. Vi'ya slapped the control and, as the doors opened to reveal the dim-lit forest outside, waved her weapon at Brandon in an ironic gesture. "Lead the way."

The ramp boomed softly underfoot as they descended. Behind them the *Telvarna*'s hull pinged softly as it cooled; Greywing could feel the warmth on the back of her neck as she reached the ground.

At the base of the ramp Vi'ya stopped and looked back.

Moments later the Eya'a emerged and glided down the ramp, their feet making no sound on its metallic surface. They did not look around, but moved swiftly in the twilight, their faceted eyes seeming to gather and concentrate the dim light, like liquid-filled diamonds. As they joined Vi'ya she led the group away from the ship.

Brandon reacted a little at the proximity of the small sentients. The rest of the crew ignored them, although they took care not to come in physical contact with them.

The eight of them started down the broad path toward the gazebo. Around them the trees loomed immense, their massive, seamed umber trunks so vast that twenty tall men could not have joined hands around them, so tall that from their base one could not see the top. They had no branches for the first hundred feet or so above the ground, so the path had the feeling of a colonnade bordered by massive living pillars.

Ivard's steps lagged as he looked around him. When Greywing caught up with him, he said in a hushed voice, "I didn't know there were trees so large."

Greywing tilted her head back to look up into the dimming sky through the interlaced branches overhead. "We sure never saw this at home, did we?"

"Home," Ivard said, his lip curling. "Home's Dis."

And if someone shoots this captain and Lokri takes over? Or someone worse? Greywing thought, but she didn't say anything. Home to her meant where you were born. Nothing more. Home like Ivard meant it—well, there was no meaning for that anymore. Like justice, it was just a word you used for something convenient.

Maybe Ivard somehow knew what she was thinking, or maybe he just decided he didn't need to walk by his sister. He rushed forward again, looking this way and that so fast he nearly tripped on the uneven ground.

Montrose, too, was gazing about him with pleasure and some awe. In contrast, Lokri sauntered a little in advance, seemingly uninterested in his surroundings. Directly in front of him Vi'ya and the Eya'a moved as a self-absorbed unit.

"These trees were planted by the first Exiles," said Brandon to Ivard. "It's said that some of them were seedlings on Lost Earth."

"If trees have memories," said Montrose, his voice rumbling in his chest, "then these are the only living things in the Thousand Suns to remember the sunlight of the mother of humankind."

Lokri looked over at Brandon with his long brows quirked, but said nothing. Vi'ya did not look back.

They moved on in silence. Around them the ordered ranks of the forest, scattered with low brush and occasional patches of bright flowers, appeared peaceful. After five days of controlled ship's air, the scents around them were strong, exciting.

Montrose sneezed suddenly, then grinned when Ivard snorted a laugh. "Just my luck," the big physician said. "We land on just about the most Earthlike planet in the Thousand Suns, and I get skipnose."

Greywing felt her own head clogging, but she could still smell the resinous duff underfoot and the heady scent of the flowers. What would it be like to have these the familiar scents of home? *If Lost Earth smelled like this, why did they leave?*

She looked at the Krysarch. He was not studying his surroundings; instead his gaze was intent on the firejac Montrose had given him. Greywing found this puzzling; it was just like hers: a worn, scratched, but otherwise well-maintained Dogstar LVI, just about the most common short-range plasma weapon in the Thousand Suns.

She looked down at her own jac. The grips were covered with some sort of rough, scaly substance, nearly worn through in a couple of places. The trigger had been polished by years of use, but the black-box finish of the finned radiants around the aperture was flawless. *It's definitely a Rifter's weapon,* she thought. *The parts that matter well maintained, but no resources wasted on appearance. I wonder if he sees that.*

Greywing also wondered, as they emerged from the forest and approached the gazebo, if the Krysarch was fighting the same curious sense of unreality that she was. He must have played here as a boy, maybe organizing his nick friends into teams, Marines against the Shiidra, like Greywing and the others had before they got to their tenth birthdays and were sold off to the combines.

Or did they play Navy captains against Rifters?

Here he was, leading an armed gang of Rifters into the Palace where he'd been born. She blinked, feeling as if they had somehow slipped into a holovid. Nothing seemed real anymore: she knew when they left here—if they left—she would never really believe she had ever set foot on the Mandala.

Overhead the first stars of evening revealed themselves behind a faint wash of high cirrus. Ahead the gazebo shone whitely against the darkening sky, rising up out of a huddle of flowering shrubs and hedges. Its ornate latticework sides shadowed the interior in mystery.

They approached carefully and found it empty, the interior dusty and splattered with bird droppings. Doves cooed under the eaves as they entered.

Lokri looked around, evincing the first interest he'd shown since their landing. "These tunnels widely used? Who're we going to meet down there?"

"Very few people know about them," Brandon replied. "There aren't any maps that I'm aware of—the computers run the transport system, so if someone decided to picnic here they'd come by air or horseback and the supplies would already be here." He looked around the gazebo, eyes narrowed, seeking something. "Galen and I searched for some of the older ones, that don't have transport in them; my father showed us one of those when we were small. When we later showed him one we'd found that opened into the Palace Minor, he said he vaguely remembered it and thought that maybe that was the one his mother had shown him when he first got started looking for them." He smiled reminiscently. "I guess it was sort of a family tradition."

"Sounds more like a family tradition for Rifters," commented Lokri, "looking for bolt-holes."

Brandon nodded as his fingers moved over the woodwork. He exclaimed softly when he found the controls. He reached under some decorative carvings near the base of one of the roof supports. Lokri and Ivard suddenly found themselves inside a circle of light about eight feet across. A gentle chime sounded. They backed out of the circle hastily; after a moment the floor rose smoothly on a slender pillar and a second platform filled the hole as the former floor integrated itself seamlessly into the ceiling above.

Brandon motioned them onto the platform. When all were within the circle he tapped the pillar, and the platform sank noiselessly back underground.

The eight found themselves on a raised dais in the middle of a large room. Its cement walls were smooth and darkened with age; there was a faint damp smell. On one side of the dais a short flight of stairs led downward, while on the other side a ramp apparently gave access for automated loaders, but there was no machinery to be seen. Across from the base of the stairs a tunnel stretched away into gloomy distance, two parallel strips of metal on the floor glinting in the dim light.

They clattered down the stairs, following Brandon as he ran over to a control console built into the wall near the tunnel opening. He keyed it to life and entered his personal code. There was a brief, almost subliminal flicker of light as the console scanned his retina; Greywing saw Lokri step back a little, his teeth showing briefly.

"Identity confirmed. Welcome, Krysarch Brandon."

Ivard's fingers gripped his firejac more tightly as the emotionless voice of the comp echoed in the chamber. The cadence of its speech was natural, but entirely neuter—there was no intimation of personality. The Eya'a made no move, and Vi'ya watched without expression.

"Status, defense systems, local and planetary."

"Local passive systems functional, with exceptions, oversight functions and reactive systems are not operational at this time. Planetary passive systems functional, with exceptions, oversight functions and reactive systems are not operational at this time."

Brandon paused, looking at the console. The others waited in silence, Lokri with one of his nasty smiles. Greywing felt her insides tighten peculiarly: So it was true. Arthelion had fallen.

"Cancel surveillance from this location, internal and external. Cancel stored images," Brandon said quickly.

"Canceled. Canceled."

He looked up at the Rifters. "The systems are still gathering information, but the machines that tie it all together are down. I've made sure no one can see us here if the system comes back up." He turned back to the console.

"Is my father in residence?"

"This system does not have that information."

"Explain."

"Numerous internal identification sensors have been disabled. He has not been detected by the remaining ones."

"Why were the sensors disabled?"

"This system does not have that information."

Brandon shook his head in frustration and turned to the others. "There's no way to tell if any of the Family are here or not. I'll see if I can get some information on activity within the Palace." He turned back to the console.

"Status, housekeeping systems."

"Housekeeping systems are operational at this time. Authorized access to services continues in the Rouge, Phoenix, and Aleph-Null quadrants. Manual access to comestible, clothing, and hygiene services by unauthorized personnel in the Ivory quadrant and Palace Minor has been enforced by recoding; other systems are still secure."

"Identify locations of unauthorized personnel."

"Most internal sensors in the Ivory quadrant and Palace Minor are inoperative. Repair functions are being hindered, but alternate circuits are being established. Current patterns of manual housekeeping requests indicate predominant unauthorized activities confined to Palace Minor and upper sublevels of Ivory wing of Palace Major."

Brandon paused a moment, rubbing a finger across the knuckles of the other hand. "Are transport activities accessible to unauthorized personnel?"

"No."

"Send a carrier to this location, eight persons."

"Acknowledged. ETA two minutes."

He turned back to the others. "There's an odd pattern here. The invaders seem to have cleared all the servants and other personnel out of the residence—the Palace Minor—and the quadrant of the Palace Major that includes the residence. Is that a Rifter custom before looting a place?"

"As if there's any universal Rifter custom other than anarchy," Montrose said, laughing a little. "But no, few are that well organized, or have that much control over their fellows."

Vi'ya spoke. "That is Dol'jharian custom," she said. "Outsiders are not permitted access to any area frequented by a Dol'jharian noble. Nothing will have been touched."

Brand stared at her, an angry flush marking his cheeks. "You think that Eusabian has taken up residence in the Palace Minor."

The Eya'a shifted position subtly, their faceted eyes fixing suddenly on the Krysarch.

"He swore a paliach against your father, did he not?"

"A what?"

Vi'ya hesitated very slightly. "A formal vengeance. Taking possession of his enemy's keep would be a part of it. I would guess that the other area is for the occupation administrators."

Brandon tightened the one fist, then dropped his hands. "So we have two choices of destination," he continued. "I know the Palace Minor best, and can direct you to any number of treasures there once I've had my shot at—"

Vi'ya moved forward slightly. "We are not here to aid you in your revenge. Our deal is simple. You can look for your family in the time it takes us to get information and loot. The *Telvarna* will need a lot of work, maybe more than we can afford."

Brandon said, "I meant my search. Anyway, the sublevels of the Ivory quadrant the computer referred to are a maze of corridors and rooms, some very old—in fact, Galen and I once found some old Hegemonic detention cells somewhere in there that had been converted to storage. There might be some prisoners there."

"And?" Lokri interjected, looking interested. He rubbed his thumb against two fingers in an age-old gesture.

"The Ivory quadrant of the Mandala has the aspect of autonomy, which is associated with the arts. Is there much of a market for fine art among Rifters?"

Montrose chuckled. "Some of the most passionate collectors I've ever known are Rifters."

"If you know the right broker," said Vi'ya, "there's nothing more profitable."

"Good. Then our goals run parallel. The antechamber to the Hall of Ivory should yield a stunning profit. The transport I've summoned will take us directly there. We'll get no help from the house system, but neither will the enemy."

A puff of air from the tunnel announced the arrival of the carrier, a long, low sled-like contrivance with a streamlined fairing at each end and flanged wheels of some dark substance that fit onto the metal strips in the floor.

Lokri let out a laugh. "Wheels in grooves!"

Ivard breathed an admiring "Oh!" and jumped in eagerly. "They're called tracks, Lokri," he said. "I've seen pictures of this sort of thing, but never in person."

Brandon seemed amused at Ivard's enthusiasm as they all got in. He tapped the keys in the small console and the carrier accelerated smoothly into the tunnel. Widely spaced lights held back the darkness; the rush of air past the fairing was loud and constant, interrupted occasionally by a muffled *whoomp* as they passed a side tunnel. The only other sound was an intermittent clicking from the rails as they passed switching points.

After a few minutes Ivard leaned toward Greywing to whisper, "This place is a maze." His voice echoed.

"Seems us Rifters have nothing on these crooked old Panarchy chatzers," Lokri said agreeably.

"Some of those crooked old Panarchy chatzers would be violently insulted to be mistaken for the Hegemonists who built these tunnels," Brandon said in an equally pleasant tone, his blue eyes steady on Lokri's cold gray stare. Suddenly Lokri grinned, a wide grin that slashed clear across his face.

Greywing let her eyes rest for a long moment on the handsome dark face, never more attractive than when laughing, or acknowledging a hit. His long curling hair blew back in the wind, his gemstone gleamed in his ear.

Then she deliberately looked away.

TWENTY-TWO

✳

Montrose sat back comfortably in the carrier, watching the younglings covertly. High amusement was his foremost emotion at the ebb and flow of their interactions. Amusement and something more when he observed the gangling red-haired pup; so would his own two have gazed around, had they lived long enough to visit the Mandala—but they had not lived, they'd been murdered, along with their mother, back on Timberwell. And so he moved through his days without ever making plans, with amusement as his goal. If he died here today, it would be nothing more than he expected; if he lived, he planned to take away a fortune and spend it all on entertainment when he could.

Nobody spoke as the cart raced along the tunnels. Ivard was too busy craning his neck this way and that, determined to miss nothing. The captain watched the accesses, cool and unreadable as always, seldom opening her mouth unless to give an order or answer a question. The two aliens were very still, the breeze kicked up by their movement ruffling through the ice-white fur. Greywing sat hunched into herself, the twisted posture enforced by her healing wound leaving her even more unattractive than usual. Montrose had not missed her long perusal of the oblique comtech Lokri. Nor had he missed the moment previous when something in the Krysarch's manner had caused one of Lokri's lightning changes of intent: the Arkad, no doubt totally unaware, had metamorphosed from adversary to quarry.

If they returned safely, Marim and Lokri would probably institute one of their outrageous bets, the Krysarch's seduction being the purpose and something either risky or costly, or both, the stake. And young Greywing would watch through that unnerving rheumy stare, her attraction to the elegant and devious Lokri only exceeded by her distrust.

If Montrose ever interfered, he would have taken Greywing aside and told her to get Lokri drunk and bed him, and then forget him, except she wouldn't forget him. If easy-hearted bunk-hopping had ever been in her nature, it had gone out of it when she arrived at Dis as Jakarr's current partner, her eyes bleak and her pale skin marked with bruises. He could have told her how to handle Jakarr, but he did not interfere, and eventually she had considered her own and her brother's place among the crew secure enough to throw Jakarr out of her bunk.

His thoughts broke when Ivard looked up and said suddenly, "Hegemonists. What is that?"

Montrose grinned. He'd never seen the boy so talkative.

"Before the Panarchy," Vi'ya, next to him, replied.

"Oh." Ivard pursed his lips, the subdued surprise in his exclamation indicating that he'd assumed—if indeed he had ever thought about it—that the Panarchy had existed forever.

"The *Telvarna* has a history chip about them, if you want to know more," Vi'ya added.

"So long as none of 'em are lying in wait for us," Lokri cut in with his good-natured drawl.

"Not likely." Montrose laughed. "They're almost a thousand years gone, and their Adamantines with them."

"So we aren't likely to come up against them," continued

Lokri. "If you want my advice, Firehead, just forget about them. They were losers anyway."

Montrose chuckled again, now watching the Krysarch, who seemed to recognize the maze of tunnels they now passed at a rapid clip. Brandon's body was tense. What did he expect? He was nearly impossible to read; either Montrose had forgotten all his Douloi subtleties, or else the shades of ambiguity and deflection inculcated into the Arkads from birth surpassed the training received by minor Houses on planets of lesser importance. A shame, really: the prospect of an Arkad, from a line unbroken for nearly a thousand years, returning to a scene of defeat promised superlative entertainment indeed.

The remainder of the trip passed in silence, until Brandon said abruptly, "We are under the Ivory wing of the Palace Major."

The others grasped their weapons more tightly; the Eya'a did not move, but somehow seemed more alert.

The carrier slid smoothly to a stop. Brandon waited while the crew followed, the Eya'a climbing out with their characteristic odd little hops that hinted at wellsprings of great energy. Then he said quietly, his voice sounding oddly disembodied in the vast, empty tunnel, "This is how to activate the carrier for the return trip."

No one said anything as he demonstrated. He got out of the carrier and moved over to a console mounted on the wall next to a ladder. "This ladder opens into an old utility closet, which is located on the lowest maintenance level. From what the computer said, it is likely not being used. There are three more sublevels above that, and then the antechamber to the Hall of Ivory. That's where you'll find what you need to pay for refitting the *Telvarna*. From there we can make our way down to the other side, where the old Hegemonic detention chambers are, and back here again."

He tapped the console, and a square of yellow light appeared overhead. He went up first and waited while the others followed. The closet was large, empty, and stale-smelling, with a single glow-bulb set in the ceiling to illuminate it. He shut the trapdoor and demonstrated how to re-open it, then went to the door.

"Wait," said Vi'ya, and motioned him away from the door. She turned to the Eya'a, and the three froze into a momentary tableau. Then she relaxed.

"They report no humans on this level. There are some above, but too far away to say how many, or exactly where."

Brandon raised his eyebrows. "Looks like we won't be needing the house system, after all."

She shook her head. "They can't tell strange humans apart, so they can't tell friend from foe until the person sees us and reacts." She smiled slightly. "At that point we won't need the Eya'a to tell us the difference."

She opened the door and stepped out into the corridor, shadowed closely by the Eya'a. The rest followed silently, weapons ready.

The corridor was paneled in a dark, subdued wood, the walls interrupted at intervals by wooden doors and occasional framed paintings on the walls.

They had walked nearly the length of the corridor when Lokri asked, "Is this area usually so empty?"

"The Palace Major doesn't have a resident staff, since its function is largely ceremonial, but even during a major function there wouldn't be much activity down here. This is only used for storage."

Lokri looked around at the subdued elegance of their surroundings and whistled derisively. "Well, pardon me," he drawled in a parody of aristocratic speech, "but I seem to have stumbled into a service corridor. I am *so* embarrassed."

Ivard snorted a nervous laugh and Montrose swatted him on the shoulder. "Keep your voice down."

At the end of the hall was a door, which Brandon opened to reveal a narrow staircase. "This goes up all four levels to the antechamber of the Hall of Ivory. It opens behind a tapestry."

They began climbing. The flights were short, with four

turns between each floor. At the top Brandon waited until everyone was on the last landing, then looked at Vi'ya.

"There's no one out there," she reported, "although they say there are some below and some distance away."

Brandon turned to the small console next to the door and keyed in a sequence. There was a flicker of red light, then a lens flashed green. "The alarms are off," he announced.

He eased the door open, separated a fold in the tapestry with two fingers, and peeked through. Then with a grand gesture, and a curious twist to his mouth that was not quite a smile, he swept the heavy hanging aside and ushered them into his world.

❊   ❊   ❊

The room was cold, and Omilov was naked, strapped to a chill-surfaced metal gurney by cuffs around his upper arms, wrists, thighs, and ankles. A slight breeze blowing from the ventilation duct high in the wall across from him added to his discomfort, but this was nothing compared to the strain of waiting.

Eusabian's Bori aide had brought him to this room and turned him over to a silent hulk of a man, instructing him with a few guttural Dol'jharian phrases. The man's long, dark face was pitted with sun-cancers, his huge hands horny and twisted with some degenerative condition, but his strength was more than a match for Omilov. He had efficiently and impersonally stripped him and bound him to the gurney; he didn't even appear to notice Omilov's resistance. The man had then shaved his head and left him to his thoughts.

Above and behind him was a console with some sort of mesh affair attached to a wire dangling from a swiveling arm. Against the walls were ranks of medical devices. Omilov vaguely recognized various types of monitoring and resuscitation equipment. Next to the gurney, where he could see it if he turned his head, was a rolling table with various mysterious and coldly glittering instruments neatly arranged on it. Omilov didn't recognize any of them, but they all seemed to involve an unpleasant multiplicity of points and edges and serrated teeth.

He looked away, trying not to think about what was coming, recognizing this time alone as the beginning of the torture.

The news of Nahomi's death had shaken him, and not only because it denied him the relatively quick death of anaphylactic shock, from the allergy to truth drugs that had been induced in him when he was named a Praerogate Occult. Contrary to the reputation she assiduously courted— her nickname had been one measure of her success—he had known her as an essentially gentle person, who subordinated her own preference for mercy to the demands of justice and fealty. She had also been a masterful administrator, wielding a deft mixture of firmness, respect, and understanding in her dealings with the Invisibles, men and women who had been entrusted with the authority of the Panarch himself, who were known only to themselves, the Panarch, and her. He would miss her greatly.

The door swung open silently and Omilov turned his head to look, the surface of the gurney cold against his cheek. A tall man with an angular, arrogant face came quietly in and stood looking at him. Another, shorter man stood behind him. The tall man's head was shaven, his scalp lacquered with a fantastic arabesque in almost metallic colors whose major themes seemed to be eyes and teeth and claws. He wore a long robe of some heavy, shimmering material the color of dried blood; the front of its sleeves left his arms uncovered to the elbow, while the back of the sleeves drooped in a fantastic spill of material almost to the floor. As he looked impassively at Omilov he absently gathered up the excess material of each sleeve and clipped the tip of it under a claw-like epaulette on each shoulder, while his assistant pinned the mid-portions to his sides. The effect was unpleasant, like the furled wings of a large carrion bird, or a demon.

When he finally spoke, his voice was soft, authoritative, his gutturals and rolled *r*'s emerging with an odd precision.

"I am Evodh radach'Enar, pesz mas'hadni to the Avatar, who has entrusted your death to me."

As he spoke his assistant moved to the head of the gurney and busied himself with the console.

"Whether or not you cooperate is a matter of indifference to me; since you are not a Dol'jharian you cannot be expected to understand the honor of your situation, nor to die well. Thus there is no honor here for me, only the extraction of information."

Omilov allowed no inkling of his feelings to show. Although the man was speaking Uni, the cultural premises behind his words rendered his speech incomprehensible.

"However, so that you may understand in part the art of *emmer mas'hadnital*—I believe you would say, 'the pain that transfigures'—I will explain as I proceed, so long as you remain capable of comprehension."

Omilov jerked slightly as the assistant lifted his head with strangely gentle hands and fitted a metallic mesh cap over it. It felt warm against his shaven scalp.

Evodh began speaking again, his eyes gazing across Omilov's body into the middle distance, his voice almost ruminative.

"There are many types of pain; all involve fear." As he spoke the assistant tapped a switch on the console, and Omilov heard a thin keening commence. Something itched inside his head, just behind his eyes.

"There are the basic fear complexes: among them falling"—Omilov gasped as the gurney seemed to drop out from beneath him—"sudden loud noises"—a prodigious explosion rattled his head, and he could even sense the pressure wave on his skin—"suffocation"—something abruptly snatched away the air in the room and his lungs ached as he fought for breath.

"There is also the fear of the unexpected, which you are already beginning to experience, and more complex and personal fears, which I will discover and exploit during your transfiguration. The mindripper can provide a variety of other effects to aid my explorations. I can diminish or eliminate any part of your sensorium . . ."

In rapid succession, each of Omilov's senses vanished and returned: sight, hearing, touch, proprioception, equilibrium . . .

". . . and I can heighten them as well."

Suddenly the surface of the gurney felt agonizingly cold and the gentle breeze from the ventilator rasped his flesh. The sour scent of his own fear and an odd, pungent scent from the two Dol'jharians filled his nose. His heartbeat resounded in his ears like the engines of a starship in emergency overload. Evodh reached down and gently traced a line down Omilov's stomach with his fingernail; it felt like he was being eviscerated with a jagged piece of metal. Then the pain stopped, instantly. Omilov felt his lip pop as his teeth met in it in an effort to repress the howl he felt building within him. Nothing in his experience had prepared him for the Dol'jharian technology of pain.

Evodh paused and looked down at Omilov. "Your culture holds that the fear of death is the greatest pang; we of Dol'jhar know this to be false. A greater pang is the fear of undeath, of continuing even after the body that has sustained you in comfort for so many years is ruined beyond redemption."

He picked up a small, stubby metal cylinder with a fine spike jutting from its underside and rolled it between his fingers. There was no hint of display in his movements, merely the unconscious gestures of an artist with the tools of his trade, which was far more terrifying than any overt threat would have been. "That is where the art begins. As its medium you will not be able to appreciate its end."

The whine from the mindripper increased and Omilov abruptly lost control of his body. He could still feel, but not move. A sour stink pervaded the room and he realized that his bowels had voided. Shame, rage, and terror warred within him as Evodh lowered the cylinder toward his face.

"We will start with stimulation of the trigeminal nerve. Later you will have an opportunity to speak, if you desire."

Omilov's terror peaked as he realized the full extent of his helplessness. Even had he wished to, he could not stop the torture by betraying his oath. He had barely time enough for a brief prayer to the Light-bearer before the needle tore into his cheek and an agony beyond anything he had ever conceived overwhelmed him.

※   ※   ※

Greywing followed the rest of the crew out from between the folds of the tapestry, and then stopped. Even the Eya'a paused momentarily, perhaps, she thought, in reaction to the others' emotions.

The antechamber to the Hall of Ivory had the form of a spacious hall, its floor covered with a plush, fine-napped carpet of midnight blue deeply incised with a complex abstract design composed of sunbursts and mandalic figurations in old gold. The high walls were interrupted at regular intervals by tall stained-glass windows, illuminated from without, of many different styles, preserving in glistening splendor a thousand years of the vitrine art. Above, just below the high ceiling, a massive crystal chandelier hung apparently unsupported, an inverted fountain of refracted and reflected light.

At the end of the hall most distant from them was a pair of ten-meter-high doors, carved in a riotous abstract design that suggested an eruption of energy from some unseen source into the phenomenal world. At the other end, near where they had emerged, a spiral staircase sprang gracefully up out of a sunburst mosaic set in the floor to a mezzanine level, its risers fashioned of exotic stone, no two alike. Whatever supported the staircase was invisible; it hung in the air like an incarnation of the flight of a bird rising from the surface of a still pond.

Scattered across the floor in a pleasing relationship to each other and the space they graced were pedestals displaying various objets d'art; similar displays hung on the walls between the windows.

Greywing looked around slowly and then moved her gaze

back again. At first the beauty hit her with the impact of a
stunning blow. Numbly she studied object after object, trying to memorize them all, for recollection later when she
was back in the ugliness that had seemed to be her place in
the universe. "Beauty" was another of those words that had
seemed to have lost its meaning, yet here it was, in forms
she could never have imagined, the gifts of unknown cultures, fashioned by long-dead hands. Suddenly she had to
see the names of the artists, though her eyes were stinging
and it was hard to read the engraved plagues: this was im-
mortality, a kind she would never achieve.

A sick kind of desolation chilled her. Except for distant,
beckoning glimpses when she was very small, there had
been no beauty in her life, and so in turn she had denied the
existence of beauty. She looked up, trying through blurring
eyes to find Ivard. Her brother bounded excitedly from figure to figure, grabbing whatever was small and stuffing it
into pockets, and when those were full, into the front of his
coverall.

Lokri, too, raced with uncharacteristic haste along the
displays, grabbing indiscriminately. He backed into something, knocking over a blown-glass figurine that glittered
with a desperate rainbow of colors before it smashed on the
floor. "Sgatshi!" Lokri exclaimed in disgust, and Ivard
snickered.

It seemed a kind of rape to Greywing, and she turned her
eyes away. Her bitterness increased when she recognized in
Ivard's laughter the hardened cynicism that she had carefully taught him as protection. It had never been his nature.

Her gaze was caught by a small silver object gleaming
against a matte-black background, just beyond her shoulder.
Closer examination resolved the object into a roundish medallion, with a broad-winged bird in flight carved on it. The
carving was worn in places, and clumsy in others, but there
was a kind of power and majesty in the soaring bird.
Around the medallion words had been engraved, in a roundish script completely unfamiliar.

She bent to look at the display plaque, and felt a thrill

spark from her brain through all her nerves when she saw the words . . . "From Lost Earth."

She lifted the medallion away from its setting, ignoring the pain in her shoulder as she lifted her arm. The cold metal was heavy against her hand. A silver bird: Greywing. From Lost Earth.

Her fingers closed around it, then she turned to look once more around the antechamber. Already many of the displays were bare. Ivard and Lokri joked back and forth as they made their way along an adjacent wall; Montrose strolled at an unhurried pace, gravely considering various items and choosing with care.

The Eya'a stood staring up at the chandelier, their necks kinked in an inhuman curve that made her uncomfortable to look at, and began keening together in a high, teeth-shivering counterpoint.

Poetry? Music? Maybe Vi'ya knew. Greywing saw her moving slowly from exhibit to exhibit, at least as interested in looking as looting.

The Krysarch alone seemed uninterested in his antechamber. Greywing saw him sitting on the stairs, elbows propped on his knees and hands dangling empty, his face pensive.

On impulse she crossed over to him. When she neared, he looked up inquiringly. "Why aren't you taking anything?" she asked, her voice coming out like an accusation. "Is this stuff boring to you?"

Brandon looked across the wide space at Ivard and Lokri and then his eyes dropped down again, so quickly she knew without his having to speak that he, too, felt the looting as a kind of rape. It made her spiraling thoughts dissolve into confusion and then take a radical turn.

"The art here belongs to the citizens of the Panarchy," he finally said. "Not to me."

"We aren't citizens," she retorted in a stony voice. "We're Rifters."

"You were once," he replied. "This won't redress our failure . . ." He paused, shrugged slightly. Gave her a twisted smile. "Better you have this stuff than the Dol'jharians use it for target practice."

She said suddenly, "If Markham had still been alive. And no Hreem attack. What would you have wanted from him?"

Brandon's eyes widened, and he hesitated a long time. This pause was as unnerving as anything Greywing had ever experienced: his answer was important to her, though she could not have told him why. And she would have died before bowing or using any of the Panarchist honorifics she'd seen and heard in vids, yet it seemed to her that this man was a part of this vast Palace and its silent hall of beauty, or else the hall was a part of him. She addressed him as equal to equal, for that was a promise she'd made to herself many years ago, but at the same time she felt the yawning gap between the Douloi Krysarch who had been bred up to power amid all this wealth and beauty, and a name-denied Rifter scantech who was scarcely able to protect one small brother.

But he did answer. "I would have asked him to join me in a rescue mission," he said. "A raid against my brother's fortress on Narbon, to free the singer he held captive to force my second brother's compliance."

Greywing expelled her breath sharply. "So you *do* believe—in justice."

"It's why I left," he said, so softly she almost didn't hear him.

"So it's not that you nicks don't care, but you don't *know*," she said. "Am I right? You didn't know about the combines on Natsu Four and the way they buy us when we're too small to know anything else, and snuff out our lives in the mines?"

Brandon's mouth tightened. "Under the Covenant of Anarchy—"

"I know about that. But *you* would fix it, if you could, am I right? Markham would have," she went on, talking faster than she ever had in her life. "He *did* try—" She stopped, swallowed. "And died for it."

"I promise, Greywing, if I can, I will." He raised his right hand.

Her eyes blurred again, and she fought to control the twist of strong emotions inside her.

"Do you know what the Eya'a are doing there?" the Krysarch went on in a light voice, his eyes on the small white figures. She recognized the change of focus as a chance for her to recover her equilibrium, and she was grateful, but she would not show that, either. "That noise of theirs might shatter those crystals," he said with a laugh.

"Vi'ya would know," she said in her flattest voice.

"Shall we go ask?" He got to his feet, smiling down at her in invitation.

She shrugged her good shoulder. "How come you aren't raiding your own art? Got better money stashed somewhere?"

He gave a slight grimace. "Prisoner of my training, I guess: I could take it, but I wouldn't be able to sell it. And where would I keep a crate of priceless artifacts? I don't seem to have an unoccupied home right now."

She felt a smile stretch her mouth at his bantering tone. Control was returning.

"So I was sitting here trying to concoct a way to get the House computer to locate and deliver some large quantities of money to me—money the new tenants think is theirs now."

She did laugh at that.

"I'll see what I can contrive when we leave this antechamber," he said.

They reached Vi'ya then, and Brandon made a gesture indicating the Eya'a. "What are they doing under that chandelier?"

"They are praising its beauty, using something akin to song." The captain regarded the Eya'a for a moment. "They rarely use speech, except in moments of great stress."

"You can understand what they say, or sing?"

"Yes, through our mind link."

He nodded. "But you're a tempath, not a telepath."

The captain studied Brandon with a measuring look. "With them it is different," she said.

Brandon seemed to sense as well as Greywing knew that no further information would be forthcoming about her relationship with the Eya'a. The Krysarch indicated the antechamber where the others were still busy. "You don't seem much interested in joining the free-for-all," he commented, nodding in the direction of Ivard, who was prying at something affixed to a wall.

Vi'ya shrugged slightly. "As captain, I receive fifty percent of everything they take." She smiled a little. "Having now seen a small portion of your home, I am not worried about being able to afford whatever *Telvarna* requires, so I can take the liberty of pleasing myself."

They had been slowly walking in no particular direction along the length of the hall and now stood in front of a pedestal displaying something that glittered softly in the light from above. It was a necklace, with a chain composed of large links—too large for a human neck—of a dark silvery alloy with an almost oily sheen to it. Suspended in a simple setting was a large elliptical gem. It was a soft gray, the indistinct color of morning rainclouds, and had no facets.

Greywing sucked her breath in, mesmerized by the eye-tricking depths in the stone.

Brandon's hand moved suddenly. He lifted the necklace from the display and held it out to Vi'ya, dropping it into her hand. Slowly the gem came to life, apparently activated by the heat of her hand. It began to flicker with a holographic medley of colors that slowly flowed up her arm, layering her in an armor of light. Against the severity of her attire and the calm impassivity of her expression the effect was startling.

"The Stone of Prometheus," said Brandon, "found in the wreckage of an alien spacecraft in the Oort Cloud around the Ndigwe system some four hundred fifty years ago. No one knows anything about the race that made it, or where they came from."

He looked around the hall for a moment, then bowed

with a flourish, his hand making an airy arc that somehow combined both grace and humor.

"As my last official act, as Krysarch Brandon Takari Burgess Njoye William su Gelasaar y Ilara nyr Arkad d'Mandala, I give this to the captain of the *Telvarna*."

Vi'ya hesitated, looking at him, her expression altering very slightly, but she did not return his smile. Her hand closed slowly over the stone, and she made a little, quick gesture—almost a nervous movement, though Greywing had never seen the captain display that emotion, even under fire.

Brandon seemed to sense it too. "What is it?" he asked, his smile changing to question.

Vi'ya shrugged, this time a sharp movement. "The captain of *Telvarna* thanks you," was all she said, and she walked past them, toward the other end of the antechamber.

"It's your moves," Greywing said. "Like this." She flicked her hand up in a parody of his mocking bow. "Don't know whether you got 'em from Markham or he got 'em from you, but sometimes looking at you is like a ghost come to life."

Brandon nodded soberly, but before he could respond his eyes went past her and then his face changed. Greywing turned to look at what had caught his attention and saw the captain approaching the big double doors.

"Got room for this one, Firehead?" Lokri asked.

"Sure," Ivard said, basking in the warmth of the comtech's friendliness.

"Good. Remember, this is another one for Marim. We don't bring her plenty, she'll hack our balls off while we sleep and have Montrose cook 'em for our breakfast."

Ivard winced as he shoved another pointy art thing down the inside of his sleeve. He could barely move; he'd have to stop somewhere and figure out a way to shift all this stuff around better.

Snorting a laugh, he thought about the fortune he was carrying inside his clothes. How he wished old Trev back on Natsu could see him now! Actually in the Palace belonging to the Panarch—and robbing it! And with one of the Krysarchs cheering them on!

He looked back to see if Greywing was having fun, and saw her frowning. Had something happened?

The captain was coming his way. He gulped and faded back defensively, but she passed by him without a glance, moving beyond him to a part of the wall that he and Lokri hadn't gotten to yet.

He craned his neck to look around Lokri, who was digging with the point of his springknife at the jewels encrusting a huge statue. The captain stopped before those big doors with the things carved on them.

"What's that?" the Krysarch said, then suddenly began walking fast, and Ivard felt impelled to follow, pulled by curiosity.

A thin yellow sash with purple blotches on it was draped across the carved doors that separated the antechamber from the Hall beyond. Its garish color clashed horribly with the old-gold of the design in the carpet. Ivard's skin prickled as the blotches resolved into the ancient and terrible symbol of the inverted trefoil.

"Radiation?" the Krysarch said sharply. "In the Hall of Ivory?"

He ran forward and pulled at the door handle. The yellow plastic sash stretched and snapped as the doors swung open under the impulse of the hinge engines, and the sight thus revealed wrung a shout of anguish from the Krysarch as he ran through—*"No!"*—and fell to his knees.

TWENTY-THREE

✳

The vast interior of the Hall of Ivory was a charred ruin, illuminated only by the light from the open doors and the few lamps left unshattered in the blackened ceiling. The tapestries on the walls were mere traceries of ash and tattered cloth; the windows—evidently destroyed by whatever energies had been released within the Hall—had been covered with opaque dyplast sheets whose fresh surface only emphasized the destruction elsewhere. The sweet stench of burned flesh still lingered faintly in the air; at the far end of the Hall the immense doors that guarded the Ivory entrance to the Throne Room were seared and blackened, their inlaid design reduced to twisted strips of metal springing from the surface in an ugly chaos.

Ivory.

The words that Deralze spoke just before he died came back to Brandon: *"Trust him. He didn't know . . . Ivory . . ."*

Now he understood, with jolting clarity, Deralze's uncertainty in the Palace, the day of the Enkainion: the hints of hidden anger, the strange speculative glances, his increasing distance on the ride to the booster field. *Lenic knew about this.*

And if it hadn't been for Markham, Brandon would have died with the others in the Ivory Hall.

The Faseult ring burned on his finger. Brandon gazed down at it sightlessly, his eyes aching, as he thought back. His ridiculous conversation with the Archonei Inesset the day of his Enkainion; the wrench he'd felt when he said his farewell to Eleris without her knowing.

Farewell. *Eleris, I thought it was I who chose danger, not you.*

He trembled, helpless in the grip of rage and grief, but he forced himself to look, and remember. Shallow or calculating, foolish or devious—as so many of them had been—none of them had deserved this.

Vaguely he heard someone come up beside him; recognized with a corner of his vision the bulky form of Montrose; heard without understanding a strident burring noise from his boswell and the one on Montrose's wrist. Without warning a pair of huge hands grabbed him under the arms and threw him backward out of the Hall. He scrambled back on his hands and knees toward the Hall of Ivory as the tall doors swung shut in his face, unwilling that his mourning should be interrupted.

Montrose picked him up by grabbing his upper arms in his huge paws and shook him, whispering fiercely, "Fool! Stay out of there! The rads in there would kill you, and not quickly—we have nothing on the *Telvarna* to deal with the likes of that!"

As suddenly as it had gripped him, the storm of emotion broke and receded.

Ivard watched as the Krysarch suddenly straightened up and the big Rifter let go of him. He took a deep breath and wiped his face with the kerchief Montrose handed him. Then his face went polite again, but this time, for the first time, Ivard could still see some of the emotions behind it.

"I'm sorry," the Krysarch muttered. "This was where my

Enkainion was held." He took another deep breath and said with a bitter smile, "Except I wasn't here, I'd gone off to join you."

"Best for you that you did," said Montrose grimly, tapping his boswell. "According to my boz'l, whoever settles into this Palace will first have to tear down that Hall and launch the rubble into the sun. Whoever it was used an obscenely filthy radiation device. There could have been no survivors."

Ivard turned his back on the blasted Hall and on the Krysarch still struggling with his reaction. Witnessing his transition from cool control to wild grief, and back again, had been more unsettling than the sight of the destruction inside the building.

He found Greywing crouched on the ground, painstakingly picking up gemstones from the floor. Looking up, he saw that Lokri was still prying stones from the statue with his knife. He caught the biggest ones, but let the smaller stones fall to the ground, where Greywing gathered them.

"There's better things," Ivard said to her.

Greywing hefted a handful of stones. "Oh, these'll bring a good price, if we don't sell 'em at once. Good bargaining." She snorted softly, lifting her chin in Lokri's direction. "Already ruined the statue anyway."

"So what? Nicks can buy themselves a new one," Ivard said.

Greywing squinted at him, and he knew he'd said something wrong. "New stones can be dug up," she said. "But you don't find things like this twice." She pointed at the statue, now scored with knife scratches and pocked where jewels were missing.

"So. These rich nicks—"

"Look, Ivard." Greywing put her hand inside her coverall, wincing slightly, and pulled out a small round silver thing—like a misshapen coin.

"That don't look like much," Ivard said, poking at the thing on her callused palm. "Won't bring a big price—"

"That's all you know," she said. "From Lost Earth."

Ivard gasped, glancing back along the hall at the things he'd passed by. Nice as these other gemmed and golden things were, he knew that anything purportedly from Lost Earth was priceless. "You could buy a ship—for us," he breathed.

"Not selling it," she stated, her eyes wide and intense. "See it, Ivard? There's only one, and when it's gone, it's gone forever."

He wanted to say, "So what?" but he could see that this was important to her. So he looked at it more closely, then discovered what the shape was. "It's a bird!"

Greywing grinned, the grin she used to flash when they were small. "Like 'Greywing,' isn't it?" she said. Her fingers closed over it. "Gonna keep it forever."

Ivard thought it over, then suddenly he thought he understood. "Like my flight medal? Except you didn't do anything for it," he amended.

To his surprise, his sister shook her bristly head. "Krysarch gave me a promise. About Natsu. They'll get their freedom too." She slid the medallion back into her pocket.

Puzzled by this odd turn of events, Ivard looked away, then made a discovery. "Hey! More stones over there." He'd help her gather them—he couldn't get anything more into his coverall anyway. He noticed the captain standing nearby, but she took no notice of him.

Greywing bent to pick up some small rubies, and Ivard saw a gleam of emerald in a corner behind a statue. He reached his hand under to grab it, then snatched it back with a yelp when a bright ribbon of what looked like green plastape rustled out and wrapped itself around his freckled wrist.

"Yow!" he yelled. It prickled, not painfully. And, "Hey!" with real fear when he tried to rip it free, and the ribbon bound tighter.

"What's that?" Lokri said from behind.

"It *jumped* me," Ivard quavered, holding up his arm. "Gimme your knife, I want to cut it off."

Montrose appeared suddenly, frowning. "Looks like Kelly ribbon," he said. "Where was it?"

"Under there." Ivard pointed. "Please, get it off." He didn't know much about the Kelly, who seemed such strange and jolly creatures, but he didn't trust anything inanimate that suddenly took on a life of its own.

"Here, I'll do it," Lokri said, producing his springknife from his sleeve. "I'll just—" Montrose put his hand on Lokri's arm, restraining him. Lokri tried to shake him off, then froze as Vi'ya, standing nearby, said sharply, "Silence."

The Eya'a emitted an ear-tingling chatter. Vi'ya spun around with her jac in a two-handed grip and fired twice at a figure who appeared suddenly at the top of the staircase at the other end of the hall. The man dropped his weapon and slumped down the stairs; the heavy jac bumped noisily down several risers and then clattered to the floor below. His body followed a short distance, then his foot caught between two risers and twisted him over the edge, leaving him hanging upside down like a carcass in a meat locker.

"Your emotions blocked the Eya'a from hearing him until too late," said Vi'ya, looking from the Krysarch to Greywing. "We had better leave here with what we have. We won't have much time once he's missed."

She pushed the Stone into her pouch with the other small items she'd chosen, and gestured with her weapon. "Where now?"

"But this—" Ivard squawked, scratching at the Kelly ribbon now wrapped tightly round his wrist. It itched fiercely.

Ivard saw the Krysarch and Montrose look at each other, and Brandon shifted his posture slightly. "I'll take care of it when we get back on board, boy," Montrose said after a moment. "Come on."

The Krysarch's face was grim as he led them across the chamber. Ivard followed as closely as he could, his attention divided between keeping up with the others and the thing on his wrist.

They passed the dead guard hanging from the staircase, a

neat, smoking hole marring the red fist of Dol'jhar on the chest of his gray uniform. Then Brandon twitched aside another tapestry to reveal a narrow door, paused, and turned to Vi'ya. Behind her the Eya'a stood unmoving, their eyes gleaming.

"This will bring us down into the old Hegemonic detention areas," the Krysarch said. "How far off can they sense humans?"

"They can localize and sense something of their minds up to a hundred meters away—walls are no obstacle. Beyond that they can sense their presence, and sometimes strong emotions, but nothing else."

"But they can't tell us apart?"

"Only humans they know. We will have to assume that anyone we meet is an enemy."

He nodded and pushed open the door, motioning them onto the landing of the narrow spiral staircase inside.

The crew filed past him and waited on the stairs. Brandon glanced back out at the plundered hall once more, then he let the tapestry fall back into place and led them down the echoing steel into the darkness below.

Almost immediately Ivard started lagging behind. He forced himself to go a little faster, but prickles and pains shot up his legs and arms from the things he'd thrust into his coverall, along with a growing ache from the green thing on his wrist.

"Ivard." Greywing loomed out of the shadows. "Why can't you go faster?"

"The things I got—" he gasped, then felt her hand run over his body.

"Dump some of it. You got enough to buy the *Telvarna* twice over."

"Not mine—got some for Marim . . ." He winced when she yanked his zipper down, but a moment later the worst of the pricks and jabs disappeared. Then clinks and chings sounded as his sister set the art objects carefully down on the metal stairway, tucked to one side.

"There. You leave Marim to me," she said grimly. "Now *run*."

She put her hand on his shoulder and pushed, and he nearly fell down the spiraling stairs in his effort to speed up. Soon he heard the others' clatter. He and Greywing caught up when the Krysarch had to stop at another passage access.

Brandon fiddled at an inset console, then turned to the crew. "Weapons ready?" he said softly. "Let us endeavor."

❋ ❋ ❋

"Why haven't you found that ship yet?" Barrodagh snarled at the miniature image of Rifellyn on the com. He carefully kept his right hand out of sight of the pickup.

"I told you, pesz ko'Barrodagh, I don't have enough techs to manage the Node as it is. Most of the Panarchists refused to cooperate, and those that did were worse than useless: if they weren't incompetent, they were busy committing sabotage. I shot twenty-three of them before I decided to expel them from the Node entirely."

Barrodagh gritted his teeth at Rifellyn's insulting use of the minimal-difference mode of address. The time was not right yet to encompass her downfall.

"With the resonance and Shield systems destroyed, my first priority is monitoring cis-lunar space and keeping an eye on our so-called allies," the woman continued, her dark brown eyes cold with dislike. "As for that ship of yours, all we know is that it came down somewhere near you, the discrimination circuits were destroyed by one of the saboteurs and we're having to inspect the satellite images manually."

Rifellyn paused, looked away from the screen for a moment at someone Barrodagh couldn't see. "I'll notify you as soon as anything turns up. Right now, I've got more important things to attend to."

The screen blanked and the Bori jumped to his feet. *Just wait, Rifellyn. My turn will come.*

He paced around the small office he had assigned himself in a sublevel of the Palace Minor, the quiet elegance of his surroundings making no impression on him. Suddenly he realized he was twisting at the Emasculizer on his thumb again and pulled his hand away hastily. No one had yet been found who knew how to remove it.

His face burned as he remembered Evodh's sarcastic laughter when he'd asked him to extract the secret from Omilov along with the information about the Heart of Kronos. "Your *tusz ni-synarrh* is no concern of mine," he'd said, using an extremely vulgar Dol'jharian term that translated literally as "lonely hand-sex." Then, compounding the insult, he'd refused Barrodagh permission to watch the gnostor's transfiguration.

The Bori pushed the memory away and turned back to the com.

"Get me Ferrasin."

Moments later the fat, sweaty face of the computer tech appeared on the screen. "Yes, senz lo'Barrodagh."

"Report your progress."

The man swallowed nervously. "We have traced most of the algorithms for surveillance, but have not yet tried to penetrate the data banks. We must proceed slowly to avoid t-triggering another worm."

"It didn't take you half this time to deal with the circuits here in the Palace and in the detention area," snapped Barrodagh.

The tech flushed and began to stutter. "That wa-wa-was accomplished manually, by physically cutting the circuits. Even so, the system c-c-continues its attempts to reestablish the connections. This is much more d-duh-delic-c-c-, *hard*, but I'm c-confident that—"

Barrodagh grimaced at the man's mangled speech. "Call me when you have something more than excuses. And don't make me call you again."

The Bori cut the connection and sat down wearily. His resources were stretched perilously thin, and it would be weeks yet before reinforcements could be ferried from Dol'jhar; the cursed treaty had forbidden them to build ships, and they were dependent on their Rifter allies for transport.

He reviewed the situation, looking again for any weak spots. The Panarchists that had not evacuated the Mandala during the first phase of the attack, after the decapitation of the government in the Hall of Ivory, were confined to the other three quadrants, where the surveillance equipment had been left intact. There was no problem there.

But in the quadrant now occupied by the Dol'jharian forces, it was not so easy. As long as the household systems could recognize them as intruders, it had refused them service; they had found it necessary to disconnect the sensory circuits in the Palace Minor and those areas of the Ivory wing of the Palace Major that now housed the Dol'jharian forces. In fact, given the continual attempts of the system to heal itself, Barrodagh had ordered the physical destruction of the sensors in the detention cells occupied by the Panarch and the remnants of his Privy Council, all destined for Gehenna. Even now, manual access to basic services was enforced by a delicate tampering with the programming that the techs warned him could still come unraveled at any time.

"You must remember," Ferrasin had said with his irritating stutter, "that this system has been running in its present form for hundreds of years. It's an enormously complicated patchwork of algorithms and adaptive systems; so complex and multilayered that I doubt anyone has really understood it for centuries.

"In fact," he had continued, with an almost fearful expression on his face, "if it weren't for the Ban, I'd say it was conscious."

Barrodagh didn't care about the Ban, no matter how the fat tech felt about it. Meanwhile, lacking automatic surveillance, he had to post guards throughout the Ivory quadrant—not just in the Palace Minor to guard the Avatar as custom demanded.

His com chimed.

"What now?"

"The Rifter from the *Satansclaw* is here."

"Send him in."

Barrodagh straightened up in his chair and hid his right hand in his lap. With his other hand he picked up a report and began to read it. The door opened to admit a tall, slender man with a vulpine face, dressed in a loose silk shirt and baggy trousers gathered into scuffed boots. The Bori ignored him for a time until he sensed that the Rifter's nervousness had grown sufficiently.

"Sit down." He stared at the man until his eyes fell. "So, Anderic, what is so important that you had to tell me in person?"

"It's about Tallis—"

"I know that, fool," interrupted Barrodagh. "He is the only reason I've wasted any time at all on you over the past year; but all you've had for me in the past is lurid tales of low-gee sexual antics and reports of his unflattering comments about me." He paused and tapped the pages of the report into alignment on edge. "Let me warn you—though it is already too late—that if this is a similar waste of my time—" The Bori reached over and dropped the papers into the disposal slot in the desk. There was a slight flash and a muted hiss as the disposal field vaporized them. "—you will not be returning to the *Satansclaw*."

As Anderic began to speak, Barrodagh held up his left hand. "Let me also tell you not to take too much comfort in the fact that Tallis has not yet returned himself. There was some question in the Avatar's mind about his performance in the affair of the nyr-Arkad's death. However, my naval liaison interviewed a number of the *Satansclaw*'s crew and reviewed the records of that encounter. It is his opinion that Tallis handled the ship brilliantly."

"That's just it," blurted Anderic, now sweating freely. "It wasn't Tallis."

Barrodagh raised his eyebrows and stared at the Rifter. "What do you mean, it wasn't Tallis?"

An odd expression crossed Anderic's face; to Barrodagh's eyes it appeared to be a compound of nausea and fear. The Rifter's voice was strained.

"He has a logos installed in the *Satansclaw*. That's what was running the ship."

The Bori shrugged. Like Dol'jhar, his world had been little affected by the Adamantine Wars; the Ban was merely words to him. *Still, it does mean that anyone can run that ship, so Tallis is expendable when and if the need arises.*

"So he has a logos. You don't imagine that the Lord of Vengeance cares about the Ban, do you?"

Anderic gaped at him. Evidently it hadn't occurred to him that observance of the Ban wasn't universal.

Barrodagh let him squirm for a while, then relented. The information was worth something, after all.

"But that might be useful knowledge. You may return to the ship." Barrodagh began shuffling through the welter of papers and record chips on his desk, indicating that the interview was over; then, horrified, realized that he'd revealed his right hand with the damnable sphere leeched onto it.

He looked up to find Anderic staring at his hand in fascination.

"Is there more?" he barked, restraining the urge to hide his hand.

"How did you get an Emasculizer stuck on your hand?" asked the Rifter.

Now it was Barrodagh's turn to gape. After a moment he asked, very quietly, "You know what this is?" No one else in the Dol'jharian contingent had ever seen one.

Anderic nodded, and Barrodagh found himself warming to him—he was the only person the Bori had encountered since the sphere attached itself to him that didn't appear to find his predicament amusing.

"Yeah. The captain on a ship I slubbed on when I first skipped out had a collection of things like that." His face twisted in recollection. "He used to use 'em for punishment."

Barrodagh swallowed, almost afraid to ask the next question. "Do you know how to get it off?"

"Yeah. I figured it out one day when it was my turn for

his twisted fun and games." He stood up and came around the desk. "Here."

Barrodagh mutely held out his hand. The Rifter positioned his hands around the sphere with his fingers in a peculiar pattern and pushed inward. There was a muted click and the sphere expanded and fell off his thumb into Anderic's hands. The Bori flexed his thumb as feeling returned; it appeared unharmed.

"Do you mind if I keep this?" asked Anderic.

"No," said Barrodagh fervently. Then, curious, he asked, "Why did you put up with such a captain? I thought you Rifters prized your freedom from authority."

"Ship's gotta have a captain," replied Anderic laconically. His success in freeing the Bori's thumb seemed to have reestablished a sense of equality, and Barrodagh was feeling too good to object. "But we didn't, finally. He tried his little tricks once too often and the crew mutinied." The Rifter turned the sphere over and over in his hands, looking down at it musingly. "We tied his hands behind his back and stuck that chatzing Emasculizer on his tongue." He laughed. "And then I triggered the reward circuit. Blunge-sucking thing tried its damnedest to bring him to orgasm—he finally choked to death."

Barrodagh suddenly shuddered. *Omilov wasn't making it up.* He looked at his thumb with a new sense of appreciation.

"I guess I'd better be going now, senz lo'Barrodagh," said Anderic.

The Bori looked at him sharply. "You speak Dol'jharian?"

"Just a little. I've been studying it. Makes sense to be able to talk to the winners, after all." He grinned. "And I understand you Dol'jharians are really stuck on titles and such, even more than the nicks. It never hurts to get that sort of thing right when you're talkin' to the one who pays the tab."

This one is much smarter than I gave him credit for. He may be worth some time.

"That's a wise attitude, but don't ever refer to me as Dol'jharian where one of the True Men can hear you. I'm a Bori, and they don't take kindly to being confused with us."

He motioned Anderic back to the chair. "But don't leave just yet. I'd like you to tell me more about Tallis and the logos. How is it controlled without the crew finding out, and how did you discover it?"

As Anderic began to explain, not without some reluctance, Barrodagh stroked his thumb lovingly and weighed the pros and cons of replacing Tallis. *But first I must judge the level of this one's ambitions. He appears intelligent enough not to overreach himself—more so than that fool Y'Marmor—but one can never tell with Rifters.*

He settled back in his chair and began to listen between the Rifter's words, measuring his character with the skills born of twenty years' service in circumstances where the slightest slip could mean an agonizing death. It didn't occur to him until later that that was an entirely accurate description of the Rifter environment too.

✳   ✳   ✳

Guardsman Remmet stood rigidly in front of the door, his cap at the regulation angle, his firejac held at exactly forty-five degrees across his chest, and tried in vain to stop the churning in his gut. He had been in the personal service of the Avatar, one of the Tarkans, for almost seven years, hardened by the savage discipline that every Dol'jharian soldier took for granted, but never, ever had he heard sounds anything like those emanating from within the room behind him. The palpable agony in them defeated every effort he made at a ward-trance; his neck muscles tightened at each new scream.

Remmet was not an imaginative man, but he could still feel the glance senz lo'Evodh had raked him with less than an hour before as he arrived to begin the transfiguration of the Panarchist. The look from the pesz mas'hadni had penetrated to every bone and tendon of his body, as if noting every vulnerable point of the fragile flesh before him and then dismissing it as unworthy of his efforts.

With all his soul he prayed to Dol in his incarnation as the Lord of Vengeance that he would never suffer the attentions of the tall man with the karra-patterns lacquered on his domed skull. He fought in vain against the traitorous part of his mind that insisted on imagining those torments, whose effects he was hearing, applied to him. The worst part was that he had no idea what they were. Then, as a particularly horrible and liquid shriek from within scraped his ears, he stiffened his spine and concentrated fiercely on the painting on the wall across the corridor from him. His watch would be over in three hours; he knew they would be the longest hours of his life.

❃   ❃   ❃

"Damn! This place is big," Lokri muttered, quickening his pace.

Montrose looked over at him. "It's a *palace*," he said, easily keeping pace with his long strides. "It's *supposed* to be big."

On his other side the little redhead chortled, his eyes wide with excitement. Montrose smiled at Ivard, glad that the boy was not worrying about the Kelly ribbon on his arm. "Enjoying it, are you, Firehead?"

Ivard looked up. "This is like a chip," he exclaimed. "Better!" He raised his jac and sighted along it as he ran. "Hope we find some o' those Dol'jharians."

"No you don't," Greywing said, thumping his arm as she ran. "Vacuumskull."

Ivard started to argue with his sister. Almost at once the Krysarch changed pace, moving next to Montrose. "Can you get that Kelly ribbon off him?"

Montrose shook his head. "I don't know," he said softly. "I have a chip on Kelly biology, but I've never reviewed it end-to-end."

"Will it poison him?" Brandon said.

"I'm afraid it might," Montrose admitted. "And whatever

damage it is going to do has been done already; even if I were to take his arm off, the ribbon's genome has likely already diffused through his body at the cellular level. It wouldn't make any difference—except, perhaps, another "ribbon" would fashion itself out of his flesh elsewhere."

"We need to find him a Kelly physician," Brandon muttered, turning his head to scan an adjacent corridor.

We? Montrose looked up, saw the captain's dark eyes watching.

"No. Down this way," Brandon said abruptly, veering. The others changed direction, following. "If they've got prisoners, this is where they'd be kept . . ." He raced ahead.

Montrose followed more slowly, watching the accessways as they progressed. Vi'ya walked next to him, her eyes on the Eya'a, who drifted forward at a surprisingly quick pace.

"If he does find any of his family?" the physician asked.

Vi'ya's lip curled. "Semion vlith-Arkad would come aboard my ship only as a prisoner."

"Would?" Montrose asked. "You don't think we'll find anyone?"

She shrugged. "Anyone brought here would be marked for execution, or for a more protracted death."

"But you let him search."

"He will lead us to the ship," she stated. "I could not find it on my own."

Ahead the Krysarch skidded to a stop and touched the wall in a brief pattern. A panel slid aside, revealing a computer console.

Montrose put out a hand to stay Vi'ya. She avoided his touch, but stopped. The others bunched up near Brandon as he began tapping at the console; Greywing drew her brother down the hall a little further and spoke quietly to him. There was a brief flicker of red light as the console identified the Krysarch.

Seeing the others distracted, Montrose said quietly, "You think his family is dead, then?"

"If it is Eusabian of Dol'jhar in possession here, it is the only possible outcome."

"Then this one"—Montrose pointed at Brandon, who was still busy at the console—"is the titular head of their government. What would that be worth in ransom—to either side?"

Vi'ya smiled, just a little, and said something under her breath. Montrose felt a prickle along the back of his neck when he recognized the harsh consonants of Dol'jharian, a language he'd heard her speak just once before. Then she said, "First we must get off this planet. Then we will plan."

TWENTY-FOUR

✳

Laughing inwardly at his own fears, Lokri stepped back when he saw the telltale flicker of a retinal scan on the Krysarch's face. Lokri watched the Krysarch as he worked intently at the console, impressed by his deft touch. Brandon's Douloi mask had slipped a little as he concentrated; he looked on the verge of laughter.

Without turning his head, Lokri observed Montrose and Vi'ya talking. He slid his hand over his boswell, tapping it: nothing. They did not want to be heard.

He risked a glance over his shoulder, only to look straight into Vi'ya's dark eyes: neutral speculation. Whatever they were talking about, then, was not him.

He was conscious of disappointment, which made him laugh silently.

Brandon stabbed at the console, giving a faint grunt of finality. The sudden motion caught Lokri's attention, and Brandon looked over at him.

"I've, ahh, resurrected a little something to keep our Dol'jharian friends off balance." A genuine grin briefly lit up his face. "We had one as a guest here once; he hated this worm."

A Dol'jharian guest? A faint memory tickled Lokri's mind, then was swept away as Brandon looked past him and motioned to Vi'ya and Montrose. As the captain approached Lokri and the Krysarch she gestured to Greywing and Ivard, who joined them.

"I reactivated a worm I built many years ago," said Brandon. He smiled ruefully. "The house system seems to have kept a lot of my childhood toys waiting for me, but this is the only one that seems useful." He shook his head, as if dispelling an unwanted memory. "Anyway, from now on you may see shadows on the walls or vague, quick movements from the corner of your vision. Don't let it spook you; it's designed to keep the Dol'jharians on edge and distracted."

His eyes went to Vi'ya, and Lokri thought he saw perplexity in the Krysarch's gaze, but then the look was gone, the pleasant Douloi mask back in place. Brandon turned and walked down the hall, trying door after door.

The passageway they were following came to an end at a cross-corridor. Brandon paused, looking back at the Eya'a. Vi'ya moved away from Montrose and then leaned against a wall, her head cocked as if listening intently. The others stood watching; Montrose turned and faced back the way they'd come, on guard.

Something scuttled across the floor at Lokri's feet, seeming to melt into the wall and disappear. He jumped, then grinned at Ivard, who was watching him—he apparently hadn't seen it. *A computer haunting.* He looked around but couldn't see any trace of the holojac he knew had to be there. Lokri glanced speculatively at the Krysarch's back as he waited, watching the captain. A worm he'd managed to write into the Palace system—in childhood?

After a moment Vi'ya turned left and went on, slowly at first, then with more assurance. They proceeded in silence for a time, passing numerous doors. The faces of long-dead and forgotten men and women stared mutely at them from faded paintings and holograms on the paneled walls.

At another junction Vi'ya paused again. Lokri noticed with surprise and sharp interest a flicker of something like pain on her face as the captain froze into a motionless tableau with the Eya'a. Then she turned to the crew.

"They are sensing someone radiating very strongly nearby. Even I can feel it now." She shook her head as if to clear it. "Someone is in great pain; resisting something, or withholding." She pinched the bridge of her nose between thumb and finger, as if to relieve aching sinuses.

Then she looked up, her eyes widening slightly as the Eya'a emitted a faint chirp in unison. "A silver sphere. The mind in torment holds an image of the Heart of Kronos."

"Who here would know about the Heart of Kronos?" the Krysarch murmured.

"The what?" Lokri asked, lounging against a piece of furniture.

Vi'ya ignored him, and Brandon gave him a distracted look. Had the Arkad been bringing some kind of arcane weapon to Markham? Lokri wished he'd tried a little harder to witness Vi'ya's interview with the two Panarchists, back on Dis.

Vi'ya motioned them down the corridor. "This way."

They were jogging now. A short time later they reached another junction and Vi'ya waved them to a stop well short of it. She crept up to the edge of the cross-corridor, knelt down, and looked cautiously around the corner, her head close to the floor. A moment later she rejoined them.

"There's a Tarkan in front of a door about thirty meters down the hall," she whispered, almost voicelessly.

"Tarkan?" asked Brandon.

Vi'ya hesitated a moment. "A Dol'jharian guardsman. The ones in black. They are Eusabian's personal guard— very dangerous. The gray uniforms are just jac-fodder—"

She stopped, wincing. All of them heard the bubbling shriek. Lokri's stomach clenched, Ivard and Greywing both looked sick. Montrose's grizzled face frowned deeply.

"We've got to stop that, no matter who it is," whispered Brandon. Another scream echoed down the corridor, seeming to come from two directions at once.

Lokri glanced back, then hit his boswell: *(Look!)*

He pointed to a ventilation grille near the ceiling about four meters back down the passageway. Vi'ya tapped her own boswell and shook her head, frowning, then she motioned Greywing and Ivard toward the corner. Both of them pulled their weapons as they took up their station as guards.

Vi'ya led the way back to the grille, gathering Lokri and Montrose with her eyes. She jerked her chin up at the grille and motioned to Lokri.

Another howl of agony echoed through the opening as Montrose swiveled his two-hand firejac around behind his back on its harness and Lokri put his hands against the wall, bracing himself.

A moment later Lokri felt the big physician's hands on his waist, and with a soft grunt Montrose lifted him into the air. Lokri walked his hands up the wall, then pulled at the grille. It came away with a faint clatter that sounded loud to his ears. Montrose lowered him, and he dropped soundlessly to the floor; back at the junction Ivard clutched his weapon in white fingers, his sister still and grim.

Vi'ya stepped away for a momentary, silent conference with the Eya'a. They moved lithely over to stand below the opening, which was all of three meters above the floor.

The Krysarch sucked in his breath in apparent surprise, as abruptly, the Eya'a leapt and vanished into the ventilation duct in two smooth motions, so fast they were almost a blur. They hadn't seemed to crouch or otherwise prepare themselves, as a human gymnast might have—one moment they were in the corridor, the next they were gone. Lokri shuddered; he still couldn't get used to them—they would be easier to take if they were frankly alien, like the Kelly.

Vi'ya motioned the rest of them back to join Ivard. "Get ready," she breathed.

❊   ❊   ❊

Remmet was clutching his weapon so hard that his hands
ached, matching the ache in his clenched jaws. Suddenly
the shrieks stopped. Remmet willed himself to relax and enjoy the respite. His gaze stayed fixed on the wall before him
until a flicker high on his right caused him to swerve, fingers tight on the trigger of his jac: nothing there. He knew
he'd seen something, though.

Ghosts, he thought. Had the Panarchist finally died? His
shade, thirsting for vengeance, walking the halls . . .

Then he jumped as a new, louder scream ripped through
the door, followed by the crash of equipment falling to the
floor.

"Guard!" he heard Evodh call, the cry changing immediately to a despairing shriek of horror and rage fully as terrible as anything he'd heard from the pesz mas'hadni's
victim, and another crash.

Remmet slapped the summoner on his belt, spun about,
and crashed through the door, his weapon ready, then
stopped, a shiver of uncanny fear racing through him.
Evodh lay on his back on the floor, his hands clenched into
claws drawn up near his cheeks, which were furrowed with
bloody stripes from his fingernails. The guardsman fought
with nausea as he saw that the man's eyes had exploded; a
hideous gray-crimson pudding was seeping from the empty
sockets and his ears and nose. Behind the gurney, where the
Panarchist lay still, his chest barely moving, the assistant
lay in similar ruin.

Remmet looked wildly around the room, his skin prickling as the superstitions of his race came welling up from
the dark corners of his soul. Tales of the karra, the demons
who'd destroyed the original paradise of the True Men, and
who still lurked in the shadows, echoed in his mind.

Then a sudden movement near the ceiling caught his eye.
He spun toward the ventilation grille, raising his firejac as
he saw two pairs of gleaming faceted eyes fixed on him. As
the faces around those eyes came into focus he had just

enough time to realize that there were worse things on this world than any karra before a sun kindled in his brain and a scream ripped his throat open and carried his life away with it.

The instant the last scream died away Vi'ya motioned them around the corner. They raced down the corridor to the open door and stopped in shock. The room stank of blood and excrement. Brandon fought a tide of nausea as he saw what the Eya'a had done to the Dol'jharians and then instantly forgot it as he recognized the man strapped to the gurney.

"Sebastian!" He leapt over the robed body on the floor, then stopped, unsure what to do next. Omilov's chest was barely moving; blood trickled out of his mouth and from small wounds here and there on his body. A thin whine emanated from some sort of machine attached to a mesh cap on the gnostor's head.

Montrose pushed past him and cast a practiced eye over Omilov's body, then looked at the banks of instruments beyond. "You know this man?" he rumbled as he placed his ear on Omilov's chest.

"My oldest friend." Brandon noticed Vi'ya step over the guard's body to join the Eya'a, who had pushed out the grille and jumped down from the ventilator duct. "He's Osri's father."

"This is the man who gave the Heart of Kronos to you?" asked Vi'ya.

Brandon nodded, his face grim as Montrose picked up a sprayjector off the floor from among a welter of ugly, glittering instruments and sniffed it.

"He's had a cardiac stimulant, which should keep him going for a while yet, but he needs attention as soon as possible." The physician motioned to the instruments against the wall, one of which displayed a wavering electronic trace. "There's something wrong with his heart—was before this happened."

"But what's that thing on his head?" asked Ivard from the doorway, his thin face greenish with nausea.

"I don't know," said Montrose, restraining Brandon's hand as he reached to take it off.

"This is a pesz mas'hadni," Vi'ya murmured, nudging the robed man with the toe of her boot. "Trained in the arts of pain. Only Dol'jharian lords have such." She looked up at Montrose, who watched her, waiting. "Free him."

"It's some kind of torture machine," Ivard whispered in horror.

Montrose glowered at the machine, his eyes running along the connections from machine to the cap on the man's head. "I can't figure it out," he said, shaking his head. "We'll just have to take a chance." He gently removed the cap, then threw his huge body across Omilov as the gnostor suddenly heaved upward in a massive convulsion. The spasm passed as suddenly as it had come; Omilov's breathing was louder now, a harsh, quivering sound resonant with pain.

Montrose levered himself up off of Omilov and turned to Vi'ya. "If he's to survive to talk, we've got to get him to the ship as soon as possible."

The Eya'a chattered suddenly. Vi'ya froze for a moment. "Patrol's coming. Can't tell how many but they're coming fast." She turned to Brandon. "How do we get back to the ship from here?"

"If we continue along this corridor the direction we were going and head down two levels—"

"All right, let's get going. You can tell us the rest on the way." To Montrose: "Bring the old man."

Montrose unstrapped his firejac; Brandon sheathed his own and took it from him. The big Rifter looked around the room for a moment, then bent down and ripped the robe off of the dead Dol'jharian with the lacquered skull and gently wrapped Omilov in it. Brandon noticed that the Dol'jharian's body was covered with scars and cicatrices, then he looked away.

Montrose carefully picked the gnostor up and slung him over his shoulder, then waited while the others filed out of the room.

Brandon motioned him out ahead, then followed and turned just outside the doorway. So the Dol'jharian rulers kept personal torturers? A flicker of memory briefly blanked the terrible scene before him: for the second time in an hour he thought of Anaris, this time remembering the threats the Dol'jharian hostage used to make.

Not that we ever listened to the nasty hulking bugger, Brandon thought, lifting the heavy two-hand firejac and thumbing it to wide aperture. *It was enough to stay out of reach of that damned saw-toothed knife of his, until I was finally sent off to school.*

He held down the trigger, hosing the room with a thick stream of sun-hot plasma. The machinery exploded into flames and gobbets of white-hot metal. Brandon let go of the trigger and stumbled backward, half-blinded, as the ceiling released a shower of foam that hissed violently and emitted a sharp chemical stench. Then he turned and hurried after the Rifters.

❋   ❋   ❋

Barrodagh came to himself with a slight start. Across the desk from him he saw Anderic waiting calmly, his eyes partially averted out of deference.

This Rifter is a quick study. It has taken him very little time to pick up the appropriate behavior. He noted the time displayed on his desk with a fraction of his attention; in the past half hour he had learned much about Rifter customs and behavior. In some ways it was a very familiar world.

One thing is certain: Tallis is not enough of a counterbalance to Hreem. I will have to maneuver Anderic into his position somehow.

"Your information is very interesting, Anderic. I will have to think about what you've told me." He smiled conspiratorially. "For the moment I'll have you escorted to Tallis' room. You may tell him that your intervention was instrumental in winning his release."

Anderic grinned back at him. "Yeah, that'll be a good

start." He stood up, stretched luxuriously, then started, his eyes flickering to the wall behind the Bori.

Barrodagh swiveled around. There was nothing there. He turned back, puzzled, then shoved his chair back in alarm as a vaguely perceived shadow scuttled out from under his desk and melted into the opposite wall. A brief shiver of fear ran through him, and he pushed it out of his mind. *Too many years on Dol'jhar, with all their demons and spirits.* But as he looked up and met Anderic's wide-eyed stare, he wasn't entirely convinced.

Barrodagh's com chimed, rescuing him from uncomfortable thoughts.

"What?"

"This is Dektasz Jesserian, over the Ivory Hall detail. One of my men was found dead a short time ago in the Ivory antechamber, and a number of artifacts are missing." The man's accent identified him as a lower-echelon Dol'jharian aristocrat; his omission of any form of address acknowledged a de facto equality between them. Barrodagh knew him as a conscientious military man with no interest in politics.

"I ordered an alert, but before I could notify you we received an alarm from the guardsman assigned to senz lo'Evodh. He is not responding to our signals. A squad is on the way and I have doubled the guard on the approaches to the Palace Minor. Have you any further orders?"

Barrodagh forgot all about the Rifter standing in front of him, and the weird shadows. Eusabian would be furious at this violation of his new demesne, but if they could capture the looters and put things right before he had to report this, the consequences would be minimal.

"No. But when you find them, leave none alive—and be careful not to damage any of the artifacts. They must be returned to the antechamber unharmed."

The Dol'jharian commander acknowledged and cut the connection. Barrodagh looked up at Anderic.

"How much of that did you understand?"

"A little," said the Rifter carefully. "Sounds like some of

the brethren got a little cocky. And greedy." He shuddered theatrically. "After reading up on Dol'jhar and some of their habits, there isn't anything that valuable, as far as I'm concerned."

Barrodagh nodded. "Perhaps you'd better stay here for the time being. I can't spare an escort for you now. You can wait in the outer office."

❋   ❋   ❋

Ivard clutched his weapon tightly to his side, running next to Greywing. Still fighting the nauseating shock of what he'd seen in that torture room, he thought resentfully that there had never been anything like that on his favorite chip, *The Invisibles*.

Not that he hadn't seen people take hits. One of their very first runs, back when Markham was captain, they'd been heading back to the second hideout to refit when suddenly they'd veered off course, and Markham had had them jack a slaveship. Ivard hadn't been allowed to help, but he'd seen it all on the screens. And he'd been part of the work detail to get rid of Totten's body, back on Dis, when Totten and Jakarr tried their takeover. But those hits had been sudden, and neat—if you held your nose around the burn smell.

He didn't know which was worse: what the Dol'jharians had been doing to the old man, or what the Eya'a had done to the Dol'jharians. He'd never seen them fry someone before, though Greywing had. She'd only told him afterward, in that voice that meant Shut Up About It, that it was disgusting. Well, she was right.

He looked over at her now, running along beside him. Her pace had slowed, and she clutched her shoulder tightly with one hand, her jac dangling from the fingers of her bad arm. He knew she wouldn't complain, though; she never did. She just went quiet and grim.

He wished suddenly that he hadn't gotten angry at her back there, when she'd called him a vacuumskull right in front of Lokri and the others, just for saying he hoped to get a shot at some of these Dol'jharian blungesuckers. Not that it wasn't time for her to stop acting like he was a baby, now that he was a full crew member.

"Here!" the Krysarch called in a sharp voice. "Through here and down the stairs. The closet we entered through is right at the bottom." He held open the door for Montrose, whose pace hadn't abated despite the weight of the man he carried.

The gnostor's eyes were half-open but he was entirely limp and unresponsive. A thread of reddish spittle hung from his lips, and with his shaved head it made him look like an aged infant. Ivard looked away and shuddered, hoping they'd be out of here soon. He no longer wanted to play with the jacs, like in a chip; he just didn't want to get caught by these mind-twisted Dol'jharians.

As they entered a wide room where several corridors converged, Ivard shied as a shadowy something swung past his head. The Krysarch's warning hadn't helped much; he couldn't help the start of fear the shadows caused—they were too much like dreams he used to have, still had.

He looked around. Scattered about them were large crates and some loading machinery, their placement suggesting hasty abandonment some days ago.

The Eya'a chattered again.

"Guards," said Vi'ya. "Close and coming fast." She looked through the door at the narrow spiral stairs. "They'll catch us on the stairs. Is there another way?"

"Yes, back that way, but it'll be a good deal further."

"No choice, we'll have to draw them off. Montrose, take the old man down to the transport. Wait for us—" She looked at Brandon.

"About fifteen minutes."

"No longer," she continued. "Don't try to communicate. Then get back and have Jaim warm things up. They must have connected us with the ship, and they'll find it soon."

"Montrose, wait a moment. Here's how to send the transport back here when you reach the gazebo." The big Rifter shifted Omilov on his shoulder and tapped his boswell to record Brandon's words.

"Go now." Vi'ya waved him into the stairs. "The Eya'a will guard you."

Montrose disappeared down the stairs with his burden, followed by the Eya'a, who alone did not seem at all tired after all that running. Ivard was sorry to see them go.

"The guards are close enough now that I can sense them myself," the captain said. "If we're lucky enough to get too far ahead of them for that, we won't need to worry." Her eyes narrowed. "Greywing. You can fight?"

"I'll be all right," Greywing said in her flattest voice. Her hand dropped away from her shoulder, and she checked the charge on her weapon. Ivard could see sweat gleaming on her scalp through her short hair, and he decided to station himself in front of her in case anything happened. She looked up at him then, and he tried to smile reassuringly. He didn't know how successful his grin was, but she did smile back, then gestured for him to check his own weapon. He looked down at it, not wanting to advertise the fact that he'd already checked it half a dozen times since they'd left that torture room.

With a few quick motions, the captain positioned them around the room with clear avenues of escape to the corridor Brandon had pointed out. Lokri and the Krysarch dragged a couple of crates to partially block it and shield their retreat. Ivard ducked into his place, trying to control the weird shakiness in his knees and wrists, and he noticed suddenly that he desperately had to pee. He sucked in a breath, held it a moment, then let it out slowly, just as Markham had taught him.

Lokri and the Krysarch had just ducked into concealment when the Dol'jharian patrol was upon them.

The gray-clad soldiers fanned out efficiently from the corridor opening. One of them had a big, ugly animal on a leash, its jaws open to display far too many sharp yellow teeth. To Ivard, it resembled nothing so much as a gaunt, misshapen dog with large, leaf-like scales instead of fur.

It emitted a harsh keening sound and lunged to one side, toward where Ivard had secreted himself. From the other

side Vi'ya popped up and needled the beast in the flank. It
went berserk, snapping at its side and its handler indiscriminately. In the ensuing confusion, as the guards fired toward
her and at the crate the animal had lunged for, the Krysarch
jumped sideways from behind a crate and triggered the
firejac.

Ivard saw at once that the unfamiliar weight of Montrose's
heavy weapon had spoiled his aim, and the blast hit the floor
in front of the guards. The flooring exploded in a hail of
flaming splinters. Brandon jerked the muzzle up; the stream
of plasma faltered and died as the charge ran out, but not before three guardsmen vanished in a cloud of bloody, flaming
steam.

The Krysarch dropped the useless weapon and dived behind Ivard's crate as the surviving Dol'jharians returned
fire. Bolts of energy sizzled into the crate, but fortunately
whatever was inside was bulky and dense enough to protect
them.

To Ivard's surprise, the Krysarch was biting down hard
against breathless laughter. Brandon looked up then, his
blue eyes gleaming, and he whispered, "I just remembered—the day I left here—I dreamed we were attacked in
the Palace . . ."

He shook his head violently, droplets of sweat splattering
the crate from his wet hair. " 'Prayers that heaven in enormous vengeance grants,' " he murmured as he pulled his
own weapon free, checking the charge.

"Arkad!" came a fierce whisper.

They both turned to see Vi'ya signaling a retreat into the
corridor. They moved cautiously back, concealed from the
enemy by the crates. The guardsmen had taken cover behind other crates; Ivard could hear guttural whispers from
them as they conferred. Another shadow sprang to life and
scuttled across the ceiling. The whispers stopped.

The five of them retreated down the corridor backward,
weapons ready, until they reached a junction. As they raced
off in the direction Brandon indicated, a jac-bolt sizzled
down the hallway they'd just quit and vaporized a holo-

graphic likeness of an archaically gowned woman with too many chins and no lips.

This isn't so bad, Ivard exulted to himself, but almost immediately he felt guilty, and slid a look at Greywing. Her face was set in a grimace of pain as she pounded along, one arm clutched tight against her. *We won't ever fight just to be fighting,* she'd said earlier. *We're going to get enough money to go back to Natsu and then we'll fight for freedom.* He liked that idea fine.

"Here." The Krysarch waved them down another corridor. "Shortcut."

Vi'ya motioned Lokri and Brandon to run behind, in case their pursuers caught up with them. Greywing and Ivard started matching pace with her, but the captain's steps slowed; Ivard realized she was using her tempathic abilities to scan ahead of them for possible attackers. He grinned, running a little faster: if she sensed any of those blungesuckers, he wanted to be ready for them. Greywing kept pace right next to him.

They clattered down two narrow hallways, then through another storage room that gave off onto more corridors. Rounding a corner, they came suddenly on two black-clad guardsmen in front of a door, who spun around and fired.

Ivard felt a terrible sense of being frozen in time; he saw the bolts of light from the weapons. He saw Greywing jerking her arm up, too slow, too late. He felt something harsh as acid bite at his wrist and flood his body: the sense of frozen time melted away and for a moment he was moving faster than he'd ever dreamed possible. His body convulsed violently, throwing him to one side, his shot going wild. He saw a shadow flicker on the ceiling, and both of the Dol'jharians look up at it, and he heard a thin, high cry before red painfire closed around him.

TWENTY-FIVE

✳

Shock stabbed through Lokri as the Tarkans' jac-fire hit the two redheads. Greywing's arms flew up and she dropped without a noise; the boy leapt aside, his body contorting, and the bolt lanced across his back.

Then Vi'ya whipped up her weapon and fired, the sound not quite drowning a guttural snarl of rage. A jac-bolt from Brandon sizzled past Lokri, and both Tarkans took hits. Their fingers convulsively clutched their weapons, which burned paths in the floor until their bodies fell full length. Something flickered again, almost out of sight; Lokri recalled that there'd been one of those flickers just as the firefight started, then he forgot it when he saw Vi'ya stiffen and shake her head violently.

Brandon sprang to check Greywing as Lokri bent over the boy, who rolled slowly back and forth, his breath wheezing. Lokri pinned him down with swift efficiency while Vi'ya reached into her pouch. "We've got about ninety seconds before the others catch up," she said as she pulled out a small ampule and jabbed it into the boy's arm.

Ivard jerked, his eyes opening wildly as the drug took effect. "It burns . . ." he moaned, his fingers crawling over his body, not toward the jac-hit but toward the arm where the Kelly ribbon had attached itself.

Lokri, looking closer, saw that the ribbon no longer had an edge; it had sunk into his skin, melding with it somehow. Lokri felt his stomach clench. "C'mon, Firehead. We're going to do a little running," he said softly.

"What happened?" Brandon jerked a thumb at the fallen guards.

"Ward-trance," said Vi'ya tersely, her brow tight with anger. "Couldn't sense them." And, to Lokri: "Back."

Lokri rolled the still-writhing boy over, and the captain popped open a pack of gel-flesh over the oozing, blackened groove across Ivard's back. The half-alive symbiont spread out and melted into the damaged flesh, sealing it against the air.

Lokri helped the boy to his feet; Ivard's pupils were dilated, his face drawn. "Greywing . . ." he whispered, lunging toward his sister.

"She's gone, boy," Lokri said. "We have to get out of here." Ivard choked on a sob and wrenched himself free, showing more strength than Lokri would have imagined the boy had, even when whole. He dropped on his knees beside his fallen sister, and Lokri moved to restrain him, but Vi'ya caught his arm.

In silence they watched Ivard turn Greywing carefully over, then his fingers plunged into Greywing's inner pocket, coming up with a handful of fine jewels and a round metallic object covered with blood. Not from the jac-bolt, which had burned neatly square in the center of her chest, but from the still-healing flesh of her earlier burn.

Ivard dropped the jewels, his fingers clutching the medallion. Then Vi'ya reached forward and took him by the chin, jerking his head up. "Now we leave. She will be angry if you follow her to the Hall of Ancestors so quickly."

Ivard blinked, his eyes still wild. Vi'ya slapped him lightly. "Run."

They started forward a few steps, Ivard stumbling. Lokri flung out an arm and held the boy's thin body against him, stopping when Vi'ya paused before Brandon, who was trying the locked doors along the corridor.

"Who were they guarding?" Brandon demanded. "Which door?"

"Someone sleeping," Vi'ya said, her eyes squeezed shut for a moment. "It might not be a prisoner, it might be one of their commanders, but we cannot stay to find out: the pursuit is nearly upon us."

Brandon gave a short nod, and then they started running again. Lokri took as much of the boy's weight as he could, and to his surprise Ivard slowly managed to gather some strength.

"Doesn't hurt—much," Ivard mumbled. "Cold. But this thing . . ." He waved his green-banded wrist. "Burning."

"Vi'ya shot you with a painkiller," Lokri said, trying to sound light. In case the boy's shock broke. "That'll keep you going until we get back to the ship. But stay out of the front line, eh?"

Ivard gave him a weak grin just as the sounds of their pursuers drifted up the corridor behind them.

When they reached another storage room, Brandon spoke. "I know where we are now. It's a portion of the old Hegemonic area, converted to food service for a nearby admin sector of the Palace Minor."

"Exit?" Vi'ya said. "They come, from three directions now." She waved her jac.

The Krysarch looked around intently, then sprang forward. "In there," he said, slapping open a door.

Gelasaar hai-Arkad awoke suddenly from a gentle dream of Ilara, unsure of what had shattered his sleep. The sound that had awakened him echoed blurrily in his memory. *Jac-fire?*

He listened intently. The door to his cell was thick, but he thought he heard voices. His ears strained to make out the words; a familiar timbre in one of the voices sent a surge of joy and hope through him.

Then he came fully awake and clamped down on his emotions. No doubt it was another one of that Bori creature's mind games. One night they had played back a recording of Ilara's last meeting with Eusabian; his throat clenched at the memory of her dying shriek. Another night he'd heard Semion's voice, the words cleverly altered to transform whatever the conversation had really been about into loathsome perversions.

He wasn't even sure that Eusabian knew about these diversions of his aide-de-camp. He had indeed misjudged the depth of Eusabian's hatred, but nothing in the man's character indicated a taste for this manner of pointless pettiness.

The voices ceased. After a moment, Gelasaar rolled over onto his side and tried to summon back the dream of his beloved.

Brandon and the Rifters plunged through the double doors into a large, automated kitchen of steel and dyplast, all but a few of the gleaming food generators silent and dark. Brandon raced across the long room toward the opposite doors.

"Wait!" hissed Vi'ya, but just then a gray-clad Dol'jharian guard pushed open the door he was heading for, carrying a tray with a carafe and several cups on it.

The man gaped at the Rifters for a moment, then dropped the tray with a crash as a bolt from Vi'ya's jac caught him in the neck and sent him flying back out the door, giving them a glimpse of more guardsmen before the door swung shut again. They could hear chairs overturning amidst exclamations in Dol'jharian; then behind them, in the corridor they'd just quit, the sound of doors opening and slamming as the two other contingents of Dol'jharians met and began a methodical search.

They hastily took cover behind some bulky metal storage cabinets. Vi'ya checked the charge on her jac, shook her head, and looked up at Brandon. "Now where?"

He had no immediate answer for her; then the door they had entered by swung open and a guardsman rolled through on the floor and came up with his firejac poised to fire. For a moment nobody moved; then the other door burst open and a flurry of jac-bolts sizzled through, followed by several guards. The first guardsman dived for cover, shouting loudly, the others stopped, staring, and then Lokri and Vi'ya stood up and burned several down where they stood. The survivors scattered, taking cover across the room and returning the fire, to no effect.

There was more shouting from beyond both doors; then, abruptly, an ominous silence. In the middle of the floor a wounded guardsman was moaning and twisting, crawling painfully toward his concealed fellows.

Brandon looked at Vi'ya; there was a faint shadow of distress on her face, which vanished as she saw him looking at her. Insight came: *What does violent death feel like to a tempath?* Then, suddenly, he understood why she had set her jac to minimum aperture: it either killed quickly or left a clean wound with minimum burns.

On his other side, Ivard crouched, his eyes roaming restlessly over the ceiling, his mouth agape as he breathed fast. Memory of Greywing's death jolted Brandon, echoing his discovery of the destruction of the Ivory Hall.

Then Ivard's head turned and his eyes met Brandon's, their expression one of pain-hazed expectancy. The boy was waiting for him to lead them to safety.

Brandon looked away from Ivard, ransacking his memory for a way out. He caught sight of a low door, no more than a meter high, on the far side of the room, across an exposed stretch of floor. *The mechwaiter access!*

He turned to Vi'ya, just as another of his worm-shadows flitted across a wall. Vi'ya's jaw clenched, and beyond the barriers, Brandon heard the harsh susurrus of Dol'jharian mutterings. *That worm is a lot more active than I remember programming it. It's almost as though it's following us.* Then he forced his mind back to the task at hand as Vi'ya looked at him impatiently.

"That little door over there leads to a tunnel used for automated food delivery," he said to her. "We can probably get back to the transport tunnel that way."

"We'll need a diversion," she replied. "They've got a clear field of fire across the floor."

A sudden motion from Ivard caught his eye; the boy was plucking fretfully at the Kelly ribbon embedded in his wrist. Only then did Brandon realize whose ribbon it had to be. *The Archon.*

Quick as lightning, fueled by fatigue and adrenaline, the images flashed before him: his first meeting with Lheri, Mho, and Curlizho as a small child, his fascination with the strange, jolly aliens, and later, the wonderful series of record chips venerated by the Kelly. Some were so old they were monochrome, of a venerable art form practiced since before the Exile. The ancients had called it by a name he couldn't recall—he did remember thinking at the time that it sounded like some sort of hand weapon for a martial art—and Brandon had been delighted by it. It was an utterly appropriate weapon against the Archon's killers; the prospect made him grin.

"We could all use a laugh right about now," Lokri said, sitting against the base of a gleaming steel table, his jac dangling carelessly in loose fingers.

"I think I can arrange a suitable entertainment to keep our Dol'jharian friends occupied," Brandon said, turning from Lokri to Vi'ya. "Cover me."

❊   ❊   ❊

Barrodagh's com chimed again. "What is it now?"

"This is Dektasz Jesserian. We have the intruders cornered in a service kitchen on level one in the blue-seven section. We took a number of casualties—they appear to have some sort of detector system."

Barrodagh jerked upright in his chair as he realized where that was. "What about the Panarch?" Maybe the intruders weren't Rifters. Maybe it was a Panarchist rescue attempt.

"The Tarkans outside his cell were killed, but he is still

there, and I have posted a squad in that hallway, in addition to the forces that have trapped the intruders. The other high-rank Panarchists are secure." The dektasz paused, Barrodagh could sense unease in his scarred features. *Is he seeing the shadows too?*

"Senz lo'Evodh, his assistant, and the Tarkan there are dead," he continued. "They were killed by an unknown weapon of great power."

"What kind of weapon?" Barrodagh demanded.

Annoyance flickered across Jesserian's face; Barrodagh reminded himself that despite the soldier's acceptance of him as a professional equal, he was still dealing with a Dol'jharian noble. He molded his face into an expression of respectful interest.

"As I said, we do not know. It is some sort of terror weapon that explodes the victim's brains without leaving any burns or entry wounds." The dektasz' mouth tightened.

Barrodagh's throat felt sour. Any weapon that made a professional Dol'jharian soldier uncomfortable was one that he never wanted to face. Then he realized that Jesserian hadn't mentioned the gnostor Omilov.

"What about the Panarchist?"

"He has disappeared."

Barrodagh suppressed a tremor of fear. His hands began to sweat. Eusabian's anger was more to be feared than any weapon. "Was there any indication of the information sought from the prisoner?" Perhaps Evodh had recorded something before he was killed.

"No. The equipment was totally destroyed by jac-fire."

"The prisoner may be with the intruders. His life is to be preserved at all costs. He has information demanded by the Avatar."

"It shall be done. I am sending in a squad in battle armor to finish them off; since the looters appear to have only hand weapons, the armored squad should be able to over-come them easily without risk to the prisoner, if he is with them. As you were concerned about the objects they stole, do you wish to observe?"

He's being very careful, and rightly so. I'd better be there to make sure those art pieces get back right away.

"Yes. I'll join you in five minutes. Do not wait for me to begin the assault, but do not search the bodies until I arrive."

"Acknowledged."

Barrodagh clipped a communicator to his waist and stepped out into the outer office. Anderic looked up from a flickering comic chip with a questioning glance.

"Stay here," said the Bori. "I can't answer for your life if you step outside this room." He turned to the Bori secretary. "If the Avatar calls for me, transfer it to my com. I don't need to hear from anyone else."

He left the office and directed one of the guards there to lead him to level one of blue-seven. The man's face was tight with anxiety, his eyes flicking restlessly about. He nodded jerkily and preceded the Bori down the hall.

As he hurried along behind the gray-clad figure, Barrodagh's mind seethed with anxiety. The gnostor was even more important than the artworks that had been stolen. But why had they rescued him, and not the Panarch? Had they been interrupted in the process? And what were those Ur-be-damned shadows? If his escort was any indication, the Dol'jharian soldiers had already decided.

That's all I need now: rumors of a haunting.

Barrodagh did not look forward to his next report to the Lord of Vengeance.

✳   ✳   ✳

The screen flickered for a moment, then resolved itself into ordered ranks of data. "We're in. Let's s-start a d-dump to our system," Ferrasin said, fighting his stuttering tongue. Fatigue and excitement made his speech even slower than usual, but the other techs, for once, paid no attention. "In c-case we fall out again."

He consulted a note window on his console, biting his words out carefully. "The surveillance system is the first priority. Have it ordered by rank."

Moments later he was staring in amazement at the first name on the list. *Brandon nyr-Arkad? But he's dead.*

But the system showed him in residence as of that evening. He tapped rapidly on the keypad, his eyes darting from window to window, the computer following in eyes-on mode.

ENTRY AT ADIT ROUGE 26 40. *That's forty kilometers from the Palace.* A still image windowed up, showing a small gazebo at the edge of a forest of immense trees. In another window a grid map located it with respect to the Rouge quadrant. He studied the map for a moment, zoomed in on the ideograph for the gazebo. It had four stylized eyes on it. His eyes flicked aside for a moment, fingers twitched on the keys; a window legend materialized.

Imagers. Let's see if we can get a live picture.
ACCESS DENIED.

He paused. A voice came over his shoulder. "That's a top-level override. Any attempt to break it will probably bring the system back down for good."

"I know that," he grumbled. Moments later he cursed loudly as the screen dissolved into garbage.

"I told you," said the tech.

"I didn't do anything," shouted Ferrasin, his stutter momentarily overwhelmed by his anger.

Suddenly it came together in his mind. *That ship. He must have come in on that ship.* He tabbed the com button. "Get me senz lo'Barrodagh."

When the aloof voice of Barrodagh's secretary answered, he stuttered, "I've g-g-got to speak to the *senxlo*."

"Senz lo'Barrodagh is not here. He has left instructions to put no one save the Avatar through."

"But—" He fought with his stubborn tongue. "But I've got critical information for him."

"The senxlo has left instructions to put no one save the Avatar through." Ferrasin could hear the amusement at his broken speech in the cool tones of the secretary. The senxlo's former secretary had been more understanding, but he had disappeared during a purge just before the attack.

"Then tell me where he is, and I'll tell him myself."

"The senxlo has left instructions to put no one save the Avatar through."

Maybe he'll pass the information along himself. He tried to explain what he'd found, but his frustration and anger had rendered him incapable of coherent speech. "The sh-sh-sh—" He stopped and tried again. "The K-k-k-kr . . ."

"If you're finished playing with your lips, I have other tasks to attend to." The secretary smiled nastily and cut the connection.

Ferrasin raised his hands to slam them down on his console, then stopped. *These Bori record everything, and never throw anything away.* Moments later he was listening to a playback of the call that Barrodagh had taken just before he left his office.

He windowed up a map of the Ivory wing, then locked his console and dashed out the door.

✳   ✳   ✳

Montrose reached the transport tunnel without incident, but his back and shoulders were aching with the strain of carrying the old man. Getting him down the ladder took every bit of strength he had. *Too many of those Briard sauces,* he thought with mild regret.

The next ten minutes dragged on endlessly. The worm-shadows didn't help. *Although, if any place were to be haunted, it would be the Mandala. The hopes and fears of trillions of people have been focused on this place for almost a millennium.*

He shook off the mood and looked down at the old man wrapped in the soiled robe. *Osri's father. I hope he's not as much of a blit as his son. One of those on board is enough.*

Nearby the Eya'a waited motionless, like statues. He wondered what their perception of time was like, compared to humans. What he'd seen of them suggested they lacked the driving urge to be always doing something that made just waiting such a torment for human beings.

His boz'l bleeped in his inner ear. He listened hopefully,

but there was no sound from above. Reluctantly he manhandled Omilov into the carrier, followed by the Eya'a, and pushed the return combination.

Back under the gazebo he keyed in the combination Brandon had given him, cursing the archaic equipment that lacked an infra pickup, forcing him to listen to the boz'l and enter the alphanumerics manually. The carrier slid quietly back into the tunnel and Montrose slapped the up key on the pillar.

Up above he could hear the wind growing in strength. Then he noticed that the shrubs and trees near the gazebo weren't stirring. He spun around, almost falling as Omilov's weight shifted, and saw a plasma cannon on a ground-effect platform skimming quietly toward the opening in the forest where the *Telvarna* lay, its barrel swiveling toward the ship concealed in the darkness.

He slapped his boz'l. "RED ALERT! PLASMA CANNON, ZERO DEGREES, GROUND LEVEL!"

❊   ❊   ❊

Osri jerked his head up, bruising his forehead against the plasma guide, as a soft paw reached out and tapped his cheek.

"Oh, Telos," he muttered. "Get out of here, you abominable bag of fur." The only response was the rumbling, saw-edged sound he'd learned meant contentment in the big cat.

"What'd you say, Schoolboy?" came Marim's cheerful voice.

Osri gritted his teeth. "I said that this guide appears undamaged."

"Wave monitor says otherwise. Give it a bang at 24-17."

Osri looked up at the metallic pipe overhead, squinted at the age-dulled dyplast label on it: 24-8. He sighed with frustration. By rights the little Rifter woman ought to be squirming along in the cramped crawl space abaft of the engines, tuning the guides that channeled waste heat to the radiants; she was the smallest of them, after all. He levered himself forward with his elbows and heels, fighting not to let his sense of confinement erupt into full-blown claustrophobia. A claw reached out and snagged his hair; he banged his head again.

Osri cursed and struck out at the cat with the tuning hammer in his right hand, and flushed with anger as he missed and hit something else with a resounding clang.

"Watch yerself, Schoolboy," shouted the little Rifter. "Put a dent in the wrong place and you'll be in there another hour."

"My skills would be better applied on the skip cavity," Osri snapped as he struggled toward the location she'd given him. "I *was* trained at the Academy in—"

"Yeah," Marim interrupted. "Day I let a nick anywhere near the fiveskip, that's the day Vi'ya plays ring-around-the-spin-axis with my guts as the guide rope."

"How's it coming?" Jaim's laconic voice was blurred with fatigue.

"Eh. How's the fiveskip?"

Osri lost the thread of their conversation as he struggled to bend himself around a particularly tight corner. *24-15. Almost there.* Then he froze as the sense of their voices returned.

". . . Palace. The loot oughta be the score of all time." Marim's voice was sharp with resentment. "Those nicks been collectin' things for hundreds of years, and the Krysarch said he knows where all the best stuff is. And here we're stuck."

Loot? Palace? Osri's head turned so suddenly he smacked his forehead on a coupling. She had to be saying it to annoy him. Except that he had seen them arming, the Krysarch among them, which they wouldn't do unless they trusted him. He thought back to the ship's actions over Arthelion. Evasive action, definitely. Had Brandon identified himself to the authorities, only to be told to surrender himself for trial? *It would be no more than he deserves.*

But if so, he had obviously refused, and the *Telvarna* had attempted to flee. That was the free-fall, diverting all power to the engines. *And the authorities would go to almost any lengths to avoid killing a Krysarch of the House Royal, no matter how debased.*

So a carefully aimed ruptor had smashed their drive and forced them down. Then, with a twist of his stomach, Osri realized that the Mandala was probably the only place Brandon had a chance of pulling off an escape: rumor had it that all Royals had override codes to the Mandalic defenses. *And to get the Rifters' help—*

Osri shook his head again. It was too hard to credit, despite the way it hung together. There had to be another explanation. Marim and Jaim were just teasing him; they had no love for the Douloi—nicks, as they called them.

He found the label he was looking for, and under Marim's relayed directions, banged a series of small dents into the wave guide, retuning it so that it could carry an intensely hot thread of plasma from the engines to the radiants without overheating. He'd reviewed chips about the effectiveness of ruptors, but now he had a visceral understanding of just how much damage they could do, even if they didn't pull a ship apart. Their rapidly alternating gee fields made a hash of the finely tuned innards of a ship's engines and fiveskip.

Marim finally pronounced herself satisfied and Osri painfully edged back the way he'd come. Back in the engine room proper, he pulled himself to his feet, suppressing a groan as his cramped muscles protested. Marim and Jaim had their heads together over a control console, discussing some problem, the little Rifter sitting perched on a console with one leg propped across the knee of the other.

Osri's eyes were drawn to the black at the bottoms of her feet; light reflecting off them showed what he had assumed was dirt was actually microfilaments. He winced, fighting revulsion; she had obviously been gennated.

Looking away, Osri stretched, then jerked his leg away as the ship's cat rubbed up against him. He looked down into the glacial-blue eyes, which were slitted with pleasure as Lucifer saw him paying attention.

Osri looked away. On another console, a security scan of the ship's surroundings played lazily, switching from view to view. Marim stepped toward him and gave him a swat on the arm.

Osri caught a whiff of some kind of flower scent mingled with heat sweat, and he stepped back, turning his head. He could smell them *both*.

"We got more for you, Schoolboy," Marim said with a laugh, clearly misinterpreting his response to the offensiveness of the Rifters' proximity. "But that's the worst of it. Next we'll—"

The security console blared with Montrose's voice, colored by the odd tonality that indicated a boswell relay. "RED ALERT! PLASMA CANNON, ZERO DEGREES, GROUND LEVEL!" Marim cursed violently and leapt to the console while Jaim spun around and grabbed a jac.

"Don't move, nick. Now lie down on the deck and put your hands behind your head."

A little confused by the contradictory instructions, and frightened by the sudden intensity shown by the normally easygoing engineer, Osri hesitated. Under Marim's hands, the console came to life, the screen displaying a mobile plasma cannon emblazoned with the Sun and Phoenix, its barrel coming to bear on the *Telvarna*. The screen flared even as Marim slammed her hand down on the console.

"*Chatz!*" she shrieked as the ship rocked. "For'rd cannon's not responding. Chatzing blunges got us." Her fingers raced across the console. "And the teslas are still off-line," she wailed. The *Telvarna* was defenseless.

On the screen, the mobile cannon rocked back, its defensive fields flaring. Then its barrel came to bear again and it raced toward the ship.

His face twisted with frustration and rage, Jaim strode forward and slammed the barrel of his jac into Osri's head, knocking him to the floor. He raised the weapon, and Osri realized that when the cannon fired on the *Telvarna* again, his life would end.

TWENTY-SIX

✳

Montrose watched as a blue-white bolt of plasma reached out from the cannon and was answered simultaneously from within the forest. The cannon's shield flared and it slewed and drifted backward for a moment, then it swiveled back for another shot. A bright, flickering glow marked the position of the *Telvarna*, but no further bolts from its cannon; Montrose groaned as he realized it had taken a hit.

Next to him the Eya'a chattered; the mobile cannon skimmed across the grass toward the *Telvarna*, then veered and hit a tree. The impact apparently damaged its ground-effect skirt; it fell to the ground with a momentary snarl as the fans dug into the duff beneath the tree, and then the engines cut out and it rocked to a halt.

Montrose shifted the gnostor's dead weight and ran heavily toward the ship, followed by the Eya'a. As he reached the ship he could hear the sound of the engines already winding up to readiness.

✳   ✳   ✳

Obeying Vi'ya's hand signal, Lokri popped up and sprayed the positions of the Dol'jharian guards with a flurry of jac-bolts as the Krysarch scrambled over to a small console set in the wall. Then he ducked back and return fire sizzled over his head and into the cabinet in front of him, sending back a spectacular spray of sparks.

A quick glance showed Brandon in the shelter of a bulky refrigeration unit as he began tapping at the keypad. The flickering light of the screen imbued his features with an odd animation.

The Arkad was beginning to interest Lokri. At first he'd assumed Brandon was just another useless high-nosed nick, of interest only to be provoked. The fact that Brandon had been a friend of Markham's was no credit; Lokri had never known anyone more willing to take people as they came.

The first counter to Lokri's preconceptions had come during the Phalanx games with the Krysarch. He was well known at the tables in the Galadium Club on Rifthaven, but Brandon had destroyed him utterly without apparent effort, even at Level Three. It had taken both him and Marim to defeat him.

More intriguing, perhaps, was the fact that Brandon's return to his home rendered him not more assured, but less. Lokri had never seen a member of a high-rank Service Family show emotion as the Krysarch had in the Hall of Ivory.

Now he watched as Brandon worked rapidly at the con-sole, a lock of his curly hair falling over one eye, his ex-pression alternating between a wide grin and a frown of concentration.

One by one the massive food generators came to life, un-til the kitchen was humming with activity. Lokri could hear harsh whispers from the Dol'jharians trapped in the kitchen with them. Just then another of the Krysarch's ghost-flickers wavered across a wall, vanishing in the shadows of a corner, causing a sudden silence among the murmuring Dol'jharians, and then a slight change in the tone of the talk.

Looking curiously at the captain, he thought he detected a stiffness to her posture that nearly made him laugh. *Take the Dol'jharian off Dol'jhar but you can't take Dol'jhar out of the Dol'jharian,* he thought, studiously looking away: keyed up as she was, he rather thought she'd kill him if she sensed the direction of his thoughts.

Across the aisle from him he could see Ivard watching Brandon too, a mixture of drug haze and trust in his eyes. Lokri was aware of a sense of disappointment, followed hard by a twinge of self-mockery. He'd never really noticed the boy's admiration except to make fun of it; he supposed it was another sign of his own perversity that he valued nothing that was freely given.

That reminded him of Greywing, and again he saw her crumple, the life and light going out of her face. He wished suddenly that he'd listened to Marim and had bedded her, except it wouldn't have erased that unswerving honesty from her face. Old anger kindled in him, and he reflected how much he detested honesty, and loyalty, and all the rest of the bindings of obligation that the weak put on the strong.

Transferring his gaze back to the Krysarch, he wondered what Greywing and Brandon had been talking about, back in the Ivory Hall. Had the little blit been about to drop on her knees and swear fealty? He snorted softly. *If he gets us out of this alive I'll fall down and kiss his feet myself.*

Just then the little door Brandon had pointed out to them slid up into the wall, and a large number of small wheeled machines scurried out, fanning out across the room to the food generators. Some of them extruded long sinuous tubes and nuzzled up to large vat-like generators like puppies at their mother's teats. Others, equipped with trays and grippers, lined up in front of food generators that were radiating heat that Lokri could feel across the room. When small hatches in these popped open, Lokri frowned in confusion.

Pies? What the Shiidran Hell is going on here?

The pies—a rather loathsome green in color—slid out onto the trays on the little machines. Other machines jostled into place to receive their loads as the first ones lined up near the edge of the open section of flooring that blocked the Rifters from escape. Some faced the cabinets sheltering the Dol'jharians, others took up positions facing each of the doors. More machines emerged from the little hatch and took up position, waiting patiently for their turn.

Lokri turned and looked at Vi'ya. She looked back at him and shrugged.

The Dol'jharians were evidently just as confused. Their harsh-toned whispering rose to a crescendo; then Lokri heard a command from one of their communicators.

"Arkad!" Vi'ya said softly. "Look out."

Brandon waved a hand at her, tapped one last set of commands into the console, and then crouched down, holding his firejac ready and motioning them to do the same.

Suddenly music blared from a grille in the wall, a stirring fanfare of brightly driving trumpets. It sounded familiar, but Lokri couldn't place it. Ivard thrust one fist forward and nodded with manic enthusiasm—he evidently recognized the music.

Some of the little machines with the snake-like nozzles on them surged forward, scurrying across the floor and disappearing amongst the storage cabinets that sheltered the guards, while a number of the tray-carriers elevated pies with their grippers. Lokri heard a series of splattering hisses behind the cabinets, followed instantly by cries of pain and rage. The guards leapt up, vainly trying to fend off streams of some steaming viscid liquid that unerringly tracked their faces.

Clang-whizz-splat. Lokri started as the front rank of tray-carriers jerked noisily and flung their pies straight at the startled guards. The pies burst against their heads and bodies, transforming them instantly into wildly capering man-shaped piles of viscous green goo. The Dol'jharians howled, dropping their weapons and wiping at their eyes; evidently something in the pie mix stung and burned.

Ivard dropped his firejac and doubled over, laughing with

drug-induced abandon. Brandon grinned a challenge at Lokri, who saluted him with his jac.

Brandon used the cover of the high-velocity pies to dash back across the kitchen. When he dropped down beside Lokri, he said, "Saves ammo, right?"

"What else did they teach you at your Panarchist Naval Academy?" Lokri said. "How to field-strip a hypervelocity custard flinger? Close-order drill with involuntary throat funnels?"

Brandon laughed. "Something like that." He motioned toward the little door, from which service machines were still issuing. "Let's go."

Outside the kitchen, shouted commands echoed. As they scrambled across the floor both doors blew open with a roar and guards in bulky battle armor thundered in, their servos whining loudly. The little tray-carriers facing the doors jerked and fired a salvo of pies as nozzled drink dispensers hosed the floor with a thick, curdled-looking grayish fluid that smelled of butter and less familiar things. The pies had no effect on the guards' momentum, but the slimy goop covered their helmets and effectively blinded them, while the slippery grayish fluid made it impossible for them to stop. With majestic inevitability, the two squads collided with a tremendous crash, like vast beasts helpless in the throes of lust.

The Rifters ducked into the little service tunnel and scrambled toward the far end on their hands and knees. They had to dodge past some of the little machines that had loaded up and were going back through the tunnel away from the main battle.

Brandon, Lokri, and Ivard were laughing as they emerged into a larger tunnel where they could stand up; even Vi'ya smiled slightly, though her eyes never stopped scanning walls and shadows. Brandon waved at the little machines that were coming out of the tunnel on their side and grinned. "Flanking movement."

As they followed Brandon away from the kitchens, Lokri could hear the sounds of the food fight diminishing behind them: amplified roars of rage from the armored guards mixed with the sizzle of jac-bolts, splattering hisses from the nozzle machines, and the clang-whizz-splat of the pie-flingers.

Moments later they rounded a corner and saw the closet from which they'd entered. They half climbed, half slid down the ladder, slowed by Ivard who was beginning to waver, piled into the waiting carrier and slid off down the tunnel.

Lokri studied Brandon's profile as the carrier sped back toward the *Telvarna. You knew how to pick them, didn't you, Markham?*

※   ※   ※

Barrodagh was panting and breathless as they neared the kitchen where the intruders were trapped. He had been rehearsing explanations for the Lord of Vengeance, handicapped by ignorance of just what he'd find when he arrived; the guard, sensing his impatience and anxiety, had upped the pace until the Bori could hardly keep up.

Now he could hear the sounds of battle: the sizzle of jac-fire, shouted commands, amplified roars of anger, and heated Dol'jharian curses. But he could also hear a noise that puzzled him: what kind of weapon went clang-whizz-splat? Then he remembered the dektasz' report and he slowed abruptly. His skin crawled. *Explodes their brains—*

A strange smell tickled his palate: heavy, greasy, with an unfamiliar bitter-sour tang to it. His imagination threw up a series of gruesome images of splattered brains dripping from the walls and sliming the floor; his stomach heaved and he stopped. His escort had stopped too, his firejac held at the ready.

Just down the hall he could see the double doors into the kitchen, with the blue-white glare of jac-fire leaking out of the crack in the middle. A tide of some lumpy, scummy grayish substance was slowly bubbling out from under the doors. Bile spurted into the back of his mouth and he swallowed repeatedly, fighting the urge to vomit. He started to back away, shaking.

Suddenly he heard something making a whining rattle accelerate from behind him. Panic gripped Barrodagh and his legs failed him as he turned around just in time to hear a sound that nearly stopped his heart—*clang-whizz-splat*.

Barrodagh screamed as the world turned green and his eyes started to burn fiercely. His brain was being boiled away by some horrible Panarchist invention! He clutched his skull, trying to hold it together. He could feel his eyes coming out of their sockets; the glop oozed into his mouth, burning and stinging as he screamed and screamed.

Clang-whizz-splat. As another blast from the terror weapon caught him square in the chest, Barrodagh's panic reached an insupportable level and he passed out.

❊　　　❊　　　❊

The crew burst out of the gazebo and raced back toward the *Telvarna*, slowing only momentarily as they caught sight of a mobile cannon crumpled against a tree.

As they approached the ship its ramp lowered and a dim light spilled out into the darkness from inside the lock, silhouetting the small figures of the two Eya'a. Brandon and Lokri were half carrying Ivard, who had gradually sunk into delirium during the transport from the Palace; the boy's arm around Lokri's neck felt clammy and he was practically out on his feet.

Vi'ya slowed as they reached the ship. Lokri saw what she was looking at: the forward undercannon was twisted and seared, evidently unable to retract into its nacelle, the hull around it discolored and warped. A slight shimmer over the scorched metal showed that the teslas were up. As they ran up the ramp the rumble of the engines increased; the trunks of the trees behind the *Telvarna* reflected in umber tones the red glow of the radiants discharging waste heat.

Vi'ya slapped the com key in the lock as the hatch cycled closed. "Montrose, Ivard's been hit."

"On my way," came the reply.

Brandon followed Vi'ya as she ran forward, accompanied by the Eya'a. Lokri half dragged Ivard toward the dispensary, then gratefully relinquished him to Montrose, who picked the boy up in his arms. "Greywing?" Montrose said.

Lokri lifted his finger, imitating a jac. Montrose frowned, then turned and disappeared back down the corridor. Lokri dashed back to the bridge and slapped his console to life.

Osri gritted his teeth as the old monster's voice erupted from the com in his cabin. "Captain wants you on the bridge right now." He levered himself off his bunk where Jaim had thrown him after holding him on the floor with his jac until that cannon attack had ceased.

Still seething at the barbaric treatment he'd been accorded by that pair of loathsome no-family Rifter scum, he stalked forward. In the corridor he passed Montrose carrying Ivard, whose head lolled on the big Rifter's shoulder, his pale face green with shock. Osri could see a charred patch on the boy's shoulder; as he passed, Ivard twitched violently and threw out his arm.

"Greywing. No." His voice trailed off into incoherence, but Osri didn't notice. His attention was gripped by something falling from the boy's pocket.

He stooped and picked up a coin, wrapped in a blood-stained ribbon of raw silk. With a jolt, he recognized the ribbon: the Piloting Award from the Military Academy. The other object, also blood-smeared, dealt him an even bigger shock as he recognized it from an art course he'd once taken. The Tetradrachm, an ancient coin from Lost Earth, the only one of its kind, part of the Mandalic Collection in the Ivory antechamber.

Rage kindled in his chest and his hand started to shake. *They were not joking. They really did loot the Palace of the Panarchs. The Mandala, fouled by these* . . . Anger burned through him as he visualized these senseless beasts rampaging through the heart of the Mandala. *Led by a Krysarch of the House Royal.*

He straightened up, and a cold certainty possessed him. *I will not let them get away with this, even if it costs me my life.* Osri shoved the coin and the ribbon into his pocket with a convulsive movement and continued forward. *And the Krysarch's. There can be no loyalty here, after this.*

When he reached the bridge the ship was already hovering under geeplane and the captain was snapping orders. He caught the tail end of Marim's response to one.

"—cut away some of the wreckage with a lazjac; I've focused the teslas over it to try'n maintain the streamlining." The little Rifter shook her head and ran her hand through her disgustingly sweat-matted tangle of hair, her attitude subdued and uncharacteristically grim. "I wouldn't push it past mach twelve or so."

On the main screen Osri could see the giant trees slipping past as the *Telvarna* accelerated out of the forest, slowly at first. He noticed that one of the consoles, the one usually handled by the red-haired woman, was empty. The Krysarch was settling in at the fire-control console, which was already lit with the Tenno configuration. He glared at Brandon's back. Everyone ignored him as he stood just inside the entrance.

The ship left the forest and leapt forward as the plasma jets ignited with a muffled thump. The ground wheeled underneath as Vi'ya pulled the ship into a tight turn and headed back over the forest, away from the Mandala. The *Telvarna* shuddered alarmingly as it went transonic; Marim stabbed at her console and the motion ceased. "Make that mach eight," she said.

Lokri looked up from his console. "There's increased traffic on some bands—coded, can't read it. Sounds like they're looking hard for us."

Finally Orsi said, "You called me." He kept his voice flat.

"You are trained in astrogation?" the captain asked.

Osri bridled. She knew very well; it was a deliberate insult. "As I informed you," he replied acidly, "I am an instructor in navigation at the Minervan—"

"Fine," Vi'ya interrupted. "Take that console and plot me a course to the S'lift. Priority ranking: minimum altitude, minimum concussion over population centers, maximum speed. Give me an ETA at maximum mach eight." As Osri hesitated, Vi'ya added, "Now," her even tone and lack of expression adding more emphasis than a shout.

Osri glanced angrily at the Krysarch, who looked back at him without expression. Then he seated himself stiffly at the console, considering his options, slowly tapping at the keys to gain time. As he worked, the meaning of her command penetrated his consciousness. Minimum concussion? He risked a glance at her, but she had turned away to her console. Why did she care about that? This escapade had already earned everyone on the ship a one-way trip to Gehenna, if the defense systems left anything for the Justicials.

"I've got Ivard stabilized, and the old man as well," came Montrose's voice from the com. "Do you need me anywhere?"

Old man? Did they grab someone for ransom? A sudden, horrid thought jerked through him and he looked over at the Krysarch, who was absorbed in his console. *No, that's impossible.*

"It's going to be rough, but if you think they will be safe unattended, stand by with Jaim on the engines."

"As long as you leave the gravitors nulled out in the dispensary the old man's heart should be all right. Ivard's in no immediate danger."

There was silence for a moment, and Osri suddenly realized what he could do. The captain had handed the ship to him; he would hand them all over to justice, and likely death.

Vi'ya turned and transfixed him with a cold stare. "I warned you, Schoolboy, I am a tempath."

Shock flooded him and his fingers hesitated on the console. *But tempaths can't read minds.* He struggled to project a feeling of innocence, wondering if the emotion came across as false as it felt. Now he knew viscerally why so many people hated tempaths.

"Pay attention to your task. Your anger could kill us all, including that old man in the dispensary."

Relief flooded him: she must have misinterpreted his feelings. He still had a chance. A slight miscalculation of their course would lengthen their exposure enough that the defense emplacements of the S'lift would ensure a swift end to this criminal endeavor. He wondered briefly if it would hurt much.

Then curiosity surfaced at the additional reference to the old man. It couldn't be, but he had to know.

"What old man?"

Vi'ya's eyes flicked to Brandon, then returned to her console and screen, concentrating on handling the *Telvarna*, which was now traveling at mach eight only a hundred meters above the ocean. The rearview showed the sea boiling in their wake under the impact of their concussion wave.

"Your father, Osri," Brandon said softly. "We found him in the Palace."

Osri's mind emptied of thought as the Krysarch's bald statement cut the world out from under him. He no longer understood anything about their situation. What was his father doing on Arthelion? How had he escaped the Rifter invasion of Charvann? Why would they hold *him* to ransom? His thoughts spun off into nonsense and he merely stared at Brandon.

The Krysarch's eyes widened slightly. "You don't know, do you?"

Osri shook his head dumbly, his fingers and a well-trained part of his mind still automatically working at his navigational task. Then his hands fell away from the console as Brandon proceeded to complete the demolition of his world.

"Arthelion has fallen. Eusabian of Dol'jhar occupies the Mandala." The Krysarch's voice was light, uninflected by emotion. Only the subtle hunching of his shoulders revealed to Osri's Douloi sensibilities the Krysarch's well-bred reluctance to be the bearer of bad news. "Your father was tortured, but Montrose believes he will recover," Brandon finished.

Osri jumped up. "His heart? I must go to him."

"There will be time for that when we have escaped," said Vi'ya. "How long to the S'lift?"

Osri glared at her a moment, then dropped his eyes before her calm gaze. He fought the impulse to touch the Tetradrachm still resting in his pocket and flexed his shaking hands. Tapping at the console a while longer, he reset the course to avoid the trap he'd tried to set. "Eight minutes," he replied at last.

TWENTY-SEVEN

✳

Ferrasin was half running, half walking down another anonymous hallway. He hadn't realized how big the Palace was, how confusing the undercorridors could be. His view had been a neater one, based on the system interconnections that he navigated so effortlessly on his console. The physical reality was entirely different. And the flickering shadows didn't help any. He was almost certain they were a computer artifact, but the gloomy byways underneath the Mandala left his certainty ever on the edge of crumbling into panic.

Up ahead he saw a small console in the wall. He ran up to it and tapped in the combination they had enforced on the house system after the sensors were destroyed. The screen lit.

Will it cooperate? They'd only managed to reprogram for basic housekeeping services; he didn't know if the system would supply him with directions.

A few moments later he sighed in relief as the console

windowed up a map. He located himself in relation to the service kitchen and ran off down the hall.

Behind him the console flickered and the map reversed itself. Then the screen went dark.

❋   ❋   ❋

Barrodagh felt a sting in his arm and opened his eyes. A gray-clad guard with the green knife of the medical service on his uniform was just withdrawing an ampule from his arm. The medic stood up and moved aside, revealing a pair of glossy black boots coated with grayish slime. *Oh, Dol! My brains—!*

Barrodagh came fully awake and realized he was still alive, his brains intact; then his eyes lifted from the boots to the thunderous visage of the Lord of Vengeance and he wondered fearfully how long that would be true.

He scrambled to his feet. "Lord," he said, bowing deeply. A dollop of green goo slithered off his head and plopped onto Eusabian's boot with a quiet splat.

"Explain this," said Eusabian. His voice was soft, a low rumble, like the thunder of a storm invisible over the horizon. Barrodagh felt a thrill of fear; that was a very bad sign.

The Bori looked over at Jesserian, standing at attention with the visor of his battle armor cocked open. The man's face was expressionless, giving him no direction. All up and down the hall Barrodagh could see the smoking, plasma-seared ruins of little machines of some sort; everything was liberally coated with the same corrosive green glop as he himself was.

"Lord, we had reports of looting in the Ivory antechamber. I gave orders for interception and execution, explicitly stating that the stolen art was to be recovered unharmed."

He swallowed; Eusabian's face might as well have been carved in stone. Barrodagh would have welcomed any expression, even that frightening, inexplicable glint of cold humor he'd seen too often lately, but there was nothing. Then, abruptly, the Avatar's eyes jumped sideways, and his expression changed ever so slightly. Barrodagh saw motion reflected in his dark eyes and shuddered; somehow his lord's acknowledgment of the shadows haunting the Palace made them something truly to be feared. He gathered his thoughts with an effort as the Avatar's eyes returned to him.

"We assumed they were just Rifters; it seemed unlikely Panarchists would bother to loot. Then they struck at the senxlo Evodh and carried off the prisoner, and attempted to rescue the Panarch, killing the Tarkans there too, but were foiled by the prompt appearance of Dektasz Jesserian's men." *There. That will help keep him on my side, if only he has the wit to understand that we're both in this together.*

"The dektasz also reported that the intruders had used some sort of terror weapon to kill the Tarkans. Despite this, I directed him to preserve the prisoner's life at all costs, as the recording equipment in the transfiguration room had been destroyed, along with the mindripper."

At least I don't have that to worry about, he thought as his mind raced ahead of his words. But that was cold comfort; Dol'jharians had perfected the infliction of pain hundreds of years before the invention of the mindripper.

"Your pardon, Lord," interrupted Jesserian. "I did not say that the Tarkans guarding the Panarch were killed by this weapon; only senz lo'Evodh, his assistant, and the Tarkan there. All the others were killed by jac-fire."

He paused, and when Barrodagh did not resume immediately, added, "They must have been Panarchists. The com system in the kitchen started playing their battle music when the—" The commander appeared to have difficulty with the next word. "—the counterattack commenced."

Eusabian was silent for a time. "This counterattack," he said, looking around. "It was apparently successful."

Barrodagh looked at Jesserian, who replied, "Yes, Lord, they escaped, but according to my men, the prisoner they had taken was no longer with them. No sign has been found of him. All the defense positions have been put on alert for departing craft."

"There may have been two groups," said Barrodagh. "Perhaps the looting was a diversion."

"How many casualties did you take here?" asked Eusabian, as if Barrodagh had not spoken.

"Three men lost to jac-fire, Lord, seven wounded. None among the Tarkans," replied Jesserian.

"I do not understand," said Eusabian mildly, "why a squad of battle-armored Tarkans was unable to overcome a lightly armed group of either Rifters or Panarchists."

Barrodagh could hear death hovering in his words. A glance at Jesserian revealed that he, too, could sense it; but they both received a reprieve from an unlikely source. With a sudden rattle, one of the little machines suddenly came to life behind them; Jesserian threw himself forward with all the speed his servos could lend him just as the device discharge its last pie straight at the Avatar: *clang-whizz-splat!*

Green glop splattered around the commander's armor as he intercepted the pie; but he couldn't stop and ran full tilt into the corridor wall, punching a huge dent in the concrete wall behind the paneling. Dust and bits of ceiling rained down on them. Another guard blasted the offending machine.

Jesserian backed carefully out of the ruins of the wall and tried to turn around, but slipped in the gray slop underfoot and fell with a crash that shook the hallway. Broken slabs of paneling clattered down on top of him.

He finally managed to get to his feet and stood back at attention in front of the Avatar. His visor had been knocked closed by the impact; he levered it open, and a flux of green slime oozed out, dripping down the front of his armor. He didn't move, blinking painfully.

Eusabian looked at the commander for a long moment. "I assume this is *not* the terror weapon you referred to." Barrodagh noted with mixed relief and trepidation that the glint was back in his eyes.

"No, Lord," Jesserian replied, relaxing slightly and wiping green slime off his face.

"Take me to the transfiguration room," commanded Eusabian, and Barrodagh realized that the reprieve might still be only temporary.

✳   ✳   ✳

"One hundred kilometers out," said Osri.

"We're being pulsed," reported Lokri. "Short-range stuff."

The ship shuddered as Vi'ya decelerated it to just below sonic velocity. On the main screen the water swooped closer; they were now only meters above the waves. Ahead false dawn stained the sky; against its faint glow the impossibly slender thread of lights that marked the S'lift stood like a knife blade dividing the horizon.

"Open our eyes, Lokri," she commanded. "Arkad, you'll have to keep them off our back for about five minutes."

The Krysarch didn't comment, concentrating instead on his console, apparently integrating the range-pulse information now flowing from Lokri's console into the Tenno grid. He paused, regarding the pattern critically, then made a slight adjustment.

Vi'ya tabbed her intercom. "Jaim, I need you to rig the radiants for thrust. How are we fixed for waste mass?"

"Full up. I ran a hose out to a stream in the forest while we were working."

Thrust from the radiants? thought Osri. That was an unusual maneuver. The radiants ordinarily used small amounts of waste mass, usually water, to vent excess heat from the engines to space; in an emergency requiring more vectors than the geeplane and positional thrusters could provide they could be used for thrust. He was beginning to get an inkling of what Vi'ya intended. The next few minutes would almost match Lao Shang's Wager for excitement, if they survived.

"Marim," Vi'ya continued, tapping at her console, "here's what I need from you. Can you do it?"

Marim whistled. "You're really gonna try it?" She cocked her head and regarded her console critically, tapped a few keys. "Yeah. Don't have much choice, right?"

Osri looked back and forth between Marim and Vi'ya. He was intensely curious but unwilling to ask. Brandon looked at Marim and raised his eyebrows.

"We're gonna head for orbit right along the S'lift cable so they can't zap us without destroying the S'lift." She glanced at Vi'ya. "We call it the L'Ranja Whoopee—Vi'ya and Markham came up with it in an all-night bilge-banger after our raid on Hipparius IV. Jakarr said it was impossible; I said we'd never have a chance to use it." She shrugged. "Looks like I was wrong, and I sure hope he was."

Osri saw the Krysarch grin, but he saw nothing amusing about it; the maneuver sounded insanely dangerous. Then an image flashed in his mind, of a time he'd seen the L'Ranja scion at a cadet gathering, his homely face animated with excitement, his big hands swooping through the air to describe some impossible flight trick. And Osri remembered some of the stunts ascribed to Markham, hallmarked by a combination of risk and tight control.

A wave of changes rippled through the glyphs echoed from the Krysarch's console to the main screen. "Incoming," Brandon said, triggering a counterstrike. Light flared in the screen; expanding gases buffeted the *Telvarna*.

In the main screen land leapt at them, a white beach with phosphorescent breakers flashing underneath as they raced toward the center of the island that anchored the S'lift. This was the staging point for virtually all exoplanetary trade; only tens of meters below the *Telvarna* a bewildering melange of tightly packed warehouses, distribution centers, and transport lines flicked by with unsettling speed.

Now Osri could see the massive terminal at the base of the orbital cable; a long sleek shape outlined in colored lights leapt up out of its roof, clinging to the cable as its magnetic drivers accelerated it toward the Node, forty thousand kilometers above. Far above he could see another carrier descending.

Fingers of light clawed at them from the roof of the terminal, to be met by equal response from the *Telvarna*. The melding of man and machine lent by the Tenno grid was so perfect that Osri couldn't tell whether Brandon or the ship's defense system had triggered the response.

A pounding roar resounded through the ship as Vi'ya

triggered the radiants into thrust mode; the resulting maneuver was part aerodynamic, part geeplane. As Vi'ya pulled the ship into a tight vertical turn the ground tilted away in the main screen, giving way to a vertiginous view straight up the thick cable—an endless string of lights outlining the carrier magtracks receding to infinity.

Moments later the descending carrier Osri had seen flashed by; he had a subliminal impression of shocked white faces in the observation bubble.

There was no more fire from the ground; they were too close to the S'lift. Vi'ya let the ship drift away somewhat from the cable. "We'll hold at this velocity until flame-out, then accelerate to three klicks and hold there until we're past the Shield generator."

"Then we make Whoopee," said Marim. "I'm ready."

Scurrying along between the whine-thump-whine-thump of Jesserian in his armor and the brooding silence of Eusabian behind him, Barrodagh felt like a criminal being led to execution. The eyes of the pictures on the wall didn't help any, especially the holographic ones, which seemed to turn and watch him pitilessly as he passed. The glop on his clothing was drying and crusting; little pieces kept falling off his collar and down his neck. They itched fiercely.

When they entered the room where Evodh and the others had died, Eusabian's face registered no emotion. The pesz mas'hadni's head had rolled to one side; the Avatar nudged it face-upward with one foot, studied its frozen expression of horror and pain for a moment.

"That is an unusual weapon. Not what one would expect from Panarchists."

Jesserian's com beeped. Barrodagh could hear an excited voice coming from inside his helmet, but could not make out the words. "Inform Kyvernat Juvaszt on the *Fist*," snapped the commander. More muffled words. The dektasz stopped and turned around.

"Lord," he said when the voice ceased. "The units emplaced around the S'lift report that a vessel matching the description of the intruder—a ship called the *Maiden's Dream*—has penetrated their defenses and is now accelerating toward the Node parallel to the cable. Juvaszt on the flagship has already been informed and will attempt to intercept, but he is presently on the other side of the planet."

More muffled words drifted from the commander's helmet com. The dektasz' face became bleak. "The kyvernat reports that since the resonance field is down, the end of the hohmann launcher—the freight-launching cable that reaches from the Node into space—is beyond radius. Since he will have to use long-range weapons, he therefore cannot guarantee capture or destruction of the intruder without severe damage to both the S'lift and the Node."

There was a long pause. Eusabian's face was thoughtful. "No," he said finally. "Post a suitable reward for the capture—alive—of the gnostor Omilov."

When he didn't continue, Barrodagh realized that Eusabian preferred losing the looted artworks to broadcasting the news of this humiliation to the Thousand Suns at large. The only question now was, would he, Barrodagh, survive the Avatar's loss of face?

❋   ❋   ❋

As they passed the Shield generator—a flattened sphere transfixed by the S'lift at one hundred kilometers altitude—Osri glimpsed a gaping, scorched-edge hole in it.

Vi'ya began to drift the *Telvarna* in closer and closer to the cable. "Ready, Marim?"

The little Rifter's fingers danced over her console. "Detuning the teslas now." She watched her screen intently, head cocked. On the main screen the cable drifted closer, features on its surface a mere blur. The planet below still filled the rear screen.

"Getting a response from the cable," she said. Then she slapped a pad on her console. "Got it! Induction successful; you two were right!"

The cable swelled alarmingly on the screen. Osri yelped

in surprise; evidently there were aspects to the Whoopee that he didn't understand. The sound of the engines rose; they were accelerating at fifteen gees right up the cable, barely far enough away from it to miss any carrier they might encounter. Even as the thought came, a carrier flashed by, so fast it was only a flicker.

His alarm peaked when Vi'ya sat up from her posture of extreme concentration, pulled her hands away from her console, and turned to Marim. "Good work. We've got about seven minutes before the Node."

What is keeping us off the cable?

Something of his alarm must have shown in his face, and the Krysarch stared at the screen in puzzlement. Marim laughed. "You should see yer faces!" She stretched ostentatiously. "Nothin' to worry about, until we reach the Node. I'm usin' our shields to induce a tesla field in the S'lift. Every time we try'n drift into it, the field in the cable converts the drift to a vector along our flight path. Nothin' to it!"

Osri shook his head, unwilling to express a distinct sense of admiration. Not only did the momentum conversion of the induced tesla field keep them off the cable, it corrected their course as well. It was a brilliant maneuver, worthy of the Academy's finest. *The Academy's finest, cashiered for insubordination.* And he remembered the conversation with Brandon in the booster, and his father's hints about the L'Ranja affair. His comfortable certainties cracked a little further, as he realized what the cost to the Panarchy and the Navy had been of the destruction of the L'Ranja Family.

He looked up to see Vi'ya's dark eyes on Brandon. "Keep your eyes open when we slow to maneuver around the Node to the hohmann. They may have had time to post some ships."

The Krysarch nodded.

With the resonance field down, the hohmann will take us past radius, thought Osri, his professional training eking further respect from him. This was one for the textbooks.

"No sign of that cruiser up there," reported Lokri.

"There's a destroyer standing off the Node, but it doesn't seem to be paying any attention."

"We'll wave to 'em as we scoot by," Marim crowed.

Osri stared at the screen. There was nothing for him to do now, but he knew the captain would not allow him to leave. He gnawed at his knuckle, wondering what the charlatan Montrose was doing to his father, hoping for the first time that the big Rifter wasn't actually the quack he'd comfortably assumed.

Ahead the Node changed from a point of light to a slowly growing circle hovering beyond the vanishing point of the S'lift cable. Minutes beyond that, he knew, lay escape. But to where, and under whose command? He glanced again at the Krysarch, but Brandon's returning gaze had no answer for him.

※   ※   ※

Barrodagh accompanied Eusabian back toward the Palace in silence, followed by two Tarkans in standard uniform. He couldn't read his lord's mood with certainty, but knew from experience that it would take very little to provoke a deadly response from him.

The Bori's office lay along their path; as they approached it he began considering how he would detach himself from the Avatar and begin dealing with the aftermath of the raid. He feared that the longer he remained in sight of Eusabian, the more likely he was to be a target of his anger.

Behind them rapid footsteps sounded. The two Tarkans spun around, firejacs ready, then relaxed marginally. It was Ferrasin, accompanied by a gray-clad guardsman. He stopped in front of the Avatar, his blubbery face beet-red and sweaty with exertion, trying to catch his breath, his mouth working.

"The K-k-k—" He tried several times, but couldn't get the words out. Eusabian was frowning deeply; the Dol'jharian nobility exposed defective children at birth, and barely tolerated physical defects in the outworlders in their employ.

With a heroic effort Ferrasin stopped, took a deep breath,

and began speaking very slowly, stuttering only minimally. "Your pardon, Lord. The computer says that Krysarch Brandon nyr-Arkad entered the Palace this evening from an adit in the Rouge quadrant. I think he was on that ship the alert was posted for."

With the slowness one experiences in nightmares Barrodagh saw the beginnings of a vast, unstoppable anger on Eusabian's face. Through a singing in his ears he heard the tech continue, "I tried to tell senz lo'Barrodagh's secretary, but he wouldn't listen to me."

The Bori grabbed the communicator off his belt. He could see in the Avatar's face what had to be done: this news had changed everything. "Get me Juvaszt on the flagship instantly!"

The response came within seconds, but it felt like hours to Barrodagh.

"Destroy that ship," he screamed.

"But the Node—our forces there—" The confusion in Juvaszt's voice was evident even through the tinny constriction of the com.

Eusabian grasped Barrodagh's arm with a merciless grip; the Bori gasped with pain as the Avatar raised the com to his lips, wrenching his shoulder cruelly.

"This is the Avatar of Dol," he said. "Destroy that ship."

TWENTY-EIGHT

✳

"Thirty seconds to radius," said Osri, his voice coming out with a slight tremor.

Nobody smiled. The maneuver around the Node had been a gut-clenching experience; even Vi'ya had a thin line of sweat at her hairline after the hull-skimming acrobatics past the edge of the Node and back to the hohmann cable. Now they were on the Whoopee again, accelerating flat out toward escape.

The tenno grid rippled violently on the Krysarch's console. As Osri watched it, the hair on his arms prickled.

"Cruiser signature," Brandon said quietly. "Missiles on the way, intersect course at radius."

"Sgatshi!" Marim snarled. "They're gonna zap us despite the S'lift!"

"Jaim, give me overload now." Vi'ya's voice was cold, but strain showed in her narrowed eyes.

The engines roared and the ship started quivering.

"No," Brandon said to Marim. "If they'd decided to sacrifice the Node they'd use ruptors. They're trying to pick us off neatly; the *Telvarna* can handle it." He triggered a counterbarrage, and streaks of light reached out ahead, dwindled, vanished.

"Overload status. You've got fifteen seconds. Fiveskip's up and ready," came Jaim's voice.

"Ten seconds," Osri put in. He was sure no one on the bridge was breathing. Ahead and off to the port side coins of light blossomed as the cruiser's missiles met the *Telvarna*'s response.

Osri looked down. On his screen he'd windowed up a graphic of the skip cavity resonance, the same image now reflected in Vi'ya's eyes as her hand hovered over her go-pad. It was flattening with dreadful slowness toward the stability that would permit the leap into fivespace.

Suddenly his ears rang with the awful squeal that heralded the edge of a ruptor pulse. Even as the sound slid down the scale toward the lethal subsonics that would disintegrate the ship, Vi'ya's hand slammed down on the go-pad. The waveform on Osri's screen convulsed, on the edge of inversion; then with a sickening, head-bloating lurch the *Telvarna* leapt out of fourspace into safety.

※   ※   ※

Rifellyn ran shaking hands through her hair and settled back into her seat, staring out through the dyplast port of the Node control room. On the main screen the flaring radiants of the fleeing ship dwindled to a point and vanished as it fled up the hohmann cable.

They'd relaxed when the Avatar had decided to spare the ship, and thus the Node; their relief had made even more shocking the sudden appearance of the ship, racing by only meters from the control room viewport. Rifellyn could still feel the hammer-like impact of panic that had swept the room; the ship had been so close that the expanding gases venting from its radiants had not had time to dissipate in vacuo before impacting the hull of the Node. She could still hear the rumbling hiss in her imagination: it was the first and, she hoped fervently, the last time she had actually *heard* a spaceship in flight.

As she waited for her heart to slow, she noticed the Panarchist tech she'd had brought in under guard that morning looking at her, an unreadable expression on his face. Despite her words to that unspeakable Bori in the Palace, she'd not given up on extracting technical information from the Node's original operators. Her own techs had finally broken into the databanks the day before, making the personnel records available; it had been a simple matter after that to identify hostages for good behavior. She'd had several Panarchist techs brought back to the Node, who now cooperated, albeit slowly. She had hopes of soon restoring the discrimination circuits of the defense systems to full operation.

A sudden movement from the Dol'jharian communications monitor distracted Rifellyn. The man was sitting rigidly upright at his console, his face filled with horror. He slapped a key on his console, and everyone in the control room heard the voice of Juvaszt on the *Fist of Dol'jhar*.

"But the Node—our forces there—"

Rifellyn comprehended immediately the import of the kyvernat's words, even as a part of her mind insisted it couldn't be happening. Then the unmistakable voice of the Lord of Vengeance filled the room.

"This is the Avatar of Dol. Destroy that ship."

Rifellyn leapt to her feet, shouting, "Disengage the hohmann cable!" She didn't know how long the disengage sequence would take—the specs varied from Node to Node, but they had very little time. Juvaszt would use his ruptors; the shock wave propagating down the cable would tear the Node apart.

Before anyone could react, the Panarchist tech stood up, twisted his probe-tool to a new setting with a decisive movement, and plunged it into the exposed circuit nodes he was working on. There was a chattering squeal, echoed from around the control room, and all the consoles went dead.

Rifellyn stood paralyzed by shock for a moment. "You fool! You've killed us all."

The tech smiled. "I hope so. That will save the hostages at least—your masters will mark it off to unfamiliarity with the equipment."

The guard assigned to the tech triggered his jac and burned the man down. He slumped against the console, his lifeless eyes transfixing Rifellyn—but the mocking smile did not leave his face.

Rifellyn turned hopelessly and looked at the main screen. Beyond the vanishing point of the cable the blue streak of a ruptor pulse fluoresced. The control room was a bedlam of shouts and screams as the techs and guards fled; but she just stood, staring. *What does it matter now? There's no place to go.*

Bleak regret possessed her mind; she'd known the nature of her employers, but the prospect of the power they had promised had been so sweet, and as long as she was fast and clever, she had always assumed their savagery would be aimed at other people. She remembered what her husband had said, years ago, when he left her upon finding out to whom she'd sold herself. *With them loyalty flows only one way.*

Looking at the body of the tech before her, she finally realized what he had meant. She walked over and closed the man's staring eyes, and was still crouched in front of the body when the shock wave tore the Node apart and her life fled into the vacuum.

❋   ❋   ❋

The long wait was beginning to get on Anderic's nerves. The Bori secretary was a real tilt-snoot; he'd rebuffed each of the Rifter's attempts to begin a conversation. The comic chip had palled on him and he was restless and bored. The occasional flickers and shadows in the corner of his vision didn't help any, either.

Suddenly the door burst open and Barrodagh stormed in, followed by an overweight, red-faced young man in sloppy clothing and a terrified expression, and a grim-faced Tarkan. Anderic goggled at the Bori's appearance: his hair was standing up in ragged spikes, covered with a crust of vile green glop, his clothing crusted with the same substance. Bits of it flaked off and fell to the floor as he moved.

Barrodagh launched into an impassioned tirade at the secretary in some language that Anderic didn't recognize, but assumed was Bori. The secretary's face gradually turned a sickly shade of gray; his eyes darted nervously to the Tarkan standing in front of the door. Even through the language barrier his replies lacked force to Anderic's ears, while the fat-faced blit seemed to slowly relax and gain confidence.

Anderic was enjoying the evident humiliation and fear of the secretary when the argument was suddenly terminated by a decisive movement by Barrodagh. The secretary shouted something and tried to scuttle away as the Tarkan strode forward, grasped his neck, and with a brutally efficient movement, crushed his larynx.

The grinding crunch was surprisingly loud. Anderic felt a prickle of uncertainty at this unexpected turn. *What's going on here?* He glanced at the Tarkan, whose eyes rested on him impassively; Anderic's belt suddenly felt light where the comforting weight of his jac would normally lie.

Barrodagh watched with a satisfied expression as the man writhed at his feet, choking his life away. Before the secretary's heels had stilled their frantic drumming, the Avatar's aide turned to the Rifter.

"Don't worry, *Captain*," said the Bori. His emphasis on the incorrect title worried Anderic; he couldn't tell whether it was sarcasm or not. Then, as Barrodagh continued, Anderic began to relax.

"Tallis made a serious mistake. It is possible that the *Satansclaw* will soon be yours."

Anderic almost laughed, but held it; the Bori's grim expression did not lighten.

"Either that, or we shall all be dead very shortly. Or wishing we were."

At Anderic's attempt to speak, Barrodagh held up a hand imperiously. "There is no time for explanation. The Avatar is waiting for us. You already, I think, know a little of the customs of Dol'jhar; do not, under any circumstances, speak to him unless he first addresses you. Do not look at him unless he speaks to you, but do not look away. Keep him in the corner of your vision so you can respond instantly if he addresses you."

He paused. "If you are as clever as I think you are, and can follow my lead, you will survive and prosper. If not, I have no use for you anyway." With that he motioned for Anderic to follow him out of the room.

As they walked, Barrodagh explained what had happened. *So Tallis' logos wasn't good enough,* thought the Rifter, then listened in stunned surprise as the Bori described in matter-of-fact terms the extent of the Avatar's attempt to stop the Krysarch's escape.

Their path took them outdoors, on a curving gravel walkway bounded by tall hedges and trees silhouetted against a bright night sky. Anderic stopped involuntarily as he saw the reality behind the Bori's words. To the south a long string of faint, blue-white points of light was slowly rising past a diffusing glow sprinkled with bright splotches and flares. Above it, several contorted lines of light sprawled across the night sky like some alien alphabet.

Now, for the first time, the Rifter truly understood the nature of the people he was dealing with. The chips on the Dol'jharian language had explained at length about the culture, trying to make some of the phrases and idioms comprehensible, but nothing had prepared him for this. *They blew up the Node and wrecked the S'lift, just to stop one ship—one man.*

At an impatient grunt from their Tarkan escort Anderic hurried to catch up with Barrodagh, who had not slowed his pace. As they rounded a curve, the Rifter saw a tall, heavy-shouldered man in black standing in front of a bulky mass of statuary, which seemed to consist of a bunch of snakes and people. As they came closer, he could see that the man was facing the statue, staring either at it or at the display in the sky above. His fingers were busy with something; as Barrodagh halted them at a respectful distance, Anderic saw that it was some sort of cord, its sinuous writhing in the man's strong fingers mirroring the agony of the statue before him.

They stood in silence for what seemed a very long time.

Tallis stumbled along the gravel path between two black-clad guardsmen, trying to hold his nightshirt closed. A few minutes ago the door to his suite had crashed open and the two guards had dragged him out of bed without any explanation; he suspected neither spoke Uni, and he certainly didn't speak Dol'jharian.

His mind, still fogged with sleep, seethed with fearful conjecture. Had Eusabian finally decided that the death of the Krysarch wasn't enough; was he, Tallis Y'Marmor, to be sacrificed for failing to supply a body? The spectacle in the southern sky merely added another set of worries. What had happened to the Node? Was the *Satansclaw* safe?

Then, as they rounded a curve in the path and he saw Barrodagh and Anderic standing together with another, taller man whose back was turned, his anxiety became tinged with anger. *I should have killed him. He's been plotting with that slug Barrodagh.*

The tall man turned around and Tallis saw that it was Eusabian. The lights lining the gravel pathway threw his features into strong relief; the contorted statuary behind him and the fluorescent destruction in the sky above gave him the stature of a figure out of some fearful legend.

The tableau held in silence for a long moment. The cool night breeze caressed Tallis' skin as though the flimsy shanta-silk nightshirt weren't there, but since every hair was already prickled up with fear, he barely noticed.

"I had decided to forgive you for the blemish in my paliach your action at Warlock created," said Eusabian, his voice soft. "As my aide pointed out, it was Hreem's foolish boast that warned the Charvannese in time to make the Krysarch's escape attempt possible."

Tallis noted without comprehension the black cord twisting between Eusabian's fingers as he spoke.

"But a few hours ago Krysarch Brandon nyr-Arkad invaded the Palace, carried off an important prisoner, and then escaped. My paliach is incomplete, my will has been defied, and tremendous damage done to what is now mine."

Tallis started to shake as comprehension of the enormity of his failure flooded him. He glanced at the night sky, now realizing what had happened. *They destroyed the Node to try to stop him. There's no chance at all for me.*

"It is only because of your brilliant piloting in that action, despite its apparent failure, that I am speaking to you now. I do not destroy talent needlessly. Is there any reason you can offer why you should not die?"

Tallis' mind froze for a moment as his fear rose up and blotted out everything else. He saw the beginning of decision in the Avatar's face, and then a sudden, stillborn movement from Barrodagh. At that moment the significance of Anderic's presence, combined with Eusabian's apparent ignorance of the logos, impelled Tallis to a desperate gambit.

"Lord," he replied. "I did not undertake to enter your service lightly, for I know that Dol'jhar punishes failure as severely as it generously rewards success. To ensure that my service would please you, I installed a logos in the *Satansclaw*, containing the accumulated knowledge of the greatest fighters of the past thousand years."

He paused, noted a faint interest in Eusabian's face, and, better yet, a tinge of frustrated anger on Barrodagh's. "I do not plead excuse on that account. The failure is still mine. But consider, Lord: if a logos could not kill the Krysarch, who among your forces could have done any better?"

He waved his hand at the display overhead, now fading away. "The night sky here at the heart of your new kingdom bears witness to the truth of my words."

❈   ❈   ❈

Barrodagh quickly smoothed his face, repressing the violent rage he felt at Tallis' brilliant improvisation. What made it especially galling was that its strength flowed from exactly the facets of the Rifter captain's personality that Barrodagh found so irritating: his love of the grand gesture and grandiloquent speech. *He's an Ur-be-damned actor at heart and it may save his life.*

There was nothing he could do but await the Avatar's decision. By offering Tallis the opportunity to plead his cause, Eusabian had made it an affair of the *nar-pelkun turish*, the "unsheathed will" that was the fundamental philosophical and emotional touchstone of the Dol'jharian nobility. Any attempt Barrodagh made to influence his lord's decision at this point would be an infringement of this, and very likely fatal.

"Well said, Kyvernat Y'Marmor," said Eusabian finally. Barrodagh cursed mentally: the use of the Dol'jharian title for captain indicated Eusabian's acceptance of Tallis' argument.

"A logos," the Avatar continued musingly. "I have heard of these devices. The Panarchists fear them greatly and have forbidden their use. You apparently have a proper sense of what it means to serve Dol'jhar."

Barrodagh's spirits slumped further as he saw his careful plans go awry. The Rifter next to him might now be a liability rather than an asset. Then he came alert as Eusabian addressed him.

"Were you aware of this, Barrodagh?"

"I only just found out, Lord."

"I see." Eusabian turned back to Tallis. "I have been told that most people in the Thousand Suns abhor devices such as the logos. How did your crew feel about this?"

"They did not know, Lord," Tallis replied after some hesitation, and Barrodagh began to see the way out of this disaster. "It spoke to me via pinbeam, and I had optical filters implanted so only I could see its visuals."

Eusabian was silent for a time. Finally he said, "You may have your life, but I will not leave you your ship. Perhaps, in time, I will have another for you.

"Y'Marmor is not to be killed," he said to Barrodagh. "Let him serve in the lowest position on his ship for a time as penance."

He motioned to Anderic. "I assume that this would be your suggested replacement for him?"

"He was the only one of the crew who realized the presence of the logos. With the optical implants he could take over without the crew learning about the device."

The Avatar nodded. "Take one of Y'Marmor's eyes and give it to this one."

Anderic started, his pleasure at the promotion and delight in Tallis' discomfiture suddenly changing to horror as he realized what was being required of him. *I can't!* his mind shrieked, horrid images from his Organicist childhood welling up. Then he noticed the dispassionate gaze of the Avatar upon him, and the impatient stance of the Bori next to him; and he remembered the fate of Barrodagh's secretary.

I don't have any choice. His study of Dol'jhar made his situation clear: refusal of Eusabian's promotion would be a mortal insult. A quick death like the secretary's would be the easiest outcome; lingering pain beforehand more likely.

But I don't have to turn it on. Even as the thought came, a part of him recognized it as false rationalization; he couldn't captain a destroyer during a war such as now raged throughout the Thousand Suns. But under the threat of imminent and painful death, he pushed the reality from his mind and bowed deeply, indicating his acceptance of the boon.

As he bowed, the weight of the Emasculizer in his belt pouch bumped against his leg. He glanced over at Tallis, who refused to return his look, and remembered some of the little "dramas" Y'Marmor had so enjoyed. *Well, Tallis, Luri is mine now,* he thought, anticipation kindling inside him, *and I can make sure that you never put the horns on me as I did with you.*

As Barrodagh ushered him away from the presence of the Lord of Vengeance, thoughts of the logos were already fading from his mind as Anderic distracted himself with schemes of revenge for Tallis' many slights. He would make out fine; he always had.

※　　　　　※　　　　　※

Marim leapt up, snapping her fingers. *"Yow!"* she crowed, making a gesture toward the screens that Osri had never seen before but which he felt had to be obscene. She added, "Lick my radiants, nacker-nose!"

The ambience on the bridge was abruptly one of celebration, with the intensity born of death defeated. A shrill ululation that raised the hairs on his neck drifted out of the intercom from the engine room; it was a sound entirely at odds with Jaim's laconic nature.

Lokri grinned, cracking his knuckles and his neck. Then he shut down his console with a careless swipe. "Good. Now to check out my loot."

Marim whirled about to face Vi'ya. "What's the take?"

"Damage?" Vi'ya inquired mildly, as if Marim had not spoken.

Marim's small hands pounced bird-like across her board. "Cerenkov suppression one hundred percent, fiveskip stable to 0.1, pseudo-velocity 0.75. Not too bad."

Vi'ya said, "We've flown on worse. Let's go home."

"Vi'ya!" Marim hooted. "What's the take? I wanna start making out my shopping list."

Vi'ya's lips quirked. "You should ask the Arkad; I can't begin to estimate it."

Brandon was smiling, color ridging his cheekbones. "The Family's been accumulating art for almost a thousand years, and I think Lokri and Ivard accounted for most of it. Some of those items were literally priceless."

"Whoo-ee!" Marim slapped one of her feet up on her

console and wiggled her long toes. "Now I can hire me a Panarchy-lady to do my toenails."

"You'll go broke first buying her nose-filters," cracked Lokri. "I'm going to check on the boy."

Marim's smile disappeared. "Comin' with you."

As they went out, Osri said formally, "Request permission to leave the bridge."

Vi'ya waved a hand, but before Osri could get up from his pod, Montrose's voice came over the intercom: "Brandon. The old man will not sleep until he's spoken with you."

Osri felt a prickle of unreasoning anger, which was only slightly mitigated when Brandon said to him, "Come. Let's see him together."

Osri got up, noticing distractedly the captain tapping at her console. Above, the screen cleared to a view of space as the ship dropped out of skip.

Vi'ya's fingers moved with precision over the keys, and Osri could see the console he had vacated flickering in response as she laid in a new course. Where was she taking them? His father would want to know. But Brandon was already at the door, so Osri caught up in a few strides, trying to ignore the watery feeling in his legs.

They'd only progressed a few paces down the hallway when Montrose loomed suddenly before him.

Osri stared up into the broad, ugly face as Montrose said, "He will live. He is awake now, and asking for the Krysarch—"

With an apologetic glance his way, Brandon walked past the physician and went into the cubicle. Osri braced himself to wait.

Brandon entered the tiny cubicle with soft footfalls.

Omilov lay on the bed gazing upward, his eyes focused light-years beyond the ceiling. His shaved head was beaded with fine sweat, his color chalky.

Montrose moved quietly in a corner, reading from a small console and tapping in numbers. At Brandon's approach

Omilov's eyes drifted down and he moved slightly on the bed. Montrose looked up, and without speaking went out. The door hissed shut behind him.

"Sebastian," Brandon murmured. "How do you feel?"

Omilov's fingers twitched convulsively and Brandon bent to grasp his hand for a moment. He would have withdrawn it but Omilov tightened his grip a little, and Brandon sank down onto the little stool which had been folded down from the wall.

"Heart . . ." Omilov whispered hoarsely.

"Your heart has been strained," Brandon said slowly.

Omilov's heavy brows twitched, his eyes ranging across the ceiling as he obviously tried to gather his strength to speak. Sudden understanding made Brandon say swiftly, "You mean the Heart of Kronos?"

Omilov's face relaxed a little.

"It is here, safe on this ship." Brandon pitched his voice to be as clear and reassuring as possible.

Omilov's eyes closed a moment, and Brandon started to rise, but the clammy hand tightened on his fingers once again.

Omilov's eyes opened, bloodshot and strained. Brandon remembered the scene in the torture room; he couldn't imagine what had been done to Sebastian to reduce him to this haggard shadow. Omilov had told the Archon that long-ago day on Charvann that he knew very little about the Heart of Kronos, but apparently he had attempted to deny even that to Eusabian. *He is a Chival of the Phoenix Gate and does not take his oath lightly.*

Brandon realized that Omilov could not know that he had succeeded in withholding his knowledge—or at least, if he had yielded, that the knowledge had died with his torturers.

"Sebastian," he said gently. "You did not fail. We destroyed everything in that room—and you were the only one to leave it alive. We not only have the Heart of Kronos, Eusabian learned nothing about it from you."

Omilov's eyes closed again, his mouth thinning. "Thank you," he whispered, his voice nearly inaudible.

"Sebastian, why don't you rest? I can come back later."

"I—have to tell you . . ." the husking voice went on, then Omilov stopped and struggled for breath. With slightly more force, he murmured quickly, "I would rather anyone else had this duty . . ." He paused to breathe slowly and deeply.

Brandon felt the tingling sense of emptiness that precedes the knowledge of loss, but let nothing of it show, saying only, "Knowledge may be a burden but ignorance is never bliss."

The platitude made Omilov's lips twitch faintly. ". . . Handed you that once . . . did I? Ah, my boy, I wish . . ." He stopped, gathering himself again. Brandon saw Sebastian's dry, gnawed lips taking on a tinge of blue, and alarm raced through him.

But then Omilov spoke. "Jerrode Eusabian has taken your father prisoner . . . plans to exile him to Gehenna. Your brothers . . . were assassinated." He took two long breaths, then murmured, "I know nothing more than that . . . Taken to Arthelion as a prisoner . . . Only information I have came . . . from Eusabian's lips."

"Both—"

Omilov nodded, his eyes shut. Brandon saw the glimmer of tears under the stubby lashes.

"Charvann?" Brandon added softly as his thumb rubbed against the warm, smooth metal of the heavy signet ring on his finger. "The Archon?"

"Dead." Omilov winced, as if lingering memory deepened the pain inside him. "And Bikara: that I saw."

Brandon shifted his grip so that his hand covered the one now trembling in his grasp. He said nothing for a time; silence prevailed in the little room, broken only by the faint blip of one of Montrose's instruments and Omilov's rasping breathing.

In his mind was only blankness, and the sense again of overwhelming grief, waiting behind some occult corner of his heart for a moment of weakness in which to overwhelm him. Through the fog of protective shock, he realized that he'd been fleeing just ahead of violent death for weeks; but each time the blows intended for him had felled instead innocents who had looked to his Family for leadership. *And now, with my father in the hands of Eusabian, and us held by these Rifters, what is my role to be?*

Omilov closed his eyes as tears burned their way free and down his cheeks. When at last he felt he had to look up again his vision was blurry; but for Ilara's blue-gray eyes the face above him could have been Gelasaar thirty years ago, regarding him with exactly the same affectionate concern. And like Gelasaar, Brandon would shut away his own reactions until there was time for them, until his presence was no longer required—Omilov realized the young man would sit there holding his hand until he felt Omilov had recovered some measure of peace.

The thought very nearly overwhelmed him again. He pulled his hand free and said hoarsely, "Doctor . . . sedative—"

The door behind them hissed open and Montrose entered, carrying a sprayjector. "Time for rest, Professor, unless you want to be tied to this bed for a year."

Brandon rose to his feet. "Sleep well, Sebastian. I'll visit you as soon as you feel up to it."

The door closed behind him, and Omilov gave in to a long sigh. Montrose slapped the little seat back up and regarded his patient sympathetically. "Shall I knock you out?"

Omilov flicked his fingers, signifying indifference. He murmured wearily, "Fortuitous timing . . ."

Montrose nodded, eyes crinkling in amusement. "Captain sent me in."

This cryptic remark surprised Omilov, but before he could turn his mind to grappling with it the sprayjector spat coolness into his arm and he found himself sinking gratefully into fog-spun dreams.

❈   ❈   ❈

Osri stared down at the crumpled, stained ribbon in his hand. The date was still visible: 955. *Markham vlith-L'Ranja. How did this get to the Mandala?*

The flight ribbon coupled with the Tetradrachm made no sense to him—but the universe had stopped making sense hours—no, days ago. He slid the objects into his pocket and then forgot them when he heard the dispensary door slide open.

Brandon came out, his face somber, his gaze inward. The Krysarch almost passed by, appearing not to see him; all his training could not prevent Osri from clearing his throat and saying: "Your pardon—"

Brandon looked up. "Sorry, Osri. Your father will live, I think. He's asleep now. I suppose you could go in to see him—" He paused, looking quickly along the hall.

He wants to speak privately. Osri did not suppose anything more could shock him, after the unnerving events of the last eternity of hours, but alarm burned in his chest. He followed, silent, as Brandon led the way to the tiny cabin that they had shared on the journey to Arthelion.

When the door was shut, Brandon said, "He was worried about the Heart of Kronos. I told him only that it is on board the ship. You'll do as you like, of course, but I suggest you wait until he's more stable to let him know that the captain holds it."

Osri nodded, signifying assent. He waited then, for he sensed that the Krysarch had more to say.

Brandon turned and touched the edge of the bunk, then turned back. "Tanri Faseult died on Charvann," he said softly. "And Eusabian had both my brothers assassinated."

Osri fell against the bulkhead as his supposition proved rackingly wrong; this latest shock, piled upon all the rest, hit him like a physical blow. Desolation made his head reel: the universe had gone nova, taking with it all meaning.

Brandon took a step toward him, speaking in a quiet undervoice. For a moment Osri couldn't make sense of it and almost didn't try. But eventually the Krysarch's words penetrated.

". . . can't be sure that they weren't listening in, though we'll have to assume that they did. What use these Rifters would make of this information, I don't know, but at least we have it as well: my father is alive." Brandon's eyes were wide and blue, his face intense. "He's *alive*, Osri. Eusabian is sending him to Gehenna, or has already. So it is up to us, you and me, and your father when he is able, to get him out."

Osri sank abruptly onto his bunk, his heart hammering painfully as, for the first time in recent memory, he experienced the rebirth of hope.

THE END OF BOOK ONE